Praise for Catherine Czerkawska's Writing:

'The narrative brilliantly describes the physical imperative they have to be together – not just the snatched times alone, but the magnetic pull they have towards one another when other people are around, their almost uncontrollable urge to touch one another and the risks that brings.'
  – *Hilary Ely, Vulpes Libris*

'It's hard to pigeonhole this book to a specific genre. It's a love story, yet sometimes defies the label. It's contemporary, yet dwells quite a bit in the past. As to its audience – I think this would appeal to readers who don't need to be led by the hand and who enjoy challenging relationships. Wholeheartedly recommended.'
  – *Gilly Fraser, the Indie eBook Review*

'Heart-warming, realistic and page-turning.'
  – *Lorraine Kelly*

'Czerkawska tells her tale in a restrained, elegant prose that only adds to its poignancy.'
  – *The Sunday Times*

'A compelling read, with a satisfying blend of history, nature and romance.'
  – *Amanda Booth, The Scots Magazine*

'Uplifting ... The reader finds themselves deeply immersed... superbly researched.'
  – *Undiscovered Scotland*

The Amber Heart

Catherine Czerkawska

Published by Dyrock Publishing

Cover image from a painting by Juliusz Kossak

ISBN: 978-0-9557364-3-8

Some of the Polish names and other words have been simplified for ease of reading, although I have tried to make them authentic. When Polish names end in 'ski' the female form is 'ska', hence Diduski, Diduska. Where the odd Polish word is included, the meaning should be clear from the text. Where it is simpler for the reader, I have used the accepted English version of words such as 'droshky'. The Polish city of Lwow is now Lviv in Ukraine, but under the Austro-Hungarian empire it was called Lemberg, and I remember my own father using that name, for clarification, when talking about his beloved Lwow. Similarly, for the sake of clarity, I have avoided the word Ruthenian, often used to describe the Ukrainian population of this disputed area. My apologies in advance to anyone who finds this upsetting. The historical background to The Amber Heart *is as accurate as possible, but please note that this is a work of fiction.*

Chapter One

MARIANNA DIDUSKA HAD LEARNED TO sit on a horse before her legs could carry her upright. Her father had perched her on a placid, broad backed mare, with a blanket for a saddle. At first, whenever she slid off, he was there to catch her. When she was older and allowed to ride about the estate alone, she had tumbled off once or twice, sliding over the side and bruising her pride more than herself. Then, she would have to find a convenient ditch so that she could coax her mount into it and clamber on again. Now, at the age of eight, she was a competent little horsewoman. She had begged to be allowed to make the whole journey from Lisko to Podlaski on horseback, even though it was much too far for her. She had made such a fuss about it that just outside the village, the carriages were halted, and she was allowed to ride up in front of her father, his arms around her. She sat there proudly, enjoying the attention they attracted as they approached the main entrance to the estate. The lodge keeper and his family were already gathered outside to greet them.

Just before they reached the gate, they came upon a group of children standing by the side of the track. They ranged in ages from perhaps three to eleven, all equally ragged and grubby, their faces pinched by hunger and fatigue. They watched with a curiosity that was quite devoid of envy, as if they were observing some intriguing fantasy passing before their eyes, something irresistibly entertaining but not quite of this world. Marianna peered at them from beneath her bonnet and shrank back against her father. Stefan felt for the leather bag of coins he had brought and bent to whisper in her ear.

'Don't be afraid, kitten. They're only village children. They won't hurt you.'

He scattered coins like a man feeding chickens, watching the children spread out and dive, squabbling, fighting for what they could find. One of them, the tallest, stood still. He was a slender boy of eleven, his hair dark and matted, his face sallow under the grime, his eyes brown pebbles in a thin face. He stood there, hands hanging by his sides, fists tightly clenched, and he stared up at Marianna, unsmiling, unmoving. She shifted uneasily. For the first time in her life, she saw a gaze of pure resentment directed straight at herself. She turned her head into her father's jacket.

'Daddy, tell the boy not to look at me,' she whispered.

Stefan's mind had been elsewhere: on his wife and her sickness, on the hundred questions that he needed to ask about the management of Podlaski, on that po-faced Austrian, and whether he could find a better tutor for his son.

He bent to her. 'What's the matter, kitten?'

'The boy. Tell him not to look at me like that.'

Puzzled, Stefan scanned the road, but the children had taken up their coins and disappeared, scared that they might be dispossessed. The dark child had gone with them.

'Look!' Stefan forced her face gently away from him. 'No-one's left. They've all gone. They're only village children. They're a bit dirty but they mean you no harm, Marianna.'

The trip to the estate at Podlaski had been a sudden impulse. Marianna adored Lisko and couldn't ever imagine leaving it, but it was her constant praise for her home that had finally prompted Stefan's decision to visit his second estate at Podlaski.

'When we're grown up,' she had said to her brother, 'We'll live here at Lisko together and I'll keep house for you. We'll have as many horses as we like and grow strawberries and do exactly as we please all day long.'

'Maybe!' said Zygmunt, with a grin. He was twelve, four years older than his sister, and he knew better. She was still the baby of the family. Antonina, their mother, said nothing, but carried on with her embroidery. Stefan had been stretched at full length on the couch. 'Resting his eyes,' he called it. He sat up.

'Come here, kitten.'

She climbed confidently onto his knee and twined her arms around his neck. She was always as lavish in her love as in her loathing.

'What if you want to marry? What will you do then?'

'But I don't want to marry. I don't like boys. Except Zygmunt. He's all right.'

'All young ladies should marry. Where would your mother be without me? Or I without her for that matter.'

'Then my husband must come here. To Lisko.'

'And what if he wants a place of his own? What if Zygmunt is already married by that time? What will you do then?'

Zygmunt made vomiting noises. He didn't much like the thought of being married either.

His mother frowned at him. 'Don't do that.'

'Come on!' Stefan bounced Marianna up and down on his knee. 'I must have an answer. What then?'

'I don't know. Go to my husband's house, I suppose. But it couldn't ever be as nice as Lisko.'

He kissed her on the end of her nose. 'We'll have to find you somewhere just as nice. What about Podlaski? That might be yours.'

'But I've never been to Podlaski, so how can I tell?'

'Well, perhaps we'll go this summer.'

The house at Lisko was a fairly recent addition to this large estate in eastern Poland. Early in the seventeenth century, a nearby lake had been drained, and the ruins of an ancient fortress had come to light. It was said that this castle had once belonged to a cruel mediaeval lord called Stanislaw the Devil. The stones of the old castle had an evil reputation but the pasture was much too good to be ignored. Armed with a bottle of holy water and a piece of the true cross, Casimir Diduski, helped by a party of brave or perhaps simply intimidated servants, had set about dismantling the ruin. Casimir had used the stones of the ancient castle to build a new house for himself. Superstitious villagers had prophesied all kinds of disasters, but those that had followed were no more than the normal tragedies that beset every powerful family in this region from time to time.

Some two hundred years passed, the Diduskis prospered and that earlier house was superseded by a more luxurious building. A grimy painting hung in the library of the pancake yellow house at Lisko. It showed the old house with only the name 'Lisko' betraying its grander origins. The house made with stones from the devil's castle still stood on the estate. At one time, it had been the Steward's house, but it had never been a comfortable place and now it was used for storing fruit and vegetables for the long winter months.

'Oh but he was a terrible, heathen fellow,' whispered nanny Nusia to the children in the nursery. Nusia had a round face and small brown eyes that glinted with pleasure at her own stories. 'And he was a magician into the bargain. They say he could turn any metal into pure gold!'

The children's eyes widened, and Zygmunt said, 'I wish I could do that. Just think of how rich we'd be if we could do that!'

The manor house at Lisko sat among green meadows interlaced with beech woods and orchards. The village of the same name was a scattered jumble of thatched farms, smallholdings and shacks, as well as a flour mill, all of which straggled around the manor house, half clinging to its shelter, half struggling to escape from its domination. Perhaps Stanislaw's ghost had laid a magical hand on Lisko, for the park was certainly beautiful, dominated by the late eighteenth century mansion. This was a long, low building, yellow as butter, with graceful wings stretching out on either side, standing among orchards of apple, pear and cherry. Marianna loved it.

'The child is growing too fond of this place,' said Stefan. 'Podlaski might be hers one day and she should see it before she's any older.'

Antonina allowed the breath of a sigh to escape from her. She was pregnant again. The thought of travelling dismayed her.

'If you think she ought to see the estate, then we'll go. But what will you do if we have a second son and a third?'

'I'll think of something. She'll probably marry and go to her husband's estate anyway. But it's time I went to Podlaski, and we may as well all travel together.'

The visit involved the transportation of the family, along with Zygmunt's tutor, Marianna's nanny, a young nursery maid called Dorota and a small group of servants. Stefan rode with Zygmunt trotting beside him on his pony. Marianna travelled with her mother, the nanny and the tutor in one carriage, while a few servants were crammed into a second, much less comfortable cart. The rest of the household had been left behind to take care of Lisko in their absence. Nusia had once been nanny to Marianna's mother. Marianna was always running to her for sweetmeats and kisses. Her baby tongue had been unable to manage Nusia, so she had called her Nunu and the name had stuck.

There was no love lost between Nusia and the Austrian tutor. She despised his haughty manners, and he thought she took unforgivable liberties with Antonina. Meissen's status lay somewhere in the miserable limbo between servant and master. He was always having to maintain his dignity in the face of Stefan's unthinking autocracy, although Antonina was invariably kind to him. He thought her very beautiful but he knew that she found him boring. Throughout the journey, he was torn between his desire to talk to her and his awareness of every weary flicker of her eyelids.

At last, he fell silent, and Antonina allowed her eyes to close against the nausea that threatened to envelop her. There had been a stillborn infant between Zygmunt and Marianna, and her last labour had been long and hard. It had been a great relief to her when she did not conceive again immediately.

The nausea subsided and she dozed, glad that poor Wolfgang Meissen was at last silent. His Polish was very limited and he spoke to her in French or German, but today it had been difficult for her to think of the right words, although she had tried hard, inspired by a kind of pity for him. He was the youngest son of a university teacher from Vienna. Stefan said that he was a good teacher and even Zygmunt admitted as much, but he lacked some essential charm.

Marianna had been fast asleep, but now she woke up and began to look out at her surroundings. It was a day of blue skies with a few high clouds casting diffused shadows on the land beneath. The leaves and grasses still had the newly-minted look of early summer. It was the week before Whitsun, and everywhere people were decorating their houses with green branches. They raised their heads to watch the carriages and horsemen go by, glad of any excuse to rest.

'Will our house be decorated too?' Marianna asked.

'I expect so,' said Nusia, comfortably. 'And we'll go to church. There's a Roman church at Podlaski and I've heard your father say that they always place a double row of young birch trees down the centre aisle.'

'I love birch trees. I like them best when they're new and the leaves are like little gold coins. Mr Meissen, don't you love them too?'

Marianna leaned over and clutched his knees in her enthusiasm.

He moved those bony joints distastefully to one side. 'They are very fine, yes.'

Nusia saw the look on his face, and turned down the corners of her mouth.

'Stiff as a poker,' she said to the Podlaski cook, later. 'The child's talking to him, and he pulls a face and moves his skinny legs out of her way!'

The cook came from the village and had been employed especially for the summer. Crimson faced from the heat of the brick bread oven, from which she was taking loaves with a big paddle, she nodded in agreement.

'Will he eat with the family when he's here?' she asked.

'Like at home, I expect. Sometimes with the family. Sometimes in his room. It depends.'

'He'll be a good bit thinner before he leaves Podlaski then.'

Later, Meissen would wonder why his fish or fowl was always more skin and bone than flesh, why his piece of game should have a liberal helping of lead shot, why his soup should be watered, and why he always found himself sitting in starvation corner. But he merely assumed that the cook was incompetent and thought with longing of the lavish cuisine of his homeland.

Chapter Two

MARIANNA SHOULD HAVE BEEN PLEASED with Podlaski. The house was warm and welcoming. There was a pony waiting for her in the stables and a squirming heap of plump, white puppies.

'Choose one for yourself, Miss Marianna,' the groom told her. 'And then, if your father allows it, you can take it back to Lisko with you.'

Normally she was a happy child but the encounter at the gate had darkened the day for her. An inexplicable gloom descended on her. She was homesick for her sunshine yellow house.

'I already have a dog at home,' she said. 'I wanted to bring him, but they wouldn't let me. I wish I was back at home now. I wish we hadn't come.'

'Take no notice of her!' Her brother had come to the stables with her. 'She always gets cross when she's tired. And she loves dogs. I'll choose one for her. What about this one, Marianna. Look at his fat tummy!'

She accepted the puppy at last and patted the pony's velvet nose, but she never rode or walked through those gates afterwards without something of that initial unease. For the first time, she realised that not everyone might love her as her family loved her. The world outside the walls of Lisko was a dangerous place.

Stefan's father had bought Podlaski from a debt ridden cousin. It had seemed like a good investment at the time, a small baroque manor house set among fertile fields and forests. He had installed a Ukrainian steward and left him to take care of the place, only very occasionally putting in an appearance to check that all was well.

After his father's death, Stefan had inherited Podlaski along with Lisko. He was a conscientious landowner, but he was also a lazy man. The old steward's son was now in charge at Podlaski, and when resentments arose, Stefan was content to let his manager act in his place. If there were undercurrents of discontent, he preferred to ignore them, so long as they didn't trouble him too much.

In church on Sunday, Marianna knelt with her mother and Nusia, looking everywhere for the dark boy, but she didn't see him. She supposed that he must go to the Orthodox church with its onion dome. At last, Nusia dug her sharply in the ribs and hissed for her to 'be a good girl now and stop spinning around like a top.'

'Why?'

'Because God doesn't like it. That's why.'

As Nusia had promised, the church was done up like a green grove, and the scent of new leaves enveloped her. She buried her face in her hands and prayed, 'God bless mummy and daddy. God bless Zygmunt. God bless Nusia and Dorota.'

When they came out into the sunlight, there were young girls all dressed in their Sunday finery: striped skirts and richly embroidered waistcoats over white linen blouses. They were singing and selling posies of spring flowers, as vivid as the flowers on their garments. Stefan bought one each for Antonina and Marianna and for Nusia too. Marianna sniffed the honey scent of violets and cheered up. God would surely take care of her if she tried to be good.

The dark child's name was Daniil Bandura, but everyone called him Danilo. He had made his way back to the hut, the only home he had ever known. He walked slowly at this lean time of year, comforting himself with the thought that soon there would be more to eat. If they could just hold out a little longer, things would be easier. His father, Pavel, had been killed in an accident in the forest when Danilo was just three years old. The bigger landowners were, for the most part, Polish. The Ukrainian country folk worked for them and for the minor nobility whose lands had been so divided over many generations that most were only a little more wealthy than their Ukrainian neighbours.

They had been tree felling, and a large beech had tumbled awkwardly, pinning Pavel to the ground. They said he had called out piteously, but there was nothing anyone could do. By the time his companions had mustered enough men to roll the tree trunk away, he was dead.

Danilo knew the exact spot in the forest where it had happened. After they had extricated the body, the tree had been left just where it had rolled. For all that the steward grumbled about the waste, nobody touched it, though whether that was out of respect for Pavel or superstitious dread it was hard to say. Now it was almost buried among vegetation, rotting away quietly. The villagers said that dogs avoided the spot when they were out hunting but it was clear that the ants and beetles had no such scruples. Danilo could not remember his father, but he remembered the funeral procession winding through the village, black against the snow, and the eerie wailing of his mother and the other women trudging after the coffin.

Danilo and his mother, Katarina, lived with his grandfather in a tumbledown cottage, little more than a shack. Having lost his father so young, he had been forced into a maturity beyond his years. Perhaps this was why he could not and would not accept his lowly status, kicking against it all the time like an unbroken horse. It seemed very unfair to him that he should have so little when his father had worked hard for the estate and lost his life in the process. It was typical of the boy that, while his fellows were scrambling about in the dirt for a few coins, he refused to follow suit, even at the risk of going hungry.

'He's got ideas above his station, that one,' said the villagers. 'He doesn't know his place. Well, he'll learn it soon enough.'

The truth was that Ukrainians – Ruthenes as the Poles called them – and Poles were not so very different. They were Slavs with a shared heritage even though they spoke different languages and didn't always find it easy to understand one another. They worshipped in different churches but on the whole they respected each other's beliefs. It was the relative poverty of so many Ukrainians that was a source of extreme tension. The poorest of the Poles were not much better off, but the Polish landowners could be unthinkingly autocratic. And there were many among the Ukrainian communities who believed that this was their land, and the Poles were incomers.

Danilo's mother helped out on the estate: dairying, gardening, washing, working long hours for small reward. Gavril, his grandfather, still worked in the forest, although his sight was failing and it was a precarious existence. Danilo had begun by working in the fields and forests too but latterly, he had tried to find ways of spending more time in the stables. There were some forty working horses, as well as the horses ridden by the steward and his assistant and the thoroughbreds kept in readiness for the family on those rare occasions when they ventured to Podlaski.

Danilo loved the horses. They responded to his voice, giving him the only real affection he had ever known. The grooms and the drivers, many of them his fellow Ukrainians, were kindly and would sometimes share their food with him. He didn't mind the smell of horses or their dirt or their parasites. In fact he preferred them to the smell and dirt of the humans with whom he was forced to live at such close quarters. The head groom recognised the boy's affinity with the animals, and told the steward about it.

'We'll pay him,' said the steward. 'But not too much, mind.'

'No. Not too much. Just enough to satisfy his family.'

'That's the idea. You think you can teach him, if he's willing to learn?'

'Oh he's willing to learn all right. And bright. He's a good stable lad. He might make a decent horseman in time. That's as far as he'll go, mind. He'd never be able to learn his letters. Neither his own nor ours.'

'Not many of them can.'

Ever since the death of her husband, Katarina had been cold and offhanded towards her son. They said in the village that she would never get over Pavel's death, but she was superstitious about showing her son too much affection. If you cared for someone, they were taken away from you. Therefore it was better to disguise affection as indifference.

When Gavril, Danilo's grandfather, had scraped together enough money, he would go to the village tavern and come home with his belly and his head full of vodka, angry with the whole world. Then he would strike Danilo hard with the flat of his hand if he didn't move away quickly enough. Most of the time, though, he simply ignored his grandson. Danilo felt like the boy in the old stories his mother used to tell him, felt as though a cloak of invisibility had been thrown over him. He could die, lost and starving, and nobody would notice him. By the age of eleven, he had acquired a suspicion of the world in general. He had learned to fend for himself as best he could. From one season to the next, and sometimes from one meal to the next, he survived.

Danilo had seen the man who owned the estate perhaps half a dozen times. From the conversations of the men around him, he learned that the present state of affairs in the country was bad and getting worse, that many went hungry while others lived in luxury, that he himself came from a proud but downtrodden people, and that you could not trust the Poles, not at all. Danilo understood all that well enough, but the truth was that he trusted nobody. The steward was fair, and Stefan Diduski was a better master than most, but the longer he stayed away from Podlaski the better they liked him.

Danilo had waited with the other children out of curiosity. He had wanted a closer look at the family. He had been rewarded with the sight, not only of Stefan, but of the child who sat up before him. Her white lace dress, tied around the waist with a blue satin sash, was just visible beneath the cape that covered it. He saw fat brown ringlets smothered by a straw bonnet, framing an inquisitive little face.

His first and overriding impression was of her cleanliness. She looked untouchable and glowing with health, as though she belonged to another universe, far removed from the world he inhabited. He stared up at her hungrily. On the edges of his vision, he saw the other children squabbling and scratching for coins in the dust, but he didn't move. He clenched his fists and stood still.

Then, she hid her face against her father, and Danilo, suddenly afraid of his own temerity, ducked aside and ran off into the woods. When his grandfather found out that some children had brought home coins and he had none, he feared he would be beaten. Danilo stayed in the forest until hunger and the gathering darkness forced him to return home.

His grandfather was waiting for him, brandishing a leather belt. 'Where have you been? The others came back with money from the master. Where's yours? Have you gone and lost it? Or hidden it?'

'I got none. Why should I scrabble about like an animal, just for a few lousy coins? I'll not crawl on the ground before them,' he said.

Gavril stared at him for a long moment.

'Your pride will be your undoing, my lad!'

Much to his surprise, Danilo got no beating. There was rye bread and a little sour milk left out for him, but the food could not ease the ache of envy in his heart. What had hurt him most, though he could not have put this into words, was the confidence with which the child had turned into the sturdy protection of her father's arms. Danilo could not remember anyone embracing him in that way.

He hated her for that.

Throughout the summer, he saw her a few times, always at a distance, playing with her nursery maid or with her formidable nanny. Danilo was wary of Nusia and took care never to get close enough to feel the weight of her hand, but Marianna herself exerted a kind of fascination on him. Sometimes he would creep through the woods to spy on her from a safe distance. Then he would hear her giggling as she played with the now long-legged puppy or ran away from Dorota. Once, he watched in genuine amazement as she stamped her foot, arms akimbo, shaking her curls. Nusia wouldn't have stood for it, but Dorota was only a few years older than her charge and nervous of the child's temper. Marianna didn't like to be crossed.

'You must do as I tell you. That's what you're here for!' he heard her say.

Danilo grinned to himself, half shocked, half envious of her self-confidence. How nice to be like that, he thought. How wonderful to have so much power.

And then, to his astonishment, she relented, her face softening.

'Dorotka! I didn't mean it. Don't sulk. Oh do come and play with me. Please.'

He saw her creep up close and kiss the girl on the cheek. Dorota was not impervious to these kisses and embraced the child, but Danilo thought, 'She wouldn't bring me round like that! She would not!'

One day, when he had been sent on some errand from the stables and was crossing the lawn at the side of the house, he came face to face with Marianna in full flight from her nursery maid. The child was carrying a doll, a foreign doll in a fashionable dress, encrusted with seed pearls and lace. They almost collided, but Danilo put out his hands to halt her. She stared at him, one arm wrapped around the doll, the other hand at her breast in a grown-up gesture copied from her mother.

'Oh, how you startled me!'

She wore so much white and yet she never seemed dirty. Why did she never seem dirty? Did they change her clothes two or three times a day?

'Boy!' she said, imperiously. 'Are you meant to be here?'

Beneath the grime, a blush spread over his thin face. Polish and Ukrainian were so intermingled here that he understood her well enough and could respond in her own language, after a fashion.

'I've been sent with a message for the steward.'

She pulled a face. 'Is that all?' She sighed. 'There's no-one to play with. Only Dorota and I'm bored with her. My brother goes off with our papa all the time and they won't let me come. They say it's business and Zygmunt has to learn all about it for when he grows up. And I'm so sick of sewing. Do you know, I took my mama's pincushion and pushed all the sewing needles into it, so that they couldn't be seen. And then I took the scissors and cut my silly old needlework into shreds. The stitches were all knots and it was so dirty. Almost as dirty as you,' she added, dispassionately, glancing at him with distaste. 'I hated it.'

'Didn't you get into trouble?' he asked, interested in spite of himself.

'Your Polish is very funny. Are you foreign?'

'No. No, I'm not foreign.'

'You make it sound a bit like singing. Yes, I did get into trouble, and they're going to make me do another, a picture of flowers, but I'll cut that one up too when I get the chance. You see if I don't.'

He believed her. Her eyes gleamed with mischief.

'I don't suppose we could play, could we?' she asked him, doubtfully. 'We could play with my doll. We could play houses. But I don't suppose they'd let me.'

'No, miss. And they certainly wouldn't let me.'

She held out the doll for his inspection. In spite of the dress, he could see that the little creature had vapid papier-mâché features, a narrow leather body and a mass of painted curls, rather similar to Marianna's own. 'Do you like her? Her name's Loulou. My papa's cousin, Floryan, brought her back from France for me. She has her own trunk full of clothes. Even petticoats and night things. Papa says she must have cost him a fortune. He says I'm his princess. He sings me the song about the princess living in a house of butter. You know the one?'

He shook his head.

She sang it to him in a high, thin voice, like a gnat.

'Once upon a time there was a princess
and she lived in a house made of butter,
and the house was full of marvellous things ...'

Again, Danilo shook his head, curling his lip in disdain at the doll and at her song. He had no idea what she was talking about. The song made no sense to him.

'Because of Lisko, you know, a house of butter,' she persisted. 'Lisko's a pancake yellow house. I don't suppose you've ever been there.'

He began to laugh at her.

'Why are you laughing?'

'Because you're so silly. Almost as silly as your stupid doll.'

She grew very red in the face. 'How dare you!'

'You needn't stamp your foot at me!' he told her boldly. 'I'll say it again, I think it's a silly old doll!'

'Say you like her!' She brandished the doll at him. 'You're supposed to say how beautiful she is. You're a very rude boy.'

'I don't care. I don't have to be nice to you. I think it's stupid. I think it's a stupid old doll. Just like you.'

He was seized with a sudden desire to snatch the doll from her and smash it down on the stone steps, smash its silly face into a hundred fragments.

'I might break it. I could, you know, and there would be nothing you could do about it. It wouldn't be beautiful then, would it? Not if it was all smashed up!'

The defiance left her. Her lower lip trembled.

'Why are you being so unkind to me? I've only been nice to you.'

The question brought him up short. He saw tears well up in her eyes and spill over. He watched as the droplets coursed down her rosy cheeks. He had not expected her to cry, not over a doll and a silly threat that he was obviously in no position to carry out. He hated her tears. He felt an unfamiliar tightening sensation in the back of his throat. Danilo never cried.

Marianna was working herself up into a storm of weeping and now she was more angry than sad.

'Go away,' she sobbed. 'I don't want you here. You're horrible, and I hate you. Go away!'

Nusia came down on him like an avenging angel. She boxed his ears so hard that they rang for an hour afterwards, snatched up the girl and shouted at him 'You dirty peasant! How dare you even talk to the child? Get away. Go back where you belong, before I set the dogs on you!'

She swept away, still carrying Marianna in her stout arms, like a baby, staggering slightly with the weight of her. Marianna was tall for her years. He was astonished to see that, over her nanny's shoulder, Marianna was sticking her pink tongue out at him and screwing up her nose. Involuntarily he put his tongue out in return.

Later, when sanity came back to him, he wondered what had possessed him to behave in that way. He waited for a summons to the head groom, for a beating, even exile from the stables. When none came, he realised that she had said nothing about him. He was no fool. It was not out of concern or kindness. It was merely that he was beneath even her contempt.

Chapter Three

AFTERWARDS, WHEN MARIANNA TRIED TO remember the good things about that time at Podlaski, all she could summon were vague images such as the warm twilight of her bedroom with the stuffy smell of old wood and camphor from the blanket chest at the foot of the bed, and the sharp humming of gnats in her ear. No matter how hard Nusia tried to keep them out, one or two would always slide in and pierce her dreams.

It was very hot that summer. The village children lost their attenuated, springtime appearance and became browner, flesh filling out arms, legs and bellies. But the heat persisted beyond comfort. There was little rain. The fields became dun and dry, and the depressions made by carts on the track through the village turned into deep, dangerous ruts. It was uncomfortable to drive along them, the cartwheels throwing up constant clouds of dust. Even in the forest the air was humid. Marianna envied the birds their wings. Oh to be up there in the cool breeze, swaying in the treetops. Only in the manor house, in the few rooms that sunlight seldom reached, was it possible to find some respite, and here Marianna would sit and draw, or play with her family of dolls and a miniature tea set that she had discovered on a top shelf in the nursery cupboard, having tea parties in imitation of those her mother held at Lisko.

In the hovels where the poorer members of the community lived, there was no escape from the weather. The water in the village well fell lower, and turned to a brown sludge. There was an outbreak of sickness and diarrhoea in the village. At last, the water began to taste so bad that they sent a man down on the end of a rope to see what was causing it. He came up hauling two decomposing cats in the bucket. The water for the manor house was pumped from an underground spring, but even so, when Antonina heard the news, she turned pale and fled the room.

Antonina had finally reconciled herself to her pregnancy, and Stefan was delighted.

'Let it be another boy,' he told her. 'Another big, strong boy like Zygmunt.'

It was late evening, and he had been watching Nusia brushing her mistress's hair. He liked to sit and watch the bristles moving gently through the shiny length of it. This was a task that Nusia jealously reserved to herself, although on the occasions when Stefan was present, their conversation was never as intimate as when they were alone.

Tonight, Antonina was wearing a long, white nightdress that disguised the bump where the baby was beginning to show. If anything, she had lost weight over these few weeks, her sickness often extending throughout the whole day. Her face looked small and wan, her cheekbones jutting out sharply beneath the curtains of hair. The hot summer didn't suit her. Podlaski didn't suit her.

Stefan stooped to kiss his wife goodnight, and held her face tenderly for a moment.

'Let it be another strong boy,' he said, on his way out of the room.

Nusia watched him go.

'Oh yes,' she said. 'Let it be a big boy! But it would be a different tale if they had to push these big boys out into the world. It would indeed!' She snorted angrily and carried on with her brushing.

'Ouch!' said Antonina, reproachfully. 'You needn't take it out on me just because my husband is a little thoughtless.'

'I'm sorry, Tonia, but it's true, isn't it?'

'Yes, it's true. But what can we do about it? And he's a loving husband in every other way.'

She sighed, and Nusia paused in her brushing.

'You're very tired aren't you?'

'Of course. I'm always like this. But it'll pass.'

The baby was due in November. It was late July, and Antonina was five months gone. The sickness should be past, but she had been sick for months with Marianna and Zygmunt, as well as the stillborn child. Her mother, Leokadia, had been the same with all five of her children. Nusia had been just a girl herself then, the first-born of a family of ten, coming nervously as nursery maid to Antonina's family home. Nusia had had enough of other people's babies, of childbearing and rearing, to last her a lifetime. Perhaps that was why she had never wanted a husband or a family of her own.

'Nusia!' Antonina broke into her thoughts. 'I wish you would keep Marianna away from the village. There's sickness in the place, you know. Or so I've heard, anyway.'

'She never goes there. Why would she? Who would take her? Besides, it was only dead cats in the well, wasn't it? That's enough to make anyone ill.'

'The water's clear enough now. But there are still two people laid up with fever.'

'I heard something of that, yes.'

'A peddler came from Olesko, and fell down dead outside the church. They say that the woman who laid out his body has been taken ill now.'

'Who has been worrying you with such tales?' asked Nusia.

'Zygmunt. And he had it from his tutor, who had it from one of the grooms when he was out riding. You know how these things go.' She laughed. 'Meissen is dosing himself with patent medicines from Austria.'

'And walking around with a bundle of herbs under his nose. I've seen him. That explains it.'

'Do you think there really is sickness in the village?'

'Peddlers and tramps die of exhaustion all the time, and he was an old man.'

'I hope you're right. But take care of Marianna. You know what a minx the child is for running off. Tell Dorota to keep an eye on her. I don't want her put in any danger.'

There was still no respite from the heat. The woman who had laid out the peddler's body was Katarina, Danilo's mother. Soon, she grew very ill. Gavril watched her in the stuffy gloom of the thatched hut. She was complaining of terrible pains in her head and lower body. She would start up from sleep and stare about her as though the room were full of devils. After a while, Gavril went to the tavern, unable to bear her delirious mutterings.

'Have a drink,' said his neighbour, Piotr. He had sold a length of his wife's woven cloth at the market that day, and was feeling generous. 'Go on. Have a drink. I must say, you look poorly yourself, Gavril, but there's nothing like krupnik for chasing sickness away!'

'It's my daughter who's sick, not me. But I'll have a drink with you anyway!'

'Never been known to refuse,' said Piotr, slapping him cheerily on the back.

The truth was that Gavril was feeling very unwell. His teeth were chattering, and his limbs ached. He drank as much as he could afford, but after a little while he felt queasy and left the inn, staggering home, his head swimming. Later that night, he took to his bed, and Danilo was left to fetch and carry for both, bringing water from the well to bathe their faces and moisten their cracked lips. His grandfather was dozing and groaning intermittently, but it was his mother who terrified him.

One moment she was asking him who he was, and the next she was clasping him close, whispering 'My little Danilo. My darling!'

It was the first show of affection he had known from her in years but now it terrified him. He laid her down and tried to make her drink. He didn't know what else to do.

After three days and nights, during which he tended his two invalids and slept fitfully whenever he could, one of the older women of the village came in, bringing some porridge in a wooden bowl and a little bread and ale. She cast a troubled glance at Katarina, who lay moaning on the thin straw palliasse that served her as a bed. Then she peered into Danilo's face.

'How are you feeling, son?'

He shook her off. 'I'm all right. But what can I do? How can I help them?'

'Give them water. Pray.'

'Why must I pray?'

'Because I saw the beggar that died.'

She went over and twitched back the ragged covers that Danilo had tucked around his mother. Katarina shuddered.

'I'm cold. I'm perished,' she muttered, fumbling for the covers, but anyone could see that her body was a torch. The old woman gestured to the red spots, like flea bites, on Katarina's breast and face. There were fleas and bug aplenty in this hut, but she didn't think these were ordinary bites.

'There,' she said. 'I guessed as much. You'll be lucky to escape with your own life. How are you feeling?'

He pushed her aside, and caressed his mother's forehead, smoothing the tangled hair. 'I told you. I feel fine. But what is it? What's wrong with them? Aren't you afraid that you'll fall ill as well?'

'No. No, I won't fall ill.'

She gestured at her face, and he saw, overlain by the brown freckles of age, the deep pock marks there. He had not noticed them before. He had always thought her simply old and ugly.

'I used to be pretty, although you may not believe so. The disease took my looks, but left me my life. Fifteen years ago, before you were born, it came back, and I took ill again, but only mildly. People seldom take this sickness twice, and if they do, it's never so bad the second time. I don't think I'll fall ill a third time. I have never known it happen and I've lived a long time. Some never get it at all. Maybe you'll be lucky.'

'Are there others in the village? Others who are sick?'

'Not yet, but there will be. I'll do what I can, but you must eat, Danilo. Even if they can't, you must. And get out of this hut sometimes. You have to keep as strong as you can, if you want to stay well. Besides, we're going to need all the gravediggers we can muster. And after that, there will be plenty of work for you, I can guarantee it.'

With this grim advice, she left him alone to scurry between his mother and his grandfather, but he spent more time with his mother. He ate some of the bread and ale the old woman had brought, finding, to his surprise, that he was very hungry. Then he went out for a while, but he didn't dare to stray far from the hut and soon he heard his mother calling him. She had been sick. He cleaned it up as best he could, but the bedclothes were filthy and smelled vile.

Later on that day, when he felt that he had been transported into a kind of hell from which there would never be any escape, there was a tap on the door that stood ajar to let the stale air out and the warm air in. He heard a quiet Polish voice bidding him 'good afternoon'. He stood up, conscious of his filthy appearance and the stench of sickness in the room.

But the women who came in smiled at him, for all the world as though she were paying an afternoon call to a friend.

Antonina Diduska held out her hand to him. He took it, and found himself kissing it, as he had been taught.

'Your name?' she asked him.

'Daniil. But they call me Danilo, my lady.'

'They tell me your mother and your grandfather are very ill.'

'They are.'

She set down a basket, and began to unpack it, behaving as calmly as though the hovel was her own parlour.

'Now listen to me. I've brought clean blankets and clothes, some food and medicine. But is there no-one to help you? You're so young!'

He drew himself up to his full height.

'I'm almost a man!'

'You must be the same age as my son, and he's not yet a man. Not in my eyes. But forgive me, Danilo. You're doing a man's work anyway. Do you have fresh water here?'

'I bring it in every day.'

Antonina took a clean linen nightdress out of her basket, and approached the woman on the bed.

'Your mother would be more comfortable in this, I think. What's her name?'

'Katarina.'

With an effort, Danilo propped his mother upright. Together, they struggled to strip the filthy rags from her. Then Antonina sponged down the thin body, talking to the woman all the while, and gently calling her by her name. Although Danilo had never seen his mother's naked body before, he felt no shame in the presence of this quiet lady. Katarina had always been modest, pinning up a blanket so that she could undress in comparative privacy behind it.

When they took off the rags, Antonina paused for an instant, seeing the red rash on the woman's body. Danilo heard a little indrawn breath and a murmured, 'Holy Mother of God!' Then Antonina carried on as though she had noticed nothing. At last they pulled the cool, white linen over the narrow shoulders, and laid her back down.

As Antonina stooped over Katarina, the sick woman's eyes flickered open, and her feverish gaze alighted on the necklace that the Polish woman wore, a large chunk of heart shaped amber, encased in intricate silver filigree. Nusia had made Antonina put on amber for the sake of her health. The buttery resin was supposed to have protective properties. A smile spread over Katarina's cracked lips at the sight of the necklace.

Danilo heard his mother whisper, 'Pretty!'

She had always been fond of beads and bright ribbons, although she had never been able to afford them, and possessed only a single string of coral, given her by Danilo's father in their courting days. She wore the coral now. Danilo had never seen her without it. But whenever a peddler or a fair came to the village, Katarina would spend as much time as she could, gloating over the brightly coloured trinkets, returning again and again to finger them. Antonina hesitated, then reached up and unfastened the necklace, placing it in Katarina's hand, curling the thin fingers around the warm, golden heart. When Katarina was laid down again, with a fresh blanket tucked around her and the necklace still within her grasp, they washed Gavril's face and hands and made him reasonably comfortable too. Then Antonina turned her attention to the boy.

'Now, what about you?'

'I'm all right. Not ill at all.'

She came over, and held his forehead. It was such a motherly gesture that he found himself leaning into the cool hand. He was surprised to feel tears scalding his cheeks. Ashamed, he tried to control them, but they came anyway.

She sat down, and held his hand while he wept. She saw the dark eyes fringed with long black lashes, now damp with tears. A tempest of thoughts and fears filled her head: pity for this child, fear for herself, fear for her own children. If only she had known. She had thought it was a simple fever, brought on by bad food or bad water or both. She had thought herself safe. Too late now. Besides, if she had known, what then? Could she have stood by and done nothing? Yes, because Stefan would have made her stay away. And perhaps he would have been right. She thought of the danger to the child inside her, and then it dawned on her that she mustn't touch Zygmunt or Marianna. She mustn't kiss them or hold them or go near either of them, until she knew.

Danilo felt her grip on his hand tighten. He thought, she's afraid she might have caught it too. Maybe she has. Maybe I have. Maybe we'll all die.

They sat there together, fearfully, and she looked down at the dirty brown hand, and thought, with prescience, this will have to do. This stranger's child will have to do for all.

She leaned down, and kissed his damp cheek, then made the sign of the cross on his forehead with her thumb.

'God bless you and keep you well. Be strong, Danielek. I'll come back if I can but I may not be able to. You understand that?'

It was the affectionate Polish diminutive of his name. She was in the habit of changing her own children's names like this: Marianka, Zygus. Brown eyes looked bravely into brown. He said 'What is it? What is this illness? Does it have a name, my lady?'

She nodded briefly, sighed as she spoke. 'Oh yes, Danielek . It has a name and you ought to know it. They call it the smallpox.'

Chapter Four

DANILO'S MOTHER DIED A FEW days later, her face a mass of suppurating sores. His grandfather survived. The crisis of the disease passed; the old man lived, though somewhat disfigured, but the young woman died. Danilo found himself wishing that it had been the other way round. He could have taken care of his mother. Worked to support her. Nursed her back to health. He didn't love his grandfather. He was attached to Gavril, only as a dog becomes attached to the presence and power of a cruel master. He had always imagined that one day his mother would praise him, would embrace him as Antonina had embraced him. Now, it would have to remain a dream.

The body was laid out by the woman who had brought him bread and milk a few days earlier. Antonina's nightdress had been washed and would serve as a fine shroud, she said. Danilo took the amber heart from his mother's grasp, leaving her to be buried in his father's coral.

'Now you're learning,' said Gavril. 'We can sell that. It'll fetch a tidy sum.'

He was sorry for his daughter's death, but if there was one thing life had taught him it was that all opportunities must be grasped.

'No. It was a gift. But I can't bear to see it buried with her, and I won't sell it.'

'What do you mean you won't sell it? Who are you to decide that? Give it to me!'

Danilo, who had put the necklace in his pocket, dodged nimbly out of his grandfather's way.

'I won't sell it and that's the end of it.'

'I'll beat the living daylights out of you,' quavered Gavril, but it was an empty threat. He couldn't have mustered the strength to beat a dog, never mind his grandson.

Danilo stayed resolute in the face of Gavril's blustering. He wanted something of Antonina for himself and – not trusting the old man – carried the amber heart about with him. Later, he transferred it to the wooden chest where his mother had kept her few personal possessions. This box contained a hidden compartment that had been a secret between mother and son; it was here that Katarina had always kept a little money, not wanting Gavril to find it and spend it on drink. Danilo left the money where it was and put the amber necklace in there too. He didn't know when or if he might have need of it, but it gave him some comfort to know that it was well away from his grandfather's greedy hands.

A few days after the funeral, Danilo went out early in the morning and saw the Diduski carriages setting off on their way back to Lisko. The servants went together in the open cart, with an indignant and mutinous Wolfgang Meissen squeezed in beside them. Stefan cantered along with Marianna seated before him, and Zygmunt kept pace on his own mount. The fine family carriage went more slowly and its windows were covered. Inside sat Nusia, who would not leave her mistress, and Antonina, who was already struggling with the first signs of the disease: fever, intense fatigue and aching limbs, all of which were only aggravated by the discomfort of the journey.

'It's nothing, nothing at all,' she had said bravely. 'I must have just caught a chill.'

But ever since she had come back from her visit to the village, she would not go near the children, nor let them come close to her, no matter how much Marianna fussed and wept over the enforced separation.

When Antonina had ventured to tell Stefan the true nature of the sickness that was beginning to spread through the village, he had tried to take her in his arms, but she had pushed him away.

'I touched the woman and the old man. Yes. They were both sick. Then I saw the marks on them, but it was too late. Stefan, you must keep away from me for a while. It's only sensible to take precautions. I don't want the children close to me, and they must have someone. It had better be you, for I know Nusia won't keep away from me. And if ...' She could not finish the sentence. 'I may need a nurse and you won't do, my darling. Nusia will be able to look after me. She says she won't fall ill and I believe her. She knows this sickness.'

'Why did you stay, when you knew? Why didn't you come away immediately? You stayed and tended to that woman. You breathed that foul air. You were there for more than an hour.'

'It was a short enough time. The child was alone, struggling to take care of two sick adults.'

'What child?'

'A boy. Zygmunt's age. He may fall ill himself. There are few who escape.'

'Boy be damned. I hope he does. What right had you to do this, Antonina? What right had you to risk yourself and our children, for the sake of some peasant who would probably be better off dead!'

'Don't shout at me, Stefan. You'll only make me cry. My head's aching.'

He would have tried to kiss her again, but she moved away. 'Go to the children, Stefan. Send Nusia to me now, and go to the children.'

The following day, Antonina felt worse. She was sick, and there were pains in her arms and legs.

The cook made a strong herbal brew, and Nusia gave it to her mistress at intervals throughout the day. Antonina said that she was feeling better, but Nusia saw the flushed cheeks, the bright eyes, and felt sick with apprehension.

'Why can't I go to my mamma?' asked Marianna. 'I always go to mama in the afternoons. Is she ill?'

'We'll just have to wait and see. But I'm sure you wouldn't like to be laid up in bed, Marianna, so you'll just have to be patient and say your prayers like a good girl.'

Zygmunt, who understood the situation better than his sister, played games with her in the gardens, but he had been warned not to leave the park, and not to approach anyone other than the immediate household, not even the horsemen or farm workers. Smallpox was rife in the village now, and Stefan was making arrangements for the family's prompt return to Lisko. So it was that Danilo saw them leave, watching the carriages in the company of one of the other stable boys. The boy was awkward, not knowing what to say about Danilo's mother. Besides, his own brother was ill now, and he was afraid for himself and his family.

'Why is the carriage shuttered?' asked Danilo, who had been hoping for a last glimpse of Antonina.

'They say the lady herself is ill now. She was down in the village giving alms to the poor and got something better for her trouble!' The boy laughed and spit viciously in the dust.

'You mean the mistress?'

'That's the one. Serve her right. Serve them all right.'

Danilo said nothing. He watched Stefan go by, his forehead furrowed into a deep frown, with Marianna huddled up close to her father, unmoving. Danilo watched the carriage until it was a haze of dust, fading slowly into the distance. Then he turned back towards the hut. His grandfather would be waiting for him. The old man would need water and a little bread. There was the heel of a loaf that one of their neighbours had brought, and some early apples, small and sour to be sure, but edible. Perhaps Gavril would like one, although it would have to be peeled and perhaps softened over the fire. In his sickness, Danilo's grandfather had become like a child, and must be humoured.

But he won't take his belt to me in future, Danilo thought.

He had become aware of his height and the strength in his arms. He had lifted his mother as easily as lifting a feather quilt, for she had been about as heavy, but he had managed the bulk of the old man too. He would grow taller and stronger yet, as Gavril grew feeble. He felt triumphant and sad. Most of all, he felt guilty about Antonina, and he wished her well, with all his heart. She had been kind to him when he was at his most needy. It would be a miserable God who repaid such kindness with disease and death, but this gave him no hope. On balance, he thought that God took no thought for him and those like him.

'Don't let her die. Don't you dare let her die!' he repeated, over and over and again.

Soon, Danilo had to leave his grandfather alone through the day and go back to work. There was plenty of work for the able-bodied, because it was harvest time and so many people were sick. Danilo divided his energies as best he could between the stables and the fields. He was well fed, and even earned a little extra money. Sometimes he brought vodka home for his grandfather. Gavril drank it and, as usual, became aggressive, but now his threats were empty. When the old man lashed out, Danilo only moved out of range and smiled.

'Don't do that,' he said quietly. 'I'll not stand for it any more!'

The man persisted for a few seconds, his arms flailing wildly, but Danilo caught at his wrists and held them, feeling the thin bones beneath the skin and the fluttering pulse, wondering how this frail person could ever have inspired so much fear in him. He marvelled at how quickly everything could change.

'Don't do it!' he repeated, and at last the old man subsided into his chair. There were tears of frustration in his eyes. Danilo felt a sudden pity for the man's helplessness. He saw fear in the thin, pitted face.

'Don't worry!' he said, more gently. 'I'll take care of you. I'll not see you starve. But keep your fists to yourself, for I'll not be beaten either. I'm a man now, and I won't be beaten by you or anyone else.'

One morning, not long after he had watched the Diduski family's departure, Danilo left his grandfather with food and water to hand and the promise of one of the village women to come in throughout the day. He made his way to the stables, and found the steward there, deep in conversation with the groom. He crept close to listen. Their conversation was all about the family. Word had come early that morning. Antonina Diduska had died. She had lost the infant boy she was carrying and then she had died, weakened by the disease and the birth. Nusia was ill too, but only very mildly, with scarcely any rash, and was expected to survive unscathed. The rest of the family were well, thanks to Antonina's foresight. Danilo went away and began to brush the pony that Marianna had ridden during her stay. It was a docile creature and craned around to caress his neck with its soft mouth. He leant in against its flank, and let the tears flow freely, for Antonina, for his mother, for himself, left alone to care for an old man he could neither love nor respect.

Marianna had caught glimpses of her mother, smiling and waving at her from windows at Podlaski and then, briefly, at Lisko, but after that, she had seen nothing more of her until just before the funeral, when she was ushered into the room where Antonina was laid out in her coffin, the dusting of white powder on her face doing little to disguise the ravages of the disease.

'That's not my mama!' she wailed, beginning to sob. 'That's not my mama at all! I want my mama!'

Young as she was, she could see that the figure in the coffin was nothing like her mother. It was an ugly, desiccated cocoon from which the bright butterfly had already flown.

Nusia was choked with tears, resigned but utterly miserable. Stefan remained well, but he was bitter and silent for weeks. Zygmunt bottled up his sorrow, and allowed himself the luxury of tears in solitude. Marianna, on the other hand, filled the house with an enraged howling, like an injured animal.

At last, Stefan lost all patience. 'Nusia, can you and Dorota not keep her in order? Surely two of you can control the child! I need some peace and quiet.'

'Sir, it's only natural for her to grieve.'

'But not to upset the whole household like this! I'm so sorry for her, but we're all suffering.'

Meissen, the tutor, had come to see Stefan that morning. He had spoken formal and flowery words of sympathy, but then he had gone on to tell Stefan that the prolonged wailing from the nursery each night was disturbing his sleep.

'I wouldn't approach you in your grief, but I'm worried about the child. Perhaps she should see a doctor.'

'Marianna has lost her mother!'

Nevertheless, the intensity of her emotions worried Stefan. His daughter always seemed to feel her joys and sorrows more keenly than other people. He didn't know how to comfort her but realised that he must try.

He found Marianna in the nursery, her face red and swollen. Her sorrow moved him to such pity that tears stung his own eyes. He took her into his arms, and she burst into tears again. She said, between sobs, 'I hate Podlaski! Why did we ever go to Podlaski? It's a hateful place with hateful people. I never want to see it again!'

Into her mind came the face of the boy who had watched their arrival at the house, a face filled with hatred and envy. She hoped he had died of the plague that had killed her mother. She hoped he had suffered too.

'Marianna, you mustn't be so wild and angry. It's God's will. Your mother would hate to see you like this. She loved you so much!'

Even as he mouthed the platitudes, Stefan knew that he didn't believe them. He would always blame himself. The child was right. They should have stayed happily at Lisko. He thought of Antonina's sweet face and the child she had been carrying, his tiny son, and sobs choked his words. He rested his chin on top of Marianna's silky hair and held her close. She reached her arms up and clung to his neck.

The scent of her reminded him of her mother. It was both painful and calming. When at last he saw that her eyes had closed, he summoned Dorota and slid the sleeping child carefully beneath the bedclothes, tucking the quilt around her chin.

That night, when Marianna cried out in her sleep, Nusia came to the room, dismissed Dorota to her own bed, and climbed in beside the child. Marianna huddled up against her. Resting her head on the soft, linen – covered breasts, she put her thumb in her mouth, as she had done years before. She murmured 'Nunu!' several times over to herself and soon fell asleep.

Chapter Five

FOR THREE YEARS AFTER THE death of her mother, Marianna ran wild about the park at Lisko. Stefan found that the memory of his precious Antonina clung like dust to every corner of the house and the gardens she had loved, but it gave him no comfort. He took himself off to the city, leaving Marianna in Nusia's care. The first year set the pattern. Stefan spent more and more time in Lemberg, becoming withdrawn and scholarly, a mere shadow of the sociable man he had once been. His cousin and her husband lived in a comfortable house in that city and they offered Stefan a small suite of rooms. They were a couple who led lives of quiet respectability. Stefan spent his days reading and writing. Whenever he came home to Lisko, it was simply to throw himself into estate business which, for much of the year, he left to his steward. He left the care of Zygmunt to Wolfgang Meissen, with occasional visits to such friends as the boy had made among sons of the local gentry.

All summer long, Marianna ran about the park and through the forest, often going as barefoot as the country children with whom she now played freely. She would take them fishing in the pond where carp were bred for the table, until they were chased away by an enraged steward. But he and Marianna knew that there was no-one with the authority to punish her. Often she would call down the wrath of the gardener by leading raiding parties on his precious strawberry or raspberry plants. The other children were keenly aware of Marianna's status, but she used it or ignored it at whim. Sometimes she behaved like one of them, running, laughing, shouting and screaming; but occasionally, she was very much the grand lady. Since it seemed to the other children to be part of some game, they did as they were told when she was in the mood to order them about, and accepted her on equal terms when she was in a kinder frame of mind. She was incapable of sustaining quarrels.

Her skin grew unfashionably brown each summer. She was growing tall. Her thin brown calves showed beneath skirts that were always too short for her, and her dark curls framed a deceptively sweet face and flowed in a mad - -tangle down her back. No fat ringlets for her now. She rode without a saddle, with her long legs thrown comfortably over the horse, not perched sedately to one side. She could use her thighs and knees as skilfully as any Cossack.

Once, Wolfgang Meissen came upon her galloping through the trees and in spite of himself felt a grudging admiration for her.

'I've seen lancers with less skill than your sister,' he said to Zygmunt, half scandalised, half charmed. 'What an Amazon the child is!'

'Oh she's a good horsewoman. Almost as good as me!' said Zygmunt.

Actually, she was better, but he would never have admitted as much.

He was sixteen now and he had grown used to Marianna's behaviour. Visiting friends would comment on his sister's strange appearance, but it was clear that they admired her. Their sisters were generally quiet, self-effacing girls. Marianna behaved like a boy, and they were entranced by her boldness and her daring. On his infrequent visits to Lemberg, prompted by some sense of responsibility, Zygmunt mentioned Marianna, but his father seemed reluctant to discuss her.

'What's wrong with her?' he asked. 'Is your sister not happy?'

'She's happy enough.'

'She's so fond of Lisko. Always has been. She wouldn't like the city at all, or I might have thought of bringing her with me.'

'I know that, father. But perhaps she needs a governess,' suggested Zygmunt, helplessly. His friends' sisters all had proper governesses.

'But she has Nusia.'

Stefan had indulged himself in his bereavement until retreat from reality became a habit that was too hard to break. His books seemed more real to him than his children. Sometimes he felt a vague sense of guilt about this, but not enough to make him want to change.

Zygmunt knew in his heart that something should be done about Marianna, that his mother would be horrified by her behaviour.

'I think maybe Nusia isn't enough,' he said, but his father was already deep in a book, and didn't hear him.

At last, Stefan went back to Lisko, bringing his cousin and her husband with him. Marianna was nowhere to be found. Dorota was summoned from the kitchen, where she had been helping the cook.

'Where's Marianna? Shouldn't you be with her,' said Stefan.

The girl promptly burst into tears.

'What on earth's the matter?' he asked.

'I can never keep up with the young lady these days. I was taken on as a nursery maid, sir, but she doesn't want me now. She says she's too old for me. That's why I'm working in the kitchen. When I try to speak to Miss Marianna I get slapped and nipped for my pains! And she calls me such names. You should hear the words she uses!'

'Be quiet!' Zygmunt tried to get close enough to kick the girl on the shins but, for once, Stefan's attention was caught.

'What words?' he asked.

'Terrible, rude words, sir!' sobbed Dorota, the persecution of years bursting out of her. 'It's those wretched children she plays with. Village children. They're a bad influence, but she won't be told. She does just as she pleases and she always has done. She sings awful songs, *drinking* songs, and she says terrible things, and takes the Lord's name in vain. And she hits me!' To Zygmunt's horror, Dorota proceeded to roll up a sleeve and display a plump arm to the assembled company. There, for all to see, was the blue and yellow print of Marianna's hand.

Nusia had been supervising the airing of long-unused bedrooms, but she came down, red faced and embarrassed by the commotion. She shooed Dorota out of the room.

'Miss Marianna will be out in the park somewhere, sir. It's where she usually is. She has her own haunts. You know how it is with children?'

'But she should be here to welcome her cousins.'

After servants had been sent all over the estate, Zygmunt took himself off to the Old Steward's House that served as a storehouse. He pushed open the heavy door, and crept up the stone stairs to the upper floor. Marianna had heard none of the frantic calling, because she lay stretched out, fast asleep, upon a bench that she had made comfortable for herself with straw and a horse blanket from the stables. There was a pile of tattered books on a windowsill, and she was surrounded by the brown cores of green apples. Her face and her feet were about equally grimy, her dress was torn, and a battered straw hat was cast down beside her. He felt his heart twist with affection for her. What was to be done with her? What could any of them do with her? Not for the first time, he wished their mother were still alive.

'Oh Marianna,' he said, sitting down on the bench.

She stirred and sat up.

'Zygmunt!' As a toddler, she had always been out of sorts when woken from her nap. She had never outgrown it and now she pouted at her brother. 'What are you doing here? You know I don't like people coming here.'

'Father has come back and Jan and Augustina are with him. The whole household is looking for you. Dorota told on you, Nusia's all hot and bothered and I don't think your dress will please any of them very much.'

She stood up and smoothed down her faded skirts as if they had been made of fine silk.

'What's wrong with me? And what has Dorota been saying?'

'She's been telling everyone how cruel you are to her.'

'Then she's a liar. I'm never cruel.'

'She has the bruises to prove it.'

'All right. I slapped her and pinched her when she tried to brush my hair. But she hurt me, Zygmunt!'

Zygmunt looked at the tangle of curls. 'I'm not surprised!' he said. 'Marianna, if you go in by the back door, you can probably sneak along to your room. You could clean yourself up before they see you.'

'Why should I?' she asked. 'What's wrong with the way I look?'

'For me, nothing. But they will find plenty to complain of.'

For answer, she picked up her hat and, swinging it cheerfully from her fingers, set off at a run towards the house. Zygmunt followed after, shaking his head in exasperation. No sense, he thought. No sense at all. Or perhaps she genuinely didn't care. He admired her for that.

Stefan and his companions saw Marianna running towards them with her face and feet smeared with mud, straw in her hair, and her dress hitched up to her knees.

My God, what have I done? he thought. And what would Antonina say to me if she could see what her daughter has become?

After Marianna had been bathed, fed and sent early to bed by a shamefaced Nusia, and after the rest had dined, Augustina tackled her cousin.

'You've allowed the girl to become nothing better than a gypsy!'

She was a woman of strong character and very definite ideas of what was acceptable behaviour.

'I had no idea that you'd been leaving her here without proper supervision.'

'What can I do?' asked Stefan, helplessly. 'I don't know how to deal with young girls. I thought Nusia could manage, but it seems I was quite wrong.'

'Nusia is all well and good for a baby, but your daughter is almost a young woman now. She must be taught how to behave, Stefan, and the sooner the better.'

'What do you suggest?'

'A French governess. I have the very person in mind. Her most recent charge has just married, and she's looking for a new situation. As soon as we go back to Lemberg we can interview her together. I promise you, she'll be happy to take your daughter in hand and make a lady of her. Leave it all to me. You'll hardly recognise Marianna the next time you see her.'

Chapter Six

THE FRENCH GOVERNESS WAS VERY fashionably dressed. Her full skirts and embroidered belt served to emphasise her tiny waist with the suspicion of rigid corseting beneath. She carried a parasol. Her bonnet was trimmed with feathers and ribbons, her sharp little face barely concealed beneath a transparent veil. She was nothing like the mousy creatures Marianna had come across in other people's houses. Stefan had taken one horrified look at Ma'amselle Jeanne, and left his cousin to make all the arrangements, relieved that here, at last, was someone who might be capable of taking his daughter in hand.

Zygmunt, on the other hand, fell in love with Jeanne at first sight and soon became her devoted slave, bringing her fruit from the hothouses, picking roses for her, snipping off the thorns, and giving the blooms to her with the dew still fresh on their petals. In return, she treated him with kind condescension.

'Ah, what a *charming* boy,' she would say, and take his offerings with a sweet, vague smile.

She had brought two trunks full of stylish clothes that she had made for herself: tightly laced day dresses with high necks and immense gigot sleeves, bonnets decorated with flowers and feathers and ribbons, alarmingly décolleté evening gowns with very full skirts. The clothes were suitable for the setting, but not very suitable for a household that had become easy-going and informal. Jeanne's presence began to change things. In the evening she would carry a fan, or fresh flowers in a jewelled holder. Dorota, the nursemaid, had been promoted to full time work in the kitchen. Not only was she happier there, but she was deeply impressed by Jeanne, and persuaded her beau to carve her a little flower holder out of wood, so that she could wave it about in imitation of her idol.

Marianna disliked Jeanne on sight. The Frenchwoman reminded her of the doll she had shown to Danilo at Podlaski. She had taken an intense aversion to the little creature. Once they were back at Lisko, she had put her and her fine clothes away at the very back of the nursery cupboard. Loulou reminded her all too bitterly of that tragic summer. But during a foray into the toy cupboard, Jeanne found the doll.

'How beautiful!' she said. 'Such a pretty face. And she has a trunk full of her own finery too!'

'I don't like her.'

'Why ever not?'

Marianna couldn't or wouldn't attempt to explain, so Jeanne insisted on putting the doll at the child's bedside, displacing the roughly carved wooden statue of a seated Christ that had stood there for as long as Marianna could remember.

'Not exactly a work of art,' said Jeanne distastefully, hiding the statue on a high shelf where Marianna couldn't see it properly. 'We'll get you a proper statue of Our Lady from the town instead of this crude thing. And meanwhile, this is a doll suitable for a lady. Let's hope she influences you, Marianna. Although I see no signs of it at present.'

Marianna had grown very tall during the past year, and she was quite unused to coping with her own height. Jeanne, who was smaller than her pupil and dainty, with tiny hands and feet, possessed a knack of making the girl feel clumsy and gauche. Jeanne was always saying how small and weak she was. Small she may have been, but the weakness was entirely fictional. Men seemed attracted to it, never noticing the steel beneath. Perhaps it made them feel strong and protective. Marianna had seen at once that there was a calculating streak running through Jeanne, that she was not weak at all, but had hit upon a means of getting her own way in a difficult world. All the girl's natural grace deserted her in the governess's presence. She fell over her own feet, fidgeted until she knocked ornaments off tables, and hunched her shoulders to disguise her height and her developing breasts.

Stefan had given Jeanne a free hand. After her first exclamations of shocked surprise over Marianna's dress and rude behaviour, she seemed determined to change the girl into a fair copy of herself. Jeanne hunted through chests and cupboards to find clothes that the dressmaker in

Kamionka could rework into something suitable for a young lady, although Jeanne had no high opinion of her skills. She thought she could do much better herself, but it would create entirely the wrong impression. Besides, sewing bored her. She even made one or two forays into Antonina's room, but when Marianna saw her mother's familiar garments draped over Jeanne's arm, she protested so loudly that the governess was persuaded to give way.

Nusia, overhearing the altercation, put in a prompt appearance and took Marianna's part.

'Have you no respect for the dead? The child's mother is only three years in her grave! You must put these things back!'

Jeanne had already realised that Nusia held a privileged position in this household. Still she thought it worth the argument.

'What's to become of these garments? They'll be eaten by moths. Such a waste of fine silk!'

'You are not to touch them. Marianna won't have it. Can you blame the poor lamb?'

Jeanne gave in with a bad grace. She thought Marianna spoiled, ugly and stupid to boot. But the house was beautiful and its owner was a wealthy widower, although she was disappointed that he spent so little time there. However, she was well paid and she would certainly make the best of things.

Jeanne was the child of a brief affair between the youngest son of a French aristocrat and a Parisienne contralto, who had performed for Napoleon at the Tuileries Palace. The aristocrat's family had fled France during the previous century's upheavals, but had returned after the Restoration. The young father had not shirked his responsibilities, but had supported mother and daughter as best he could. The truth was that his private resources were not large. When Jeanne was seventeen, her mother had died of the consumption that had lent her body such delicacy and her cheeks such a fascinating bloom. When her father, too, died after a short illness, his family had refused to recognise Jeanne as his daughter and she had been left to make her own way in the world. She often thought that it might have been different if she had been born a boy, but what couldn't be cured must be endured. She had already been given a decent education which was more than could be said for many girls at that time, although she had not inherited her mother's lovely voice. She had a good deal of sharp intelligence as well as a natural vivacity. She was a clever seamstress when she chose, so she could muster a fashionable wardrobe on a shoe-string, reworking many of her mother's old gowns. But life was a struggle and there had been times when the wolf was so close to her door that she could practically smell his breath, hear the scratching of his claws.

She had come to Poland because a friend of her late father had recommended her to a post with a family in Lemberg. The Poles confused her. They were polite, romantic, and yet full of a kind of earthy physicality. She had had admirers in plenty in Lemberg, but after the marriage of her pupil, she had refused them all, and had taken up this offer of another post, aware of the size of the estate and the history of the family. The fact that Lisko had a reasonably young, wealthy, widowed owner was a bonus. But Lisko had not really lived up to expectations. Stefan seldom visited. She found the countryside a trial. Her skirts were always muddy, her shoes were ruined and there were insects everywhere: flies in the butter, gnats and moths in the bedroom, long lines of ants marching through the whole house. Mice gnawed at the walls or scurried about the attics in the night.

In addition to all that, the child was impossible, almost feral and certainly wilful.

With Stefan out of the way, she felt free to take Marianna in hand. She found a stay-makers in Yarychev and took the child, protesting, to be measured, giving directions as to how the stays should be made. Soon Marianna was encased in a cruel contraption of whalebone, steel and buckram. Each morning, Jeanne herself forced Marianna into this, pulling on the laces, pausing for breath, then pulling again until Marianna's growing body had achieved the desired shape.

'There now,' she said. 'Look at yourself. Isn't that better?'

Marianna gazed at herself in the mirror. There were little wads of padding squashed into the two half cones that covered her developing breasts. She put her hands on her hips and turned this way and that, pulling a face.

'Well?' Jeanne demanded again. 'Isn't that so much better?'

'I look like an ant,' said Marianna.

'An ant?'

'Yes. And I think you look like an ant too, if you want to know. How can I sit down? How can I run?'

'Young ladies shouldn't run. They should walk at a sedate pace. Not rush about like nasty, rough boys.'

'I can hardly walk, never mind run. I can't breathe. Look!' She made a sudden stooping motion, the stays gave way with a bang and she fell flat on the floor, giggling.

Jeanne kept her temper with difficulty, laced her into the stays again, and quickly dressed her before she could try the same experiment twice. The gown was a frilled imitation of Jeanne's own, just a little shorter, with pretty cambric pantalettes visible beneath the skirt, in acknowledgement of the wearer's youth. Marianna protested loudly that since she was already much taller than Jeanne, the pantalettes were both embarrassing and superfluous. Her hair was washed, put up at the back and combed into ringlets at each side. Jeanne had even trimmed her a bonnet with lace and ribbons.

Nusia gave a gasp of grudging admiration at the sight of her transformation.

'What a lady!' she said, half pleased, half shocked.

'I hate it, Nunu,' hissed Marianna, when Jeanne was out of earshot. 'I look ridiculous. I can hardly move. I'm afraid to get dirty. And I can't ride either. She tells me I must sit like a lady and wear a riding habit, but how can I go for a good gallop if I do?'

'Ladies should never gallop,' Jeanne had told her, severely. She could never understand the Polish obsession with horses. She thought they were nasty, smelly creatures, unless they were pulling a smart new carriage or a fancy sleigh, when they might be tolerable.

There were, it seemed, a great many things that ladies shouldn't do. Young ladies must never consort with peasant children. It was best to ignore them altogether, but if that were not possible, young ladies must be carefully condescending towards their inferiors. Ladies must not run or shout, whistle or even sing aloud, unless in company, when they were permitted to entertain visitors with a suitably well-rehearsed song or two. They must not climb trees, or eat green apples, or let down their hair so that they could feel the wind and the rain in it. They must not frolic in the stable yard with the hounds, or kiss the puppies on their noses, or rub down ponies to help out the groom, nor must they sneak into the kitchen to be given slices of bread and sour cream with sugar sprinkled on top. Instead they must wait for proper mealtimes, when eating was not made any easier by the fearsome stays.

Marianna might have grown very thin, but for the fact that Nusia would smuggle bread and cheese and pieces of apple cake up to her at night, after Jeanne was safely in bed. Nusia had been banished from Marianna's bedroom, and Jeanne slept in a room along the passage, but she was a sound sleeper and many a midnight feast was consumed by a ravenous Marianna in her own bed, while Nusia stood by, brush in hand, ready to dispose of the incriminating crumbs.

Marianna was not one to give in gracefully. Three years of freedom had given her a taste for independence, and she was a strong-willed child.

'I won't do it!' was her repeated cry. 'I won't do anything you tell me.'

There was a constant battle of wills between Jeanne and Marianna, but Jeanne had authority on her side and Marianna had to give in, even if it was under strong protest. She still escaped, still played with the village children, but now she was hampered by her new clothes, and she could not decently rid herself of them since her old, comfortable garments had been consigned to the kitchen fire.

When she was dressed in her new clothes, her old friends treated her differently. Jeanne's anger at the sight of mud on the fine cambric pantaloons was so terrible that even Marianna was afraid of it. Once or twice, Ma'amselle had flown into such a rage that she had slapped Marianna hard five or six times across the legs and buttocks, holding her still with steely fingers. Once, after a particularly bad transgression, the hand was even drawn sharply across Marianna's cheek, and the previously unknown pain so shocked Marianna that her defiance collapsed for a time.

'Now she knows what it feels like,' said Dorota, in the kitchen. 'Serve her right.' That'll show her!'

Jeanne found the constant battle to tame this wild soul a wearisome business. She knew that waging such a war earned her the dislike of those servants who were fond of the child and that was most of them. Zygmunt and Dorota might admire Jeanne, but Nusia was her bitter enemy. Even the housemaids and stable servants thought Jeanne too proud for her own good and showed it in an offhand manner that verged on rudeness.

Jeanne's one great ally was Zygmunt's tutor, Wolfgang Meissen. He had been here so long that he knew all there was to know about the family, and sometimes he would even consent to walk with her, very decorously, in the park. They made a strange couple, the little Frenchwoman so smart and dainty, the Austrian so tall and thin and straight, striding beside her with his hands firmly fixed behind his back, while she pattered along in thin shoes, trying to keep up with him.

'It was quite different when Antonina Diduska was alive,' he told her. 'Much more civilised.' He was forever comparing the cultured Viennese unfavourably with the Poles and the Ukrainians – Ruthenes, he called them.

'I wish I had known her!' She steered him carefully towards a more private part of the gardens.

'Oh, you would have liked her. The whole house was better run. The children behaved themselves. She was a very kind lady.'

'But surely you get on well enough with your pupil?'

'I used to, but he has little need of me now. I've taught him all I can, and must go back to Vienna very soon. But I shan't be sorry to get back to civilisation, I can tell you.'

The thought of him going to Vienna alarmed her. He had become her ally. She questioned him closely and, heartened by her interest, he described his city to her so vividly that she longed to be there too. It sounded very much like her beloved Paris, and she sometimes thought that it might be a more-than-acceptable substitute.

Jeanne and Wolfgang presided over the dining table 'as though they were father and mother, which they're not and I hate it and I hate them!' said Marianna to Nusia in a fury of loathing and resentment. 'And Zygmunt is no help at all. All he does is make cow eyes at her.'

Zygmunt ate with eyes only for Jeanne. Wolfgang looked straight ahead and seemed embarrassed by mealtimes, though he ate heartily enough, while Jeanne toyed with her food. Marianna watched them scornfully, despising her brother and his moonfaced hankering after the object of her hatred.

'I have an appetite like a bird,' Jeanne remarked, complacently.

'So has Marianna,' said Zygmunt, kicking his sister under the table. 'A vulture.'

The maid smothered a giggle. Meissen mopped his mouth.

'Really, Zygmunt,' said Jeanne, without even the ghost of a smile. 'I don't expect such uncouth remarks from a young gentleman, and certainly not at mealtimes. Eat up your spinach, Marianna.'

Marianna had an aversion to spinach. There was something about its metallic taste and furry texture that made her retch. When Jeanne had discovered this, she seemed to take a perverse delight in ordering that the vegetable be served up two or three times a week. The kitchen gardens were full of it.

'Come now, child. It's good for the complexion, so finish it up,' she told Marianna one lunchtime, over sieved spinach and cold poached eggs.

'I can't! I do hate it so. Everyone knows I hate it. My daddy never makes me eat it.'

'But your father is away now, child, and he left your upbringing in my hands. And it is the hallmark of a lady that she eats whatever is set before her, uncomplainingly.'

'How would you know?' muttered Marianna.

'What did you say?'

'I said how would you know anything at all about what a lady does and doesn't do?' asked Marianna with venom.

Jeanne chose to ignore this open declaration of hostilities, but couldn't help colouring a little.

'Eat up your spinach, Marianna, like a good girl.'

Marianna pushed the soggy green mound to the side of her plate and finished the rest of her meal.

At supper, the spinach appeared again, cold and congealed in the middle of an otherwise empty plate. Marianna left it. That night, Jeanne mounted guard outside her bedroom. Dorota had told her of Marianna's midnight feasts, and she was determined that Nusia should not feed the girl cake and fruit on this occasion, at least.

At breakfast, Marianna was again presented with the spinach and only the spinach, drying a little round the edges. There were mutterings of protest in the kitchen, angry whispers among the servants.

'It isn't right!' said Nusia to the cook. 'The child's mother will be turning in her grave!'

Nobody dared to oppose the little Frenchwoman. At lunchtime, even Zygmunt protested, but Jeanne was adamant, and Marianna finally forced the green slime down her throat. Immediately afterwards, she got up and left the room with her napkin clutched to her mouth. She ran out of the house and vomited violently into a flowerbed, tears of rage and frustration running down her cheeks.

'I hate her,' she said aloud. 'I hate her! I wish she were dead!'

Chapter Seven

WHILE MARIANNA WAS SUFFERING AT the hands of her governess, Danilo was honing his skills as a horseman at Podlaski. He had given almost no further thought to his encounter with the spoilt little girl, but he remembered her mother from time to time, taking the amber heart out of its hiding place and staring at the butter-yellow resin in its delicate filigree case.

At sixteen, Danilo had grown very tall and spare, but the hard physical labour in forest, field and stables had given him the strength of a much older man. As he had grown stronger, Gavril had become more frail. Gazing at his grandfather's yellow face and trembling hands, when he stumbled in from the tavern in the evening, Danilo had no idea how Gavril managed to survive each winter, but survive he did, like a dying tree that puts out a few green leaves every spring. He could do very little productive work, beyond picking through baskets of mushrooms in the autumn, on the look-out for poisonous interlopers, or repairing and polishing bits and pieces of worn tack that Danilo was allowed to bring home from the stables. Danilo was the keeper of the purse, and it was he who doled out a few coins to his grandfather now and then, so that the old man could go out for a drink or buy himself sweetmeats from the occasional visiting peddler. He had a sweet tooth and would hide honey cakes under his straw mattress so that he could chew at them in the night, softening them on his tongue, since he had so few teeth left. He was a pathetic old soul, and Danilo couldn't help but feel sorry for what he had come to, marvelling at the way in which time had so transformed the monster of his childhood into this wailing ghost of his former self.

The small farmers at Podlaski were contracted to work for the estate in return for their houses or a little land. They were free men and women and liked to proclaim as much, but since local power lay with their landlord or his steward, their wellbeing depended very much on their masters. There were a few men who owned the freehold to their property, mostly Poles, mostly the descendants of the old Polish gentry, the *szlachta*, although these smallholders had come down in the world. They behaved like princes but lived, if not like paupers, then with only a few more resources than their neighbours.

Austria saw the fertile province of Galicia as a source of wheat, fighting men and trouble in about equal measure. On the principle of divide and rule, they did what they could to exaggerate such divisions as already existed between Pole and Ukrainian, between Pole and Jew, between Orthodox and Roman Catholic. God forbid, thought the politicians in Vienna, that the people of Galicia should come together, independent of their Hapsburg masters. The estate owners were heavily taxed and it was a good steward who could make the land pay. Ignacy, the Ukrainian steward at Podlaski, walked a fine line between keeping his workers reasonably content and running the estate in a way that would satisfy Stefan. A single bad harvest could spell disaster.

As a Ukrainian in this disputed territory, Gavril had the roof over his head and a tiny patch of stony ground upon which he still grew a few wormy vegetables each year. Beyond that, Danilo was given a small amount of money in payment for his work, enough to keep body and soul together, but not much more than that. Still, he was good with the horses and the steward would sometimes chat to him, treating him as a valued worker rather than the troublesome boy he had once been. He was earning a modicum of respect and he liked it.

Several years passed before Stefan ventured to Podlaski again. The estate had to be cared for, but he would communicate with his manager by letter. He would probably have sold the place if he didn't still have a dowry for Marianna in mind. He was afraid that any money from such a sale would simply be absorbed into Lisko itself, a large estate that needed money and resources. At last, problems arose that demanded Stefan's attention.

There had been an unusually wet and windy spring and summer, quite the opposite of the one that had brought smallpox to the village, but just as deadly. Streams overflowed, the fields were knee deep in mud, and horses and men alike struggled to work in miserable conditions. The fires in the cottages smouldered and smoked, regularly dowsed by the rain that came down the chimneys. There was too much water everywhere, and yet drying anything had become an impossibility. The men's working clothes were caked with layers of mud. When they went home to cottages where water leaked through the thatch, the heavy trousers and coats would be laid in front of the fire to dry, filling each house with the stench of baking mud, wet wool, and human dirt. The clothes would dry overnight, after a fashion. But no matter how much they were brushed in the morning, just getting dressed became an agony, with dried earth tearing at flesh. Lice were an ever-present misery. Danilo remembered that the big house had warm racks in the laundry where clothes and bedding would dry in no time, and all for a Polish landowner who never deigned to visit, although Danilo was sure that the steward and his wife made the most of their privileges.

Quarrels broke out between Polish freeholders and Ukrainian villagers with each side finding the other to blame for a situation that was the fault of neither. Small arguments quickly threatened to turn violent. Sensing rising undercurrents of unrest, Ignacy reluctantly wrote to Stefan asking for advice. The Lisko steward was too occupied with that estate to be spared so, for once, Stefan gritted his teeth and made a solitary journey on horseback to the place that still reminded him of the saddest time of his life.

It was a long journey and in his anxiety to get there and back again with all speed, Stefan over-pressed his horse, with the result that the black stallion was lame by the time he arrived at Podlaski. He would have to stay longer than he had intended, while the animal recovered.

With the rain still teeming down, a quarrel had erupted between a widowed Polish smallholder and a Ukrainian who worked on the Pole's land in return for the use of a cottage. The Ukrainian had a daughter called Alyona, seventeen years old, a diminutive girl with a waterfall of thick, light brown hair, and the Polish farmer was accused of enticing her into his house and assaulting her. He denied it. He had, he said, simply invited her in to dry herself before his kitchen fire. The girl herself had not complained at first but, urged on by her father, had started to protest that the farmer had laid hands on her as she stood drying her legs in front of his fire. With astonishing speed, the quarrel had escalated. Neighbours took sides, with the Poles declaring that the girl was a flirt, while the Ukrainians indignantly pointed out that it was no minor allegation. Alyona's reputation (and consequent marriageability) was at stake. The Orthodox and Catholic priests tried to intervene but only added fuel to the flames.

By the time Stefan arrived to consult with his steward, the two communities were barely on speaking terms, and gangs of young men were roaming the village, armed with knives, spoiling for a fight.

'How could such a small thing cause so much trouble?' he asked Ignacy.

'Sir, you know what it's like. It doesn't take much. And the weather doesn't help.'

Stefan sighed. 'You'd better bring them here. Let me speak to the girl and her father, and the farmer too. There must be some solution.'

Danilo had been watching these goings-on from the sidelines. As usual, he confined himself to the stables whenever possible, preferring the company of the horses. He was tending to Stefan's horse when the master came to the stables to check on progress.

Stefan didn't recognise Danilo. He saw only a sullen peasant who, Ignacy said, seemed to have a way with sick horses in spite of his youth.

'Can you sort him out?'

'He was ridden too hard, sir. He needs rest as much as anything.'

'I'd rather not be here for long.'

'Then he'll be lame again by the time you get back to Lisko. If you get there at all!'

Stefan frowned. 'Are you always this blunt?'

He was surprised to see a grin overspread the boy's thin features. 'Only about horses, sir.'

'Well, I can't blame you for that. I appreciate your honesty. Do what you can. I'll postpone my journey. This lad is one of my favourites.'

'Thank-you, sir.'

Stefan rubbed his hand up and down the horse's neck. 'What's your name?'

'Daniil Bandura. Danilo, sir.'

'Ignacy has some regard for you, it seems. For your ability with the horses, at any rate.'

'I like them, that's for sure.'

'That's obvious. And it's clear that they like you.'

'You know where you are with horses, sir.'

'Unlike people, you mean?'

'I suppose so.'

'Well I'm with you there. Tell me. This girl. The one who's supposed to be the cause of all the trouble ...'

'Alyona, sir.'

'She must be about your age.'

'A year older.'

'But you know her?'

'I do.'

'Is she telling the truth? Did the man assault her?'

'I don't know.' He shrugged. 'It's what she says. Now.'

'And is she a truthful girl?'

Danilo sighed. 'Mostly. She flirts. Oh, I don't blame her for that. She's pretty, and men go a bit daft over her. But she's a good girl.'

'And the man she's accusing?'

'Tomas? He's all right. He lost his wife a year ago and he has a couple of children. I haven't really had any dealings with him, but they say he's honest.'

'So he doesn't have wandering hands?'

'Not that I've ever heard. He seemed to be very happy with his wife. If you want a man with wandering hands, the miller's your man. Nobody's safe with him. Well, no woman, anyway. Even the old *babushkas*.'

'So what do you think happened?'

'Oh, sir!' Danilo shook his head.

'You don't want to get involved?'

'I'd rather not.'

'But if it were to go no further than here and now? Just between the two of us?'

'Just between the two of us, she likes the man.'

'She *likes* the man?'

'There was a time, through the winter, when she had eyes for no-one but him. Why else would she have gone in to dry herself in front of his fire? He didn't drag her inside. Nobody says that. Not even her. And no unmarried girl would put herself in that position. No good girl, anyway.'

'Well, I did wonder about that.'

'He's a Pole, she's one of us, but there are plenty such marriages. They're near neighbours. He's young and free and sorely in need of a wife as far as I can see.'

'Then why on earth ...?'

'I think she was trying to force his hand. He wants her, and the children need a mother, but he feels he ought to be mourning his wife. Or he did. It all went wrong, sir. Her father got to know about it, whatever it was. A kiss maybe? Nothing worse than that. And flew into a rage. She thought her father would try to arrange a match between them. Instead it sparked a war. It's madness.'

Stefan stared at Danilo for a few moments, and then started to laugh. The younger man found himself chuckling too.

'Thank-you, Danilo! I'm very grateful to you. I'll tell Ignacy what a help you've been. You're a very astute young man.'

A little while later, after a meeting between Stefan and all the parties concerned, a betrothal was announced between the Polish farmer and the Ukrainian girl. Stefan himself had sweetened things with a gift of money for the couple and a small parcel of good land for the girl's father. There were some in the village who muttered about underhanded deals being done, but since the couple in question were so obviously happy, things calmed down for the present. Danilo was surprised when the steward sought him out.

'You seem to have made a good impression on Mr Diduski.'

'I did my best, sir.'

'Better keep up the good work, then. You never know, if you work hard, you might finish up as one of the grooms one day.'

Chapter Eight

In the spring of Jeanne's second year at Lisko, Wolfgang Meissen caught a bad chill and took to his bed. A day or so later, Jeanne succumbed to the same infection. As usual, Stefan was in Lemberg. Zygmunt had seized the opportunity of his tutor's illness to spend a few days with friends at a nearby estate, hunting during the day and drinking more than was good for him at night.

The illness was not serious, but Jeanne felt very miserable for three days. No-one came near her during that time, except servants bringing trays of plain food. At her lowest point, she cried into her pillow, wishing herself anywhere but in this yellow house, full of people she despised, who seemed to return the dislike with interest.

In the midst of these recriminations, she heard a hesitant knock on the door and when she called out 'come in', she was amazed to see Wolfgang Meissen.

'I thought you might be lonely. I'm feeling very much better and I wondered if I might perhaps chat to you or even read to you.'

'But someone may come!' she said, clutching the bedcovers close to her chin.

'They've all gone out.' He wouldn't have had the courage to come to her room otherwise.

It was mid afternoon. Nusia and Marianna had gone to pay a courtesy call on the Orthodox priest, and most of the servants had taken the chance of some free time for an hour or two. Wolfgang's face creased with concern at the sight of Jeanne's shiny nose and swollen eyes. Even he could see that it owed more to sorrow than a cold in the head.

'Have you been crying?'

Jeanne blew her nose on a square of cambric that was quite inadequate for the purpose. She said, 'I'm feeling very low.'

Wolfgang saw the broderie edging of her linen nightdress and the little fingers clutching at the sheet and felt a sudden desire to comfort her. He thought her very vulnerable and womanly. He sat down in the chair beside the bed and seized one of her hands.

'Oh, my dear,' he said, and suddenly smothered her fingers in kisses.

The broderie at the cuff tickled his nose. He pushed it back, turned the hand over and kissed the wrist where the skin was soft and fragrant.

'Oh, my dear,' he repeated fervently, surprising himself.

He had, she thought, a nice enough face, with freckles and a sandy moustache. It was pleasant to be kissed by him. But when they heard the laughter of returning household servants, she pushed him away from her.

'You must go now!'

'Am I to come back?' he asked, humbly.

'Of course you are. Of course.'

That night, she dreamed about him. When she woke, she decided that perhaps her illness should last just a little longer. She was tired of the constant battles with Marianna. The next afternoon, Wolfgang came to her room again and this time she allowed him to put his hand between the folds of her nightdress and caress her breast.

'Save yourself for the right man,' her mother had told her. But the right man had been a long time in coming, and she had lately felt her youth slipping away. She was almost thirty. When she gazed in her mirror, she could see faint wrinkles around her eyes. What if the right man never came? She wanted marriage, a home of her own and children.

'Come at night,' she said, breathlessly, as he left her. 'The door will be open.'

That night, Wolfgang waited, expectant and nervous, until well past midnight. Through his open window, he heard the sounds of hunting owls in the park. He heard the silvery chimes of the French clock in the drawing room, and still he waited. Then he crept along the corridors from his room into the central part of the house, past Marianna's door. He paused for a moment there, but Marianna had been roaming the park all day and she slept soundly, exhausted by the unaccustomed exercise. He found Jeanne, awake and alert, her eyes shining like those of some small animal. He saw that she was naked beneath the sheet. He was going to extinguish the candle he had carried with him, but she stopped him.

'No,' she said. 'No – it's better to see.'

He felt foolish in his nightshirt, not knowing whether to keep it on or take it off, but she summoned him with a gesture and carefully lifted the shirt over his head. Then he crept in beside her, and she ran her fingers over his body, immediately arousing him.

She said, 'You're new to this, Herr Meissen, aren't you?' and he nodded dumbly.

'Well, so am I,' she said. 'Believe it or not I have never done this before. Not with any man. But all the same I think I know more than you.'

One unbearably stuffy night, in late summer, Marianna had gone to bed early with a headache and a sense of oppression that she blamed on the thundery weather. In the early hours of the morning, she was woken by an unaccustomed ache in her stomach. She sat up and went to tug aside the curtains, to let the moonlight shine in. She was disturbed to see a stain of something dark on the bed and on her white nightdress too. She must have injured herself. She was seized by the idea that she was going to bleed to death, for blood this most certainly was, although the moonlight milked it of all colour. Then clouds swallowed the moon, and she saw the first flash of lightning and heard the rumble of the thunder that had been threatening all day.

Normally Marianna's first thought would have been to go and seek out Nusia, but Nusia was spending time with one of her brothers who was dangerously ill. Suddenly she remembered that Jeanne had once told her, quite matter-of-factly, 'Child, if you ever find blood on your clothes or in the bed, tell me at once.'

She had not understood at the time, and had asked in some alarm, 'What do you mean? I bleed if I cut myself. But why should there be blood in my bed?'

'It means you'll be a woman.'

She moved to the door, her hands clutching her stomach as a knife of cramp tore into it, but the pain faded as quickly as it had come. She tiptoed along the corridor to Jeanne's room. There was a faint glow of light from inside. Jeanne might have fallen asleep over a book, leaving her candle burning. Pausing, Marianna was surprised to hear noises coming from inside. They were sounds such as she had never heard before, and she thought at first that Jeanne, too, must be in pain, whimpering like an animal. She stood still for a moment, listening and wondering what to do, her own discomfort forgotten in her surprise. Another noise had imposed itself upon the first: deep masculine groans and the sound of the bed, rattling and moving rhythmically on the wooden floor. Marianna stooped down and applied her eye to the narrow space between the double doors.

She wasn't totally ignorant. She had seen animals mating, had come to accept this in the matter-of-fact way of all country-born children. She had heard stories about adults from the peasant children and from Zygmunt too. All the same, her first thought was that Herr Meissen was attacking Ma'amselle Jeanne. But that could not be, for Jeanne was laughing. Marianna stood still, fascinated by the sight of the two bodies entwined on the bed. There was a flash of lightning that illuminated the whole room, immediately followed by a crash of thunder. In that brief moment, she saw Wolfgang Meissen, braced above the governess, her legs, protruding from beneath his thighs, looking so ludicrous that Marianna almost laughed.

It occurred to Marianna that she had never seen Ma'amselle's legs before, except for the odd glimpse of them, clad in black or white stockings, as she walked on a windy day. Marianna turned away from the door and sank to the floor, resting her back against the wall, a prey to revulsion and excitement, all mixed up hatefully together. Her cheeks were burning. Inside the room, the cries died away, turned to sighs and whispers.

Outside, the thundery rain began to rattle down. The trees in the park groaned under the sudden onslaught of water. Her belly gave a great twinge of pain. She crawled back to her room and lay down on her bed, shivering. The following morning, she approached her governess, apprehensively carrying her bloodstained nightdress. Surprisingly kind, Jeanne explained about her monthly cycle and supplied her with folded rags. Briskly, she reiterated her statement that Marianna was a woman now and this was to be welcomed, not feared.

'What do you mean?' asked Marianna.

'It means you are ready to have a husband.'

'I almost woke you in the night,' said Marianna, who didn't think she wanted a husband at all.

The look that Jeanne cast her confirmed that the vision had been no dream.

'But the thunder frightened me a little and I thought I would wait till morning,' she hastened to add.

At breakfast, the sight of Wolfgang Meissen, so upright and careful, made her blush and choke on her bread, so that she had to leave the table.

'I felt sick,' she lied when Jeanne came looking for her.

'It sometimes happens that way the first time,' said Jeanne. 'You'll be all right in a day or two. A good long walk is what you need, my girl.' She suited the action to the words and proceeded to drag Marianna round the park at a spanking pace. The exercise, unwelcome as it was, made her feel better.

As the days went by, the memory of that night preyed on Marianna's mind. She lay awake for hours, listening for the footfall in the passage outside, and sometimes she was rewarded with a stealthy sound, followed by the creak and muted thud of a door opening and closing. At last, unable to bear her curiosity any longer, she crept into the corridor and applied her eye to Jeanne's door once more.

Three weeks later, Nusia, her brother having unexpectedly recovered, returned to Lisko, and immediately noticed Marianna's secretive behaviour. There were whispers among the servants, and Nusia made her own enquiries. That night, she lay awake, considering what she ought to do. In the early hours of the morning, she got up, wrapping a shawl around her nightdress, and went to Marianna's room. She was determined to speak to the girl as she used to, without the intrusive presence of the governess.

So it was that Nusia came upon Marianna kneeling outside Jeanne's door, peering into the room. She took in at a glance the girl and her unnaturally tense posture, along with the sounds that came from inside. With great presence of mind, she retreated along the curve of the corridor. She opened and closed the door of an empty room, loudly enough for Marianna to hear but not so loud that it would disturb the lovers. When she peeped into the passageway again, it was empty. She padded cautiously along the corridor, applied her eye briefly to the spy hole to confirm her suspicions, and then let herself into Marianna's room, where the girl lay feigning sleep.

She knelt down beside the bed and touched the girl's shoulder. It felt rigid and cold.

'How long has this been happening, love?'

'What do you mean?' Marianna turned over and stared at her.

'You know full well what I mean. I saw you just now, Marianna. And I saw what you were watching.'

Marianna began to cry. At last, it all came out. Over and above the story of what Marianna had seen in the candlelight came other, darker tales of beatings, of stays laced too tightly, orders to do this and fetch that, all on the whim of the governess. Nusia quietly cursed Jeanne, and Stefan too for his lack of care. Most of all, she cursed herself for not being more watchful.

The following morning, she went to the steward and demanded that he write to Stefan, asking him to come to Lisko at once.

'Tell him it's urgent. Tell him it concerns Miss Marianna.'

Stefan came with all speed. Nusia had her faults, but she was incapable of lying to him.

'I must speak to Marianna. I must question her.'

'It would do more harm than good, sir. And besides, what could you say?'

He paced about the room with a stricken face. 'Oh God, if only Antonina were here.'

'But she isn't and she never will be again and something must be done now, sir.'

'Of course. The woman must be removed. And Meissen is to go anyway. Zygmunt no longer needs a tutor, thank God. I should have sent him away to school.'

'What will become of Marianna?'

'I don't know,' he said helplessly.

Whether it was instinct, or whether Jeanne had been forewarned, perhaps by Dorota, who had been indulging in a little eavesdropping, she pre-empted them all. Messages were sent to the miscreants, but they were nowhere to be found. They had set off together, apparently for a walk in the park, but had not returned. The day wore on and there was still no sign of them. Nusia looked in their rooms to find in each, a box, packed and corded and ready, cupboards and drawers empty, and in the tutor's room, a note in his thin, precise hand, addressed to Stefan.

'We realise with great sorrow and regret,' it read, 'that our shameful secret has been discovered. I have arranged transport in the village to take us to the coaching inn at Yarychev, and thence by stages to our ultimate destination, Vienna, where you may be reassured to hear that we plan to marry. Perhaps you would be so good as to send our boxes to my father's house, at the address you know of. I can only apologise for any trouble brought on your family by myself and Mademoiselle Jeanne who is, however, very soon to be Frau Meissen.'

The letter was signed by Wolfgang Meissen. From Jeanne there was no word, nor was there any communication from the couple again, except for a brief wedding announcement forwarded anonymously from Vienna some weeks later.

Chapter Nine

MARIANNA FOUND HERSELF IN LIMBO. She was twelve years old, and the children with whom she had once played were now kept busy, working in the fields or the stables. Almost in spite of herself, she had learned a great deal under Jeanne's tutelage and not all of it had been bad. She was glad to cast the terrible stays into the kitchen fire and, with Nusia's help, resume her old, comfortable mode of dress, but even that was something of a disappointment. Nothing seemed right.

Autumn made Marianna even more restless. She would lie awake for hours, getting up to sit beside her window, watching the moon as it sailed through ragged clouds above the park.

'What's wrong with me?' she asked Nusia.

'You're growing up. That's what's the matter,' said Nusia. 'And there's no remedy for it. Save to become a woman and like it.'

'But I don't like it. If this is what it feels like, I don't want it.'

'What *do* you want?'

'I don't know. The moon maybe. I think I want the moon. Sometimes I see it reflected in the lake and it's so close that I feel I could reach out and touch it. But if I do, the image breaks up and the water runs through my fingers and all I have is cold hands.'

Nusia frowned. 'What nonsense you do talk to be sure. Nobody can have the moon.'

So Marianna fretted in the house or rode aimlessly about the park or tramped along through the autumn mud, wearing her brother's riding boots. And who knows what might have become of her, had not her father's cousin, Floryan Yelitowski, come to Lisko with his wife Wanda. They made the journey from their home at Milatyn some forty kilometres to the south east, before the winter snows made travelling difficult.

The estate of Milatyn was owned by the great Yelitowski family, the main stem of which the Diduski cousins were merely branches. If Lisko was beautiful in the conventional, Austrian style, the house at Milatyn was a fabulous eccentricity with white walls, a heavily sloping tiled roof and an extraordinary carved wooden balcony, that ran the entire length of the back of the main building and along its two side wings, making a sheltered cloister of the gardens beneath.

There was a portrait of Floryan Yelitowski in the house at Milatyn, a picture in the heroic style of a stern man with a fantastic moustache; a warrior who habitually wore the long robe of another century, fastened with a broad sash, embroidered in gold and silver thread. He had fought through and survived the heroic years of Poland's many insurrections against partition. Afterwards, dreaming of even greater glory and in the habit of worshipping heroes, he had followed Napoleon.

By the time Floryan was thirty, the thrill of battle had begun to pall for him. He no longer thought himself immortal. He had seen too many men die, and his body and mind bore the scars. He returned home and, after the death of his father, began to tend the land at Milatyn and dream up schemes for improving the lot of the poor workers. Floryan's years of fighting had given him a strong sense of justice and he loved the house at Milatyn, the estate and all its people, Polish, Ukrainian and Jewish, with a fiercely protective affection. Above all, he refused to keep the Ukrainian and Polish peasantry in deep poverty while reaping rich rewards for himself and his family. Those who knew him well soon perceived that he was far more approachable than his portrait suggested: a generous friend and an indulgent father.

Floryan presided over this small rural world, his contentment only disturbed by the devastating loss of three wives in succession. The death of his womenfolk was the only sorrow to trouble his hard-won peace and that was down to God, not man. He believed in God, all right, a very personal and vengeful God, upon whose broad shoulders a great deal of blame could be heaped. His estate workers were loyal, and even the independent smallholders of the village accorded him a grudging respect. Others might cast envious eyes upon his prosperity, but for many years, he and his family seemed magically safe from outside interference.

Floryan's first wife had given him his eldest son, Stanislaw, but did not survive the birth of a second stillborn child. Soon after that came dainty Julia, who had died of consumption. His third wife, Teresa, was the daughter of a far travelled Polish father and a Tatar mother, from the east: small, dark and very pretty, with high cheekbones and pale cream skin. She was always laughing. She made Floryan laugh, didn't mind the dogs, and was good to Stanislaw. Besides that, she had inherited all the genius with horses of her mother's race. She scorned the lady's pommel saddle and when they went out hunting, she rode astride like a man, declaring that it was far too dangerous to ride side saddle at such speed. Which was true, because she rode like a warrior. This caused something of a scandal in the neighbourhood, but Floryan loved her for it and boasted proudly of her achievements. For all her spirit, Teresa did not survive the birth of her first child, leaving him with a tiny, wailing, premature daughter to remember her by. This child was also christened Teresa, and proved to be a perfect replica of her mother. Reluctant to leave the infant to the care of hired nurses, who might be prejudiced against her race, he looked about for a new wife.

While Marianna Diduska was still toddling about Lisko or sliding off horses, Floryan had married for the fourth time. Wanda was the grave and rather quiet daughter of a neighbouring landowner. When they married, she was already in her thirties, a widow who came to Floryan with a ready made family of two girls, Sylvestra and Helena, and then bore him two sons, Julian and Anton. At first Wanda was simply content, which was far more than she would have expected from the match, but later she realised that she had grown to love her husband very dearly.

When she and Floryan were regular visitors at Lisko, little Teresa had become friendly with Marianna, for the two were about the same age, but after Antonina's death, the visits had ceased. Floryan had been very fond of Antonina but found Stefan's company a poor substitute. Besides, the man was hardly ever at home and Floryan didn't care for Lemberg.

Time passed and it struck Floryan that he had not been to Lisko for some five years. Then, news came to Milatyn of the hurried and simultaneous departure of the French governess and the German tutor. Wanda remarked that they really must visit cousin Stefan and see what was happening. 'If only in memory of dear Antonina,' she said, slyly, aware that this would touch Floryan's heart. A few weeks later, Wanda and her husband set off for Lisko, taking Teresa with them.

Shy at first, Marianna was soon glad of their arrival. Floryan made her laugh, Wanda was kind and Teresa was a friendly chatterbox. For the first time in her life, Marianna felt truly happy to be with a girl of her own age. Wanda watched with approval as the two girls began to spend more time together, and as she saw Marianna's sullen face break into the occasional smile.

At the earliest opportunity, Wanda cornered Stefan.

'Let's walk in the gardens. There are still a few roses and I believe you have some varieties here that we don't have at Milatyn.'

'They are from England, I believe.'

Short of direct rudeness, which was not in his nature, Stefan couldn't escape the reproachful gaze of her brown eyes.

'You do know that you are ruining your daughter's chances of making a good marriage?'

'What?' he said, in astonishment.

'Forgive me, but what would dear Antonina say to you if she were standing here today?'

'What's wrong with Marianna?'

'She seems so unhappy. She was such a pretty little thing when last I saw her. So full of life and spirit. Now look at her!'

'But she had a governess.'

'Who ran off with Zygmunt's tutor and, according to Nusia, treated the girl very badly into the bargain.'

'She and Nusia never got along. The woman was certainly too strict. And indiscreet. But if Marianna had been badly treated she would have told me.'

'You were never here, Stefan, were you? You were in Lemberg with your nose in your books. Or too busy on estate business, even when you were at home. What was the child to do? She is not yet thirteen. These are difficult years and she needs help of the right sort.'

'I thought that was what I was giving her.'

'Look at your daughter. Can't you see what she has become? She has no conversation and no spirit. I hardly know what to make of her!'

Stefan sighed. He motioned to a stone seat, where the last roses of summer hung their heads in the chilly air and, when Wanda was settled with a shawl about her, he sat down beside her.

'She looks so dreadful, for one thing. Her clothes are appalling. All wrong for her. But what's much worse, she seems so very unhappy!'

'I should have married again, given her a new mother, as Floryan did for his little Teresa.'

Wanda burst out laughing. 'No. I didn't mean that exactly, Stefan.' She paused. 'But did you never think of marrying again? There are plenty of women who would have been glad to accept your proposal. You would have been a very good catch. You still are.'

'It wouldn't be fair. My heart wouldn't be in it. Some people can forget.'

He stopped.

'Like your cousin Floryan and myself,' she said. 'I know. Floryan can put bad memories out of his mind when he wants to. He isn't callous. He just lives in the present. He wanted a mother for Teresa and I badly needed protection. As luck would have it, the arrangement was more satisfactory than we could ever have believed. But some people are afraid to try again. And with good reason.'

'I don't think it's fear, Wanda, so much as lack of inclination. I had so much joy with Antonina. And her death was so quick, so appalling. I think I blamed myself. Still do, if I'm honest. I don't really want another wife.'

'Then why don't you send Marianna to our house for a few years? We're nothing if not sociable. She'll meet people and learn the right sort of behaviour by absorbing it, rather than having it forced on her. She needs attention. Good society, good food as well. Time to grow up.'

She saw him waver and pressed the point home.

'Zygmunt has you and he has the estate. And I believe he has friends nearby. He's old enough to ride over there himself and be sociable.'

'Yes. There are boys at Feliksa and Banunin. I don't worry so much about Zygmunt. But I worry about Marianna all the time.'

'Then let her come back with us. We'd love to have her, Teresa in particular.'

'But what about Floryan? Would he mind?'

'One more young person in the house makes no difference to Floryan.

We've spoken about it and he agrees with me. He was very fond of your wife, and he'll love Marianna on that account alone.'

'And what about Nusia? Should she go too?'

'Oh I don't think so. I think Marianna has outgrown her. Not that she doesn't love her and will go on loving her. But I still think it would be better if Nusia stayed here and kept house for Zygmunt – and you when you're here. Marianna will come back for holidays. Nusia will see quite enough of her darling, don't worry.'

Marianna's first few months at Milatyn were spent in sad indifference to her surroundings, but soon Floryan and Wanda began to notice a gradual improvement in her spirits. She began to take a genuine interest in her clothes and had to admit that Wanda's taste was pretty as well as practical for a young lady who might also want to run and jump and play games with her friends.

Julian, Floryan and Wanda's eldest son, was twelve years old by the time Marianna arrived at Milatyn, a quick-witted and studious boy. During her first few months at the house, when she was withdrawn and homesick, it was he who made her feel she belonged, dragging her around the house to show her this or that ornament. Floryan was an inveterate collector and the house was a treasure trove of old weaponry, uniforms, and other militaria.

One day, not long after her arrival, Julian took her into the room where Floryan kept his collection of weapons: fearsome Turkish knives, jewelled shields, cases full of beautiful Polish sashes, long bands of woven silk, patterned with leaves and flowers and geometrical designs in pink, green, red and gold, so beautiful that she gasped and lifted one out and wound it around her like a scarf.

'It looks nice!' said Julian, shyly. 'But don't let father catch you wearing it. They're very old. Two hundred years, some of them. And made in Turkey too. They may have been our enemies, but we loved the things they made. Although I suppose some of these things were the spoils of war.'

'You mean they were taken in battle?'

'Some things for sure. The weapons in particular. But come and see our winged hussar.'

'You have the hussar armour?'

Nusia had told her and her brother all about the battle with the Ottoman army, at the gates of Vienna, long ago, and how the Poles had come to the rescue of the Hapsburgs, and how the Polish King Jan Sobieski had led his winged hussars to a great victory. She had heard all about the eagle armour of the old cavalrymen, but she had been unprepared for the size and menace of this ancient suit, the blank stare of the helmet and the great arcs of eagle feathers that towered above it. The armour was priceless, the breastplate encrusted with precious stones that glistened in the dusty sunlight of the room. When several thousand cavalrymen had charged at the same time, the wind had rushed through them and set up a roaring sound that froze the enemy's blood and caused them to turn and flee. It was as though some of the horror it had originally inspired had seeped into the very materials of the armour, making it an artefact of beauty and menace. Marianna thought that it was like something the warrior Archangel Michael might have worn.

She recoiled from it, but couldn't take her eyes off it.

'It's beautiful, but it scares me,' she said, at last.

'It's meant to be frightening! There's no shame in being scared of it. Although I shouldn't like Stanislaw to think me a coward.'

Stanislaw teased his young step-brother mercilessly for his bookishness and his gentleness.

'I won't say anything to him.'

'Father says it will be mine some day. He says all this,' the boy gestured to the surrounding militaria, 'will go to me, and nobody else, because I understand it and I love it as he does.'

'And is he right?'

'It's true that I love it. But Stanislaw is the soldier of the family. I think I should like to be a doctor. I want to make people well, not fight them. I expect I'll finish up here at Milatyn, running the estate. Unless I can get somebody else to do it for me.'

Chapter Ten

MARIANNA GREW TALLER THAN EVER. Finally, she had outgrown everyone in the family except her own brother. Aware of her unfashionable height, she continued to hunch her shoulders and fold her arms around herself, until Wanda forced her to stand upright by thrusting a thin board down the back of her dress and making her look in a mirror.

'There. Isn't that better?'

'Yes. But it's very uncomfortable.'

'Of course it is, darling. Then you have to remember to do it without the board. Stand up tall and don't be ashamed of yourself.'

The atmosphere at Milatyn was easy-going and there were few rules. The daughter of the village doctor came in every day to read with the girls and teach them a smattering of Latin, French and English, as well as the rudiments of History and Geography. Marianna found that she knew more than Teresa, so perhaps she had learned something useful from Jeanne after all. Wanda taught them to draw and there were dancing and riding lessons too, but Marianna and Teresa were already accomplished horsewomen, and that proved to be another bond between them. Marianna grew in confidence and blossomed into an eccentric beauty.

Wanda could see that even Marianna's occasional *gaucherie* could be very becoming. She would have her choice of eligible husbands. There was little else for a woman to do but acquire a husband and family, and if an unsuitable match could be a sore trial, it was a sad life for those who did not marry at all. They would become maiden aunts, relying on the charity of married relatives.

When Marianna and Teresa were sixteen, they went to Lisko for a summer visit. Zygmunt was tall and handsome now, with thick brown hair, the same hazel eyes as his sister and a wonderful moustache, of which he was very proud.

'What a fine man your brother has become, Marianna!' whispered Teresa.

Marianna was more critical. He drank too much at dinner and when he did, he became extremely silly, telling tales about his exploits with the other young gentlemen of the district. He spent most of his time hunting, and had told her proudly that he had begun to fill the big hall at Lisko with a collection of trophies, stuffed and mounted. Marianna shuddered at the thought, but Teresa would sit and listen to him for hours on end.

'I think your brother is much more handsome than mine, Teresa!' said Marianna with a little sigh.

At the age of twenty five, Stanislaw had returned to Milatyn from Vienna a few weeks before the girls had left for Lisko. He was shorter than Zygmunt, but with fine features and an elegant manner. He had spent some years in the army and had the erect bearing of a military man. At balls and receptions the young women fluttered about him like moths drawn to the flame of his courtesy, his elegance and the promise of all those Milatyn acres. Stanislaw enjoyed being the centre of attention, but on the edges of his vision he was always catching sight of Marianna Diduska's admiring face. He enjoyed the flattery, but still thought of her as the shy young girl who had come to Milatyn and spent weeks skulking in corners.

'Oh I do so love Lisko!' said Marianna impulsively, when she and Teresa arrived at her old home. She had never forgotten the house. Now, seeing its butter yellow walls again, she was flooded with happiness.

Nusia greeted them with open arms. 'I hardly recognised you. Two grown up ladies! Aren't we lucky to have you here?'

The truth was that Lisko seemed very quiet after Milatyn, and Marianna soon found herself impatient to return to her foster family. Yet she knew that no sooner had she left Lisko than she would begin to be homesick all over again for the pancake yellow house. As for Teresa, she did nothing but moon about after Zygmunt all day, admiring his bloodthirsty trophies or sketching idealised versions of his face. After some initial incredulity, Marianna began to see the advantages of a little matchmaking.

'It would be wonderful if you were to marry my brother. I've always hated the idea of him marrying, because when my father dies, Lisko will belong to Zygmunt and his wife. I'm to inherit a place called Podlaski and I don't like it at all.'

'At least it's something to have your own house. I'll have a house of my own if I marry but even then it won't really be mine. It'll be my husband's.'

'I have bad memories of Podlaski. My mother caught the sickness that killed her there.'

'I forgot. I'm sorry.'

'It isn't just that. I never liked it. Even before everything went wrong there. I love this place. But if you and Zygmunt were married, it would be like visiting a sister. I would always feel welcome.'

The plan seemed so perfect that the girls imagined it was almost achieved. Teresa declared that she loved him madly, and Marianna agreed that her cousin needed only a go-between to tell him of her true feelings, whereupon they would become engaged and it would all be settled. One evening, when Teresa had already gone to bed, Marianna approached her brother. He was seated at their mother's old desk in the drawing room, writing a letter, squinting at the page in the lamplight, for he was a little short-sighted. She came up behind him, sliding her arms around his neck. This was as good a time as any.

'I suppose you've guessed that Teresa is madly in love with you.'

Zygmunt threw down his pen, making a large blot in the middle of the letter. Then he burst out laughing. This was not what she had expected, but perhaps his emotions had overcome him. She persevered. 'Don't you think it would be wonderful? I know she's a bit young, but lots of girls are married at sixteen.'

He realised she was serious and stopped laughing. When he didn't reply at once, she said, 'Well perhaps it might be better to wait a year or two after all.'

She was disconcerted when he burst out laughing again.

'Oh, Marianna, what a baby you are!'

'What do you mean?'

'I'm not marrying anyone just yet and when I do, it won't be that little Tatar.'

'Don't call her that!'

'But it's what she is.'

She flew at him in a rage, slapping and scratching him until he held her hands firmly at her sides.

'Don't do that! You're a big girl now and those slaps hurt.'

'I hate you for saying those things.'

'I'm only speaking the truth. She'll never find a husband.'

'Floryan married her mother.'

'Yes but he's eccentric. All those years in France I shouldn't wonder.'

She began to cry in earnest then, and he relented. He never liked to see her cry.

'I'm sorry, Marianna but I don't love your little Teresa. I like her and I admire her as a horsewoman. But I don't love her and I'll certainly never marry her. I'm setting my sights higher than that.'

Teresa was waiting eagerly for her return. They were sharing a bedroom, out of companionship, for there was no lack of rooms in the house.

'Well, what did he say?'

'He says he likes you very much but he doesn't want to marry anyone right now.'

'But he likes me?' Teresa was young enough to be optimistic.

'Like a sister I suppose. He didn't take me seriously. He thinks I'm a child. So does your Stanislaw for that matter.'

She bounced angrily on her bed but Teresa lay back, contented for the moment with Zygmunt's liking.

'Never mind. There's time enough yet. I don't know that I want to be married so soon anyway.'

'Neither do I. But it would be good to be kissed. What do you suppose it's like?'

'I kissed one of my cousins once,' said Teresa. 'We were very young. Only nine. It was in the old barn at Milatyn. It was a dare and I did it.'

'On the lips?'

'Yes, but very quickly. And not with tongues.'

'What do you mean with tongues?'

'That's what people do,' said Teresa, matter-of-factly. 'They stick their tongues into each other's mouths when they're in love.'

'I don't like the sound of that at all.'

'Me neither, so I didn't do it. But in any case it wasn't very nice. He'd been chewing wild garlic.'

The girls began to giggle. Every time one of them stopped, the other began, until they were breathless with laughter.

Then Marianna whispered, 'I saw someone *doing it* once.'

'Doing it!' Teresa echoed her. She sat up on the bed. 'You mean ...?'

'Yes. It was my governess and Zygmunt's tutor. Before they ran away together. I suppose they had to run away together. I mean you have to get married if you do it, don't you? They went off to Vienna together and got married there. Nusia knows but you must promise never to tell anyone else.'

'I promise, but are you sure that's what they were doing?'

'Of course. I'm not stupid. They were in her room. It was when I was twelve. Before I came to Milatyn. I watched them several times.'

There was a pause while Teresa absorbed this information. A trapped wasp buzzed against the windowpane.

'What was it like?' she asked at last. 'Was it wonderful?'

'No. It was absolutely disgusting. I couldn't believe it. He was on top of her. I thought he was attacking her at first. Then I realised it was ... something different. She seemed to be enjoying it. I can't imagine why.'

'How could you see?'

'Her room had double doors – you know? It's the big one along the passage there – and there's a little gap between them. There was a candle burning. I suppose they wanted to be able to see each other.'

'How could you bear to watch?'

'I didn't mean to. I just couldn't move away.'

'Weren't you afraid they'd catch you?'

'I was. But I couldn't stop myself. And then I went back quite a few times. And then Jeanne ran away with Mr Meissen and they got married, and I came to your house. There was a great fuss about it all. I didn't understand why at the time. In fact I still don't quite understand why they had to run away, why they couldn't just get married here, but I'm glad they did. I hated her.'

'I suppose everyone has to do that when they're married.'

'If they want any children they do. I think that's how you get children. It's how the dogs make puppies isn't it?'

Teresa giggled. 'Yes, but not that way round!'

Marianna blushed and laughed too. 'I think men expect it. Nunu says that they have coarser natures than women. Women just have to put up with it if they want a husband.'

'But you said your governess looked as if she was enjoying it.'

'Yes, she was. But perhaps she had a coarser nature too.' Marianna giggled again, irrepressibly.

'Maybe Nunu doesn't know it all' said Teresa sagely. 'Maybe it is possible to enjoy it.'

'I hope so. I suppose it depends on the man! With some people, an embrace would be enough,' she said, romantically, and indeed that was what she dreamed of: Stanislaw clasping her close to his smartly clothed, cologne scented chest, and telling her that he loved her.

When the girls came back to Milatyn, Stanislaw was still at home. That summer had changed Marianna. At sixteen, she was fractionally taller than Stanislaw, but she no longer needed padding in her stays. She was as shapely as a statue. It was as though something had flowered in her face, or perhaps the months of her absence had allowed him to see her differently. Whatever the reason, when he came forward to kiss her hand, his lips lingered. Then he raised his eyes to hers, stepped closer and kissed her on both cheeks.

'Marianna. My dear cousin. How good to have you back with us again,' he said warmly.

Marianna hurried to her room, where she spent a long time dressing for dinner in a watered silk gown of pale blackbird egg blue. Wanda's maid had been sent to put her hair up, sweeping the dark curls away from her face and lacing silk ribbons and flowers through them. When Marianna saw herself in the mirror, she seemed unfamiliar and too grown up; quite different from the girl who had run through the forests at Lisko and climbed trees and turned shameless cartwheels on the grass. Briefly, she felt the loss of that child, a sharp pang of regret. But then she remembered Stanislaw and his warm breath on her cheek. Conscious of her skirts that rustled and billowed around her, she descended the stairs in happy anticipation of whatever the future might hold.

Chapter Eleven

FOR THE NEXT THREE YEARS, Stanislaw Yelitowski courted his cousin. His visits home became much more frequent. Marianna found their conversations enjoyable but faintly unsatisfactory afterwards, rather like eating a great deal of something sweet and sickly, that left your hunger all unsatisfied. She thought her cousin very much her superior in every way and blamed herself for her lack of experience. She tried to display just enough wit to keep him amused. She found it tiring, always being on her mettle like this. She never relaxed in his company for long enough to discover what lay beneath the veneer of his courtesy. It was enough that he was her hero.

He talked a great deal, but he asked her very little about herself.

Floryan and Wanda watched the growing attachment between the pair with satisfaction, though they did nothing to force matters. If anything, Wanda was more hesitant than Floryan about the match, aware that there was a fervour about Marianna that Stanislaw would never understand. She comforted herself with the thought that Marianna might be good for Stanislaw. Maybe they could be happy together. Stefan had already confirmed that the estate at Podlaski would be his daughter's dowry. It had been well maintained and Floryan couldn't bear to think of it slipping out of his eldest son's grasp.

'He's almost thirty. He needs a wife and family to steady him and land to occupy him.'

'Yes, but is he what Marianna needs?' Wanda asked. She couldn't help feeling that Stanislaw might not make Marianna happy, but she couldn't explain why.

'I don't see why not. I think it will be a good match.'

Stefan too saw no reason why his daughter shouldn't marry her charming cousin. The couple could start their married life at Podlaski, and then he wouldn't have to worry about the place any more. If he had stirrings of superstitious unease about Podlaski he managed to quell them. The young couple would be able to make changes to the house and when there were two or three children running about the place, he was sure that Marianna would settle down there. He only wished that Zygmunt could make a similarly happy match, but his son showed no signs of wanting to marry. Instead he seemed to prefer drinking and gambling with a crowd of his friends.

At first, Stefan had put it down to the usual transition from boyhood to manhood, but at last he was forced to admit that it had gone on for too long. Zygmunt was twenty three and undisciplined, spending money thoughtlessly. He would promise to reform, but time after time, those promises had proved worthless. So it was with relief that Stefan gave his consent to his daughter's marriage. At least she would no longer be a worry to him.

Stanislaw chose his moment carefully, when they were alone on the veranda at Milatyn. She was sitting in a basketwork chair, wearing a dress of cream silk, edged with blue satin, and a modest bonnet of the same colours. She looked so demure that when he knelt at her feet in the approved manner and said, 'Marianna, will you marry me?' he was genuinely moved by her beauty and thought himself the luckiest man in the world.

'Have you spoken to my father?'

'Of course. He's agreeable, so long as you are. And my father will be delighted, I know.'

'Then of course I'll marry you!' Impulsively, she enveloped him in her warm embrace. He could smell the eau de cologne scent of the hollow between her breasts, warm and musky. 'Oh Stanislaw, my dear, I've loved you all along. I thought you'd never ask me!'

Somewhere deep inside him came the smallest stirring of distaste. A really maidenly young woman would surely have hesitated, would have asked for more time before replying. How like madcap Marianna, he thought, a little contemptuously. How like Marianna to rush so passionately into consent. But he forgave her because he loved her. He forgave her because she so obviously loved him.

The wedding took place at Milatyn in June. It was a fairy-tale event: the beautiful young lady and the handsome young gentleman, with the happily-ever-after assured by their joint fortune. No expense was spared. Marianna wore an elaborate dress of white silk satin, with a net overdress, heavily embroidered with lilies of the valley, and with a little spray of the same flowers in wax, tucked into the v of her breasts, so that she could keep it as a memento afterwards. The church and house were full of fragrant flowers, and champagne was brought from France specially for the occasion. The vodka flowed freely, the food was delicious, and celebrations went on in the village for several days. Little work was done on the estate for a whole week. Even the house dogs ate too much beef and chicken and lay in the hallways with distended bellies.

Marianna and Stanislaw spent their wedding night in a bedroom lit with many candles and decorated with flowers and greenery. She left the party long before Stanislaw and went upstairs to bathe in water that was scented with violets, and then Wanda and Teresa and two giggling maids helped her into a new nightdress. Wanda had embroidered it with Marianna's new monogram in fine silk, stitched on white cambric.

By the time the women had finished and left her ensconced in the great goose-feather bridal bed, she was trembling with suppressed excitement. As she heard her husband's footstep in the passage, her breathing quickened and her heart pounded in her ears. From downstairs, she could hear the music, the rhythms of one wild dance following another.

Stanislaw had been drinking champagne, but not too much. Perhaps if he had drunk a little more, it might all have been easier. As it was, he stood in the doorway and gazed at her. Her smile of welcome became foolishly fixed. The moment was so intimate and so strange that she could think of nothing at all to say. Then he closed the door and extinguished the candles one by one, but still said nothing to her. She began to tremble, her teeth chattering, although it was a warm night.

Summoning all her courage, she said, 'Should I take off my night-dress, Stanislaw?' partly for something to say, because the silence was so terrifying, and partly because she didn't know what was expected of her.

With a note of alarm in his voice, he said 'No – no – that won't be necessary,' just as if she had asked 'Shall I take off my shoes?'

He blundered about in the dark for a time. She imagined him

undressing. Then she heard a rustle as he slipped his linen nightshirt over his head, and at last he approached the bed. She felt the darkness around her like a solid entity, suffocating her. He reached out for her and pulled up the fine cambric of her nightdress in a business-like fashion, then clambered clumsily on top of her. The unexpected weight of him made it hard to breathe. Automatically, defensively, she locked her knees together to stop them shaking.

Not knowing what else to do with them, she rested her hands on his back and was horrified to feel, beneath his nightshirt, the bones and straps of the corset that he had worn ever since a riding accident had strained his back a few years before. Did he never take it off then? She almost giggled. Her next thought was, 'What will Teresa say, when I tell her?' and then she remembered that this was real, this was her wedding night, and she couldn't talk about it to Teresa. She could never tell Teresa about the corset, for that would be disloyal to her husband. She must learn to behave like the respectable, married woman she had so suddenly become.

He was fumbling at her knees and at last exclaimed testily 'Open your legs, can't you!' She realised that he was terribly embarrassed, so she opened her legs obediently and prayed that it might soon be over.

He pushed his way roughly inside her. After the first sharp pain, that made her cry out but passed very quickly, her chief emotion was one of surprise at the intrusion of a stranger into her body, surprise that such a little ceremony should give him absolute right of possession over what was hers, or had been hers, until yesterday. She felt him thrust hard a few times, then he gave a shuddering groan and, much to her relief, rolled off her and far away to the other side of the bed. There was a merciful space between them and she could breathe again.

Something warm and wet slid down her leg. She wriggled until her nightdress covered her, and turned on her side. From the void on the other side of the bed, her husband said, just as if nothing had happened, 'Goodnight, my dear.' It was exactly the tone of voice that he had always used when bidding her a fond farewell.

'Goodnight, Stanislaw,' she said, surprised by the sound of her own voice.

For a little while, she felt as if she might be going to cry, but what good would crying do? This was not at all what she had expected. Wanda had said nothing about what to expect from her wedding night, but she had heard servant girls giggling, and older country women making coarse jokes and laughing about it. Always, beneath their laughter, ran a current of something exciting and forbidden. But if it was like this, what point could there possibly be in it? Was it, as the priest had said, only for the procreation of children? Was there something wrong with her, that Stanislaw could not bear to look at her while he was doing it? She fell asleep at last, puzzled and very low in spirits.

The following day, they set off on their bridal journey. Marianna enjoyed the travelling immensely but viewed the approach of each night with apprehension. Sometimes they managed to secure separate rooms, and then Stanislaw would accompany her to the door of her room, kiss her chastely on the cheek and let her go. On the whole, she viewed this with relief. Sometimes, they were thrown together in a big bed, and just occasionally, he would repeat his detached assault upon her body. This invariably happened in near silence, punctuated only by his sighs and groans. She felt nothing except a little discomfort. He never spoke to her until afterwards, and then only to wish her the same courteous 'good night'.

It no longer hurt her, but neither did it give her any pleasure. His scrupulous avoidance of her breasts, his obvious distaste at the touch of her flesh or her bodily hair aroused a sense of shame in her. There must be something peculiarly repulsive about her for him to react in this way. Just occasionally, her body would give her some notion of its own capacity for pleasure, but she had been brought up to distrust these sensations. By night, she lay swathed in long nightdresses. By day, she was covered in layers of muslin and calico. The sheer quantity of clothes needed to disguise her body weighed her down and oppressed her.

Only a few weeks after the wedding ceremony, not long after his return to Lisko, Stefan Diduski collapsed while riding along the estate boundaries. His men brought him back, half conscious and slumped over his horse, his head almost touching the animal's mane. He had insisted on riding home himself. Nusia summoned the physician, but before he could arrive, Stefan had become unconscious. A few days later, he died, with Nusia and Zygmunt at his side.

On hearing the news, that had taken some time to reach them, Marianna and Stanislaw cut short their travels and returned home, much too late for the funeral. Marianna would have liked to stay on at Lisko for a while, sleeping in her old room, coming to terms with her bereavement, but it was not to be. Almost immediately, Stanislaw decided that they should travel to Podlaski, and so they set off for that house, leaving Zygmunt trying hard to reconcile his jubilation at his sudden inheritance with his genuine sorrow for his father.

Marianna came back to Podlaski for the first time since her mother's death, wearing deep mourning for her father. She had endured many a sleepless night at the idea of returning to the house but she had hoped that the bliss of marriage would exorcise any lingering ghosts. Now, grief at this new bereavement possessed her, so that she hardly noticed her surroundings. In spite of their gradual estrangement, Stefan's death had left a gap in her life, and she wept bitterly for him. Stanislaw did his best to comfort her, but although her grief was a pale shadow of the way in which she had mourned Antonina, it embarrassed him a little. He sometimes found his new wife too ardent. Her impetuousness alarmed him. He thought that, like an unruly young mare, she would have to be tamed, somehow.

She had been dreading her first sight of the estate, but the summer of her mother's death now seemed distant to her, as though it had happened to another person altogether. The house was quite small by comparison with Lisko and Milatyn, and Stanislaw was already making plans for extensions and changes. She had remembered big, echoing corridors along which she had once run, searching for her mother. Now, all she saw was a gloomy but well furnished home; the once great trees and meadows of the park seemed tamer to her adult eyes. Much to her relief, they occupied separate rooms. Stanislaw took a keen interest in the management of the estate, and his room was cluttered with papers and books on farm management. He would stay up working at his desk late into the night, or reading beside the fire. She had no idea what time he came to bed, but he seldom troubled her with his presence.

Stanislaw was never violent or cruel towards her, and he was always considerate of her well-being. He simply believed that women were helpless creatures. On the increasingly rare occasions when he came to her bed, it was as if this same chivalrous stranger had thrust himself into sudden, unwanted intimacy with her. She found it both alarming and distressing. Although she tried very hard to disguise these feelings, he seemed to notice them, and she was relieved when his visits ceased altogether. Perhaps he was relieved too. In the space of a few months, their relationship had become polite and formal, friendly enough, but almost completely without physical intimacy.

Chapter Twelve

Marianna had forgotten all about the boy called Danilo, who had so frightened and fascinated her that summer before her world fell apart. As the carriage paused at the lodge gates on her return, his image briefly crossed her mind. She thought he too had probably died in the smallpox epidemic that had killed her mother.

Some weeks after their arrival, Marianna and her husband rode out to pay a call on their neighbours. There were great houses within a day's ride of Podlaski, but within easy calling distance there was only a young couple called Poniatowski. They led an uncomfortable, hand-to-mouth existence, with their four thin children, twin boys and two little girls, all with white faces and persistent coughs. They lived in a crumbling manor house some few miles from Podlaski, with a handful of badly paid and consistently exploited Ukrainian servants, and an assortment of starving hounds. But they were 'people of the right sort' as Stanislaw was fond of saying. He could ignore the shabbiness of their clothes and draperies, the cold, damp rooms, impressively vast but gloomy, the general decay of the building, so long as their connections were sufficiently highly polished.

The house reminded Marianna of Lisko, a sadly tumbledown and neglected Lisko, to be sure. Amalia Poniatowska could talk of nothing but her children and her sincere worries about their health. She hardly seemed to notice her surroundings. Marianna sympathised with her, but she was miserable company. The only benefit to be gained from these visits, as far as Marianna could see, was that they made her appreciate Podlaski more. At least it was better than this vast and chilly place. After a few hours spent in the drawing room there, her skirts and petticoats would be heavy with the moisture that seemed to linger in the very air itself. She was always relieved to return to the comparative comfort of her home. She was still in mourning for her father at that time, but her black riding habit was, Stanislaw felt, a smart compromise. He always took an interest in her clothes. She wished he took as much interest in herself.

It was a fine afternoon and they had decided to ride to the decrepit manor house. The countryside seemed empty, small sounds only serving to emphasise the quietness. The day was warm, the fields already ploughed and utterly silent beneath a pale blue sky. Marianna still loved to ride, though she had never been able to rid herself of her resentment at the restrictions of her ladylike saddle. Stanislaw rode beside her. Every now and then he made some polite comment about the weather, about the estate, about her comfort, as though he were riding with a stranger. She wished he would be quiet so that she could listen to the ominous approach of winter over the fields. She wished she were simply riding out for pleasure, and not for these ridiculous visits, where laughter itself seemed to be rationed, alongside the glasses of weak tea, the dry cakes that threatened to choke you as you swallowed them.

They returned later that afternoon, after a party of such insipid refine-ment that it had almost bored Marianna to tears. At some point in the interminable afternoon, two whey faced little girls and two identical but equally ghostly little boys were brought into the room by a nursemaid, so attenuated that she put Marianna in mind of a skeleton in a threadbare linen gown, like a shroud. The girls, shivering in thin and much mended white dresses, curtseyed in unison. More shrouds, she thought. The boys, faring somewhat better in terms of warm clothes, bowed and clicked their bony heels together. They stood in a line, eyeing the visitors with shy solemnity. Then the girls sang a sad song, interrupted by a great deal of coughing, and the boys recited a grim poem about the terrible fate that befell naughty children, with much prompting from their mother. Their audience of five, including the nursemaid, applauded sedately, whereupon their proud father handed out four small sweetmeats, one apiece. Then the whole procession turned and left the room, but not before one of the dogs, more boisterous than the rest, had almost taken the feet from under the last in line, the most fragile and ethereal of the girls. Marianna half rose, but the child righted herself, leaning on the dog, and trotted off, her hand still resting on its head.

'Charming,' said Stanislaw. 'Quite charming!'

On the way home, Marianna found herself thinking of Milatyn, so full of people and laughter, with mead and wine to drink, and endless supplies of good cake. She became aware of long, slow waves of misery washing over her. How could she bear it? And winter was coming, when even travelling a few miles to a neighbouring house might be difficult. Before the wedding, she had imagined herself and her new husband blissfully cocooned together against the wintry weather. Now, the prospect made her wretched.

Stanislaw stopped at the gates of Podlaski to speak to one of his men who was working there, clearing a patch of woodland of a summer's undergrowth. Marianna drew ahead of him.

'Stashek, I'm so thirsty. There wasn't enough tea and the cakes were very stale. I'll ride on up to the house if you don't mind.'

'I won't be long, my dear. But do as you wish.'

She was anxious for the pleasure of riding alone among the oaks and beeches and hearing the swish of the horse's hooves through the fallen gold. The carriage drive was a long one, and soon she had left her husband far behind, trotting quietly homeward, feeling better for this interval of solitude.

Danilo was twenty three years old. He had survived years of privation and he had not caught smallpox, nor any of the multitude of diseases that occasionally ran rife through the community. He had grown tall and strong. He was rather handsome now, with a thin, swarthy face and dark eyes regarding the world from beneath a pair of black brows set in an almost permanent frown. Life had not been particularly kind to him. His grandfather, Gavril, was still alive, but frailer each year, his sight almost gone. He and Danilo rubbed along together well enough. They had grown so used to arguing with each other that it had become a habit, and even represented a kind of affection between them.

Danilo still worked with the horses, ploughing and harrowing the manor fields in season or hauling felled trees, but he also did whatever else was demanded of him, mending walls and fences, digging potatoes and other vegetables, harvesting apples and pears. He was a hard worker who never seemed to tire and he earned enough to pay one of the village women to look after his grandfather's meals when he was away from home.

For the first few weeks, he had seen Marianna only from a distance and always with her husband, remembering both his dislike of the small girl with the imperious manner and the fatal kindness shown him by her poor mother. Unable to reconcile these two feelings, he had resolved to put Marianna out of his mind, for she was the lady of the house now and as far removed from him as the mountain peak from the meadow beneath.

It was a quiet autumn evening, the trees beginning to turn golden, and he was making his way home to the village along a side path, when he saw her cantering slowly homewards, riding side saddle. He stopped, partly to avoid intruding on her privacy, and partly to watch her, prompted by curiosity. He wanted to see if she was anything at all like the little girl he remembered. Afterwards he was to remember the vision of her that eclipsed all previous memories. He saw a tall young woman wearing a hat and black veil, an absurdly masculine collar, tie and jacket, and a skirt so long and full that it almost reached to the ground. He was half scornful of the absurdity of her clothes, half admiring of the shiny newness of her. She looked fresh and young and graceful. She looked like her mother. She still looked more pretty than anything he had ever seen.

He lurked among the shrubs, clenching his fists and scowling as he had scowled at her once before. The turn of the track brought her closer to him. Would she call him a dirty peasant, he wondered, and tell him to be on his way? But her face showed no sign of emotion. She was locked somewhere far inside herself. She didn't even see him. He held his breath until she was past, and then released it in a great sigh.

Marianna stopped in front of the house and, to her dismay, remembered that the length of her skirts would prevent her from dismounting without help. Where was the groom? It would be so undignified to have to shout for help. She would be forced to wait until Stanislaw came, or ride back to meet him. Perhaps she should just go straight to the stables but that would mean a walk back to the house along muddy pathways and she was already tired. She looked around for assistance and saw Danilo, about to plunge back into the shrubbery.

'You, boy!' she said sharply.

Immediately the words were out, she regretted them. He was hardly a boy. She felt a twinge of apprehension. Did he work on the estate or was he some wandering vagabond?'

He turned to stare at her, scowling still, and reluctantly came closer. He dipped his head briefly, scarcely a bow at all.

'My lady?'

'What's your name?'

'Danilo, my lady.' He almost added, 'Don't you remember me?' But he managed to restrain himself.

'Do you work here, Danilo?'

'For the gentleman, your husband, yes.'

She could hear his nationality in his accent. Not Polish then.

Stanislaw had not made himself popular with his workers. The villagers were already resentful of him. Usually Danilo kept his own counsel but he had not liked what he had seen of his new master so far, and couldn't help but agree with their judgement.

'Danilo, would you be so good as to help me dismount?'

This was unexpected and embarrassing. He looked helplessly at his grubby hands.

'Never mind your hands,' she said, with a little of the old imperiousness in her tone. 'Just help me down if you would and if you would be so kind as to take Essor to the stables for me ...'

He reached up and lifted her down, her face briefly close to his as she swung past him. She smelled clean and fresh as honey. He set her on her feet and stepped back quickly, bowing again, and turning his attention to the horse. She raised her veil, throwing it back over the hat and shot him a dazzling smile.

'Thank-you so much, Danilo,' she said and, gathering up her skirts, ran into the house.

Chapter Thirteen

STANISLAW WAS PROVING TO BE a very poor landowner and a worse farmer. He had expected to have to wait for his inheritance, since Floryan had other children to provide for, so he was well pleased to become master of such a good estate. The workers and staff at Podlaski, especially the Ukrainian steward, had gone their own way for many years. As long as the estate more or less paid its way, Stefan was satisfied, and it had been in all their interests to keep things running smoothly. Now they found it hard to disguise their resentment at their new master's overbearing ways. Stanislaw had learned to imitate his father's attention to detail but not that man's sensitivity to the feelings of others.

Stanislaw was obsessed with his rights but neglected his responsibilities.

He soon made his unwelcome presence felt on the estate and in the village. Not long after his arrival, suspecting irregularities in the accounts, he dismissed Ignacy. The error was his own, but he would not admit as much. The steward had a reputation as an honest man. He readily found a position on another property some miles away, but resented his treatment. When a traveller from Podlaski told him what Stanislaw was saying about him, he went to his new master and complained bitterly.

'I gave many years of good service on that estate,' he said, indignantly. 'Mr Diduski never had a bad word to say about the way I ran things. And I won't be slandered now. I did nothing wrong, sir!'

His new employer tried to calm him down. 'Nobody believes what young Yelitowski says. Not in this village, anyway. And not in Podlaski either. It's all so much hot air. Nobody likes either of them much. Well, they visit the Poniatowskis from time to time. Good luck to them! They'll not grow fat on *their* hospitality. You should be glad to be away from Podlaski and I'm certainly glad to have you here. Yelitowski has too many of his father's vices and few of his virtues. Forget about him!'

The steward tried to forget, but the insult rankled with him, and he was by no means the only enemy Stanislaw made at Podlaski. In a country already divided, he seemed to despise Ukrainian and Jew alike, and tolerated his Polish workers only a little better. It was impossible to please him.

Early the following year, he insisted on changing all the planned crop rotations, with the result that the harvest was not good. He blamed the workers who tilled the fields, the horsemen, and even the ex-steward for fomenting trouble. Inevitably, Ignacy heard the accusations and his loathing for Stanislaw grew. Few in the village and on the estate could muster a good word for him. Like her mother before her, Marianna worried about the desperate poverty she knew existed in too many parts of the village, but she tended to shy away from visiting, reluctant to allow grievous memories to come flooding back. Had she been married to a different man, warmer and more kindly, she might have been better liked, but the Ukrainian and Polish farm workers judged her as they judged her husband.

'Thinks she's too good to come down among us,' said one old woman.

'Mistress High and Mighty,' said another, with cruel emphasis on the word 'high'. They had all noticed that she was taller than Stanislaw, that she hunched her shoulders in order to minimise the difference between them.

Lonely and miserable, Marianna wrote to Nusia, suggesting that her old nurse might like to come to Podlaski, but Nusia had evil memories of the place. Besides, Marianna had a husband now. Young Mr Zygmunt had only Nusia to keep house for him and make sure that he ate properly. She didn't tell Marianna that Zygmunt was drinking and gambling to excess. It was all she could do to wake him up by mid-day and get some food into him. At this rate, Lisko would go to the dogs and Zygmunt with it. Nusia could not leave, for fear of what he might do in her absence.

Marianna wrote to Teresa, begging her to visit as soon as she could. Though her letters were careful, they were so frequent that they must have betrayed at least something of her unhappiness. Teresa, however, had preoccupations of her own. She had fallen in love with a man who loved her in return. The one great drawback was that Michael was an artist from Lemberg, the son of a small tradesman and totally penniless into the bargain.

Floryan had invited Michael to Milatyn in the first place. He wanted a portrait of Wanda and had heard that the young man was both talented and cheap. Floryan loved a bargain. Michael had duly arrived, flamboyant and handsome. When the portrait of Wanda had proved flatteringly successful, he had managed to secure further commissions to paint Floryan's family and so, said Wanda afterwards, he had no-one to blame but himself.

As Michael painted Teresa he fell in love with her.

There was something about her face and the way the light fell on it that enchanted him. After he fell in love with her image, he lost no time in falling in love with her smile and then he fell in love with her altogether and told her so, and showed her what he meant by it. She didn't object and soon after, he began a different painting, in the privacy of his room, a painting of the softly sprawled flesh of the woman he adored, and who loved him.

Michael was an honourable man and when he tentatively approached Wanda about the possibility of marrying the girl, he received some encouragement. Michael seemed set for a successful career. His portraits of the gentry were becoming fashionable, and he had even been asked to exhibit in Vienna.

When she told Floryan the news, however, the old man flew into a rage and vowed that never, ever would his darling Teresa marry a penniless artist. Michael was ordered to leave the house, and Teresa took to her room in passionate protest.

'I hate you!' she screamed at her father. 'You've ruined my life. I'll go into a convent and never see anyone again.'

In despair, Teresa wrote to Marianna.

'Why don't you come and stay with us for a while,' replied Marianna, but Floryan forbade the visit, suspecting a conspiracy between the girls, and Stanislaw wouldn't let his wife go to Milatyn either, though she begged him.

'My father is right as usual,' he said complacently. 'Teresa will come to her senses in time, my dear. Your place is here with me. I would miss you too much if you were to go away.'

She was tempted to ask him what it was about her that he might miss, since he was out on the estate all day and never came near her at night, but she held her tongue as usual. Her next letter from Teresa came three months later, in November.

It had been practically impossible for the family to keep Teresa in her room for any length of time. At last, she had pretended that her passion for the young artist had died away, but her heart was hardened and her mind made up. She loved her father but she loved Michael more. With the connivance of her maid, Lidia, she managed to get a message to Michael. It was almost time for the autumn fair in the nearby town of Peremyshlany, and Teresa had persuaded Wanda to let her go there with Lidia and with Wanda's two daughters, Sylvestra and Helena, as sensible chaperones.

The traders sold wonderful beads, coral and amber, as well as embroidered ribbons in bright colours. Teresa's eyes shone when she spoke of them and even Wanda thought her completely over her love for Michael.

'So you think she's quite cured, do you?' she asked Lidia.

'Quite, quite cured, my lady.'

Wanda sighed. 'Well, I think I would have been more faithful to such a talented young man. Perhaps if she had been more determined, her father might have agreed eventually.'

'You liked him then, my lady?'

'I did.' Wanda hesitated, always unwilling to admit any disloyalty to her husband. 'I would have welcomed the match, but her father thought otherwise. And maybe he was right after all, if the fancy was such a passing one.'

The fair was busy and the streets of the town were engulfed by a pandemonium of noise: the clatter of hooves, the chorus of animals and birds, and the raised voices of a hundred men and women haggling over prices, bartering eggs for salt, cheese for nails, chickens for oil. It was the fair at which servants and farm labourers were hired for the following year and also the last fair at which smallholders could sell animals or produce to make some extra money to see them through the hard winter ahead.

The Milatyn coachman drove the girls to the fair in an open droshky. He was young and susceptible, and while Lidia plied him with hard vodka and soft bread rolls and flattered him with compliments, the girls descended on the stalls. When the time came for the coachman and the maid to retrieve their charges, only Sylvestra and Helena were to be found. They swore that Teresa had been with them all the time; then they burst into tears and declared that they couldn't remember when they had last spoken to her. Ten minutes ago, perhaps? Or might it have been a whole hour? They had been so preoccupied with toy birds that nodded and tiny clay whistles that made a sweet sound, not to mention the performing monkey, dressed in a red waistcoat and hat, who danced for them and grimaced, showing yellow teeth and clapping his little hands in time to the music of the violin.

The panic-stricken coachman, accompanied by the maid, hunted high and low, though a keen observer might have noticed that Lidia could be seen smiling to herself every now and then, aware that she was leading him in quite the wrong direction. Finally, they learned that in the early afternoon, a smart, hired carriage, containing a dark haired young woman and a fair haired man, had been seen heading off along the Lemberg road.

At Milatyn, the girls sobbed out their story, but Lidia couldn't bear the painful uncertainty of her mistress and confided in Wanda. Teresa had run away with Michael, but the artist had no intention of behaving dishonourably. They were planning to marry in Lemberg and leave for Vienna almost immediately. They would be very grateful if Teresa's things could be sent on, along with Lidia herself if she could be spared, for the young wife would be badly in need of a maid.

Wanda was half horrified, half amused at the impertinence of these requests. For some hours she kept the news from Floryan, fearful that he would go after the couple in a murderous frame of mind. But when at last she plucked up the courage to tell him, he shook his head, left the room and walked up and down outside the window, seemingly deep in thought. When he came back inside, she was surprised to find him quite cheerful.

'The little fool,' was all he said.

'He loves her. I'm sure they'll be happy.'

'They might be. If she doesn't mind doing without money.'

'I don't think she'll have to. Or not for long. I think Michael is going to be very successful. You employed him, Floryan.'

'More fool me.'

'I think he'll do well in Vienna. He has talent.'

'He has a talent for flattery!'

'People like to be flattered. And you'll give her something? Now that they're married.'

'Not a penny!'

But he spoke in the bluff tones he had used to his younger children when he wanted to frighten them with false threats. Floryan had a grudging admiration for his daughter's bravery. It was, he thought, what her mother would have done under similar circumstances. His anger dissipated as quickly as it had come. At least Michael loved her. Which would make him a better husband than the younger son of some poverty stricken nobleman, marrying her for her dowry alone, without passion or affection.

He made arrangements for Lidia, together with all Teresa's clothes, to travel in comfort to Vienna, sending a brisk letter, the astringent words softened by the value of the wedding present and the large sum of money that accompanied it.

Marianna learned the details of all this in a long and confiding letter from Teresa, established in a small apartment in Vienna, and gloriously happy.

'It isn't disgusting at all, is it?' Teresa wrote, cryptically, in a postscript. 'The thing that we used to talk about. In fact it's endlessly fascinating.'

Although she was delighted for her cousin, and wished her nothing but good, Marianna was ashamed to find tears starting into her eyes. It was not fair. She had wanted Stanislaw for years. Now she had got him, she had better make up her mind to be content too.

Chapter Fourteen

Autumn gave way to a long and bitter winter. It seemed to Marianna that she could hardly name each day of the week, so uniform did her days become. Her life seemed to be a tedious round of writing letters or sewing, and then changing her clothes in order to eat poorly cooked meals. Stanislaw was as conservative in his eating habits as in everything else. Good plain food, he called it, but she hated the game, bitter and tough, or the bony fish that were their chief diet.

They still paid occasional calls on the Poniatowskis, at first by draughty carriage along roads that were rivers of mud, and then by sleigh, which was better, driving home by moonlight, wrapped up in furs, with the hot breath of the three horses steaming and the jingling of harness in the frosty air. The Poniatowski children looked more poorly than ever. Marianna wondered if they would survive the winter. One or more of them would always be confined to the nursery. Now their mother was expecting another baby. How would they cope? The sleigh with its piled furs was warmer than the Poniatowski's house. Even Stanislaw admitted as much, and would take a flask of spiced vodka to drink on the way home, passing it over to his wife for her to take the occasional mouthful. He didn't approve of women drinking liquor, but he had to make an exception in this case, since the chattering of her teeth was so distressing.

Podlaski was a chilly house too, albeit not nearly as bad as the Poniatowski mansion. Marianna didn't remember Milatyn or Lisko being so cold, but both Floryan and her father had insisted on keeping the tiled stoves burning day and night in every room, even those where the indoor staff slept, all through the winter. There was no shortage of wood, but Stanislaw didn't seem to feel the cold in the same way as Marianna, or perhaps he was simply more active. Marianna tried to wrap up in shawls all the time, but even so, as the winter deepened, the chill seemed to eat into her bones.

'You surely can't be cold,' he would say, pursing his lips.

'But I am, Stashek. I'm perished.'

'Your blood must be thin. Go for a brisk walk, Marianna. I can recommend it!'

'I don't *want* a walk,' she told him, peevishly.

'All right. But don't get angry about it, my dear.'

She had soon read almost all that the limited library had to offer. She had begun to try to improve her small command of English from the few books in that language she had found tucked away on a top shelf: Shakespeare, Milton, a frayed Pilgrim's Progress and a few tattered English novels, brought to the house by some visiting lady or lady's maid, many years ago. These were crammed with villainous counts, bandits, ladies in distress, mad monks and handsome young heroes. They gave her some respite, but they weren't easy to master. Stanislaw didn't mind the enforced isolation, but Marianna found it unbearable. Her only relief came from riding or walking around the park or skating alone on the frozen pond. This always brought a flush to her cheeks and a corresponding lightening of her spirits, but although she asked him to join her, Stanislaw would never come.

'I don't really consider skating a dignified occupation for a man of my station,' he said, implying that he didn't consider it suitable for her either. She chose to ignore his disapproval, and skated whenever she could escape her husband's censorious gaze.

One day, Danilo came upon her, gliding smoothly over the big, shallow pond beside the ice house. He had been sent to fetch a block of ice, cut from the surface of the pond earlier in the winter and stored in straw, before the ice became too thick to shift. She was all dressed in black, with her hands tucked into a black fur muff. She reminded him of the dark swallows that swept back and forth over this pond in search of insects every summer. He didn't show himself, but lurked in the gloom of the cellar and watched her for a long time through the low doorway, captivated by her skill and her self possession, as she moved over the surface of the ice, curving and turning. Again it seemed to him that she was locked somewhere deep inside herself.

When at last she went to the edge of the ice and sat down on a rock to remove her blades, he saw that her eyes were shining and her cheeks were flushed. She looked happy, and he found himself smiling at the sight. He waited until she had gone and then he slipped quietly away through the trees, carrying his ice in a leather pouch.

Occasionally, she and Stanislaw would have guests to dinner, people from estates further afield who might stay for a night or two. The men would discuss hunting and politics while they ate strong meat and drank heavy red wine, but the women would often remain silent, listening to their menfolk with smiling indulgence. Stanislaw would hold forth at length about the untrustworthiness of the Ukrainians, the dishonesty of the gypsies, the cunning of the Jews. Marianna was ashamed of his vehemence, but his neighbours seemed to find nothing odd in his behaviour, although occasionally she intercepted a smiling glance between her guests. She suspected that, privately, they despised Stanislaw's bombast. She could hardly believe that she had been so foolish as to marry him. What on earth had possessed her?

On other occasions, she would preside over a silver samovar filled with glowing charcoal, handing glasses of sweetened tea in filigree holders to ladies who talked about family relationships all the time, keen to give Marianna her proper place in these annals. They would compliment her on the quality of her cherry confiture, eating it daintily out of porcelain dishes with tiny silver spoons. She had had no hand in the making of it – it was entirely down to her cook – but she would nod and smile. What else was she to do?

Marianna had some respite when the couple spent Christmas at Milatyn, largely on the insistence of Floryan. Even Stanislaw could not disobey his father and, much to Marianna's relief, they spent the best part of a month in pleasant company. She behaved as if she were a girl again, chatting, laughing and skating on the frozen lake every day, arm in arm with Floryan who noted with approval the way colour bloomed in her cheeks, the pink so becoming against the cream of her skin, the dark brows and lashes, the deep brown of her hair.

'My dear, you look well again,' he remarked, when they were walking back to the house. 'To tell you the truth, I've been worried about you. We all have. When you arrived, I thought you must have been ill, though my son assures me you've been quite well.'

When she didn't reply, he persisted. 'Is there something wrong, Marianna? You must tell me if there is, you know. Is it Podlaski? Does it hold evil memories for you? Your poor mama, God rest her soul.'

'There's nothing wrong.' How could she tell him? 'It's just that it's very lonely at Podlaski. I'm used to more company. That's all.'

'You'll not be lonely when the children start to come along.'

'No,' she agreed, rather wistfully. 'No, I'll not be lonely then.'

The Christmas Eve supper, begun as the first star appeared in the sky, was traditionally meat free but with courses of many different kinds of fish. They finished off with the old Galician dessert called *kutia*: boiled wheat, poppy seeds, honey and cream. It was a particular favourite of Floryan's who would go into the kitchen to supervise its making, urging 'more honey, more cream!'

After the meal, each guest drew out a strand of the straw that was scattered under the linen banqueting cloth, a reminder of the manger in which the Christ Child was laid. Floryan's strand was very long, which was said to foretell a long life. The company observed that Stanislaw's piece of straw was shorter than any other. Nobody took much notice and Stanislaw threw it aside. He despised all superstition. Once the Christmas celebrations were over, he insisted on their early return to Podlaski, worried that the estate workers would slip into their easy-going ways, if he were not there to chivvy them along.

The one great disappointment for Marianna had been Teresa's absence. She had written, 'I'm in an interesting condition and have been very sick. Michael will not let me stir, but brings me sweetmeats to tempt my appetite and wine and water to drink, and generally cossets me, so perhaps it's worth all the misery. And what about you, Marianna? You and your husband must hurry up and make a cousin for my baby!'

Stanislaw came to her bed so seldom these days that conception was unlikely. She was partly relieved, partly saddened. She would have liked a child, but with each moon her body demonstrated its disappointment.

She was barely twenty. All the years of her marriage stretched before her. Unlike the heroines of her English novels, nobody had forced her. She had married him entirely of her own volition. Now, she was bored to the point of madness, and she had no-one to blame but herself. There was mending and embroidery, to be sure, but she had never liked sewing. She had brought sheet music with her from Milatyn, and Stanislaw had promised to buy her a pianoforte from Lemberg in the spring, when it might be transported more easily. All these things seemed to be ways of filling the time until the real business of living began.

Belatedly, she tried to overcome her fears and take an interest in the village, thinking that she might do something about the dreadful poverty there, but Stanislaw controlled the purse strings and although he was generous with his wife, giving her money for new clothes and the occasional piece of jewellery, a writhing serpent in blue enamel with a spray of diamond petalled flowers in its mouth, or a gold and ruby pendant from Vienna, that was the limit of his charity. He loved to see her wearing the latest fashions, but it seemed to her that she was like an expensive doll, to be kept very clean and splendid, but untouched. In her more despairing moments, she thought that he would have been content to see her fade away and die for love of him, as long as he no longer had to engage with the real flesh and blood woman. In any case, he strongly disapproved of any attempts at philanthropy.

'It's enough that you give a little, now and again, where you think fit,' he said, when she approached him with an idea for new houses for the estate workers. 'There are those who may deserve help, but not many.'

Marianna had reached some kind of compromise with her fear of the village by sending servant girls in her place with clothes, blankets and baskets of food, but Stanislaw disapproved.

'We give them gifts at Christmas! They are allowed to take kindling and fallen wood from the estate. Do you want us to impoverish ourselves, so that they can live in palaces?'

'Hardly palaces,' she said, mildly, unwilling to antagonise him further.

His father's expansive virtues seemed to have become vices in a personality much too narrow to accommodate them. He was too blinkered and proud to see the resentment that people might be harbouring against him. He came to Podlaski and bullied where he should have been firm and steady, demanded blind obedience where he should have fostered co-operation.

He made many enemies.

Sometimes, during the long, lonely nights, dreams full of colour, warmth and sensuality would come to her. They would involve some man who made love to her with shameful passion, but the man himself was always a vague, indistinct figure and she could never put a face to him, except that he was nothing like Stanislaw.

One morning, on her way to visit her favourite horse, Essor, she came face to face with Danilo in the stables. He stood back respectfully to let her past, and she cast a quick glance up at the thin face, the teeth very white, the hair long and straight and dark.

She said, 'I've come to see Essor. They tell me he isn't well.'

Danilo's rather sullen manner changed immediately at her mention of the horse.

'Colic. He chewed at a loose piece of wood in his stall. I was worried. But he'll be fine. I've been tending to him myself.'

'Have you?'

Under his breath, he muttered, 'Better company than my grandfather.'

'What did you say?'

'Nothing, my lady.'

'You're very good with the horses, aren't you?'

The estate kept some thirty working horses, the small, sturdy Polish 'koniks', as well as four trotting horses for the carriage, and a couple of valuable thoroughbreds for riding. Taking care of them was a big under-taking but only a few of the young grooms were trusted with the more valuable mounts. Danilo was one of them. Essor was Marianna's own, a young gelding, as sweet natured as Stanislaw's stallion was fierce, and she loved him.

'I don't like to see them troubled. I walked him around for half the night until his pain eased, and then I thought I might as well spend the rest of the night here. Sometimes they're like human beings. They get lonely in the night. Especially when they're unwell.'

Not only horses, she thought.

'By morning he was much better.'

She was grateful. She had grown very fond of the horse, a gentle chestnut, a colour Danilo called 'sorrel'.

'You really do love the horses.'

He grinned, suddenly. 'Better than I love people, my lady.'

Afterwards his words stuck in her mind. She found them sad and yet she could identify with them. Her friendships here seemed all to be among the animals rather than the people of the estate: the horses and hounds and even the farm cats. All these could be both undemanding and demonstratively loving: better company than humans, anyway.

The truth was that Danilo had become obsessed with Marianna Yelitowska. No village girl was good enough for him. Although he would have found it impossible to describe the emotion at that time in any but the most simple words, he was infected with a kind of courtly love, and wanted only to be her cavalier. He knew this was madness but he was powerless to stop it. During the harsh months of January and February, he saw little of her, except for glimpses of her on the ice or out on a horse-drawn sleigh with her husband, and he tried to put her from his mind. But he thought about Antonina a great deal. He wondered if Marianna knew that his mother had been the cause of her own mother's premature death. He wanted to tell her and also to tell her how kind her mother had been to him, but he never found the opportunity. There could be no real conversation between them, so how could he ever broach such a topic? That too was a kind of madness.

Then, spring came and he began to see more of her: in the stables, trudging alone through the muddy park, riding out with her husband. Each sight served to reinforce a reluctant sympathy for her. He concluded that the villagers were wrong. She wasn't proud. She was just unhappy, and quite unlike the self confident little girl he remembered from all those years ago. Then he would say to himself, 'What does she know of real suffering, with her fine clothes and fine house and good food? Why should I feel any sympathy for her?' Resentment would flare in him, but it was always short-lived, for something in her face touched him and made him pity her more than he could say.

Chapter Fifteen

THAT SUMMER WAS LUSH AND warm, although not as hot as the summer when Antonina had contracted smallpox. One fine afternoon, Danilo had been sent with a message to a neighbouring estate. It wasn't often that he managed to escape from work and from the demands of his grandfather for a while, and he made the most of it, electing to walk where he could have ridden. On the way back, his errand completed, he halted some distance from the village and stretched himself out in a meadow, among long grasses and flowers. He dozed for a moment or two in the luxury of sun and scent, but woke to the sound of singing.

'Anna, my Anna, I do not understand
Why, as I mounted my horse today,
You would not take my hand.
As I sat astride my sorrel horse,
You turned your pretty head aside.
Are you false or true?'

He rolled over and, peering between grass stems, he saw Marianna, wandering towards him, singing to herself as she walked, her arms full of meadow flowers. She wore a dress of pale muslin and, still clutching the flowers against her breast with one hand, she took off her bonnet with the other. Then, holding bonnet and flowers together, she pulled the pins out of her hair, throwing them away, with a gesture that was at once angry and abandoned. Having escaped from her confinement, however briefly, she seemed determined to be free in every possible way. He watched her hair tumble down her back in a shining brown cascade. She shook it out, lifting her face to the sun.

Dizzy with sudden desire, he crouched low, but when he saw that she was coming his way, he didn't know what to do, so he turned over and feigned sleep hoping that she wouldn't see him. Instead, she almost tripped over him, and a cascade of blue cornflowers, yellow cockle and crimson poppies, already wilting from the warmth of her hands, fell on his upturned face and on his shirt, so that he had to pretend to wake up, and then leap to his feet and dip his head in a bow, and try to gather up the flowers for her.

He saw her blush as crimson as the poppies against the white of her dress, and found himself reddening too. He could feel the heat on his cheeks. Awkwardly, she took the flowers from him, all the while clutching the blue ribbons of her bonnet.

'Thank-you, thank-you. I'm so sorry to disturb you. I thought there was no-one else here.'

She kept trying to touch her hair, conscious of its abandoned state, but she was hampered by flowers and bonnet, and he saw that she was watching his lips as though transfixed by them.

She was turning to go, when he said, 'My lady!'

She paused, looking back at him.

'Do you not remember me at all, my lady?'

She shook her head, puzzled and anxious. 'From the stables? You looked after Essor for me and I was glad of it.'

'No. I mean when I was a boy. You came to Podlaski. You had a doll called Loulou.' He had always remembered the doll's name. All these years later, he still remembered it.

He saw the light of recognition in her eyes. A shudder ran through her as other, more painful memories surfaced.

'You were *that* boy? Good heavens! You said you would break my doll!'

'I was very rude. I must apologise. I was sorry later.'

'And I stuck my tongue out at you.' She began to laugh, then stopped short, not knowing how best to respond. She stood like a tall, white pillar, holding her flowers close.

He rushed on. 'I must also tell you that your mother was very kind to me. And to my mother.'

This admission confused her even more; she put up her hand as though to ward him and his words away from her, dropping more flowers. He bent to pick them up again.

'Leave them be!' she said. 'There are plenty of flowers.'

'My mother was ill. Your mother was very kind to me and my family. I wanted you to know.'

'Your mother? It was *your* mother who was so ill, that time?'

'I'm sorry. I shouldn't have spoken. It was wrong of me. I'm so sorry. Good afternoon, my lady.'

He bowed again and strode quickly out of the meadow, looking back once, from the edge of the forest. He saw that she was standing very still, with the afternoon sun beating down on her unprotected head, clutching her flowers and her bonnet and watching his retreating figure. What had he done? What had he said and why? Would she hate him now? For the second time after an encounter with Marianna, he expected retribution of some kind, punishment or dismissal, but nothing happened.

A day or two later, when each family brought a wreath or bouquet of flowers to church to be blessed, to mark the octave of the holy day of Corpus Christi, he watched her alight from the estate carriage carrying a posy of herbs and wild flowers. He recognised some of the flowers as those she had been gathering in the meadow. She saw him watching her and raised the posy to her face, sniffing at the blossoms. She looked as though she might be about to dissolve into tears. Again, anger at his own misplaced sympathy supplanted desire, and he resolved to put her out of his mind completely.

At harvest time, when Marianna and her husband had been at Podlaski for little more than a year, a group of gypsies came to the village. They helped with the harvest, in return for food to see them through the winter. They were a small, cheerful group, accompanied by quantities of bold children, well-kept horses and mangy dogs. They worked hard and played hard. The locals were half fascinated by them, half contemptuous, and accused them of stealing everything from chickens to children, although Danilo observed that they seemed to have plenty of ragged infants of their own without needing to acquire more.

Danilo was helping out with the harvest too. In the fields he found himself working alongside a gypsy girl called Rozalia, who took a great fancy to him. Most of the gypsy girls were shy and very chaste and wouldn't look twice at Ukrainian or Pole, but for some reason Rozalia was headstrong and confident. For the duration of the gypsies' stay in the village, Danilo went in fear of being attacked by her fiercely protective brothers, but the girl was cunning and made sure that her brothers knew nothing of her liaison with the young Ukrainian.

On a dusky late summer's evening, Rozalia pulled him behind a newly built hayrick and, with the swallows dipping and crying fiercely overhead, encouraged him to make love to her, but stopped him from going too far. He was surprised by her wiry strength when she held him off.

'I know how babies are made!' she said. 'But there are plenty of other ways of giving and taking pleasure.'

She made him feel foolish. No woman had ever spoken to him like this before.

'I thought women were always quiet.'

'No wonder they're quiet if you push and pull them about like that. You may be a big handsome lad, but you're a fool as well. Women's pleasure is different.'

'I didn't know women felt anything at all!'

'Neither do most men – or women for that matter.'

He was momentarily angry with her, but she began to laugh and kissed him.

'Listen,' she whispered in his ear. 'I can teach you how to give a woman so much pleasure that you'll be able to make love to anyone you like, Danilo, from the rich lady at the big house to the poor peasant girl in her cottage!'

He heard her words with a little start of shame. Could she read his mind, he wondered?

'What must I do?' he asked her, with unusual humility.

'Perhaps I'll show you.'

When they next met, they went up into a warm hayloft, where she took hold of his hand and showed him how to please her. She made him explore her body with lips as well as hands, and whenever the sensations threatened to become too much for him, she would bring him back to himself with a ferocious pinch or scratch, making him cry out in pain and frustration that was not entirely without its own pleasure.

'Think of something else,' she would tell him, laughing. 'Think of your grandfather, think of cabbages and turnips, think of anything but me!'

She showed him which parts of her body were most sensitive to pleasure. She made him touch her with exploring fingers and then with his tentative tongue.

'If a woman really wants you, you'll know. If she doesn't, then you'll hurt her and there'll be no pleasure in it for either of you. Take your time. There's no need to rush.'

Clumsy at first, but with an increasing sense of wonder, he discovered the delight to be gained from the pleasure of another person. Only at the very last moment would she relinquish her role as teacher, even while he abandoned himself to his own joy. He grew very fond of her. He thought afterwards that she had liked him very much without loving him at all, that the affection had mostly been on his side. But sometimes, he closed his eyes and pictured, not the gypsy girl, but the long body of Marianna Yelitowska, moving with pleasure in response to his touch.

One day, Marianna chanced to see them together. She had planned to go out riding. On her way to the stables she saw the girl emerge, stand on tiptoe and kiss Danilo lightly on the lips, her hands at his waist. It was a fleeting but intimate caress. As she watched the way he gazed after her, with obvious admiration, Marianna's heart was filled with anger against the girl. It gave her a sharp sensation, a physical pain in her chest. She waited until the gypsy had gone, and then called out for Danilo. In some confusion, for he would not normally be in the stables at this time, he came out to assist her.

'I want Essor saddled! I'm going riding. Just around the estate.'

To his embarrassment, she came in to watch him work. Instantly his fingers became clumsy, fumbling with the straps on the saddle.

'Who is the girl I just saw leaving?' she asked. 'Is she your sweetheart, Danilo?'

He caught the acid in her voice with surprise and a certain amount of gratification.

'No. No, she's just one of the gypsies who seems to have taken a bit of a fancy to me, my lady. They never stay long in one place.'

'And you've taken a fancy to her, it seems.'

'All gypsies are fond of horses. She likes to come to the stable and pet them. That's all. She means no harm.'

'But she seems to be fond of men, too. Well, one man in particular.'

He looked her straight in the eye and nodded, sure of her jealousy now. She flushed, and bent her head. It struck him that if she had been a child, she would have stamped her foot or slapped him and flounced away. He tried not to smile.

With a sudden, fierce edge to her voice, she said, 'You can saddle the grey and come with me today.'

'My lady?'

He didn't think that Stanislaw would approve at all. This time, she did stamp her foot, and he was reminded sharply of the little girl clutching her doll, so peremptory and proud.

'Do as I say! Saddle the grey for yourself, and come with me. I want some company and it will have to be you, because there's nobody else. I'm sick of riding out alone.'

He did as he was told and soon they were picking their way along the bridle path, with Marianna in front.

Presently, they came to a broad track along the edge of a field, the field where she had spilled the flowers over him, and she summoned him to ride alongside her. He didn't know what to say, and it was Marianna who spoke first.

'I'm surprised you're not yet married, Danilo.'

'Me? Who would have me? What have I got to give any woman? A hut to live in and an invalid grandfather to look after. I'm not much of a catch, am I, my lady?'

He knew that his manner was too informal, but he was feeling reckless. And she had broached the subject first. She frowned and he could see that the dreadful reality of his poverty had never really crossed her mind. He felt as if the air between them had grown hot and heavy. He couldn't draw a full breath. He wondered if she felt the same. He glanced across at her.

'Do you think we should turn back? We're a long way from the stables, and it'll soon be dark.'

'Aren't you enjoying this, Danilo?'

'I'm enjoying the fresh air.'

'But not my company, it seems.'

'My lady?' He was quite at a loss how to answer this. What did she expect him to say?

'Never mind!' She drew Essor up sharply. 'I have to dress for dinner. We have to go back now!'

They rode back to the house in absolute silence. Still without speaking, she allowed him to help her dismount, turned, and left him holding the reins of her sorrel horse and his grey. He stood and watched her go indoors, but she didn't look back.

That evening, over dinner, Marianna said to her husband, 'Those gypsies should be moved on. They're only causing trouble in the village. There have been fights and thefts, and their dogs are everywhere.'

'They've been helping with the harvest as they do every year, I believe. People grumble about them, but they do no real harm.'

You knew where you were with gypsies, thought Stanislaw. He neither liked nor trusted them himself, but then he didn't trust any of his workers, and at least the gypsies could be persuaded to do a very good day's work without becoming a burden on the estate.

'I caught one of them in the stable tonight, eyeing up the horses! You know about gypsies and horses, I suppose. Don't blame me if your beloved stallion goes missing.'

She spoke with such acrimony that Stanislaw looked at her in alarm.

'Do you think that's a possibility? Have you heard rumours?'

'No. No rumours. I'm only telling you what I saw.'

The next day, Stanislaw had the gypsies moved on, just to be on the safe side. After all, the harvest was almost finished. Rozalia left without regret, but with a skein of pretty ribbons from Danilo, which was all he could afford to give her. She told her brothers that the ribbons were a gift from the lady of the house. Danilo would always be grateful to her. About Marianna's behaviour he was more equivocal. It intrigued him. He knew that she was quite capable of having the gypsies moved on out of spite, but could she really be so jealous of his friendship with Rozalia? And what did that signify?

Chapter Sixteen

Autumn, the couple's second at Podlaski, drew nearer. Danilo had been sent to rebuild a section of the estate wall that had been partially demolished by a drunken farmer, taking a corner much too fast. He had survived intact, which was more than could be said for the wall or his poor horse, which had broken a leg and had to be slaughtered. Danilo wished it had been the carter who had been killed rather than the horse. He had never liked the man anyway and the horse had been a gentle, biddable creature.

It was a hot, airless day and as Danilo worked, cursing the cause of the accident, Marianna rode by with her husband in the open droshky that they used for trips to the Poniatowskis. Naked to the waist, Danilo rested for a moment, his hair straggly with perspiration, his skin darker than ever after exposure to a summer's sunshine.

Stanislaw drew the trap to a halt, and Danilo squinted across at them through the sunlight.

'You! Come over here!'

Danilo came over to the droshky and stared up at them.

'Yes, sir.'

He dipped his head quickly in a half hearted gesture of respect, and then looked up again, unsmiling, into Marianna's face. She was acutely aware of his brown shoulders and arms, gleaming with a thin layer of sweat. His gaze made her blush and half turn away. No servant should look at her in that way. Nobody had ever looked at her in that way, let alone a servant. He saw her embarrassment and a slight smile, hardly more than a twitch of the lips, crossed his face. He thought of all he had done with the gypsy, and wondered again what it would be like to lie with Marianna in the same way.

Stanislaw surveyed him with distaste. 'Boy, you must not work here in the gardens as if you were out in the fields. It's an affront to the lady. Put your shirt on.'

'Yes, sir.' Danilo cast a glance over his shoulder to where his coarse linen shirt lay carelessly across a fallen log.

'And don't you know that you must kiss my hand?'

'Which am I to do first, sir?'

To Marianna's horror, Stanislaw's instant response was to raise his whip and draw it sharply across the side of the younger man's face.

'That's for your insolence. Now get on with your work!'

Marianna drew in her breath as she saw a red welt raised over the sallow cheek. But Danilo didn't flinch or even put his hand to the wound afterwards. Stanislaw gathered up the reins and drove on. Unable to restrain herself from turning around, Marianna saw Danilo standing very still, staring after them. He was passing a heavy stone from hand to hand, as though testing its weight. It was so hot that the birds had ceased their singing, though the crickets were chirping incessantly. Her lips felt dry. She passed a hand across her forehead.

There's going to be a storm, she thought, and her skin tingled in anticipation. She wanted to go back to the safety of Podlaski. She didn't want to visit the Poniatowskis at all. One of the thin little girls had passed away while she and Stanislaw were at Milatyn for Christmas. But now there was a new baby in the house, another girl. Marianna had seen it once or twice, kicking up its legs on a rug beneath the trees. It looked well and contented enough, but then it hadn't experienced the house in winter.

'There are none so lazy and mean minded as these wretched peasants,' remarked Stanislaw, flicking his whip over the back of the pony as carelessly as he had flicked it across the young man's cheek, albeit with less force. 'You talk about gypsies, but these Ukrainians would steal the coat off your back and manage to justify the theft to themselves in some way. Sly, shifty, untrustworthy. They lie about everything.'

'Your father doesn't think so.'

'Then my father grows weak-minded in his old age.'

'They're poor and overcrowded. It would be strange if they didn't envy us. I've often wanted to do something about their poverty.'

'But you do, my dear. You send food and clothing to the poorest. You ought to remember what happened to your mother.'

'I do,' she replied quietly. 'I remember it all the time. That's why I can't bring myself to go to the village on my own account. But I should, you know. If she could, I should. And the poorest are very poor indeed.'

'Then it's God's will. They were born to it, as we are to what we have. Each man should accept his station in life.'

'Perhaps. But those words come much more easily out of the mouths of those who have plenty!'

Stanislaw pursed his lips and made a series of irritated tutting sounds. 'Who has been putting such nonsense into your head?' he asked. 'My brother Julek, perhaps? Well, he has always had ridiculous ideas!'

'Not Julek. No. But it's what my mother would have said. She was well loved. I doubt if they could say as much about me. And besides ...'

'What?'

She sighed. 'I don't know. There's something wrong.'

'What could be wrong?'

'Don't you feel it in the air? The servants in the house feel it. I know they do. They fall silent when I walk into a room, but I know that they've been whispering among themselves. It's like this, Stashek, like the stillness before a storm.'

'Nonsense. There's nothing wrong except the usual incompetence and insolence.'

She shuddered, remembering the hatred in Danilo's eyes as he had gazed after them, remembering his words about her mother. Would he think of her as a good lady? She doubted it.

'Then why do I feel so afraid all the time?'

Stanislaw turned to her in astonishment. 'But what could happen to *you*, my dear. You can't be afraid of that insolent young peasant, surely. If so, I can have him dismissed, instantly. Or beaten. Just say the word.'

'No, no. You mustn't do that. It has nothing to do with him. I wasn't talking about him in particular. He's quite harmless. And he's a genius with the horses. Essor loves him. There's no-one so good or so willing to work with them. He's a little brusque that's all. I can forgive him a lot for that, and so should you.'

'Don't tell me what I should do!'

'No. And I'm sorry. I just meant I don't think he intended to be insolent. He's always perfectly polite to me. And he's so good with the animals.'

'You're too concerned about that horse of yours, Marianna,' said Stanislaw. But he was willing to indulge her on this point. Even he knew that the wellbeing of the horses was vital for the smooth running of any estate.

'I was thinking of my mother,' she added. 'It hurts me to remember what happened to her. It gives me a bad feeling. And I think there will be a storm. The sky is so dark. Drive on Stanislaw. Drive on, do.'

One of the servants at Podlaski was a boy of twelve called Ivan. He was employed to tend to the fires, run errands and do a hundred and one tasks for the cook, the butler and even the kitchen maids. He was the lowest of the low in this household and slept in a kind of cupboard off the kitchen, his body growing grimy with grease and wood ash. Occasionally, the cook, unable to bear the sight or smell of him, would take him out and pump cold water over his head until he looked tolerably clean. He was well fed, but the horses in the stables received more affection than this solitary child, and Danilo, meeting him occasionally about the estate, was bitterly reminded of himself at the same age.

Ivan could remember neither mother nor father. As a small child he had travelled about with the tiled stove setter, a man he called Uncle Victor, although he was not even sure that this man was a blood relation. They had moved from village to village, building and repairing stoves. Victor had been brusquely kind to him, he had worked hard and had been happy, or at least too busy to consider whether he might be unhappy. But one year, Uncle Victor had fallen ill at Podlaski and had died soon afterwards, leaving Ivan to the uncertain mercies of the villagers. Nobody in the village could afford to keep him, but the big house had absorbed him, and he had been grateful for the shelter, even if so many of his chores were of the dirty, unpleasant variety that others despised.

In spite of his difficult start in life, Ivan was a smiling, ingenuous lad, rather simple, very religious and fond of the wild birds that he fed each day, with scraps that the cook gave him. He had more than once felt the weight of Stanislaw's riding crop across his shoulders, but seemed to bear his master little resentment on that account. He thought he must deserve punishment if it was meted out to him.

One December day, he was on an errand in the village when a surly farmer peered out of the door of the tavern and called him over.

'Come here to me!'

'What do you want?' asked Ivan uneasily. The man had never been kind to him in the past.

'Ivan,' the man said, and slipped a small coin into the boy's hand. 'Will you do me a favour?'

'What kind of favour?'

'Nothing too difficult.'

'What, then?'

He glanced around, pulled the boy closer and muttered in his ear. 'I want you to leave the kitchen door open tonight, up at the house. Well, not exactly open. Just make sure it isn't locked and bolted, there's a good lad. Will you do that for me?'

Ivan's immediate reaction was one of surprise, rather than suspicion.

'Why?' he asked. 'Why would you want me to do such a thing? What can you want in our house? Are you planning to steal something?'

'Don't be stupid!' said the man, winking at Ivan. 'How could I steal anything from the big house? I'd be caught right away, wouldn't I?'

'What do you want, then?'

'Don't you know I'm madly in love with your kitchen maid, Aniela?'

'Are you?' Ivan's face fell a little.

'Aye, and she likes me. She told me you would be sure to help us. You will, won't you? You're a good lad.'

Ivan liked Aniela too She helped him whenever he brought an injured bird in, sometimes with a bad grace, it was true, but usually she would provide him with a space near the stove to keep his feathered refugees warm while he fed them and nursed them back to health.

'All right,' he said. 'If it's for Aniela, I'll let you in. Cook bolts the kitchen door before she goes to bed, but I think I can draw it back.'

'Quietly, mind. And don't mention it to the girl. Or anyone else for that matter.'

'Why not? Is it to be a surprise for her?'

'Oh yes. That's what it is, Ivan. A very big surprise. Besides, if she knew, it would only embarrass her. And if anyone else knew they might not like it. Then Aniela would be very disappointed.' The man grinned. A little group of his friends, standing behind him, had overheard the tail end of the conversation. They nudged him and laughed out loud.

'When will you be coming?' asked Ivan, nervously.

'In the middle of the evening. In the quiet time after dinner.'

'Yes, the kitchen's always quiet then. Once the washing-up's done and the fire's banked up for morning. The cook always goes to bed early.'

'Does she now?'

'She does.'

'What a helpful lad you are, Ivan. I'll be sure to tell Aniela. And I don't want your master or mistress poking their noses out to see what I'm up to either. They don't like servants having followers, do they?'

'No. No, they'll be in the drawing room. The butler has a cottage on the estate since he married, and cook goes to bed as soon as dinner is cleared. Master always checks all the locks himself, but that's much later on, before he goes upstairs. I have the kitchen to myself most evenings.'

'You'll be waiting for me then?'

'Of course,' said Ivan. 'I can do that!'

'And mind you don't fall asleep.'

'No. I won't fall asleep if I know you're coming.'

Usually he curled up near the embers of the stove and slept like a puppy, only retiring to his cubby hole and his blanket in the early hours, in case the maids should come down and find him there in the morning.

'Good lad.' The man pressed another small coin into his hand. 'There'll be more where that came from, don't you worry! You just do as you're told and see what happens!'

Chapter Seventeen

IN THE WINTER OF 1846, a number of wealthy Polish landowners had been plotting a rebellion against Austrian rule. The people of the various nations that comprised the great empire of Austria-Hungary were always plotting rebellion of one kind or another, but Stanislaw Yelitowski had not been among the conspirators. He was comfortable at Podlaski and, although his support had been canvassed, he had followed his father's advice and rejected any idea of uprising.

The Hapsburg authorities had spies everywhere. They learned of the intended rebellion and deliberately spread word among the Ukrainians that the Poles were planning an uprising, one that would enslave them once and for all. Infiltrators encouraged disaffected Ukrainians to revolt against their Polish masters. At Podlaski, these sparks of revolution had fallen on the dry tinder of resentment against Stanislaw. He had already made plenty of enemies. Many of the men he had dismissed or punished judged that they had little to lose, and were eager to take their revenge on him.

They hadn't been sure whether Danilo would join them or not. Gavril would have been a different matter if he were not so frail. You knew where you were with Gavril, but Danilo was his own man. It was not that they judged him to be in any way fond of the Poles. He had little reason to side with them. They knew him as a brave but sullen fellow, who kept his own counsel and went his own way without fear or favour. He was a formidable adversary, when he could be bothered to fight, and he suffered fools not at all.

'A better friend than an enemy, that one,' said the former steward, the one whom Stanislaw had dismissed.

In the event, Danilo pretended to go along with them. It was not hard to dissemble. He thought that Stanislaw deserved everything that was coming to him. He would not have lifted a finger to save him from the consequences of his own folly, but he wondered what on earth he could do to save Marianna from the tempest he realised must soon be coming. Could he warn her? Impossible. She wouldn't believe him, and if she told her husband, as she surely must, the consequences for all of them would be terrible. He could not betray his own people, but nor could he see Marianna destroyed in the impending conflagration. So he must come up with some other plan. Afterwards, it struck him that he had not hesitated for an instant. His only uncertainty had been about the best way of ensuring her safety and his own survival. But her safety came first.

That night, Ivan heard the low knocking at the door and leapt up to let Aniela's supposed lover in. He was alarmed to find a whole band of villagers filing into the kitchen. He recognised Ignacy among them, the man who had once been the steward on the estate, and he grew very frightened. Most of them had been drinking and were fired up with a combination of vodka-inspired courage and bitter hatred of Stanislaw.

When Ivan tried to stop them, one of them cast him aside. He bumped his head on the hot metal of the stove and lay dizzily for a few moments, blood running down his cheek, before getting to his feet and crawling to the door, knowing instinctively that he must escape, that running away was his only option. But where could he go?

In the doorway he met Danilo coming in with the tail end of the mob. Ivan recognised him as somebody who had been brusquely kind to him in the past. He looked up at him in mute supplication, but he saw to his horror that Danilo was carrying a pitchfork from the stables. The tall man gazed at him, frowning. Then he reached down and pulled him roughly to his feet, shaking him as a dog shakes a rat.

'Ivan! Jesus, I forgot all about you.'

Ivan stood, suspended foolishly from Danilo's grasp, his head still buzzing from its contact with the stove.

'Ivan,' hissed Danilo again, but lowering his voice. 'Are you listening to me?'

Ivan nodded, as vigorously as he could, although the action made his head spin.

'If you've got any sense at all in that thick head of yours, you'll get away from here, now, as fast as you can.'

Ivan saw that Danilo was sober and deadly serious.

'But where shall I go? What's happening?' asked Ivan, tears leaving little runnels in the grime of his face.

'Something that you don't want to see. You mustn't be here. They'll destroy you too, if they think you're a threat. Go quickly. Go to the village. Run as fast as you can, Ivan, and stop for nobody. *Nobody*, do you hear me? You've seen nothing, you've heard nothing. You've just run away.'

'But where shall I go? What shall I do?'

Danilo hesitated briefly. 'Go to my grandfather, Gavril. Gavril Bandura. You know where he lives?'

'Yes, sir. I do.'

'Say that there are terrible things happening up at the big house and that you have been badly hurt. Say nothing else about your part in any of this, not if you want to live afterwards.' Danilo shook him again. 'Later on, you can tell my grandfather that I sent you. But only him. Nobody else. Do you understand what I'm saying?'

'I think so.'

'Then go now and don't look back!'

The boy went, sobbing, running, falling and getting to his feet again. He found Danilo's hut on the edge of the village, found the old man asleep in bed and very resentful of being woken. There was an air of suppressed excitement elsewhere in the village, cries and whispers and lights flickering where most people should have been safely abed. Soon women and a few older men came to the hut and some of them said, 'Now they will get what's coming to them!'

'Perhaps more than they deserve,' observed Gavril. He wondered uneasily where his grandson was.

'No, no. We hate Yelitowski. Let him suffer. Her as well. Too proud to mix with the peasants. Let all the Poles suffer! Let's teach them a lesson they won't forget in a hurry!'

Most of them ignored Ivan. He huddled onto Danilo's bed, making himself as small as possible, his teeth chattering with cold and fear. After a little while one of the older women made him drink vodka from a bottle, just one swig, the first he had ever tasted. 'Did they hurt you, lad?' she asked. 'There's blood on your face!'

'I hit my head on the stove when they pushed past me into the house. But then I was frightened so I got up and ran away.'

'Best thing you could have done. If anyone asks you, later on, just say you were in the village all the time, sent here with a message. Pretend you weren't up there at all. There'll be hell to pay for this night's work, no matter what happens. Get into bed and try to sleep, son.'

Soon he fell into a restless doze, pulling Danilo's blankets around him.

At the manor house, the men milled about the kitchen. Their initial silence had been replaced by shouts, taunts and insults. Many of them were very drunk. They had found a big flagon of vodka and were passing it round, pouring it down their throats. The Polish cook came to see what was going on, but she completely misjudged the situation and rushed at them with a mixture of outrage and panic.

'Get out! Get out, you filthy peasants!' she shrieked. 'Get out of here before I call the master!'

All of them had screwed up their courage to this point and were not going to be deterred by an enraged woman in her nightclothes. Nevertheless, none of them expected what happened next and many of them were shocked by it.

The miller had sidled up behind her. He caught at her hair, pulled her backwards and deliberately cut her throat with a single stroke of his knife, before she could say another word. She gurgled, choked on her own blood, fell, her limbs twitching.

'There now,' he observed, grinning at his fellows. 'That's settled that one! And there's no going back now, lads, is there?'

There was no going back.

Timidly, little Aniela had followed the cook, afraid of what she might see, but afraid to remain in her bed. Terrified and confused, she tried to run away, but slipped on the cook's blood and fell. The men seized her. The murder of the cook seemed to have triggered something bestial in them. Or perhaps all too human. As Danilo watched them from the doorway, he thought that they were no longer individuals. They were a pack and just as savage, just as heedlessly dangerous as wolves or wild dogs. It seemed to him, when he thought about it afterwards, as though something else was in the room with them. Visions of that terrible night haunted his dreams throughout his life. Danilo had little use for religion, but he thought that there was something demonic here. As though the vicious murder of a helpless woman, who had done no more than shout at them, had allowed something devilish and pitiless to enter in and take possession of them.

Several of them held Aniela down on the kitchen floor and raped her, taking turns, egging each other on. Danilo turned away. He could do nothing to help her, knew that he had to remain silent and complicit, or he too would be dead, and Marianna would die with him, the girl too. The sight of the savage assault made the bile rise to his throat and that too stayed with him for ever, the terrible guilt of it, although he tried to move away, tried to make himself inconspicuous. They cut her breasts with their knives, but they did not kill her, only turned her out, naked and bleeding, into the wintry park where she wandered about in a dazed state until morning. She was trying to get to her mother's home in the next village, but her body was found days later on the borders of the estate, where she had collapsed with shock and exposure and loss of blood, and had died where she lay, her poor little body huddled on the ground with the crows pecking at her.

After that, events moved with hideous speed. Danilo had made careful preparations, but he saw that the situation was unpredictable, his own position precarious, and that he must respond to events as best he could, rather than follow any real plan. Already sickened by the scene in the kitchen and close to vomiting, he followed a group of men as they ran to the drawing room. The pitchfork was his badge of honour, proof of his involvement, proof that he was with them rather than against them, and he clutched it close, his hand sweaty with fear.

When the men burst into the drawing room, they found Stanislaw and his wife huddled together in the centre of the room, appalled by the noises from the kitchens at the rear of the house. Vodka and resentment had given these men a courage they might otherwise have lacked in the face of their habitual respect for Stanislaw. But Stanislaw was no coward. If there had been a weapon to hand, he would certainly have used it and taken a few of them with him but there was no weapon. As it was, he stepped forward and pushed Marianna behind him.

'What the devil do you think you're doing in here?' he shouted. 'Get out! Get out of my house now!'

So deeply ingrained was their habitual deference to his authority that, even then, they hesitated. But he lacked the presence of his father. He was without friends and unarmed. These men felt no loyalty to him whatsoever. Why should they? He had shown them nothing but disapproval and disdain. They stared at him, their voices hushed, while they circled him warily.

'At least let my wife go! You have no quarrel with her. Let her go!'

The leader shook his head. 'She has eyes to see, ears to hear. That's our quarrel with her!'

Still they faltered, each reluctant to make the first move, until one, more daring or perhaps more crazed with resentment than the rest, stepped forward, knife in hand. He knocked aside Stanislaw's arm that had automatically flown up to protect himself, and managed to thrust the blade deep into his neck. The blood spurted out in a wide arc, defacing a fine old tapestry of Venus and her Nymphs, turning their pink, naked bodies all crimson. The sight of it seemed to trigger something in the rest of the men. They were, said Marianna afterwards, like fiends from hell, bent only on destruction, pulling down pictures, smashing porcelain, even gouging at the furniture with their knives and axes.

She stooped down beside her dying husband and cradled his head in her lap. Perhaps it was that that saved her from the first ferocious assault. The blood gushed out of his neck in a deadly stream. She was aware of warm blood soaking the silk of her dress and her hands. She would always remember the smell of it. She saw Stanislaw glance about him in utter surprise, close his eyes, shudder and lie still. She could only think, incongruously, of how he would hate to see his precious possessions treated like this. She crouched there, unmoving, while the destruction went on around her and it seemed to her as though she was at the calm eye of some terrible storm. She waited for the blows to rain down on her too, anticipating pain, then oblivion, wishing for it to be over, praying for everything to end with as little pain as possible. In sudden terror, she felt hot breath on her neck and rough hands grasping her, seizing her from behind, pulling her away from her husband's body. She heard coarse laughter. And then, she was aware of Danilo, pitchfork in hand, towering in front of her and whoever held her from behind.

'Leave her!' Danilo said, his voice a dangerous growl. 'This one's mine! Leave her to me! That was the agreement!'

Her captor hesitated. Over her shoulder, she could smell his sour breath, feel the heat of it on her neck. Deliberately, Danilo levelled the pitchfork in his direction, his voice low and menacing.

'I said this one's mine. I've waited too long for this to be robbed of my prize now! Don't you cross me or you'll pay for it!'

There was a moment of vacillation. Then the man laughed again. He was very drunk. He shoved Marianna towards Danilo and she stumbled against him.

'Take the bitch and welcome. I've no quarrel with you, Bandura!' the man said, thickly, spreading his hands wide. He laughed. 'Besides, I can wait till you've finished with it!'

Danilo tossed the pitchfork aside, grasped Marianna about the waist and half dragged, half carried her towards the door. She would certainly have met the same fate as her husband, butchered there in her own drawing room, with her blood soaking into the carpet, had not Danilo hauled her along corridors towards a small side door, used mainly by servants bringing produce for the kitchen. He had used it himself when he was younger. He held Marianna fast, while he fumbled with the heavy bolts, grazing his fingers on the cold iron, swearing under his breath. Avoiding the front of the house, where other men waited with weapons and torches, hoping that she wouldn't scream, he dragged her roughly down a pathway that led into the forest.

She resisted him at first, turning her head anxiously this way and that, beside herself with fear.

'Come on! We must hurry! Do you want to live?' He drew her close and hissed the words savagely into her ear. She could feel his heart pounding, or was it her own that she could hear, her own frightened panting? She was very cold. Her gown was of thin watered silk with a full skirt and short sleeves. Stanislaw had liked to see her in fashionable gowns. Now he would never see anything again. She drew in her breath and let it out in a great sob. Those eyes would see nothing again. Panic rose inside her, and she quelled it with an effort. Then, quite suddenly and surprisingly, the trance of horror left her and in its place came a fierce desire to live, to save herself at all costs. She had survived so far. Perhaps she could live to tell Floryan what had become of his son.

It was a frosty night. Their combined breaths made a fog around their faces. She had only thin slippers on her feet. She felt the cold and damp strike through them as they slithered on the icy mud. Danilo was still half dragging her along. The great weight of her underskirts hindered her, the silk of her dress tearing on twigs and thorns, her breath constricted by the whalebone and metal that compressed her upper body and waist. Her mouth gaped wide as she tried in vain to take in more air.

They were passing the naked stems and withered leaves of the cherry orchard and then they were through a wooden gate and the darkness of the beech forest closed around them. Just before they plunged into the trees, she glanced back towards the house and saw a red glow beginning to illuminate the sky.

'Oh Holy Mother!' she exclaimed.

Danilo stopped, but never loosened his grasp on her.

'They are burning his house,' he said in her ear. 'They are burning him in his house. They would have burned you too, believe me! They would have burned you too!'

Her hands clutched at the damp skirt of her dress and when she realised that the dampness was her husband's blood, such intense fear came over her that she lost consciousness and fell against Danilo, there on the dark path. He picked her up, bundling the skirts together as best he could, and carried her over his shoulder, as he might carry a sack of grain, along woodland tracks that he knew from memory. The darkness was absolute. It was warmer in here too and he felt safer, less afraid of pursuit. They would all be occupied with the destruction of the house and the looting of its contents now. They would not even remember Marianna until it was too late. He had saved her life, but what would he do with her now?

Chapter Eighteen

STILL CARRYING HIS BURDEN, DANILO reached a clearing beside a wider track where, some hours earlier, he had tethered Essor and a long wooden cart full of straw, with a blanket he had taken from the stables that afternoon. The horse was moving uneasily, aware of danger, but he quietened at a word from Danilo. With an effort, he managed to push Marianna, still unconscious, into the straw, and then climbed up beside her. All was quiet here. A smudge of moonlight filtered through the thinning trees, and he crouched in the cart, staring into her face. In this light it looked pale as ash. Very gently, he reached out and touched her cheek.

All at once, he felt confused and afraid. She had been hurt enough.

'Oh, Marianna!' he said.

He saw her eyes flicker open at the sound of her own name. She felt the prickly sensation of straw against her neck and struggled to sit up but he pushed her back down.

'No, no. Lie down in the straw. You'll be warmer that way.'

She did as she was told. Besides, she was very dizzy. She could smell his sweat and his fear and something else. She could smell desire on his breath as he looked down at her. She had never been aware of this before, never experienced it before, but she knew what it was as surely as if he had told her, 'I want you'. All unexpectedly, she felt a faint, answering response in her own body. It horrified her. How could it be? In these circumstances? With more self possession than she felt, she said, 'Danilo, will you take me to my father-in-law's house? Please. You'll be well rewarded when we get there.'

'But Stanislaw is dead. Old Floryan is quick tempered, so I've heard. He'll blame me, believe me part of the conspiracy, kill me. Perhaps I *was* part of the conspiracy. How would you know? Why should you trust me?'

'I do trust you! You saved me! He'll give you money. He'll be grateful to you. I promise you.'

'I don't want his money,' he muttered. 'Or yours.'

Her hand flew to her neck where she often wore a simple necklace of pearls that Stanislaw had given her on their marriage, but she remembered that the catch had come loose and she had left it off that morning, intending to have it mended.

'I have my rings,' she said, desperately. 'You can have those. And I promise you there will be more.' She peered up, trying to see his face in the dark, trying to read his thoughts, but she could barely make out his features.

'I don't want your rings, either.'

'Then what do you want? I have nothing else to give you!' Even as she said it, she knew it wasn't true. But his answer surprised her.

'I just wanted you to live. That's all. I couldn't bear to see you hurt.'

'Then take me to Milatyn, please!'

'I will.' He drew a deep, shuddering breath. 'Yes, I can see that I must do that. It's the only thing to do. Podlaski won't be the only massacre, the only rebellion. God knows what terrible things are going on elsewhere. I hope all's well at Milatyn. But we must be gone before daylight if you're to be safe.'

'We must. Oh Danielek, we must.'

Her cold hands searched for the comfort of his in the dark. His fingers were hot and dry. Even that small contact sent a shiver through them both.

He leaned down and kissed her on the lips. There had been occasions when she had allowed herself to imagine this man kissing her. When she had seen him with the gipsy, she had imagined herself in Rozalia's place. She had lain alone in her bed and thought about him. Even so, the sudden explosion of sensation in her body amazed her. She had known nothing like it before and she couldn't help but respond. When he released her, she fell back on the straw, still holding his hands.

'Your husband never kissed you like that.' It was a statement rather than a question.

'No' she whispered. 'No, he didn't. But he's dead. My poor Stashek!'

'I had no hand in it. You must believe me. I hated him. But I feared for you. So much. I had to find a way to save you.'

'Why?' she asked him. 'Why are you helping me? Is it because of my mother?'

'No. Your mother was kind to me. But don't you understand? This is only because of you, Marianna. Only because of you.'

She reached up to him, taking comfort from his strength and his warmth. Her arms slipped around his neck. Sure now of her consent, he gave in to his own inclination and began to kiss her lips, her cheeks, her forehead. Each kiss gave him more confidence. She lay back on the straw, dazed by his proximity and her own response to it. In the gloom he began to cast up her petticoats, skirt after skirt, seeing the ghostly gleam of cambric and lace, muddy from the pathway, stained with blood, another gleam of linen, the softer feeling of scalloped flannel beneath his fingers and the coarse horsehair petticoat, bound with straw. He smelled the stale scent of it and, beneath it, the clean, musky perfume of her body. He wondered briefly if this was all a dream, for he had had many such dreams over the past few months, but he had always woken up, sweating and anguished. He drew out his knife, glad that she couldn't see, because it would have frightened her. Then his fingers found the tapes that held the last petticoat in place, and he cut them, pulling it down and tossing it out of the cart.

She lay still, amazed and excited by her own acquiescence. She felt the cold penetrating her lower limbs, a sensation that was very strange and new. Desire surged through her. She heard Danilo groan. At last, his hands travelled up over the silk stockings, torn and muddied, and found the flimsy divided drawers. He paused, wishing for daylight, wishing for a glimpse of what his fingers now sought. She lay very still, blinded by her own linen, but desperately wanting him to go on. Again she felt the sudden chill of night air on her naked flesh. She was more aware of her body than at any time in her life before.

Then his fingers were parting her and there was another entirely new sensation. She gasped. As the strange, unbearable feelings blossomed inside her, she moved to accommodate him. Pleasure, raw but undeniable, knifed through her. So this was it. What Stanislaw had done to her had been an act of duty: shameful and grudging. Perhaps he knew no better. Perhaps he treated all women so. But this was different. This sensation of abandonment was what made servant girls risk everything for the sake of a few stolen moments in a hayrick. She began to moan softly and Danilo pulled her closer.

The thought came into her mind that at least he had not killed Stanislaw. But he had done nothing to prevent the murder. Guilt flooded through her. How could she permit this? And then, she knew that there was no stopping it or herself. She wanted him, had wanted him for months and he had saved her life. She moved beneath him and gasped his name, terrified in case he should stop, straining to be closer to him.

He slipped inside her while she was wet and open to him, and they cried out together in the darkness. Afterwards, he sought for her face and kissed her again, his hands in her hair, tearing at the careful arrangement of plaits and ringlets. She returned his kisses and pulled him close, exhausted and overwhelmed.

At last, he pulled the blanket around her shoulders and got down from the cart. Then he drove them both away from Podlaski, down long forest tracks, until they emerged into open country. As the cart veered around, Marianna could see the dying glow of her burning home. She sat back amid the straw, wondering at the pleasure she had felt at such a time and place and with such a man.

She remembered the day he had helped her to dismount from Essor. When he had held her for that brief moment, a sudden unlooked-for desire had flared in her. She remembered the day by the wall and how her eyes had been drawn again and again to him. She remembered other occasions when she had felt him staring at her and had returned his gaze with interest before looking away, afraid of her own feelings. More than anything, she remembered casting the flowers on him in the meadow and how he had looked up at her with what seemed very like love, and how she had felt as if something in her heart was yearning towards his. She had tried to dismiss it afterwards because it was all too foolish and impossible. But Danilo had been in her mind all the time, and when she had seen him with the gypsy, she had felt as though she might die of the jealous rage that possessed her. Now she felt a renewed thrill of desire mixed with shame and guilt, as though her passion for this man had somehow precipitated the death of her husband. But perhaps it was simply that the proximity of death had given her a fierce desire for life at all costs. Perhaps Danilo felt the same way. There was no help for it. There had been an inevitability about it and she couldn't regret it.

With the first light of morning, Danilo stopped the cart in a copse and went and begged bread from a nearby cottage, while she relieved herself, smitten with sudden modesty, beneath the trees. She did not think of leaving him. She knew that whatever happened, he would defend her with his life. They ate and drank and he held the leather flask of water to her lips and put the bread into her mouth with his own grimy fingers, looking at her tenderly and hungrily all the while, as though he could never see enough of her. With the light, she saw the ugly brown of dried blood, her husband's blood, on her gown, and the mud on her skirts.

In the light of day, he seemed more vulnerable, his body weary, his face haggard, her desire for him less improbable. How could she not love him? If he looked ragged and dirty she must appear little better. They were both very young, their bodies each reflecting the other, mirroring each other, their limbs achieving an unconscious symmetry. They drove on and she dozed, leaning against him, taking pleasure in his proximity. When a wintry sun rose in the sky, he stopped again to feed and rest the horse, finding water for it, breaking a thin film of ice in an old horse trough at the edge of a smallholding. Then he came back to sit beside her and warm himself against her. The countryside was deserted, quiet and empty, as though shocked by the events of the night before. People were keeping to their houses, afraid of retribution. There was a smell of burning in the air, though whether this was from normal winter pursuits or other more sinister reasons, they could not tell.

'I'm sorry if I frightened you,' he said. 'I was frightened for you. I thought they were going to kill you. I was mad with worry. I've loved you for a long time. I didn't know what to do. I still don't.'

'I didn't know,' she said, simply. 'Danielek, I didn't know it was possible to feel like this.'

She began to caress him, tentatively at first, but with growing confidence, and they made love again, still encumbered by the remains of the terrible petticoats, so he took out his knife and cut the tapes and tore off more flannel and then he braced himself above her so that he could see her face, open and intimate, with him deep inside her, and could hear her crying out with the intense pleasure he gave her.

Then they drove on, touching each other compulsively as they went. She looked at his long brown fingers and wrists as he held the reins and thought, 'I may never see him again. I can't live with him. But how can I live without him?'

At the boundary of Floryan's estate, they met a peasant staggering home in the late afternoon under the weight of a great bale of kindling. Danilo asked about Floryan and his family, reluctant to leave Marianna until he was certain that her in-laws had not met the same fate as her husband.

'No,' said the old man, looking up at them curiously. He was anxious to get home before dark. 'No – all is well up at Milatyn as far as I know. There have been terrible goings on elsewhere, that I do know. But not old Floryan. Nobody would touch old Floryan. They wouldn't dare, or want to for that matter.'

Danilo seemed half relieved, half disappointed by the news. He drove as close as he dared to the house, and then Marianna climbed down, but not before he had wrapped the blanket around her.

'What about you?'

'I'll manage. I have a coat and it's a long walk through the park.'

Almost at once, she turned back to him. He got down from the cart and took her hands in his.

'How can I leave you?' she asked him. She marvelled at the suddenness of love. Or was it only desire, coming like a thunderbolt? They could see the long splendour of Milatyn, glimmering whitely through the dusk.

'Where will you go? What will you do?' she asked him, anxiously.

'I'll not go back to Podlaski, anyway.'

'No. Of course you can't. That would be madness.'

'There'll be reprisals.' He thought of his grandfather. Would the old man survive? Who would look after him now? Ivan perhaps. Maybe that had been fortuitous. Maybe the boy would stay and take care of Gavril.

'Then why don't you stay here?' Her voice broke into his thoughts. 'Floryan will find you work. You could stay here on this estate.'

'No.' He shook his head. 'How can I?' She saw that there were tears in his eyes. 'What do you expect me to do, Marianna? To stand in my working clothes and bow when you pass by in your finery. Do you expect me to hear you bid me a polite good morning, when I have heard you cry out with pleasure? Do you expect me to kiss your hand submissively, when my lips have ...'

But she was embracing him again, kissing his face, his eyes, his cheeks. 'Don't. What will I do without you?'

He put her away from him, more calmly than he felt.

'Go now, my lady,' he told her. 'Go – quickly – to your father-in-law. There's nothing for us. This must be the end of it. This must be enough for us. I'm like the green pasture that loves the mountain, but may never climb there. The wind must just carry songs between us two. I'm strong. I'll find work somewhere. I'll survive.'

'But I want you to stay. Oh can't you stay? Just for a little while?'

'No. Not even for a little while. They would ask too many questions. You know it. Say you escaped. Say you were helped. That's all. I must go.'

'Must I lose everything I love?' she cried, in despair.

He was silent and sad, thinking of his own mother.

'And will I never see you again?' she asked him. 'My darling, give me some hope at least.'

Against his better judgement, he said, 'Do you think you'll stay here at Milatyn?'

'I don't know. I'll probably go to my brother eventually, to Lisko. It's my old home. Do you know where it is?'

'I know where it is.'

'Listen to me. I don't know what will happen. But that's where you might find me. If you are ever able to. You could come there and find me. You have to give me some hope.'

He stared at her. He seemed to be restraining himself with a great effort. 'We may meet at last. Who knows? Take care of yourself.'

She went back to him one last time and seized his cold hands in her own, kissing them, calling his name, again and again.

At last he said to her wearily, in Ukrainian, 'Go away, Polish lady, go away. For the love of God, walk away from me, Marianna, or I shall die.'

He climbed onto the seat, took hold of the reins, clicked to Essor and was soon out of sight. She stood still for a long time, straining to hear the very last jingling of harness. Then she made her way up to the house, aware suddenly of pains racking her body as well as her mind.

Chapter Nineteen

MARIANNA HAD ALWAYS THOUGHT OF the house at Milatyn as a noisy place. It was generally full of children, the rooms ringing with their games and squabbles, and all of it accompanied by the excited barking of dogs. Today, however, the house was quiet, voices hushed, the dogs, for once, sent outside. She had walked the whole length of the park in her thin shoes, the stones and twigs tearing at her feet, glad of the opportunity to allow Danilo to get well away from the place. By the time anyone might think to pursue him, he would be long gone.

At last, utterly exhausted, she stumbled through the door, calling for help, practically fainting at the foot of the stairs. They rushed to her aid, made her drink brandy and helped her out of her soiled clothes. When she had recovered enough to speak she brought them the news they had been fearing. The only thing that comforted them was that she herself had, by some miracle, survived. She told them nothing about Danilo, other than that one of the loyal workers on the estate had helped her to escape, a tissue of lies and truth that made her feel sick with guilt.

Wanda had Marianna's ravaged clothes burned, all except a single bloody fragment of cloth that Floryan took for himself, vowing vengeance for his eldest son's life. They had grown apart, and he had not really approved of the man that Stanislaw had become, but blood mattered. Family mattered. He remembered his son as a small boy toddling about Milatyn. There had been love between them, then.

Later came the news that the Poniatowskis had been killed in the massacre as well, the whole family, with a savagery that seemed beyond all understanding. Marianna was distraught. The thought of those pale, slender children, a threat to nobody, the mother and her baby too, all dead, ruthlessly slaughtered, was more than she could bear. But it made her own escape seem even more miraculous. She began to have a clearer idea of the extraordinary risk Danilo had taken in saving her. Men who could kill small children without a second thought would not have baulked at killing herself and Danilo too if they had been caught and in the cruellest way possible. He must have known it and still he had come to her rescue. She had no doubt that she owed him her life.

Floryan was not without influence in Vienna. Some weeks later, he had his retribution. Many men from Podlaski and the neighbouring villages were arrested and executed for pursuing a cause that had been Austrian-inspired in the first place. Gavril was judged to be too old and frail to have participated in any plotting or violence. Alarmed at the thought of being left alone and with no idea what had become of Danilo, Gavril let the investigators assume that Ivan was his grandson who had been with him all the time. Nobody betrayed them. Ivan was under strict instructions to keep silent and the officials who came to the village thought only that the boy was a little foolish and left him alone. Ivan had nowhere else to go. Glad of a roof over his head while winter deepened, Ivan tended to Gavril's needs as best he could and undertook various small jobs around the village. He was a willing if clumsy worker and he managed to earn enough to keep the wolf from the door.

The big house at Podlaski was a burnt-out shell. Nothing was ever found of Stanislaw, nor of such servants as had been trapped, terrified, on the upper floors, while fire raged through the building. Surprisingly, the frightened horses had survived as had the other beasts, the stables far enough away from the house to escape the fire. Gradually, a garbled tale filtered through the community that Marianna had escaped, but nobody knew how. Essor was missing and so was Danilo. There were those who could put two and two together, but since they had not been in the house that night, they deemed a discreet silence best.

After a while, when he could bear to do it, Floryan Yelitowski travelled to Podlaski and spent a few weeks in the steward's house there, re-organising the estate. His first act was to engage a new steward. The position was well paid and soon filled. The remains of the house were razed to the ground but the land itself was productive. Not everybody in the village was culpable. Floryan wouldn't see the innocent starve over the winter because of the crimes of a small group of people. He was, however, relentless in pursuit of the murderers, and all of them paid the ultimate price.

Danilo was not among them. He never went back to Podlaski. Before darkness fell, he had already driven the horse and cart some way from Milatyn, but Essor was exhausted, and Danilo knew that he would soon have to stop. Besides, the animal was an unnecessary encumbrance, needing food and shelter where he himself might possibly go without. When he came to a hamlet where there was a well kept inn, he sought out the owner, an old Jewish man with a kindly face. He had almost no money and thought that he might be able to sell the horse and cart. He had left his savings where he knew that Gavril would find them, bringing with him only a few coins and the amber heart, kept safe inside his shirt. He could feel it, warm against his skin, like a talisman. Even at the risk of starvation, he would not sell it. He wondered again if Ivan would stay with Gavril and care for him as he had once cared for all his lost fledglings. Too late to worry about that now.

'The horse is a thoroughbred,' he said to the innkeeper. 'It would suit a nobleman. Or noblewoman. I'll sell you the cart too. I need the money.'

The innkeeper stared at him with grave suspicion. 'And where has it come from, that you wish to rid yourself of it so quickly and so late at night?'

News of the previous night's events in the surrounding countryside had already reached the inn. The man was anxious to distance himself from any involvement. These were dangerous times.

'Ask no questions and you'll be told no lies,' said Danilo.

The innkeeper looked at the young man's frowning face and wondered how to respond. 'Be reasonable, lad! The horse is clearly exhausted, and I've no wish to turn you from my door. But if the beast is stolen, I could be signing my own death warrant. It's a gentry horse for sure, and how do I know what has become of its owner?'

Danilo made a swift decision to trust the man. He had no other option.

'Suppose I tell you how you could return it to its rightful owner?'

'Where? Where should it be returned?'

'There's a young lady at Milatyn. You know the manor house there?'

'Yes, of course I know it. Old Floryan Yelitowski's estate.'

'There's a lady at that house who will want to have this horse returned to her. She was in great danger. You know the kind of danger I mean. You know what has been happening.'

'I do indeed.'

'The truth is that she would have been killed, but I helped her to escape. I saved her life.'

'How can I believe you?'

'That's down to you. She loves this animal. But I can't go to that house. It would be dangerous for me for reasons I can't even begin to explain. Better that I don't explain, in fact. I have divided loyalties.'

'I'm sure you have.' The innkeeper looked at him shrewdly.

'But I'm guilty of nothing else.'

'I take it she's a Polish lady as well. While you ...'

'I'm Ukrainian and proud of it. Pay me a little money so that I can be on my way, and the horse is yours. Its name is Essor. Make whatever discreet enquiries you want and then take it back to Milatyn. You'll be well rewarded. And I'll be gone from here. Long gone and I promise you I'll never be back again. You can spin whatever tale you want about me and keep the cart for yourself. But I swear to you – the young lady will pay you more for this beast than any smallholder would ever give you. She has a particular affection for it. She knows its true worth.'

The man gazed at him. 'You have the face of a ruffian. But I'll give you something for the horse. It's a fine animal.'

'I need a bed for the night, some food and a small amount of money to see me on my way. That's all. Also sir, I'll be frank with you, I need to be rid of this horse, but it is too fond of me. I have tended Essor so well that if I let him loose, he will only follow me. And I would like to think of him being returned to the lady.'

'Her name?'

'Marianna. Her name is Marianna Yelitowska.'

'Isn't she the one who married ...?' The old innkeeper stopped. The less he knew about this matter, the better. He said 'Very well. I'll trust you so far and I'll get a message to the lady somehow or other. But you'll forgive me if I feel the need to blacken your character a little.'

'Do whatever you like. She knows the truth, and I don't care what you say about me.'

That night, Danilo ate chicken soup with bread, and slept restlessly on a bed of straw in the stables. He was very weary, too weary to sleep well, and his body still ached for the woman he had left at Milatyn. He floated on the surface of consciousness and his dreams were full of Marianna. In the morning, he was aware only of an ache in his heart that nothing could assuage. He washed in icy water at the pump, which at least roused him a little. Then he breakfasted off bread and ale, and took as much bread and cold meat as he could carry with him, a heavy winter coat that the innkeeper's wife had found for him, and a pair of ill fitting but intact winter boots. They were too big for him, but the woman handed him a pair of much darned woollen socks and when he had pulled them on, the boots fitted well enough.

She had peeped in at the young man as he slept and felt a sudden rush of pity for the pale, exhausted face. She had grown-up sons herself and thought that if any of her boys were in such dire straits as this young man, she prayed that they would receive similar charity. Her husband paid him something for the horse and cart and sent him on his way.

After waiting a day or two to let Danilo get well away, the innkeeper made tentative enquiries at Milatyn via a nearby smallholder who was courting one of the maids at the house. From there he heard the alarming news that Floryan's daughter-in-law, Marianna, had arrived home in a dreadful state and that Floryan's son was dead, murdered and burned at Podlaski, the body along with the house. He cursed the young Ukrainian roundly. What was he to do with the horse now? Surely it would be recognisable, and then it might bring terrible trouble to his door.

At last, after much discussion with his wife, who would only say 'I think he had an honest face', he managed to send a discreet message to Marianna.

'I believe I have a piece of your property and would be glad to return it to you at your convenience,' was all he wrote.

He was very surprised when, a few days later, the lady herself was driven out to his inn in a smart droshky. He had half expected to see an avenging Floryan wielding a sabre at him, but to his great relief, the little trap contained only two women: Marianna and an older lady, very smart and sensible looking, who he judged must be Floryan's wife. The younger woman stepped down, all eagerness. He hardly knew what to say to her, but he led her round to his stables. When she saw the horse, she fell on its neck, kissing it and stroking it. The innkeeper admired her dark good looks, though she seemed very unwell, with circles under her eyes and pinched cheeks.

'Where did you get him?' she asked, fearfully, glancing around at the droshky where Wanda waited. 'For God's sake, tell me. How did you come by this horse? Nobody died? Nobody was killed?'

He was taken aback. 'No. Of course not. A young man brought him, my lady. Said that I should take good care of him. He told us that he belonged to you and that you would be glad to have him back.'

'And he was right. I'm delighted to see Essor again. We're old friends. But what was he like? This young man?'

'He was Ukrainian. A tall, swarthy fellow with dark hair. My wife tells me he looked honest but I couldn't see it myself. I thought him a bit of a villain.'

'That will have been my groom from Podlaski. He's a good man. Your wife was right. His looks belie him. You heard the news of my husband?' When she referred to the terrible events at Podlaski, her voice was oddly monotonous and quite devoid of emotion.

'Yes, my lady. I'm sorry. But why would your groom leave this beast with me?'

'He would have been afraid to bring it all the way to Milatyn. He wasn't involved in the murders at Podlaski. In fact he helped me to escape. But he would still have been afraid of my father-in-law's anger, and with good reason. He's desperate for revenge.'

'I see.' It seemed a reasonable explanation. Besides, thought the innkeeper, it was none of his business. The horse, joyfully nuzzling his mistress, was certainly happy.

Marianna wondered why Danilo had chosen to relinquish the animal, but perhaps he would find it easier and less conspicuous to travel on foot. Wherever he was going.

'We have taken good care of him for you. He was exhausted.'

'And what of the young man?'

'Oh, he seemed exhausted too. But I gave him some money and fed him and I believe my wife gave him warm clothing and we sent him on his way. It will be a long trek back to Podlaski, if that's where he's going, but no doubt he will survive.'

'No doubt. I must thank you for that. He was a loyal servant to me. And you're out of pocket. I'll speak to my father-in-law, sir. You'll be paid the full value of the animal and more for your charity.'

'You see!' said the innkeeper's wife afterwards. 'I told you and you wouldn't believe me. But women have an instinct about these things. That young man was honest. I saw it in his sleeping face. May God guide him home in safety.'

Chapter Twenty

MARIANNA WAS UNWELL. ON THAT terrible morning when she had stumbled into the house with news of Stanislaw's death and her own miraculous escape, they had bathed her and tried to feed her, but she would eat nothing, so they put her to bed. She slept for hours, like a sick animal. Later, they tried to question her about events at Podlaski. Although she told Wanda as much as she could about the attack on Stanislaw, her account of her own escape was more confused.

'One of the grooms saved me. He managed to get me out of the house and away through the woods. They were so intent on destroying the house and everything in it that I don't think they noticed what was happening to me. It was Stashek they wanted to kill. Poor, poor Stashek. But I'm sure they would have killed me too, if this man hadn't managed to get me out of there.'

'And it was this same man who brought you here?'

'He had a horse and cart waiting in the woods.'

'So he must have known what was planned. He could have warned Stanislaw.'

'I don't know and I was in no condition to question him. I was scared out of my wits. Maybe he was in the stables when it all started. I think that was it. He often stayed there late. If one of the horses was unwell.'

She began to cry, tears streaming down her cheeks.

'Marianna, you mustn't upset yourself. I just thought it might help Floryan to know more about what happened.'

Wanda handed the girl a handkerchief. Marianna wiped her eyes and blew her nose.

It's all right. You and Floryan need to know what I know. But it's all very patchy in my mind. I fainted a couple of times. He was kind to me, Wanda.'

'And this was a man who worked on the estate?'

'Only a stable lad. He was good with the horses. I liked him for that. I thought he was a kind man. I know he couldn't save Stashek, but he did what he could at the risk of his own life and he certainly saved mine.'

'For which we are all grateful.'

'He brought me as far as the park, but he would come no further. He said he was afraid of being accused of complicity in the murders. I can't blame him. Maybe that's what would have happened. He would have had to betray his fellow Ukrainians and I doubt if he would have wanted to do that.'

'No. I doubt if he would have wanted to do that.'

The return of the sorrel horse, Essor, and the innkeeper's tale of the swarthy young man had relieved Marianna's anxieties a little, but the weather had turned very wild, and her heart quailed at the thought of Danilo, homeless and wandering in such conditions. She would sit at the window, watching the snow and singing snatches of song. 'Give me your hand in the green meadow, Anna, my Anna.'

Then, without warning, her mind would take her back to that terrible evening at Podlaski. Again and again, she found herself reliving the violence, the blood, the terror of it all. It was only the thought of Danilo that calmed and comforted her. Not their lovemaking. In those first weeks, she could hardly bear to think about that without a creeping sense of shame. How could she have behaved so wantonly, so soon after the violent death of her husband? And with a man who was both her enemy and her inferior as well! How could she have done it? But still, when her mind was full of horrific images, it was Danilo she thought about, the comforting sense of leaning up against him, while he broke bread for her, the warmth of him, his unexpected tenderness towards her. She knew why the horses loved him so much. When her dreadful memories were at their worst, she clung to this image of Danilo, the sensation of his body next to hers, his arm around her, an anchor in a sea of troubles.

Julian took every opportunity to spend time with Marianna. The manner of his brother's dying filled him with horror and pity, but the thought of what might have happened to Marianna herself was even more dreadful to him. He was a studious boy who had never deviated from his desire to study medicine, and Floryan had agreed that he should go to the University of Lemberg. When he was at home, she would lie on a couch in the library with her head propped up on goose feather pillows, and he would sit at her feet and chat or read to her. She liked to be with him. He was a point of stillness and solace for her in this busy household. But when Julian was occupied with his studies, Marianna would take herself off to some secluded part of the house or to a quiet corner of the gardens and sit in silent contemplation.

'She's still grieving for her husband,' the family told each other.

Once afternoon, Julian found her in the stables, standing with her hand on Essor's mane, tears streaming down her face.

'Do you miss him so much?' he asked, sympathetically.

She nodded. 'Oh yes' she said. She looked up at him.

'I miss Stashek,' she said quickly.

'Of course you do. You had such a short time together.'

At the end of two months it became obvious to Marianna that she was pregnant. At first she tried to pretend that it was not so, but at last, the changes in her body, the strange and unfamiliar sensations that so possessed her, convinced her that it must be true. She managed to conceal it from her family for some weeks, but after Wanda found her one morning, pale and sick, clinging to her washstand, she broke down and sobbed on the older woman's shoulder.

'Yes. There's a baby.'

'Floryan will be so happy,' said Wanda.

Marianna's shoulders shook with weeping.

'I know, my dear,' said Wanda. 'I know it must be very disturbing, but at least you'll have something of Stanislaw. This is a very precious baby and you must give it all the love you can.'

'I will love it. You can be sure of that!'

Floryan was elated at the knowledge that Stanislaw had managed to produce an heir before succumbing to what the old man thought of, with a kind of resigned bitterness, as the result of his own folly. And at least the death had been avenged.

As for Marianna, she thought about Danilo every day, wondering where he was, whether he had survived the winter. It struck her that she knew almost nothing of him beyond his kindness to animals and to herself, and his skills as a lover. As her pregnancy advanced, she began to think of him with a constant ache of thwarted desire. She told herself that she would never see him again, and so she had better stop thinking about him, but she could not put him out of her mind for more than a few hours at a time. Besides, the baby that moved within her was a constant reminder of the lover who had certainly fathered it and about whom she could speak to nobody.

Zygmunt came on a visit from Lisko and suggested that Marianna might like to stay at Milatyn to have the baby.

'I think you need the company of other women just now,' he said.

The change in him alarmed her. He had obviously made an effort to smarten himself up, but nothing could disguise the bloodshot eyes and the puffy cheeks. It was plain to Marianna that the thought of coping with a pregnant, bereaved sister appalled him. He pitied her but he didn't want her at home with him. So she chose to stay at Milatyn. Besides, the thought of returning to Lisko filled her with misgivings. How could she cope with Zygmunt as well as a new baby. And what if Danilo went there, looking for her? What if he were to find her there, with a child that bore his face, but not his name? So Zygmunt returned alone to Lisko, pleased to be able to go back to his friends and his card games, leaving her in the capable care of Floryan and Wanda.

Chapter Twenty One

AFTER HE LEFT ESSOR WITH the Innkeeper, Danilo made his way slowly across country, begging food from smallholders, although they had little enough to spare, sleeping in barns and outhouses when he was lucky, beneath a hedgerow or in the shelter of a copse of trees when he was not. Where there was work to be had, he would stop for a while, sometimes for a week or two, but it was winter and there was little work to be had. People had scarcely enough food for themselves and they were suspicious of a young beggar where they might more easily have accepted an older man. Even when he said he was an experienced stable lad and could help with the horses, they were mistrustful.

Without any conscious intent, he found himself heading north west, going very slowly in the direction of Marianna's old home at Lisko. If he had gone as the crow might fly, he would have been there within a few days. Instead, he wandered aimlessly for many weeks, making long detours, but invariably finding himself back on the road to Lisko. He was lucky enough to spend Christmas Eve with a family of fairly prosperous Polish smallholders who had been dismayed to discover that sickness in the family had left them with an odd number of guests at the table for their festive supper. Since this meant that one of their number would die, for sure, during the ensuing year, the head of the household rushed outside, looking for somebody, anybody, to make up the numbers.

Danilo had been lurking not far from the house, wondering whether he could pluck up the courage to beg for food at the kitchen door, on this night of all nights. He could hardly believe his good fortune. He washed as best he could in the butt of water at the back of the house, breaking a film of ice to do so, and the farmer's wife found him a well-worn but clean linen shirt, in honour of the occasion. His eyes were dazzled by the light, and the heat of the room bemused him, making his head swim. He swayed and clutched at the back of a wooden settle to steady himself and tried to mind his manners.

In each corner of the room stood sheaves of rye, wheat, barley and oats. There was straw on the floor and a thin layer of hay on the table-top that was covered with white linen. The company sat down to eat. The farmer broke the blessed wafer, thickly spread with honey, and handed it to each guest in turn, including Danilo in this ritual with a smile.

'Welcome, stranger! Welcome in God's name. Join us, eat and drink on this blessed eve!'

The supper was plentiful. The family had been saving for this all year. Danilo ate his fill of beetroot soup, cold pike set in jelly, fried carp, smoked eels and pierogi, dumplings shaped like little ears, filled with a mixture of mashed potato, onion and cheese. There was dense, creamy cheesecake, spicy honey cake, luscious poppy seed roll called *makowiec* and the traditional dish of *kutia*. At the less decorous end of the meal, the young boys vied with each other in tossing spoonsful of the grain and poppy seed mixture up to the ceiling. When it stuck there it signified luck and a good harvest for the following year. The family were scrupulously polite to Danilo, attending to his needs but asking him few questions. These were troubled times and there were plenty of displaced people on the roads. It didn't do to enquire too closely what had befallen strangers, why they were destitute or where they might be travelling. As long as Danilo behaved himself they wanted to know nothing else about him.

After the meal, there followed a convivial few hours with cherry vodka and violin music. One or two of the women led the company in singing traditional Christmas songs. They were mostly lullabies to the Christ Child: 'sleep baby Jesus, my little pearl, sleep my heart's darling.' Danilo recognised the melodies and even knew the words of some of them, but he was shy of singing aloud and only mouthed the words along with the singers. They brought a lump to his throat, though he couldn't have said why.

When the family had gone to bed, Danilo was allowed to sleep beside the kitchen fire. It was the most peaceful night he had spent in a long time. He woke in the night with a sense of warmth and wellbeing. The house was quiet. He could hear the faint snores from the farmer and his household, replete with good food and drink and the pleasures of the season. It was dark in the kitchen but not oppressively so. When he turned his head, he could see the comforting glow from the embers of the fire, banked up for morning. The kitchen cat was sharing the space with him, drawn to the warmth of his body, and he luxuriated in the sensation of its sleek fur beneath his fingers. It purred contentedly and the sound soothed him and sent him back to sleep. In the morning, he went on his way, laden with a supply of food, a worn but serviceable woollen jacket and a blanket to wrap around himself at night.

January was a bitter month and the food did not last long. One particularly cold night, he was given shelter by a kindly Roman Catholic priest who allowed him to sleep in his church, with a promise of possible work. He wrapped himself in his blanket and stretched out on one of the pews, but the following morning, an old woman, her nose and cheeks crimson with the cold, came in early to clean the place, woke him with a blow of her broomstick and sent him packing.

'Get out of here, you thieving gypsy!' she screamed at him. 'Away you go before I set the dogs on you!'

He might have gone to find the priest, but hunger and cold had induced a weary acceptance in him, and he just took to the frozen roads again. He grew thinner and weaker and less able to take on the few tasks that were offered him. He developed a racking cough and his hunger deserted him, which was a relief, even while a sensible part of his mind realised that this was a very bad sign. He knew that he was ill and growing worse by the day, but what could he do to remedy it?

At night, dreams of Marianna tormented him. They gave him no comfort, because they were inextricably tied up with images of violence from that terrible night at Podlaski. Drifting between sleep and wakefulness, he was always trying and often failing to save her. He would wake in pools of his own perspiration, with his hands and feet icy cold and his forehead burning. He didn't know where he was going and didn't much care. Sometimes, he thought it would be good to be dead, to be forever enveloped in comforting blackness. Still, he didn't give up entirely, but as the weather grew colder, he managed to find some kind of shelter each night, knowing that his first night spent outside at this time of year would probably be his last.

One February evening, half starved, crawling with lice and desperately ill, he fetched up at the lodge cottage of an estate called Banunin. The lodge keeper was away from home, and his mother was there alone. It was probably this that saved Danilo, for Yuri, the keeper, would most likely have given him short shrift and sent him on his way, in which case he would have been found dead in a ditch when the winter snows melted.

Danilo felt so bad that no matter what happened now, he could not move on. Let them kill him, he would welcome the oblivion. His head was swimming and the one small light burning in the lodge house seemed to advance and recede as he swayed towards it. There were blisters on his feet, but they had burst and the flesh was rubbed raw beneath them. He tried to knock on the door, but instead he fell against it and slithered down onto the step, groaning a little at the pain in his limbs and his back.

Yuri's mother Marysia was a robust woman of eighty. The strange sound at her door frightened her, but she had enough spirit to investigate rather than tremble all night at a sound that might well be a cat or some other animal seeking shelter from the snow. She opened the door, muttering prayers to the Holy Virgin and all the saints to keep her safe, holding a lantern high in her trembling hand. Danilo literally tumbled into the cottage. She said afterwards that she was very scared, but she felt too close to a meeting with the good Lord Jesus to have some poor mother's son on her conscience for all eternity. When she was telling the story, she liked to say that even the lice that fell from his body were starving, which was probably true.

Certainly she would have had a job to turn him out. He was crawling across her floor towards the heat of the kitchen fire, whimpering like an injured animal, and although he was powerless to stand, she could not have dragged him outdoors again. She stooped and looked at his face in the light of her lantern. Then, talking to him all the while to make him seem less frightening, lecturing him as she would her own son, she warmed ale and honey on the stove.

'There now,' she said. 'What a state to get yourself into! How could you let yourself get so ill? I wonder who you are and where you come from? But what am I to do with you? Well, we'll just have to see, won't we? And what will Yuri say when he comes home? That's what I'd like to know.'

Danilo lay semi-conscious, panting and shivering in front of the fire.

When the ale was ready, she poured it into a beaker and encouraged him to turn on his side and try to drink. He was shaking so much that he spilled some of it, but the warmth percolated through his fingers and he drank at last.

'That's right,' she said. 'Drink it down, son. It'll do you good.'

His teeth stopped chattering. She refilled his mug, adding a dash of vodka as well as honey, and sat opposite him, surveying him with a gap-toothed smile.

'Here's a fine state of affairs. Me, entertaining a young man while my son's away. What would he say to that, do you think?'

Danilo couldn't reply. His limbs felt like lead, and even his tongue seemed too heavy to move. His eyelids drooped. Presently, she took the mug away from him, pushed an old feather pillow beneath his head and covered him with a blanket. He slid into a doze before the fire. She sat for a while and listened to the wheeze and rattle of his breathing, put another blanket over him, and then took herself to her own bed, behind a curtain on the other side of the room, with the thought that he would be either dead or alive by morning. She had much better leave it until then to decide what to do with him. There was nothing more she or anyone could do. It was in God's hands.

In the morning, he was still alive but very feverish. All day, he lay on her floor, in a delirium. She brought him a fresh pillow and a coarse, well darned linen sheet to cover him, tucking it around him beneath the blanket. She wasn't going to ruin her good wool and linen on such a filthy individual. When she stooped to feel his forehead, it burned beneath her fingers, and he called out in tones of such anguish that her heart was moved. She coaxed him to drink a little of her own herbal brew mixed with a good measure of vodka, but left him where he was. By evening, she was relieved to see the flush leaving his thin cheeks, to be replaced by beads of sweat that broke there again and again, running down his face like tears. He managed to stagger out to the icy yard to relieve himself and came back in, shivering again. This time, because the delirium seemed to have left him, she persuaded him to lie on a high-backed bench that she had made into a bed with a rolled up blanket. She wrapped him in more blankets and he slept again, soothed by the warm wool and the faint crackling of the kitchen fire.

The following morning she was woken by the sound of him coughing very violently. The air that filtered into the cottage had a chill clarity about it. It had snowed very heavily in the night and the forest tracks, manor park, trees and sky were one dense white. She moved slowly about the room, rekindling the glowing embers of her fire from a basket of dry timber, boiling potatoes, getting out sour milk and butter. He watched her in silence and when she placed a laden dish in front of him, he managed to croak the words 'Thank-you. God bless you!'

She dipped her head in acknowledgement of the blessing and motioned him to eat. His appetite was very poor, but he ate a mouthful or two and drank some sour milk.

She said, 'You're starving, son. I recognise that grey look on your face. I've seen it often enough in my lifetime. And yet you don't eat, now that there's good food before you.'

'I'm sorry. I will. I haven't eaten for a long time. I've been travelling for weeks.' He wondered how far he had come. Latterly, every step had been painful. He began to cough again.

'I'll make a poultice for your chest today. I gather the herbs in summer, you know, and dry them,' she added, proudly.

'You're very kind.' The room was spinning around him. He pushed his plate aside and lay back down again, huddling into the blankets.

'My Yuri would not be so kind, but he's away from home. I think he'll be away for some days yet in this weather, so you may stay if you please. Looking at you, I doubt very much if you could move.'

'No. I don't think I could. What place is this?'

'Banunin. This is the lodge house. The gentry went away to Lemberg for Christmas, but they'll be back in a week or two.'

'What family lives here?'

'Komorowski is their name.'

'Are we far from Lemberg?'

'I don't know. I've never been there. What's your name, young man?'

'Danilo.'

'Well, Danilo, I've never been there yet, nor do I intend to go. But they tell me it's some two hundred furlongs. Perhaps more. My Yuri says it's a long day's ride in winter.'

He stirred and tried to sit up. She motioned him to stay still. 'You're as weak as a baby, my lad! Lie down and take your rest.'

'Do you think there might be work for me on this estate?'

'Work?' She chuckled. 'What work could you do?'

'Plenty, when I'm well again. I know all about horses. I've worked in stables for years and on the land too.'

'Then we'd best get you all cleaned up and well before my son comes back, hadn't we? Where do you come from, Danilo?'

'To the east,' he said vaguely. 'To the east of here.'

'And you're one of us. That's something.' She meant he was Ukrainian, like herself and her son. 'But I can't imagine what a young man like you is doing roaming the land and begging his bread in the dead of winter. If you were an old, religious gentleman, a holy pilgrim, it might be different.' Danilo remained silent. 'No doubt you were dismissed from some estate somewhere. But what for? That's the question. Dishonesty perhaps?' He shook his head but she continued, looking at him shrewdly. 'Stealing your master's corn. Or horses. Or money. Or something worse perhaps. Who is Marianna?'

'What?'

'You were calling her name. While you were so ill.'

'She was a girl I knew. That's all. Just a girl. I wasn't dishonest and I stole nothing. I was caught up in the troubles last year through no fault of my own, and I had to leave my home. But I swear to God I have committed no crime.'

She looked at him with comprehension in her faded eyes. She knew all about the troubles. Yuri had been on guard at Banunin all night with heavily armed men and well trained dogs.

'I see. We'll say no more about it then. Can you walk properly yet?'

'I don't know.'

'You can have my son's bed until he returns. What he doesn't know won't harm him. But not the way you are. You stink and you're running wick with lice, son. I'll warm some water later on and you can have a good wash. Your hair too. Get some of that grime off you and let's see what you look like under it all. And you can borrow some of

Yuri's clothes, although he's a good deal shorter and fatter than you are!'

She bathed his poor feet, tut tutting over the state of them, although they were already less fiercely inflamed than they had been. Later, she chopped away at his hair with a big pair of kitchen shears, and tugged a fine-tooth comb through it. Cleaner, well fed, warm and clothed in a linen nightshirt, Danilo slept himself well. Marysia seemed to enjoy mothering him. She had given birth to six children, five of whom had died in infancy. Her only surviving son, Yuri, had never married, and she had felt the lack of grandchildren keenly. She was a soft-hearted woman and would have taken in a suffering dog had Yuri allowed it. Now, with his absence prolonged by bad weather, she could indulge her maternal feelings to her heart's content.

One morning, more than a week after his arrival in Banunin, Danilo woke up feeling cool and clear headed. It was a good feeling, as though his body had finally regained control of itself. When he set them to the floor, his legs buckled beneath him, but he ate well and soon began to regain his strength. Before Yuri returned, even later than his mother had supposed and half mad with worry about her, Danilo was already chopping wood for Marysia, making sure that the log store was replenished, or hauling up water from the deep well when the well head was frozen. He had even repaired an outhouse roof that the weight of snow had damaged.

'Now that you're clean and fed,' she told him, proudly, 'you make quite a presentable young man.'

For the time being at least, it seemed that luck was on Danilo's side. Yuri arrived back only just ahead of his master from Lemberg. Yuri, small, fat and irascible, had expected to be away from home for a day or two, but an injured horse and the sudden and persistent snowfalls had detained him. He had been worrying about his mother for days. Presented with the *fait accompli* of Danilo's presence, he grumbled but accepted responsibility for his mother's foundling. The intense cold of February had finally done for one of the elderly stable lads at the manor, and he had died of pneumonia that very week. Danilo, therefore, was given the job, on the back of another's tragedy and on the recommendation of Yuri, who scolded his mother for taking in strangers in his absence, but also admired the neat job Danilo had done on his outhouse roof.

Yuri made no enquiries about Danilo's background, having learned as much as he wanted to know from his mother. If he suspected her of tender-heartedly allowing Danilo to take advantage of her, he said nothing to her about it and nothing to Danilo either. Reluctant to hurt his mother by turning the young man out, but equally reluctant to feed him for the rest of the winter, Yuri recommended him to the head groom as the son of a distant cousin. It was the sort of lie that was so commonplace as to be conventional, a kind of code for 'I don't know much about him, but I think he's all right'. Danilo moved his few possessions to the bed allotted to him in the stable loft, and again found comfort in the warm, undemanding presence of the horses below.

Chapter Twenty Two

MARIANNA HAD AN EASY PREGNANCY. At Wanda's insistence she abandoned her tightly laced corsets and wore old, high-waisted gowns that they had found packed away in trunks. During the rest of the winter, Marianna wore these high-necked, long sleeved velvets and brocades, but as the summer advanced and the weather grew warmer, she and Wanda dug deeper, coming up with enchanting dresses in muslin, tulle, gauze and taffeta, with short sleeves, full draped skirts and low necks. These came out of their wooden chests, fresh and sweet as they had been packed away, smelling faintly of lavender and other herbs. They were very becoming, these dresses, even to the heavily pregnant Marianna, and since the fashions were those of Floryan's youth, he approved.

'Ladies today,' he remarked, 'they never look so fine as they used to in my young days. Sometimes in the summer my friend would deliberately dampen the fabric of her gown.'

'Floryan!' said Wanda. 'You'll embarrass the girl!'

Floryan kissed her hand affectionately. 'I was seventeen,' he said, sighing at the memory. 'Where have all the years gone? She was twenty six. When we parted, she gave me a keepsake.' He gazed around the room. 'Where is it, Wanda? You know what I mean.'

His wife looked at him severely. 'I know what you mean. But I don't approve of it at all.'

'Nonsense. It's a thing of great beauty.'

She opened a glass-fronted cabinet and took out a green and gold enamel box, exquisitely erotic. Around the curve of the sides lay miniature nymphs with gleaming green robes spread out beneath them, while on the hillock that formed the lid, a nude golden woman reclined, one hand supporting her, the other touching her breasts. Opposite her, a muscular naked man entwined his long legs with hers. They were a god and goddess, disporting themselves in their own green and gold paradise.

'Oh my goodness! I never saw this before!' said Marianna.

'My Wanda keeps it hidden away for fear of embarrassing the young ladies. It's the work of an Italian artist and already a good deal older than I am. Marianna – you're carrying my son's only child. If you give birth to a boy, this will be yours to keep.'

He put the little box back in its place. Then he came over and took Marianna's hand again.

'Don't mind me, child,' he said. 'I mourn for my son. For what he might have been. Any child of his will be most welcome, boy or girl.'

As her time drew nearer, she became consumed with an overwhelming desire to confide in someone. Terror filled her at the thought of dying with the secret on her conscience. In the cool of the evening, she walked in the garden, leaning on Julian's arm. He was tall for his age and a little gangly, but already filling out into the handsome man he would become. They sat down on a bench among the roses where the scents of the old bushes enveloped them. Julian stole a sidelong glance at Marianna. From the village came the distant sound of a woman singing, a plaintive song with a strong, chilling vibrato that carried on the evening air.

Marianna shuddered. 'Who is that?'

'Lubka. She sings to call the beasts in. She does it every evening. They come to her.'

'But what is it? The song. It sounds so hopeless.'

'I can't make out all the words, but I know the song anyway. It's about love. All their songs are like ours. About love and death. Two hearts that can never be one. The meadow cannot come to the mountain just as I cannot come to you, my love. That's what she's singing.'

She was silent for so long that he said, 'Marianna, is there something the matter?'

She smoothed her hands over the loose muslin of her dress, shaping it to the huge mound of her belly. 'Can't you see what's the matter, Julek?'

'Don't be silly. You know what I mean. I'm not a child any more, so don't make a fool of me.'

'No. You've been a good friend to me these last few months.'

'Good enough to see that there's something wrong with you. Something more than just the baby. Sometimes you seem so desperate.'

'Do I?'

'Is it Stanislaw? The memory of what happened to him that night?'

'It isn't that. Though it was a terrible night. And it comes back to me often as if I were there all over again. Sometimes in dreams. Sometimes even when I'm awake. But there's more. Oh Julek, I mustn't burden you with this. You're so young.'

'I'm seventeen. Old enough to fight for my country, as father's always telling me. You can confide in me.'

'If I do, you must tell nobody else. Ever. Not while I'm alive. And perhaps not even when I'm dead. Will you promise?'

'Is it so serious then?' he asked.

'Yes it is. And if you don't want to hear any more, tell me to stop now, and I will.'

'Will it help you, to tell me this great secret?'

'I think I'll go mad if I don't tell *someone*.'

'Then tell me. You know you can trust me.'

Even so, she was quiet for a long time. In his innocence, he thought she was going to confess that she hadn't loved Stanislaw. He was prepared to reassure her, to tell her that he too had found his brother a difficult person to love.

She whispered, 'You see, this isn't his child.'

She was slumped on the seat, her belly forcing her knees apart.

'Are you talking about Stanislaw?'

'Yes.'

'Not his child?' he echoed, feeling foolish.

'No.'

He looked so taken aback that she wished she could recall the words.

'What are you saying? Whose then? Whose child is it, Marianna?'

'Somebody who helped me to get away that night. The men from the village would have killed me otherwise. This person helped me. He worked on the estate and he knew me.'

The colour had left his face. He took her hand, unable to disguise his anger, leaping to conclusions. 'And he did this to you, this man. He did this when you were helpless? Oh my dear, dear cousin!'

She was struck by the impossibility of explaining to this boy the nature of her relationship with his brother and her feelings for Danilo. He would never understand. She hardly understood herself. And even if he could be made to understand, he would still be terribly shocked.

'It just happened. He didn't hurt me. You must understand that, Julian. He didn't hurt me.'

'But he took his reward for rescuing you, all the same.'

'It wasn't like that. He didn't hurt me.'

'That's no excuse.'

Still she couldn't quite bring herself to say that she had been his willing partner. Instead, she said, 'Everyone thinks the child is Stanislaw's.'

'But surely there's a chance ...'

'I know it can't possibly be his!'

She was so vehement that he gazed at her in dismay.

'I don't understand you.'

'There's no chance at all. We hadn't been together for months.'

She looked at his horrified face and saw that at last he understood, reluctantly, and even then not fully.

'But I can't say that, can I? I would be shamed. And heaven help me, it would destroy Floryan. So what else can I do but pretend and go on pretending?'

'What about the man who ...?'

'He's dead,' she said quickly. 'He was executed afterwards. His name was on the list. But he saved my life.'

Julian still had her hand in his.

'Yes,' he said. 'I see now that you must pretend. My poor Marianna.'

'And you won't say anything to anybody?'

'I promised and I never break my promises.'

He offered her his handkerchief and she mopped her eyes.

'You know,' he said at last. 'I admire you. You're so strong. You're worth ten of Stanislaw.'

'No. No I'm not.'

'Yes, you are.'

He helped her to her feet. 'The insects are biting. We'd better go in.'

They walked through the garden. Down in the village, Lubka had finished her song. The birds had gone to roost but the gnats sang on, piping their sad melody in the gathering dark.

Marianna Yelitowska had a long and difficult labour. Helped by Wanda and an old woman from the village, Marianna pushed her daughter into the world on a scream of pain. Exhausted, she stared down at the bundle that was presented to her, wrapped up tight as a parcel in soft cotton, its face screwed up in surprise and outrage.

'A girl!' said Wanda. 'A beautiful little girl. And as dark as yourself, my dear. Not like her father at all, but I don't think Floryan will mind, as long as she's healthy. What will you call her?'

Marianna had not thought of names. She said the first thing that came into her head.

'Zofia.'

'The gentleman will be disappointed,' said the old woman. 'He will have wanted his son's son, surely.'

'Be quiet!' Wanda told her sharply. 'He'll be just as delighted with a grand-daughter.'

Much against the advice of the old woman who had counted on supplying a wet-nurse and taking a cut of the fee for herself, Marianna put the child to the breast. Little Zofia suckled for a while and then fell fast asleep with a dribble of milk running from her rosebud mouth. Marianna gazed down into her daughter's face and saw that Zofia was very like her father. Nobody else in this household would notice it. The baby was very like her mother as well.

Marianna fell asleep with the infant swaddled in the crook of her arm. It was August and as she fell asleep, she was aware of the soft bump of insects hurling themselves against the window panes in a crazed attempt to reach the lamplight. She thought, keep out, keep out, you will only singe your wings on the flame and then you'll never fly again. She tried to say this aloud, but sleep claimed her. When she woke up, it was to find that Floryan had crept in for a glimpse of his new grand-daughter and left the little green and gold box beside her bed.

For a few days after the birth of her daughter, Marianna felt well. Then, without warning, pains seared through her belly. Floryan sent for a doctor to attend to her. He prescribed medicine and fixed leeches to her stomach, a treatment that filled her with indescribable horror, although after they had sucked their fill, the pains seemed to abate somewhat. She was ill for several weeks but gradually, health and strength began to return to her.

'She's lucky,' said the doctor. 'I've seen women die of this same condition.'

Later, he asked to speak privately to Wanda.

'You know that the girl might have problems with another pregnancy? I've seen it happen. She may find it difficult to conceive or to carry another child to term. But then she's a widow so perhaps it doesn't matter.'

'She's a very young widow. My husband and I both hope that we might find her a suitable husband before too long. Or that she might find one for herself. She has land and an inheritance and I think there will be no shortage of suitors when she has recovered.'

'Well, if the occasion arises, she might be told. There may be difficulties; there may not. I think I would remain silent, but I leave it to you to decide, my lady.'

On the whole, Wanda thought it best to remain silent.

Time passed, and Marianna, almost wholly occupied with her growing child, didn't think of leaving Milatyn. Her thoughts strayed to Lisko from time to time, but she wasn't quite ready to go back there. Zofia was growing into a precise, pretty and remarkably healthy child. She had her mother's creamy skin and brown curls, her father's dark eyes and brows. She liked things neat and tidy, liked to keep her toys just so, with a place for everything and everything in its place. She was good humoured, but if her young cousins borrowed or broke one of her playthings she was capable of throwing a fit of temper that would raise the whole household.

'Tantrums and nonsense!' said Marianna, disapprovingly.

'Just like you, when you were young,' said Wanda.

When Zofia was three, Julian went away to Lemberg to study medicine, returning only for holidays. The child pined for her uncle, asking all the time when he would be coming back. Marianna's brother would sometimes visit, but he was no substitute for Julian. He would play grand rough and tumble games with his niece, but he had neither patience nor imagination and was too easily bored to become one of her favourites. Zygmunt brought the news that Nusia was well and missing her darling. She sent laboriously written notes for Marianna, gifts for Zofia, sweetmeats and wooden toys bought from passing peddlers. They would make vague plans for a return trip to Lisko, but Marianna always put it off till later. She had heard nothing at all of Danilo. She doubted if he even knew how to read and write. At last, she had become convinced that he must be dead or gone from Galicia altogether.

But she had not forgotten him.

How could she, when every glance at the dark flower of her daughter's face reminded her of him? To her surprise, people had told her how like Stanislaw the child was, in spite of her colouring, and she had learned to accept such comments gracefully. People saw what they wanted to see.

Afterwards, she was to remember those years as among the happiest and most contented of her life, with few worries beyond the child's occasional sickness. She was reluctant to break the spell of peace that held her and her daughter in safety. It still seemed to her, superstitiously, that any move she made might ruin things, that if once she broke out of the charmed circle of her present life at Milatyn, things would never be the same for them again.

Still, she had loved Lisko. Now and again, she would sing her daughter to sleep with the old lullaby about the house made of butter:

'Once upon a time there was a princess,
and she lived in a house made of butter,
and the house was full of wonderful things.'

As she sang the familiar words, she knew that one day, she was destined to go home to the pancake yellow house. She dreamed about whatever might await her there and woke with yearning in her heart.

Chapter Twenty Three

FOR FIVE YEARS AFTER THE birth of her daughter, Marianna lived contentedly at Milatyn. When the changes came, they were both unexpected and tragic. In the summer of 1852, the year that Zofia was five, Wanda fell ill and died. For Marianna, it was like losing her mother all over again. Wanda had given birth to a stillborn boy in the seventh month of a late and unexpected pregnancy. Her labour had been long and difficult, and she had never really recovered her strength. Gradually, over the ensuing weeks, she dwindled to a shadow of her cheerful self. Floryan summoned doctors from the city. They debated treatments, gave her purgatives and bled her, but nothing worked. Julian came home too, but was helpless in the face of her sickness, and at last she died as quietly as she had lived. For several months afterwards, Floryan raged around the house, cursing his own robust good health.

'It should have been me,' he told anyone who would listen. 'It was my fault. I should be dead, not my dear Wanda.'

Zygmunt Diduski came from Lisko for the funeral and Marianna was shocked by the change in her brother. He had lost weight. There was a yellowish tinge to his skin, as though he had spent far too many days and nights in smoky rooms with dice or cards for company. He began drinking early in the day and stopped only when sleep took him. There was no talking to him. All conversations descended into miserable arguments, with Zygmunt on the defensive, accusing his sister of 'nagging him to death.'

Afterwards, Marianna thought that he might have listened to Floryan but he was too sunk in his own grief for Wanda. Zofia would sit on her grandfather's knee, and trace the deep lines on his face with her finger, trying to make him smile. Floryan's older children were married and gone and the house seemed unusually quiet, although Julian's younger brothers were desolate without their mother. Julian mourned her quietly and alone. Once, Marianna found him sitting on his mother's bed with one of her dresses on his lap and his face buried in the fabric. When he raised his head, she saw that there were tears on his cheeks. She sat with him in silence for a while, patting his shoulder, remembering the way the familiar scent of her mother's clothes had once comforted her.

'Nothing helps. Except time. You won't forget her. But time takes the edge off the grief.'

'Does it?'

'Yes. All grief. No matter how terrible. It doesn't go away. You just build a new life around it.'

She was thinking of Danilo, who had saved her from certain death, Danilo whom she had loved as no other. Even her grief for him had faded to the extent that she could put him from her mind and get on with living, although he still came to her in dreams.

Some six months after Wanda's death, Zygmunt was driving home to Lisko in a pony trap, very late one night. He had been drinking in the small town of Yarychev. He was, said his companions afterwards, very drunk. They had tried to reason with him, and one of them had offered him a bed for the night, but he was determined to go home. He ran the trap off the road and himself into a ditch, where he bumped his head on a stone, knocked himself unconscious, and drowned in a few inches of sluggish water. Had the stream dried up altogether, as it did in high summer, he would have survived with nothing worse than a headache.

Marianna was filled with remorse at the manner of his death. His visits to Milatyn had been few and far between, and they had never really talked intimately about their hopes and fears, dreams and desires, not as they once had when they were children. Too late, Marianna began to wish that she had gone back to Lisko and kept house for him, taking Zofia with her. Things might have been different. He might have been alive today. And then she thought that, after all, he had not asked her to come, had seemed to enjoy his unencumbered possession of the fine butter-yellow house. He would not have welcomed her intrusion. So why should she feel guilty?

It was Floryan who, as kindly as he knew how, brought matters to a head.

'My dear, I suppose you're aware that you're going to be quite a wealthy young woman now.'

She hadn't thought about what Zygmunt's death meant in terms of her inheritance.

'I suppose I will be.'

'You'll have all the young men and many of the old beating a path to your door. Two fine estates: Podlaski and now Lisko. You're going to have to make some decisions and make them quite soon.'

Floryan had paid for a new house at Podlaski. Modern and comfortable, it had been built some distance away from the ruins of the old. Floryan had been determined that Marianna should not lose anything of her inheritance, especially after the birth of his grand-daughter. But once the building was finished, apart from the new steward, and a couple of servants, nobody ever visited the ill fated estate.

'Lisko is by far the better of the two,' he continued. 'And it has such potential, given a good steward. You'll have to think about all this.'

'I have been thinking about it.'

'And have you come to any conclusion?'

'With your permission, I think I should like to sell Podlaski. Perhaps you would sell it for me, Floryan.'

'Are you sure?'

'I could never go back there. The very thought terrifies me. I kept it for Zofia's sake. So that she should have a dowry, or at least a source of income. Now that I have Lisko, I don't need it. Besides, I think Zygmunt has been very extravagant. I don't know what state the place is in, but I know I'll need money if I'm to improve things there.'

'You're right. Podlaski would have nothing but bad memories for you. I feel the same. And with the new house there, I think we'll soon find a buyer.'

Floryan and Julian went to Lisko to attend Zygmunt's funeral and to see to the various legal matters connected with his death. Everything had been left to Marianna, to do with as she saw fit. The Lisko estate manager, who had struggled for years to take care of the place while Zygmunt was frittering away the family fortunes, seized the opportunity of his employer's death to move away. He had found Zygmunt difficult and saw little reason to suppose that the spoilt sister, of whom he had disagreeable memories, would behave any better. Floryan, therefore, made discreet enquiries in the district and appointed a new steward, a young man about whose honesty and capability he had heard much that was reassuring.

'My dear,' he told Marianna, 'you should know that he's a Ukrainian.'

'Is that wise?'

'I knew it might worry you after what happened at Podlaski, so I made extensive enquiries. He's young and intelligent and a good, hard worker. A married man too, with a Polish wife and a child to support, so he'll be steady. I've interviewed him. I liked him and Julian seemed to approve. Your Nusia will stay on to take care of the house, of course, and the young man will manage the estate. It needs a firm hand and a certain amount of energy, Marianna. It's very run down. But I don't doubt that with an efficient steward in place, everything will be safe and secure there until you decide what you want to do next.'

Marianna found Lisko preying on her mind. Now that it was hers, the responsibility of it weighed on her. There was no doubt that the new steward was making a good job of managing the land, because Floryan himself demanded frequent reports, but the house itself was standing empty, except for a few servants. She heard that Nusia had been unwell, and she worried about her. Her mind was finally made up the following spring when Floryan announced that he was about to be married again, this time to Ursula, the daughter of a Lemberg doctor.

Julian had rather liked the girl himself, only to see her swept off her feet by the charm and, just possibly, the affluence of his elderly father. Still, he accepted the match philosophically enough, and Marianna concluded that he had not really loved the girl after all. But the wedding only helped to confirm her own decision. Before the spring was out, she had decided to return to Lisko.

'Are you sure you're doing the right thing?' asked Julian. 'And won't you miss us?'

'I miss you all the time, Julek,' she said reproachfully. It was true. He was her best friend and more of a brother, she sometimes thought, than Zygmunt had ever been. 'But since you're almost never here these days, it will be just the same at Lisko. And you'll visit us, won't you?'

'We'll all visit you. But it's such a big house for you and Zoshka to be rattling around in.'

'There'll be plenty of people to fill it. Nusia and some of the old staff are still there. And the steward and his wife have a little boy, I believe. It won't be lonely at all.'

'They're not your family.'

'I know that. But I always dreamed of going back there one day. I loved it dearly when I was a child. I still do, and I've neglected it for far too long.'

'You always know your own mind, don't you, Marianna?' said Julian, with the mixture of admiration and misgiving he always felt about her.

One fine morning in early summer, Marianna climbed into the open carriage that was to take her and some of her possessions back to Lisko. The rest would be sent on, packed into trunks and boxes. Zofia, clutching her favourite wooden doll, was lifted in beside her mother. She was full of excitement about the journey and the house she had never seen. She reminded Marianna very much of herself, on that long ago journey to Podlaski, although she hoped for a much happier ending for the child.

All day, they drove through lush countryside, along dirt roads fringed with lindens and tall poplars. Hooves and wheels threw up the dust in tawny clouds. They passed scattered villages, untidy conglomerations of thatched houses and farmsteads scattered among dark beech woods and broad, sunny fields where people worked. Zofia waved to everyone they passed. It struck Marianna that her daughter had no real idea of the permanence of the move. For her, it was a delightful excursion. Most people waved back, glad of the chance to ease their aching backs and pause for a moment to watch the carriage go by.

That night, they stopped at an inn, where rooms had been arranged for them: a bedroom with a big feather bed and a sitting room with a good fire, although the night was warm. Very early the next morning they set off again, stopping for food and drink at another inn. Then Zofia slept through the afternoon, leaning against Marianna. It was late in the day when they came within sight of the collection of smallholdings that was Lisko village.

When she caught sight of the familiar onion dome of the Orthodox church rising through the trees, she knew that they were almost home. She half rose in her seat, straining to see the house, waking Zofia in her excitement. There it was, elegant and butter yellow, a jewel among green parklands. At the lodge, the couple who had lived there since her babyhood came out to greet her and admire the child they had waited so long to see.

'My lady, you're welcome home at last. The new steward is waiting for you up at the house.'

'Everything looks just as it should. He must have worked very hard.'

'He soon licked everything into shape. Your father would have approved. He's a good man. Not afraid to put his foot down. He cares for the place as if it were his own.'

'Then my father-in-law chose well for me.'

They drove on.

'Look!' She took Zofia's hand. 'There's the old linden. It must be two hundred years old. That's what your grandfather used to tell me. It's older than any other tree at Lisko. Oh and the orchards are still in bloom!'

The orchards of apple, pear and cherry that surrounded the house were still cloaked in a mass of blossom, and she wondered why she had been so long away from this place that she loved above all others, and why she had not brought her child here sooner.

Impulsive in her happiness, she thought, 'Why should I not marry again? Why should I not forget the past, bring a new husband here, somebody who loves me, and fill this house with children? I have money and a home. I can take my pick.'

As they drove up the avenue towards the house, a sudden breeze, coming with evening, blew down a shower of pink and white petals, covering their skirts, their shoulders, their heads. Zofia laughed, brushing them away.

'It's like snow,' she said, delightedly. 'Warm pink snow.'

The driver was drawing the carriage to a halt in front of the main entrance to the house. She saw a small group of people with Nusia's smiling face among them, older, more wrinkled, but otherwise unchanged. Above all, she was curious to see the man who had cared for Lisko so well in the months during which she had debated about her return. The groom steadied the horses. Zofia was clamouring to step down and meet all these new people. Marianna didn't see him right away, as she brushed petals from the child's hair and skirts.

He waited quietly, respectfully, dressed in his best for the occasion, from his smart woollen coat to his well polished boots. He stretched out his hand to the child. As he did so, he remembered another season, another place. He thought of himself, seven years ago, taking a woman briefly into his arms as he had swung her down from her mount. He thought of the desire that had flared in him and all that had followed.

Marianna gave her daughter into the man's arms and, for the first time, looked directly at him. She gasped and put out her hand to the leather seat to steady herself. He ignored her for a moment and held the child away from him, looking into her face, smiling. She grinned back. Brown eyes met the same dark brown. His hands trembled.

'Welcome home, little Miss!' He set her on her feet. She ran to Nusia, who was coming forward with outstretched arms, and instinctively thrust her head into that lady's starched apron. The steward turned his attention back to the mother, clicking his heels smartly together, bowing his head.

'Welcome home, my lady,' he said, gravely.

Behind him, the small group of staff echoed him. 'Welcome home, my lady!'

He would have kissed her hand, but she didn't offer it. Afterwards, folk said that was a strange thing, for it was the custom, but perhaps she was tired after her journey and shy of this rather grim stranger, with his swarthy face and dark hair. He offered her his hand, very formally.

'My lady, may I help you down?'

She avoided his eyes, forcing a smile for the other members of her household. Then Nusia came forward to kiss her, still holding Zofia by the hand, and the others followed more diffidently. There were a few newcomers, but most of the old servants had stayed on, waiting to see whether she would return after her brother's death.

Suddenly, Marianna felt very tired. The long day's journey and its ending had exhausted her. He saw her sway and was at her side immediately, offering his arm . Reluctantly, she took it.

'You are?' she said for the benefit of the others, for she knew the answer well enough.

'Bandura, my lady,' he told her in his sing-song Polish. 'My name is Danilo Bandura. I am your new estate manager and your most loyal servant.'

Chapter Twenty Four

DANILO BANDURA'S PROGRESS FROM VAGRANT to steward of one of the more desirable estates of the area had been unexpected but not unprecedented. It had come as a shock to him to find out that Banunin was adjacent to Marianna's old home at Lisko, but he never had occasion to go there and although he sometimes heard gossip about her, the consensus seemed to be that she would stay at Milatyn after the birth of her child. News of the child had come as a shock to him, but he had locked his suspicions deep away inside. He mustn't even think about her. That way, madness lay.

At Banunin, they soon noticed that the new worker had a way with horses. He had a calming voice and a gentle but firm manner that suited the animals, and he could even handle the master's temperamental stallion that no-one else but Komorowski would dare to approach. He remained solitary and unsociable, but if a horse were ill or in discomfort he would give far more than was expected of him. When one of the mares had difficulties giving birth, it was Danilo who helped the foal into the world, Danilo who stayed up all night with mother and daughter, just to make sure that nothing else went wrong.

He made few friends among the other stable lads or the men who worked with the horses, but the under-manager, Bogdan Wilk, approved of this detachment. Close fellowship with other workers meant that you put them before the interests of the estate and that was not what Bogdan sought in his man. He looked at Danilo and saw a certain intelligence. When Danilo had been working at Banunin for almost a year, Bogdan summoned him to the estate office and demanded, 'Can you read or write in Polish?'

'Sir, I can neither read nor write in any language. Not my own. Nor Polish. I was never taught. It was not ... necessary.'

'Then would you like to learn? You look to me as if you might be anxious to make your way in life.'

'But who would teach me?'

'I would, if you were willing. I could spare you an hour or two each night.'

Danilo was touched. Few people had ever been so gratuitously kind to him. Only Antonina and then Yuri's mother. No man, ever.

'I'd be grateful,' he said.

'I see no harm in letting you know the true position. You're aware that Mr Lipka, our steward, is a very old man.'

'The men say he's well into his eighties.'

'He is. Which means that more and more of the work falls on my shoulders. But he's been a good manager and Mr Komorowski has said that he must keep his place to the very end. Well, I've no quarrel with that. He's given good service. But the master has also asked me to train up a young estate worker to give me some help, effectively to become my assistant.'

Danilo had had few dealings with the acerbic old man Lipka, few dealings with Bogdan Wilk either. He was surprised that he had even been noticed.

'There must be people who have been here far longer than me. People who can read and write.'

Polish men, he thought, but didn't say it.

Bogdan eyed him, shrewdly. 'Maybe. But not so many as you might think, and besides, I have a feeling that you're an honest man. And my instinct tells me that, given the right kind of teaching, you could be clever. I've followed my hunches all my life and they've never let me down yet. You've already given more than you need to this estate, and without much reward.'

'I like the work.'

'Don't let this go to your head, Bandura. I'm doing you no favours. I neither like nor dislike you. It's not my way to have favourites. I simply think you might be an asset to the place, given half a chance.'

Before long he was proven right. Danilo learned, not without difficulty, but very eagerly, as though his brain had lain fallow for too long. At first he struggled, reduced almost to tears by letters and words that danced before his eyes. Even worse was quill and ink and the incomprehensible black squiggles that flickered across the page in the candlelight and seemed determined to become big blots. But though Bogdan was not a patient teacher, Danilo kept at it. Gradually, it became easier, so that towards the end of his second year at Banunin, Danilo found that he could read with comparative fluency whatever books Bogdan could provide. Reading was the key that unlocked a new world for him. With the master's permission, he was given limited access to the library at the manor house, and soon he was educating himself, poring over books in the deserted estate office long into the night, teaching himself the rudiments of history, geography, mathematics and a little of the sciences. When old Mr Lipka died and Bogdan Wilk took his place as steward, Danilo became under-manager of Banunin, and began to learn something of the real practicalities of running an estate, with all the judgements, calculations and responsibilities this entailed.

Halina Olech was eighteen when she first set eyes on Danilo Bandura. She had been nursery maid at Banunin since the age of fourteen, a shy Polish girl who had lived in the village all her life. The young Komorowski children, a boy and a girl, liked her well enough, but they took advantage of her, managing to get their own way with her most of the time. They were not above putting frogs and spiders in her bed or sewing up the arms of her nightdresses when the mood took them. She took it all in good part, but her apparent forbearance was the result of a reluctance to make trouble. She flinched from any sort of upset, and hated to find herself the centre of attention. Instead, she flitted about the house, annoying the children's mother with the tears that sprang to her eyes if she should be taken to task about anything.

'I can't bear it,' said Julia Komorowska to her husband. 'If I complain about anything at all to the girl, she just starts to cry. I feel like some kind of monster. She drives me wild.'

'Then find another nursery maid. One with more spirit.'

'But she's a good girl and very honest, and the children seem to like her. I'm not at all sure that I want a nursery maid with spirit. Do I?'

'Then you must just put up with her other failings, my dear.'

'You're no help. No help at all.'

'If she's as biddable as you say, she'll make some fortunate man a fine wife,' observed Komorowski, with feeling.

The old steward had died just after Christmas. Candlemas, the feast of Our Lady of the Thunder, fell almost immediately after Danilo's promotion. In the kitchens at the manor they made candles of beeswax, and Halina showed the Komorowski children how to decorate them with coloured ribbons and dried flowers, as she had done every year since her own childhood. She was always happiest when she was making things: jam, cakes, pot pourri, candles, decorated eggs at Easter, it didn't matter what. She was dexterous, loved to see things taking shape beneath her fingers.

The candles were taken to church and blessed by the priest on the morning of the feast day. During thunderstorms, people would light them and stand them in their windows to protect the house from thunderbolts. After much agonised debating with herself, Halina knocked on Danilo's door. Along with the added responsibilities of under-stewardship of the estate, Danilo had been given a one-roomed cottage. She tapped so timidly at first that he didn't hear her, but when she plucked up the courage to knock more loudly, she heard his footsteps. The door swung open.

'Sir? I thought you might like a thunder-candle.'

'So you think I need protection from storms, do you?'

'I made them myself. I thought you might like to have one. I always give one to Mr Wilk, you see, and even Mr Lipka used to take one.'

'Did he, now?'

'He was always kind to me, Mr Lipka.' She was very tender-hearted. He saw her eyes fill up and took the candle to forestall any weeping. He didn't like tears.

'It's very pretty.' He looked straight at her and his rather grim features dissolved into a smile. He couldn't help himself. She blushed again, joy welling up inside her.

'Do you think so?'

'I do. You're the nursery maid, aren't you? At the big house.'

'That's right.'

'What's your name?'

'Halina, sir. Halina Olech. But everyone calls me Halka.'

'You're Polish?'

'I am.'

'And I suppose they lead you a merry dance, those children?'

'Sometimes they do.' She smiled up at him, shyly. 'They're a handful, for sure. Spirited, Madam calls them.'

'Spoilt. That's what I'd call them. Spoilt rotten. I've seen their like before.' He held the door open for her. 'Thank-you for the candle, Halka. I'm sure it'll keep me safe.'

Towards the end of March, the villagers at Banunin celebrated the ancient festival of *Marzanna*. They made a figure of straw that represented winter, carried it in procession around the village and ceremoniously drowned it in the pond. Danilo, who had errands in the village that day, came to watch, and found himself standing beside Halina. Caught up in the moment, she plucked at his sleeve and stared up at him with shining eyes.

'Winter is dead!' she cried. 'Winter is dead and gone and the spring is coming! Oh, sir – aren't you glad?'

Her good humour was infectious. He smiled down at her in spite of himself.

'Yes,' he told her. 'I *am* glad, Halka!'

Impulsively he picked her up, swung her round and set her down again. She was as light as a bird in his arms. Lighter than Marianna. The remembrance of that night in the forest came back to him, but he pushed it away, resolutely. That life was gone. Over and done. Now he must concentrate on his future.

Later that day, when Halina returned to the manor, her thoughts were full of him and when she might contrive to speak to him again. Gradually, her concern for him overcame her shyness and she found excuses to place herself in his way. Love lent her boldness. She brought him cool drinks when he was working in the sun and loaves of fresh bread and sweet cakes that she begged from the kitchens. In summer she would fetch him baskets of wild strawberries and bilberries. When she took the children for walks, she would make sure that they passed by wherever he happened to be working.

At first he was mildly irritated by her presence, but gradually he began to find it soothing. It was clear that Halina thought him very handsome, and she was attracted to his self-confidence and his power. She loved him with a dangerous yearning to drown herself in what she saw as the strong, sure current of his life.

Danilo had furnished his cottage in a rudimentary fashion, but Halina was convinced that it needed a woman's touch. One day, when the children were visiting friends with their mother and Danilo was out in the forest, she dared to venture inside the austere little building and worked all afternoon, cleaning and polishing the bits of furniture, trimming the place with fresh flowers and a few bright fabrics that she had begged from Nusia. Then she sat down to wait for him, trembling in anxious anticipation. Late in the day he stooped through the low door, looking around in surprise and a certain amount of irritation.

'I know you don't like to be disturbed, sir, but I thought ...' She hesitated. 'I haven't pried into anything. I haven't opened anything or disturbed anything important or private. I've just touched the surface, really.'

He saw her expression: afraid, eager, hopeful, and he relented. He could no more scold her than he could be casually cruel to the puppies or kittens that the Komorowski children held up to him to be petted.

'You thought you would try to make it nice for me?'

'Yes, sir, I did.'

He sat down and began to pull off his boots. She came and stood over his leg and helped him, tugging at the muddy leather, an intimate action that aroused him a little. Then she brought warm water and washed his feet, touching the white flesh tenderly, paying special attention to the parts where the boots had rubbed and bruised him. She had prepared food for him. She was a good cook, and he ate with enjoyment.

'Why don't you join me?'

'I must go back to the house. The children will be coming home.'

'But you have an hour or two, surely?'

'Well, maybe, sir.'

He said 'You needn't sir me so much, Halka. You're not my servant. I thought we were friends.'

'We are.'

Then call me Danilo. Everyone else does.'

When the meal was finished and still she hovered, watching him hungrily, he gave a sigh of capitulation and took her over to the wooden bed across which she had flung a threadbare but brightly embroidered coverlet in scarlet and blue. He didn't kiss her, but pulled back the bedclothes and made her kneel up on the linen sheet, standing beside her. Carefully and without speaking, he loosened her clothes and removed her dress so that she was in her petticoats. Then he reached around, gently unfastened the buttons of her chemise and began to massage her breasts until the nipples grew firm. When he felt the tension begin to leave her, he allowed his hands to travel down her body, caressing its small contours. All at once, she relaxed completely. He slipped his fingers beneath her petticoats, held her narrow hips for an instant and then moved his hands further around, from behind and at last touched the soft mound of hair.

As he did so, he felt her start of surprise and stopped.

'You've never done this before?'

'No. Never.'

'Then I should stop.'

'No. No!'

'Are you sure this is what you want?' he whispered in her ear. 'If you want me to stop, tell me now, Halina. I won't mind. You can just get dressed and go away. We'll still be good friends.'

'No. I want you to go on.'

She leaned back against him, trying to turn into his arms, but he wouldn't let her. Instead he made her bend forwards over the big pillow, arranging her limbs carefully to suit him. She felt him come into her from behind, cautiously at first. She gasped, and he was still for a moment. Then his hands slipped around her again. All at once she forgot the small moment of pain and pushed her buttocks back against him, crying out his name. He heard the muffled gasp against the pillow, took his own pleasure and buried his face briefly in her hair.

She pulled her skirts down, sitting upright.

'Was it what you wanted, Halka? Was it what you expected?'

'I didn't know what to expect.'

It was true. She hadn't. But it had been at once more puzzling and more exciting than she had anticipated.

'I didn't hurt you, did I?'

'No. There was more pleasure than pain.'

He said 'Good. But look. There's blood on the sheet.'

'I'll wash it.'

'You don't have to, you know. I can fend for myself. I've done it for years.'

'Do you want me to come back again?'

He reached out and touched her hair, very gently.

'Again?' he asked.

She was puzzled by his apparent indifference. And yet he had been kind to her.

'Yes. Should I come back?'

'If you like,' he said.

'But do you want me to?'

'If it pleases you. Yes. Why not?'

Halina came to the cottage often, that summer. Each time, he would make love to her, meticulous in giving her pleasure, but meticulous too in not allowing her to see his face, in not looking into hers until the lovemaking was done. Halina knew very little about these things and accepted it as Danilo's way. In autumn she came to him with a face full of woe, and when he pressed her to tell him the reason, she confessed, hesitantly, that she thought she was carrying his child. She had had no show of blood for two months now, had been sick in the mornings and, although it was not noticeable to others, her clothes no longer fitted her so well as they once had.

He looked at her with a sinking heart and knew that he was responsible. There would have been no other man in her quiet life. He would not insult her by making the enquiry. The child must be his. But at the thought of a child, he felt his spirits lift. Why not marry her and have done with it? He could do far worse than gentle Halina. A child would be something of his own, something to cherish. If he could not have one Polish lady, why not another?

He said, 'Don't worry, Halka. I'll not desert you. We'll be married if you'll have me.'

Her cheeks glowed with relief and her eyes shone. 'You mean it, Danilo? You really mean you want to marry me?'

'I wouldn't say it, if I didn't mean it. Did you think I would reject you?'

'I'm never very sure what you'll do, Danilo. But I'll be a good wife to you. No-one will ever love you so well or take such good care of you. I'll make you meals fit for a king!' She chattered on. 'I'll spin and weave and sew for you and you'll wonder how you ever managed without me.'

Her happiness touched him so much that he could almost imagine himself really in love with her. When next they made love, it was face to face. Afterwards, he went to a chest in the corner of his room and from its depths, drew Antonina's amber necklace. He had carried it with him the whole time. Now he hung it around her neck as an affirmation of faith.

'Oh, Danilo! How beautiful! I feel like a great lady in this.'

'You're a hundred times better than any great lady, Halina,' he said, kissing her on the lips.

When the child was born, a boy christened Pavel, Danilo was smitten with such affection for the infant that the mother too was encompassed by the genuine love he felt for his tiny newborn son.

During the first years of their marriage, Halina was blissfully happy and Danilo took his cue from her. All would have been well if news had not come of the untimely death of Zygmunt Diduski over at Lisko. Everyone agreed that he had run the estate into the ground, and that it was badly in need of a good steward. For a little while, Danilo wondered if Marianna would come back and take over the estate herself, but Bogdan Wilk remarked that this was unlikely and Danilo felt a strange combination of relief and regret at the news.

'However,' Bogdan said, looking sidelong at Danilo, 'Old Floryan Yelitowski and his son Julian are coming here to sort things out. It seems they plan to appoint a new steward to try to lick the place into some sort of shape.'

'That'll be a job and a half.'

'It will. A job for a young man. An ambitious young man. One with a family to support. I hear they sold Podlaski, so they won't be short of money.'

Danilo shook his head. The thought had crossed his mind but he had dismissed it as impossible. 'They'll want a Pole, surely.'

'Not necessarily. I gather Floryan wrote to Mr Komorowski asking if he could recommend anyone.'

'And?'

'And he asked me what I thought and I recommended you.'

'Oh sir, I don't think it's the place for me.'

'Why not? I can find another assistant, but you won't find a better position round here, except for Banunin itself and I don't intend to give that up any time soon.'

'I don't have the experience.'

'You do. I've taught you well. They've asked me to sound you out. Because Komorowski agrees with me. It would mean a much better house for you and your little family, more responsibility, more power, but I don't think you'll abuse it. You're honest, and an honest man is hard to find.'

'That's true enough.'

I think you'd do your best by the estate. The master was very fond of Stefan Diduski and his wife, and hated to see what their son had done to the place. The sister that owns it now, she'll never come back here. Too comfortable at Milatyn. But Komorowski says she cares about the estate and the people who work there far more than her brother ever did.'

'Perhaps she does.'

He hardly knew what to say, his mind in turmoil. How could he refuse the promotion, for promotion it undoubtedly was? Bogdan Wilk saw his hesitation and put it down to his natural diffidence.

'Think about it. Talk to Halina. It would be a step up in the world for all of you. Let me know what you think in a day or two. If you want it, the job's as good as yours and I can't think of anyone else who would do it so well or so conscientiously.

Chapter Twenty Five

THE SERVANTS AT LISKO PUT Marianna's silence down to a combination of fatigue after her journey and the strain of returning to her childhood home. A meal of hare meat and vegetables was placed before them in the dining room, but they sent it back almost untouched. Marianna remembered her father and her brother's strong tastes in game and thought that there would have to be some changes made in the kitchen. She sent for bread and milk for Zofia and bread and cheese for herself. She nibbled at it with a little wine and water. The wine was French and excellent. She supposed it must be whatever remained of her father's once extensive cellar. But Zygmunt had probably made great inroads into it and there couldn't be much left now.

'I must take stock,' she thought, confusedly. 'I must take stock of what I have and what I need to do.'

She sent for Jacek, the butler who had worked at Lisko in her father's time. He was growing very frail now and, late in life, had managed to find himself a middle-aged wife. He didn't sleep in the house, but went home to his cottage on the estate each evening, where his wife massaged his rheumaticky limbs with goose grease and plied him with Gdansk vodka, in a sincere effort to prolong his life.

'Can you tell me what's left of my father's wine cellar?' she asked.

'Very little, I'm afraid. Your brother ...'

'I know,' she interrupted him. It was too painful to think about Zygmunt just now. 'You had better contact my father's old wine merchant. You know what he would have bought.'

'I still have the account books. Your brother did some buying, but mostly ...'

'Mostly he drank what was here. I can imagine. I'll leave you to order what you think we might need, but don't spend too much until I've had a chance to look at the household accounts. We'll certainly be doing a little entertaining, and I wouldn't like our neighbours to think us mean or provincial.'

He bowed and kissed her hand. 'As you wish, Miss Marianna. And may I say how good it is to have you home again!'

He seemed genuinely happy to see her.

'I'm delighted to be here.'

He hobbled out of the room, smiling to himself. She hoped the Gdansk vodka would have some effect. She couldn't bear to lose all her ties to the old days.

Grazyna, a young girl from the village, had been engaged as nursery maid, and she came to take Zofia upstairs. For the first time that day, the child looked frightened. Marianna accompanied them, lamp in hand, to the nursery that had once been hers, checked that the bed was well aired, and installed her daughter safely, with her wooden doll clutched close.

'She's afraid of the dark,' she told Grazyna. 'If she wakes, you must light the lamp immediately and don't be afraid to call me. I shan't mind. And I'll look in on her later. I used to be afraid of the dark myself so I know how frightening it can be.'

In one corner of the old nursery was a shiny tiled stove that gave out great gusts of heat on this summer night, clicking and rustling as the logs settled inside it. In spite of the heat of the day, the servants had lit all the fires to air the house against Marianna's return. She was glad of it. It would be comforting for Zofia. It had always seemed to her like a fat and friendly person, keeping watch, winking at her in the night and fidgeting occasionally. You couldn't be lonely or sad when the tiled stove was lit.

She looked around the room at the carefully arranged furnishings. There was the wooden rocking horse with a face like a benign dragon, brought from Sweden for her grandmother when she was a little girl. There was the woolwork coverlet her mother had made before her marriage, the wooden cradle painted with scenes from the nativity and decorated with gilded fretwork, given to her parents by the villagers on the occasion of her own christening. Best of all, beside the bed was the little figure of Christ, perched upon a low wall, his chin resting pensively on his hand. This Jesus looked friendly and ordinary, or so she had always thought when she was small. Now, he had been reinstated from the distant corner to which the French governess had relegated him all those years ago. Marianna thought that tomorrow, she would pick flowers from the gardens and begin to make a pot pourri of lavender and rose petals, banishing the faint but unmistakeable odour of disuse that had fallen over the house.

'I love this place,' she said to Grazyna, impulsively.

'Yes, my lady.'

The girl seemed nervous of her, and Marianna thought of poor Dorota, her own nursemaid, and how she must have tormented her. Dorota was married now, living in the village with children of her own, and Marianna hoped that she herself had long been forgiven her bad behaviour. She must send presents for the children, mend fences.

'I was very happy here when I was a girl. Before my mother died. it was a good childhood. I want Zoshka to have the same.'

Grazyna's brown eyes filled with sympathetic tears, and Marianna saw that she was a soft hearted soul, a pleasant enough companion for her daughter, though soon the child would need to learn reading and writing. Marianna intended to teach Zofia herself. There was a good library at Lisko. Some of the books were old and precious. When she was a child, it was not considered helpful for a girl to be too bookish, but now, with no husband to consider, she could please herself. In spite of her earlier ideas about filling the house with children, she was in no hurry to commit herself to marriage again. There was one problem only, a problem that she kept trying to push to the back of her mind, not wanting to think about it now, when she was so weary from the journey.

What on earth was she to do about Danilo?

If it wasn't for her steward and the dangerous truth of his relationship to her daughter, she could be truly happy here. She looked down at the child, her cheeks rosy in the candlelight. She must never know. She must always think herself a Yelitowska. And then a thought struck her. Why shouldn't she lie to Danilo? Years had passed and he was a married man, presumably a happily married man, or so Nusia said. She had lied to everyone else except Julian, but Julian only knew half the story and would surely keep the secret. Besides, he believed that Zofia's father was dead. He would make no connection between a competent Ukrainian estate manager and a rebel from a distant village. So why shouldn't she lie to Danilo too? He couldn't presume to argue with her.

She went back to the small room that she had asked to be prepared for her own use. This had once been her grandmother's private sitting room. The furniture was French and English: a comfortable couch, curved armchairs with tapestry seats, a gilded chair, almost too beautiful and fragile to sit on, a bureau of inlaid satinwood and a table with a Dutch marquetry top of flowers and birds in walnut and cherry. On the wood-panelled walls, that lent a sweet, resinous scent to the room, there were family portraits from the last century, ladies and gentlemen, powdered and bewigged. The wooden floor was covered with silk rugs from Bokhara in the East. Even the stove was beautiful, decorated with mellow Delft tiles. It was a deeply feminine room with gilded Sevres vases and Meissen figurines on tables. Marianna's grandmother had brought some of these lovely pieces with her when she first came to Lisko as a young bride in the 1770s. Here, amid the possessions of her grandmother and her mother, Marianna installed the green and gold enamel box that Floryan had given her.

She sat for a while, deep in dreams of the past, and then she rang for Nusia.

Nusia was past seventy now and beset by rheumatism and other vague ailments that she always described as 'liver troubles', though she was still very active and capable. She had not been able to manage Zygmunt, but she managed everything else.

'My darling Marianna, It does my heart good to see you back here again. We thought that you might marry elsewhere or stay on at Milatyn, and then what would we all have done?'

'I've been away for much too long. I want to know everything. Tell me about the estate. This young man – Bandura. What is he like? Do you think I should keep him on?'

Nusia lowered herself onto the couch. 'You'd be a fool if you didn't,' she said, forthright as ever. 'He's honest as the earth. I'll tell you now, Miss Marianna, and not wanting to speak ill of the dead, but your brother had let things get well out of hand. Your father left the estate in good order but your brother had a stab at ruining it and himself into the bargain.'

Marianna said nothing. It was as she had suspected, as Floryan had hinted.

'You'll pardon me for saying this, my lady, but if he hadn't gone when he did, God rest his soul for I loved him dearly, the place could never have been pulled back in so short a time. Then along comes your father-in-law and your dear brother-in-law – how kind he was to me,' she added. 'He gave me so much good advice about my rheumatism – and they had a good look around and went off to Banunin to ask the Komorowskis for advice. When they came back, Danilo Bandura came with them. Well, your father-in-law saw to it that all the debts were paid, and as for Mr Bandura, why, he's worked miracles!'

'Has he?'

'Oh, he has. If anyone proves to be a slacker, off they go. He won't stand for it. If anyone quarrels, they're told to save their anger for a more suitable time and get on with the job in hand. And most folk don't mind, because he's not above mucking in and helping out himself whenever a job needs doing.'

'He sounds too good to be true.'

'Oh no!' Nusia shook her head, smiling. 'He isn't what you'd call good. Not what you'd call an angel. He's a strong man and quick tempered too, so no-one argues with him. Just after he'd arrived, one of the foresters, Kiril – he's always been a lazy bully, that one – stood up to him, pulled a knife on him and in a moment, so they tell me, he was flat on his back, and young Bandura kneeling astride him with the blade hard against his fat throat. So he had no more trouble from that direction. He made one or two mistakes and one or two enemies, but he's always fair, and they mostly came round to him in the end. Even those who won't admit to liking him say they've got to admire him.'

'It seems that he has a champion in you, anyway,' observed Marianna, dryly.

'He has so, Miss Marianna. I speak as I find and I find him honest.'

'Where is he from?' she asked, cautiously. 'Is he a local man?'

Nusia looked rather vague. 'No. He's not local. But he was working as under-steward at Banunin when your father-in-law came here to make the funeral arrangements for your poor brother. Where he was before that, I can't say. I remember old Marysia over at Banunin telling me that he'd fetched up at their lodge gate one February night, half starved and freezing and crawling with lice into the bargain. That was some years ago though. She was scared to take him in, but it was either that or leave him to die. And it turned out that he was quite a presentable young man when he was cleaned up and fed, and besides that, he had a real talent where the horses were concerned. A job was found for him and they soon noticed that he had a talent for managing men too. So when old Lipka died and Bogdan Wilk took his place, Bandura got Bogdan's job. They say Bogdan taught him reading and writing.'

'But how did he come to Lisko?'

'Your father-in-law heard them speak well of him over there and asked Komorowski if he might "steal" him.'

'Didn't Komorowski mind?'

'Maybe he did, but you can't stand in the way of a man with ambition, can you? I believe they summoned Bandura and asked him if he would like a job with more responsibility. Left it up to him to decide. The next thing we knew, here he was. I'll say this for Bandura, he's always very civil to us older folk. Very civil and courteous.'

This, coming from Nusia, was praise indeed.

'And he's a married man, so I hear?'

'Oh yes. He met her over at Banunin. She was nursery maid to the children there. Halina Olech as was. She's Polish. A little mouse.'

'A mouse?'

'You know the type. Nice enough, but very quiet. She runs about after him as though he were King Jan Sobieski himself, always fetching him titbits, clinging to him. I think she embarrasses him sometimes. But he does love his son. Pavel. Now he'll be younger than little Zoshka. She's, what, almost six? He'll be about three, I think. '

Nusia paused and came up for breath. Marianna had forgotten her propensity for gossip, her avid interest in people and their relationships, but was rather glad of it now.

'I don't know where Halina was today,' remarked Nusia, thoughtfully. 'She should have been there with the others to welcome you. But she's very shy so maybe that was it. She sometimes helps out in the kitchen, you know. She's a good cook. But there was no sign of her or the child.'

'Never mind. I'll meet her soon enough. That reminds me, Nusia, could you have a word about the food?'

'What about the food?'

'I don't have the same tastes as my brother and I have Zoshka to consider. We shall want more eggs, fish, fruit and cheese. Less game. Much less game. More cakes. Can you tell the cook very tactfully please? I don't want her walking out on us.'

'She wouldn't go, my lady. Not her. She's too comfortable here to make a change now. But a growing girl needs meat you know.'

'I know. But Zoshka won't eat game with the lead shot still in it and I'm not going to force her. I had enough of being force fed when I was a child.'

She thought of Ma'amselle Jeanne's cold spinach and shuddered. She had never been able to eat it since. 'No spinach,' she said with a grimace.

'Oh definitely no spinach!' Nusia yawned widely and apologised. 'Excuse me, my darling, but it's been a very long day and you must be tired. Bed for you too, I think,' she added.

Marianna had asked that the room prepared for her should be close to the nursery so that any crying in the night would be sure to wake her too. It was her mother's old room with a big feather bed and wooden presses against the wall. She undressed, washed in cold water and donned the nightdress that had been laid out for her. Feeling the room stuffy from the heat of the stove, she eased open one of the windows and sat beside it, staring out into the night.

The moon was almost full, so large that it looked just a little frayed around the edges. It rose high in a clear sky, throwing the grassy slopes and buildings into sharp relief. She could make out the white gleam of the carriage drive, winding away from the house among the trees. The breeze brought the scent of linden from the ancient tree that stood sentinel over her property. A covey of bats winged swiftly past and an owl flapped, ghostly, across the lawn. Distantly she heard the sounds of dogs barking, whistles and shouts from the village. People were leaving the tavern. A woman's voice was raised, high and scolding, then it ceased, perhaps quieted by a blow, perhaps by an embrace. A baby wailed suddenly in the night. She thought for a moment that it might be Zofia, then knew it was too far away and much too young. There was silence. She waited breathlessly.

A man was singing in Ukrainian, his voice clear and metallic, like some strange instrument. It was a love song with a repetitive, haunting melody.

'I brought you flowers from the meadows,
But you cast them down and trod them under your feet.
I have cast myself down to kiss your white feet.
Love me or I shall die.
Love me, girl, or like the flowers,
I shall wither at your feet.'

The song made her shiver. She thought of Stanislaw, falling to the ground with that look of wounded surprise on his face. She thought of Danilo, making love to her in the long cart, his face dazed with desire, and her own impassioned response. She craned her head out of the window to see where the song was coming from, but it was hard to make out the whereabouts of the singer in the dark. The last notes died away. In the ensuing silence she was rewarded by a glimpse of a dark figure moving through the trees and out of sight.

Fear gripped her. She didn't know whether it was the memory of Stanislaw's death, coming upon her suddenly, or fear of her future here at Lisko, but her heart pounded in her ears and she found herself panting as though she had been running. She looked up at the stars and felt her mind spin away towards infinity. She said aloud, 'Oh help me!' but there was no-one to hear. She banged the window shut and climbed hurriedly into bed, reaching out to extinguish the candle. Then she closed her eyes against the dark and her mind against her body, and fell into a restless sleep.

Chapter Twenty Six

MARIANNA SUMMONED DANILO TO HER the following morning, as he had guessed she would. He had taken some trouble with his clothes. His wife had put out a freshly laundered linen shirt, his boots were polished, the dark blue woollen top coat well brushed. She received him in her sitting room. He saw that she too had dressed with care, plainly, almost severely.

As she stood up to receive him, she extended her hand, keeping him at arm's length, and his lips just brushed her fingers. He clicked his heels smartly together. He knew that his manners were much improved since his Podlaski days, that the years at Banunin had lent him a certain polish. Not quite knowing how to behave, she fell back on formality. He took his cue from her and was coldly efficient.

'I hear that you're making a very good job of restoring my estate to its former fortunes, Mr Bandura. Nusia tells me you've done well.'

'I do my best, my lady.'

He hardly knew what he was saying. She looked very proper in a day dress of lavender-sprigged muslin with a high neck, long sleeves and lace at her throat. Her hair was parted in the centre and pulled back neatly, only to escape in a flurry of side ringlets.

Involuntarily he thought of the last time he had seen her on that winter's morning outside Milatyn. He remembered the brown curls tangled in his fingers. He thought of her long body, moulding itself to his. She had loved him once. Could she really have forgotten how she had loved him? How he had loved her? He gritted his teeth into the semblance of a smile and tried to concentrate on estate business.

'Will you sit down, please?'

She indicated a carved chair. He waited while she sat on the couch, waited for her to arrange her skirts. Then he perched nervously on the chair, afraid that it might crumble beneath his weight. Why did she have to receive him in this place? This was a room for stitching and sewing, for feminine banter, not for the serious business of running an estate. It put him off balance. He saw, from the slight smile on her face, that this was her intention. Of course. He made an effort to pull himself together.

'I'm so glad to see you well and happy,' she said, primly. 'I often worried about you, you know.'

'Rightly. For I almost starved.'

She frowned. 'But you're fine now. Aren't you? You've done very well for yourself.'

'Better than I expected, or deserved, that's for sure.'

'And I'm glad to see it. I hope you're well settled here? You're not going to desert us? I'd be sorry to lose such a good steward. I would, truly.'

'No. No, my lady. I'll not desert you.'

'As soon as we're properly settled in, I'd like you to tell me all that you've done and all that you plan to do. Podlaski is sold now, you know, and I want to use the money to improve Lisko.'

This was safer ground.

'I can think of a hundred ways of using your money. We need more horses to start with, and the old stables will have to be repaired to make room for them.'

'Well, you would say that, wouldn't you?'

The ghost of a smile crossed his face. 'Well, maybe. But it's the plain truth. We have some twenty pairs of working horses but we need at least twenty five pairs, possibly thirty to be really efficient.'

'And I suppose that means we'd need better stabling.'

'Which would be good for your own horses as well as the working animals.'

'That sounds reasonable. What else?'

'We could do with more milkmaids. They can work in the kitchen gardens too. We could get a good price for our soft fruit if only it could be picked efficiently and sent to Lemberg quickly enough, while it's still fresh. And we need better cottages for the estate workers. With respect,' he added, as an afterthought.

'Do we?'

'Go and see for yourself, my lady. Oh, not for me. My house is a good one. But the row of cottages across the park is a disgrace.' His detachment deserted him. 'They are damp and dirty and they need replacing. When there is sickness, it spreads among the families like wildfire. Too many children die. You know how these things are.'

'I do indeed,' she said gravely. 'But would new buildings help? Isn't it just the way they live?'

'I think our Ukrainian children deserve warmth and cleanliness just as much as Polish children, don't you, my lady?'

'I meant no insult. Forgive me. Of course we must have new cottages, if you think they're necessary.'

'I don't believe in unnecessary expense. But you should make up your own mind, madam. It's not my decision to take.'

'That's true, Mr Bandura.'

'Oh, some of them are feckless, right enough, but the same could be said for all people. Even your own brother was not the most caring of landowners. Most of them do the best they can in difficult circumstances.'

'Mr Bandura, you mustn't speak of my brother like that.'

'I apologise. But I feel so passionately about all this.'

'I know, and you may be right about the houses. I'll go and see for myself, and if something needs to be done then something will be done. But you must give me time.'

He said nothing, only nodded.

'You must give me time to settle in,' she repeated. 'It will all take time, don't you agree?'

There was a long pause. 'Your little girl ...' he began, but she forestalled him.

'Yes. Isn't it wonderful that I should bear my husband's child, even after his death? Isn't it wonderful?'

He had been wondering how she would cope with his presence. When he had learned that Marianna was coming back to Lisko, it had given him many a sleepless night. Now, he saw how it would be. She was already deceiving everyone, herself included. She was trying to pretend that none of it had happened, none of the passion that had drawn him, cold and starving, in the direction of Lisko, none of the passion that he remembered each night before sleep finally took him. Even as he made love to Halina, he would imagine that it was Marianna crying out with pleasure and returning his love with interest. But Halina never cried out with pleasure now, only gave a soft sigh and turned away. He was sure that she loved him, but perhaps she felt that he didn't love her enough. Perhaps she was right.

His passion for Marianna had given him a sense of his own worth, but she must feel only shame at the memory. How could he bear it?

With dignity, he thought. At least he had that. And he would have to make some effort to come to terms with her.

'I was very lucky to be taken in at Banunin, you know. I almost died. But this – I never intended this. It just happened. Fate, if you believe in fate. I want you to know that I never expected to be offered this position and even when I took it, I believed that you would never come back. Your father-in-law said as much. I didn't have any expectations, nor do I now. Except to be a good steward to your estate. Please believe me.'

She seemed close to tears. She whispered, 'I believe you.'

When he had worked at Banunin, it had been enough to be close to Lisko, to the place that he considered hers. When Halina had fallen pregnant, he had married her quickly because it was the right thing to do, because he could not bear the hopelessness on her face, perhaps most of all because he was sure that the child was his. He had wanted the child most desperately.

When they had been offered the position at Lisko, he had still not expected Marianna to come back. Floryan had been adamant in his belief that Marianna would either marry again or stay at Milatyn. Danilo too had convinced himself that she would do this, marrying some young nobleman and giving him sons and daughters. He had heard about Zofia and had thought about her often, but he had never expected to see the child.

If he had imagined that one day he might be sitting in this room with Marianna, discussing estate business, he would never have taken the position at all. But it was as he had feared all those years before. He must bow when she passed by in her finery. He must kiss her hand submissively and wish her a polite good morning. There was no-one to blame but himself. How could he bear it?'

'I do believe you, Danilo, ' she said again.

Abruptly, he said, 'My lady, with respect, I think you must call me Mr Bandura don't you? Otherwise eyebrows will be raised in the village and that would never do, would it?'

His eyes strayed round the room and alighted on Floryan's enamel box. She saw the direction of his gaze, the sudden flicker of amused surprise at the openly erotic posture of the figures.

'And you're married, so I hear, Mr Bandura?'

'Yes, my lady. At Banunin.'

'Well that's excellent news. A steward needs a wife. A Polish girl, so they tell me.'

'Yes. It seems to be my misfortune to love Polish girls. If it can be called misfortune.'

He turned the bold, brown eyes of the old Danilo on her for an instant and then gazed intently at the pattern on the Indian rug beneath his feet.

'And children?' she persisted.

'We have a boy called Pavel. I'm very fond of him.'

'And many more to come, I shouldn't wonder. You must let him play with Zoshka sometimes. She'll be lonely otherwise. She's used to company.'

'Gladly, my lady, if you don't mind.'

Suddenly he was very weary of these games. Deliberately breaking the rules, for it was up to her to dismiss him, he stood up.

'My lady, I have no wish to be impolite but there is a very great deal of work to be done today so, with your leave, I'll return to my tasks.'

'Oh of course. You must go, Mr Bandura. I'm sorry for detaining you.'

She saw that she would have to come to terms with him or else let him go and find herself a new manager. She was the lady of this house now, and must establish a proper relationship with him, otherwise he would take advantage of her. Disconcertingly, he read her mind and echoed her thoughts.

'My lady, if you want me to leave the estate, just say the word and I'll go. There'll be no trouble. There are many men capable of doing as good a job or even better.'

'No!' She shook her head vehemently. 'No, I don't want you to go. Don't put words into my mouth.'

He bowed again and walked to the door. He didn't offer to kiss her hand. He didn't think he could have done it just then. Before he left the room he heard her say, 'Danielek!' in a low voice.

He stopped, his heart momentarily lifted by her use of the affectionate version of his name. 'Yes?'

'Were you singing, last night?'

'Singing?'

'In the park. I heard singing in the park. Yesterday evening, just before I went to bed.'

'It might have been me. Sometimes I take a walk, last thing, to check that all's well. Sometimes I sing. Songs my mother used to sing. Do you want me to stop? Does it disturb the gracious lady in some way?' He was as formal as his Polish permitted, which was very formal indeed, to the point of absurdity.

'No, no. I liked it. It was very beautiful. I had no idea you could sing.'

He smiled at her.

'And I can dance the *hopak* too. I'm a man of many talents,' he said. 'You of all people should know that, my lady.'

He had opened the double doors, stepped through them and closed them silently behind him, before she could think of any suitable reply.

Chapter Twenty Seven

ZOFIA WAS HIS. HE KNEW it in his blood and felt it in his bones. Sometimes he met the child playing on the short grass in front of the house or walking through the woods with her nursemaid, asking questions and stamping her little foot like her mother before her, when Grazyna was too slow in answering. Each time he looked at that sweet face or caught a glimpse of those brown eyes, gazing in wonder upon her new surroundings, he knew that she was his daughter.

He had attempted to broach the subject with Marianna only once more. Towards the end of one of their formal meetings, he had said, 'Zofia. I must know.'

The colour flamed into her cheeks. She turned away for a moment and when she looked at him again, he saw that all the lines of her face were set, but her hands were shaking. She said, 'I don't understand what you're saying, Mr Bandura.'

'You understand me well enough, *my lady*!' He spat the word at her, suddenly desperate, hating her for her self control.

'I do *not* understand what you are saying, Mr Bandura!'

She turned on him a face of such cold fury that he was cowed by it. He backed away.

She said, more gently, 'Danilo, you are a very good steward to me. I would find it very hard to replace you. But if I had to, I'm sure I could.'

He didn't reply, so she continued.

'Don't misunderstand me. I would be very sorry indeed to see you go. But when you speak to me of Zofia, I will *never* understand what you are saying.'

He bowed his head in capitulation and walked stiffly to the door, like a man sleepwalking.

Danilo went about his business that day with a morose face and an acid tongue. That night, when Halina tried to fuss over him, caressing his head as he sat eating his supper, he pushed her away from him.

'Leave me be, can't you? Don't paw at me!'

He had never been so impatient with her before, but he was in the grip of some emotion that he was powerless to control. Halina retreated into a reproachful silence. Later, he would feel sorry for his bad behaviour, but at that moment, everything about her irritated him, even the way she chewed her food, the way she moved so quietly about the house. Instead he went to his son, stroking the smooth forehead as the child lay in bed, whispering marvellous promises for the future into the pink shell of the boy's ear.

After that bruising encounter, Danilo and Marianna met regularly but spoke only of estate business. He grew used to it and even welcomed the impartial elegance of her sitting room. Marianna surprised him by her knowledge of the intricacies of running the estate, her interest in the welfare of her workers, and her command of the finances involved. He sometimes felt that he was still learning as he went along, feeling for footholds in the dark, but he had not realised that a young woman could be capable of such understanding. Helped by Julian, who sent her newspapers and books from Lemberg, Marianna had embarked on a programme of study. She had plenty of time at her disposal and filled it profitably.

Mindful of Zofia's need for company, she also called on her neighbours. She made friends with several of the young married women of the district, but although some of them tried matchmaking, she was reluctant to give up her new-found freedom. She enjoyed chatting and even flirting with the young men who kissed her hand, poured wine for her and made her laugh, but when she saw them covertly eyeing her acres as well as her person, she turned away in revulsion.

She wished often and fervently that she had never laid eyes on Danilo Bandura. If she had never known physical pleasure, perhaps she would not now be dreaming about it in such frustration. Sometimes, it seemed as though every part of her body, from the hairs on her head to her toes in their soft silk slippers, ached with a painful longing to be close to

Danilo, to feel his arms around her, to rest herself against him. But she could not. It was unthinkable. He was the father of her child, but he was her steward and her inferior. Besides, he was married to somebody else.

Pavel, Danilo's son, loved Zofia on sight. During the whole of that first summer at Lisko, he ran after her, his chubby legs struggling to keep up with her. He was not yet four, but he was still small for his age, dark like his father. His plaintive cries could be heard floating through the trees.

'Zoshka! Zoshka! Don't run away! I can't fiiiiind you!'

He spoke in an odd mixture of Polish and Ukrainian, switching between both, mid sentence. Zofia mocked him at first, but she could never be truly malicious, and when she saw the fat tears oozing from beneath his eyelids she began to cry too.

'You silly little thing!' she said, mopping her own eyes and then his, with her white petticoat. 'Why on earth are you crying?'

'Because you're cross,' he said, the tears drying, miraculously. He sniffed deeply and wiped his nose with the back of his hand.

'Don't do that,' she scolded him. 'It's very impolite. Where's your handkerchief?'

'Not got one,' he said, cheerfully.

She wiped his face again with her petticoat. They were sitting in a clearing under the trees, close to Danilo and Halina's cottage. 'Don't you have any manners, child?' she asked him. It was what Nusia sometimes said to her.

'No,' he said. 'I don't have many toys.'

Zofia giggled. 'You can play with some of my toys then.' She leaned over and kissed his cheek. 'I'll be your best friend. And you'll be mine. Won't you?'

He nodded. 'Best fends,' he said.

Danilo was coming down the path to the house, rather weary from his day's labours. The children stood up and Pavel ran to him, shouting, 'Daddy!' and clinging to his long booted legs. Zofia stood back as Danilo swung his son high up into the air, kissed him and then set him down again. She looked mutinous and sad. A frown had settled on her high forehead between the dark arches of her brows.

'Zoshka says I can play with her toys, daddy.'

'Does she now? Well, I call that generous.'

He was inclined to irony, as a kind of protection against his true feelings towards the child. He glanced quickly around. There were no nursemaids in evidence and no sign of Nusia or Marianna. He strode over and squatted down so that his height should not intimidate her. He took her dimpled hand in his own and kissed it very gently.

'Good day to you, my little miss,' he said, with his engaging grin.

She blushed furiously and hid her hands behind her back, but he could see that she was pleased with the grown-up greeting. Her face had cleared, and she beamed at him.

'Good day to you!' she replied, as she had been taught, dropping a curtsey for good measure. 'I'm very pleased to meet you, sir.'

'And I you.'

He wanted to pick her up and swing her round as he had swung his son, but he didn't dare. She would tell her mother.

'I hope you'll be kind to my Pavel. He's still very young, you know, and you're such a young lady now, aren't you?'

She said, 'Do you like my new dress, Mr Bandura?'

She pirouetted ingenuously for his approval. Again, he remembered her mother saying, 'Do you like my doll?' but this child, although equally spoilt, seemed much less imperious.

He nodded. 'I do.'

'Nunu made it for me from one of mamma's old ones. My mama won't get me many new clothes because she says I only tear them on the trees.'

'And do you?'

'Sometimes. But Nunu says I'm a good deal better than my mama when she was a little girl. And I'm to have a new blue silk gown for best.'

'Well, I think you look very pretty, anyway.'

Grazyna was calling through the trees, a diminuendo of pet names. 'Zofia! Zoshka! Zoshkunia! Where are you? You're to come in now.'

The child turned reluctantly in the direction of the voice. Danilo was still crouching beside her with his arm around Pavel, who had come running up to him possessively.

'You're wanted,' he told her. 'You must go, Zofia, Zoshka, Zoshkunia!'

'But I may play with Pavel again?'

'Whenever your mother allows it.'

'She says I may if I want to. But only if you agree.'

'Does she?'

'Oh yes. She said "Ask Mr Bandura if you may play with his little boy, but don't make a nuisance of yourself."'

'You'll never do that, sweetheart.'

Impulsively, she came closer and planted a kiss on his forehead, then ran off through the trees towards the house.

He watched her go, still with his arm around Pavel, then turned to see Halina standing in their doorway, smiling at them both.

'What a nice child she is!'

'I suppose so. But we hardly know her.'

'She has a pretty face.'

'She's a little madam who's too used to getting her own way.'

'She's taken a fancy to you, anyway.'

'Do you think so?'

'Oh that's plain to see! And why not?'

As so often now, Halina's sheer delight in him gave him a twinge of irritation. He tried hard not to show it, and she seemed unaware of it.

I don't love her at all, he thought in sudden despair. I should never have married her. She's a fine woman, but how can I possibly love her when my every waking thought revolves around somebody else?

He washed in cold water and sat down to eat the meal that she had so lovingly prepared for him. She was a good cook and he should have enjoyed the food, but guilt threatened to choke him and he left half of it untasted.

'Are you all right?' she asked, anxiously.

'Of course I'm all right. You should know by now, I'm never ill, Halka.'

'Then there was something wrong with the food maybe?'

'The food was good. It always is. Don't fuss so much. It drives me mad. Leave me be.'

Her face crumpled but he steeled his heart against her. He fetched a big glass jar of vodka flavoured with bitter rowans and drank himself slowly into oblivion. At last he threw himself on the bed and fell asleep. She undressed him with great care, kissed him and covered him tenderly with a blanket.

Chapter Twenty Eight

ONE SATURDAY IN EARLY AUTUMN, Marianna had been invited to dinner at the neighbouring house of Banunin. The family found the pretty young widow an asset to their dinner table, and they couldn't understand why she hadn't been 'snapped up' as they put it. Julia Komorowska, who fancied herself as a matchmaker, would invite various eligible young men, always hoping that sooner or later, Marianna would look favourably on one of them. So far, greatly to her disappointment, it hadn't happened.

Marianna usually returned very late from these parties, for there would be dancing after an early dinner, and maybe a late supper after that. Zofia had a cold in the head, and Nusia had promised to put her to bed early. The Komorowski family dressed with great formality on these occasions and expected their guests to do the same. Consequently, Marianna had taken a lot of trouble with her dress: a russet silk evening gown, flounced and heavily embroidered, with a half length, outdoor cloak, trimmed with white fur to keep out the autumn chill. She had found some late rosebuds of pale yellow in the garden. Nusia had drawn her long hair back loosely in a bun at the nape of her neck, threading the buds through the dark strands.

Marianna passed a pleasant evening at Banunin, flattered by the attentions of her host and a young gentleman from Kamionka, who had known her brother. He thought the sister a much nicer proposition altogether. Marianna smiled at him and chatted to him but gave him little more encouragement than that.

'May I call on you and your daughter?' he asked. 'I used to spend time at Lisko when your brother was alive, and I miss your lovely gardens.'

He didn't miss the gardens at all, and she knew it. He missed the cards and the wine cellar. She said brightly, 'If you care to, of course you may call. Zofia always loves company.'

'And may I be allowed to take you home tonight?'

She shook her head. 'Thank-you, but no. My coachman is coming for me. I can't possibly give him a wasted journey.'

'A pity,' the young man said.

Marianna had arrived at the house in the Banunin carriage. It had been passing Lisko that evening, bringing Julia's spinster aunt home from a visit to a friend. Marianna had arranged for the one horse droshky to come for her, driven as always by the elderly Lisko coachman, Waldemar.

It was a clear autumn night with a full moon and a nip of winter in the air, but no rain. Told that her coachman had arrived, she was escorted onto the carriage-drive, but was disconcerted to find Danilo waiting to help her into the open trap.

'You are to be driven by your steward tonight, I see,' said her host. 'Good evening, Mr Bandura.'

Danilo bowed to Komorowski. 'Good evening, sir!'

'Where's Waldemar?' Marianna asked, in some confusion.

'My lady, his wife made plum dumplings for his supper.'

He handed her into the droshky and would have tucked the rug around her knees, but she seized hold of it, shrugging him away.

'You're creasing my gown,' she said.

In the moonlight she saw the ghost of a smile cross his face.

'What do plum dumplings have to do with anything?' asked Marianna's host, intrigued.

'Well, sir, she makes excellent plum dumplings. In fact I can vouch for them, having tasted them myself.'

Marianna made an impatient movement with her hands. He saw it and smiled again, a faint, crooked twist of his lips.

'Waldemar ate not wisely but too well, and is now confined to his bed, groaning. Forty dumplings I believe.'

'Forty!'

'I was passing his cottage on my late rounds, when I heard him moaning, and his wife scolding him. He really is in no fit state to move. So I said I would oblige him by coming to collect my lady myself.'

'I'm sure she's grateful to you. Though she would have had plenty of offers of help here too. In fact she would have been very welcome to stay.'

Komorowski kissed his visitor's hand, bade her a warm goodnight and went back into the house, still chuckling over the coachman's forty dumplings.

Marianna sat in silence until they were trotting steadily along the driveway. Unable to contain herself, she burst out, 'Was that true, Danilo? About the dumplings?'

'As true as I'm sitting here, my lady. Would I make up such a story?'

'You might.'

He laughed. 'Yes. I suppose I might. But on this occasion I spoke only the truth. Waldemar was all for waking the groom and sending him out, but I said that since I was already wide awake and it was such a fine, moonlit night, I would come for you myself.'

'And here you are.'

He turned to look at her. 'And here we are.'

'Keep your eyes on the track, Mr Bandura.'

They went on in silence, turning out of the gate of the big house, past the dark lodge where Yuri and his mother had been asleep for many hours. The driveway led between tall lindens that gradually thinned until they were on a narrow track. Flat fields stretched away for a great distance on either side, broken only by lines of poplars and beeches that showed where a web of other tracks ran here and there. Occasionally they would see a distant lamp, glimmering faintly from a cottage where someone kept late hours, but most of the houses were in darkness. The moonlight silvered the ploughed earth and all was still and silent, save for the jingle of harness and the occasional snuffle of the horse. Marianna found herself thinking of that other night, that wintry night when she and Danilo had driven away from Podlaski. She had drunk a good deal of champagne and it had left her feeling reckless and happy, just the kind of dangerous mood in which she would not have wished to encounter Danilo.

Suddenly, with a muffled exclamation, he reined in the horse and swivelled round in his seat to gaze across the nearby field.

Immediately on her guard, she asked, 'What is it? What's wrong?'

Amazement overriding formality, he said, 'Am I going mad? Tell me if you see it too!'

'What do you see?' She peered out across the field. 'What is it?' she repeated but the words died on her lips.

The field was full of hillocks where cow and horse dung had been left in great piles to be spread out later on, after the frosts had got to them and broken them up.

'There,' he said, pointing. 'Look. What *is* that?'

The horse stamped and snuffled in the chilly air. Danilo shushed her down. Marianna felt her teeth begin to chatter in spite of her warm cloak and the rug tucked over her knees. Throwing caution to the winds, for she was beginning to be frightened, she clambered up beside him, greatly hampered as usual by her skirts. He moved over to make room for her, and then pointed across the field again. She followed the line of his gaze.

'Wait,' he said. 'Wait and see if it does it again.'

It was standing up at the far end, very erect, on one of the piles of manure, smaller than your average man but too big to be an animal. A child maybe? She caught her breath. It did not, somehow, have the look of a child. Nor the shape. But then the moonlight cast such very odd shadows that it was impossible to tell its exact shape. As they watched, it bent itself right over backwards like a bow, an impossible contortion. Marianna gasped in disbelief. As it bent, they heard it cry out in a loud, high-pitched voice that carried across the field to them.

'Hehee!'

Suddenly, as though some tension had been released, it sprang up and hooped forwards upon the mound, crying, 'Hahaa!'

They both saw it leap, sure-footedly, onto another pile of dung, and repeat the same impossible manoeuvre, the same high pitched call.

'Hehee! Hahaa!'

Marianna's mouth fell open in disbelief. All the tales she had ever heard about the demons that haunted the fields, the noon ghosts and the night time devils, came flooding back to her. She put her hand on Danilo's arm.

'I thought for a moment it was a vision,' he said softly. 'But I haven't been drinking tonight.'

'What is it?'

'I don't know. I've never seen anything like it.'

She said, 'Let's drive on. Mr Bandura, Danilo, please. Let's drive on.'

The fear that had gripped her at the sight of the ludicrous but somehow menacing figure had stripped all her authority from her.

'Hehee!' called the creature, bending backwards and, 'Hahaa!' as it sprang from one mound to another.

Seized by some devilish impulse, Danilo let the reins fall and half stood up. As Marianna watched him in stunned disbelief, he cupped both hands to his mouth and shouted as loudly as he could across the field, 'Hehee! Hahaa!'

There was a pause, while the creature stood in the moonlight, casting about it in a horrible manner, seeking the source of the shout, rather, thought Marianna, as though it were *smelling* them out. All of a sudden, it turned and came bounding rapidly in the direction of the cart, coiling and uncoiling, like a spring in awful motion.

Marianna crossed herself. 'Holy Mother of God! Danilo!'

'Shit!'

Danilo sat down, seized the reins and whipped up the horse that had already caught something of his panic, until the trap was rattling at a spanking pace along the rutted road. 'Shit!' he said again, half laughing, half horrified. Marianna clasped his arm fast and hid her face against his shoulder. For a time, all Danilo's attention was fixed on controlling their headlong dash for home, but when no demonic retribution seemed to have overtaken them, he nudged her and said, with a flash of the old devilment, 'Look behind us, Marianna. See if there's anything following!'

'No. No, I shall *not*. Just keep going. For the love of God, Danielek, just keep going!'

She was almost beside herself. She stayed with her face buried in his sleeve, and her arm threaded through his, her nails digging into his flesh even through the cloth of his coat, until they were well within the boundary of Lisko. Then, Danilo slowed the sweating mare to a trot and looked down at her dark head, nestling against him. He was helpless in the face of his feelings for her. He thought he would always love her, no matter what became of them.

At last, she raised her head and began to laugh. She laughed until she ached, folding her arms against herself and bending over them like the creature.

'Oh how could you! How could you do that!' she said. She couldn't stop laughing. 'But what in God's name was it?'

'I haven't the slightest idea!' he replied. 'Some demon of the fields, maybe!'

'I don't believe there are such things.'

'Then *you* tell me what it was!'

'And what on earth possessed you to call out after it like that?'

He shook his head, still laughing. 'I don't know.'

'Never do anything like that to me again. Or as God's my witness, I'll demote you, Danilo. You can be my stable boy again.'

'I like it better when you call me Danielek.'

They were approaching the silent house. He had told the suffering coachman that he would see to the horse himself before he went to bed. She had moved to separate herself from him and was already, he knew, attempting to slip into the role of his superior again. She would be calling him Mr Bandura next and the moment would be lost. Full of the recklessness of the evening, while she was still weak with shock and laughter, he grasped her shoulders and kissed her. As he held her, she responded to him. When he released her, she slumped against him, weary of all pretence.

'We must see to the horse after such a gallop. Will you help me?'

She nodded, dumbly, so he drove to the stables where he unharnessed the horse. In spite of her finery, she helped him to walk the animal for a while and install her, rubbing her down and covering her with a blanket. But all the time they worked, she could not take her eyes off him. Her body betrayed her, inclining towards him, desperate to touch him again, desperate even for the passing brush of hand against hand, skin against skin. Her lips itched with longing to taste him. It felt like a sickness inside her. She thought she might die of wanting him.

When the horse was comfortable, and still she lingered at his side, he took her hand, gently.

'Marianna, I know where we can go. Where no-one will see us. We can be together for a while. If you wish.'

She hesitated.

'Please, Marianna.'

'Where?'

'The Old Steward's House. Come with me before I go mad. Before we both do.'

'Yes. All right, I'll come.'

They walked through the silent park, arm in arm. He carried a bunch of keys at his belt and opened the oak door. The grating of metal on metal seemed loud to her ears but the Old Steward's House was set well away from prying eyes. Moonlight flooded in at the windows, making another sweet-scented world of the old house as Danilo led her between barrels of cabbage and boxes of fruit: pears and apples, carefully and separately laid up in straw for the winter.

They conversed quietly, their voices ringing hollow in the old building.

'I used to come here when I was little. I had my own special place.'

'Where? No. Let me guess. Up above. A big wooden bench in the window.'

'Yes. Is it still there?'

'I knew it. I've seen it. I even found one or two books that you had left there, though the mice had chewed them. But your name was on one. Marianna Diduska. I'm afraid I took it for myself.'

'Did you?'

'I did.'

'I've never been here at night. I always thought it would be frightening in the dark, though I liked it well enough by day.'

'And is it frightening?'

'Not with you here. But it's supposed to be built with stones from the devil's castle you know. That's what they say in the village.'

'So I've heard. But they're only stones, when all's said and done. Let's go upstairs.'

They climbed the uneven steps to the upper storey and there, sure enough, they found the wooden bench where Marianna had loved to lie during those sad years following Antonina's death, reading and eating green apples.

She perched on the edge of it, suddenly shy of him. 'It brings it all back to me. Oh, I ran wild, you know. After my mother died.'

'You were wild before.'

'But not in the same way. I was just a wilful little girl. I thought every-one loved me. But afterwards ... '

'I remember your mother.'

'You shocked me so much when you told me that. That day in the meadow. Do you remember?'

'I've never forgotten. I remember every meeting between us two. I don't think I've forgotten a single moment.'

'Neither have I. But you see I didn't know, until then, that my mother had been visiting your mother. I knew she caught smallpox in the village but I didn't know ... it seemed so strange. Such an uncanny connection between us.'

'She was very kind to me.'

'She was a kind woman. And I was so unhappy to lose her, so miserable. I never saw her after she came back from your house that time, or at least only distantly. And then not at all. They said she was too ill. But it was to save us from getting the sickness I suppose. And perhaps because she was so disfigured by it.'

'It's a terrible sickness. Terrible.'

'They let me see her in her coffin. Her face was all powdered. It looked nothing like my mother. I learned afterwards that she lost the baby first and was in great pain from that too. What a cruel world it is, Danilo.'

'I'm so sorry that it should have been my mother's sickness ... '

'She would have visited whoever was sick. It was in her nature. She would have caught the disease anyway.'

Suddenly, he took off his long coat and spread it on the wooden bench beside her. 'I don't know!' she said. 'We shouldn't be doing this. It's wrong.'

'Don't be afraid of me. Take your cloak off. I'll keep you warm.'

He took her hands in his. He remembered Antonina, holding his hand, stroking his forehead. He remembered her tenderness.

Marianna tried to do as he suggested but her fingers were cold and clumsy on the fastenings, so he helped her and gently removed the cloak from her shoulders. 'So many clothes, as usual,' he said, with a wry smile.

She stood up so that, with slow decorum, he could help her to take off the russet evening dress. Then he laid it carefully to one side. One by one, very gently, he removed her petticoats until at last she stood, tall and graceful, in an embroidered slip and camisole. The camisole he also removed and fingered the stays beneath. She showed him how to unfasten them from the front.

He held the garment up and looked at it, shaking his head. 'Why do you women wear such instruments of torture?'

'None of my dresses would fit.'

He flung the corset aside. At last she stood naked before him in the moonlight, shivering. It was very cold in the old house.

'Lie down,' he said. 'Lie down and cover yourself with my coat.'

She lay down, feeling the pleasant friction of the wool against her skin. The garment was still warm with the warmth of his body. It smelled of Danilo. Soap and sweat. She inhaled deeply, dizzy with the scent of him.

In the moonlight she watched him as he stripped off shirt and trousers and his own undergarments. He smelled clean and sweet. She realised that he must have washed in preparation, planning or at least hoping for this. He came over and held the coat aside for a moment, staring at her intently. Then, as she began to shiver again, he pulled the big coat around them both, so that they were warmly rolled up in it together. As their bodies touched, he let out a great sigh.

'Oh, my darling, I thought I would never lie with you again.'

'I never thought I would let you.'

He braced himself above her and looked down into her face. 'Then why did you? Why have you?'

'Because I'm so empty without you. Because I want you all the time. Every minute of every day.'

'Then why wait for so long? What were you afraid of?'

'You're in a position to take advantage of me.'

He forced her legs gently apart with his knee. 'I am now.'

'Don't mock me. And don't hurt me.'

'When have I ever hurt you? When would I? You already trust me with your estate. Why won't you trust me with your body as well?'

He bent down and kissed her again. Beneath the coat he moved his head to kiss her breasts and then returned to her mouth, running the tip of his tongue around her lips, savouring them, biting at the soft, wet flesh. All at once, he moved on top of her, pushed her legs apart and thrust into her, trying to control himself, grasping her so tightly that – in spite of his promise and intention not to hurt her – his fingers left faint marks on her shoulders and breasts.

'Do you want me? Say you want me!'

The sensation was so sharp and sweet that it took her breath away. He paused, and she lay very still.

'Danielek. Please!'

'Then say you love me! Tell me that, at least. For it's true, Marianna. Isn't it? Isn't it?'

'I love you. You must know it. Of course I do!'

He felt her come to meet him and mould herself to him, her hands moving on his back. She could hear someone crying out and knew that it was herself. Then she heard nothing for she was all sensation, all one with him. He paused for the last time, braced above her body.

'Tell me you love me as much as I love you!'

She pulled him deep inside her. She felt herself convulse, her body racked with waves of intense pleasure as he moved with her, crying aloud, and she didn't know which was his body and which was hers, but she called to him, 'I love you. Oh God in heaven, Danielek! I love you so much.'

For a long time they lay together, their eyes closed, each feeling the nearness of the other with a yearning pleasure, all the more piquant because they knew that they could not stay like this till morning, but must soon separate. When she stirred, he groaned and said, 'Not yet. Oh not yet' and held her close, fiercely protective. 'I want to slow time down!' he whispered. 'I never want this night to end!'

They slept for a while and woke to make love again, but more gently this time. He lifted the coat that covered her and stared at her body, white in the moonlight, and then bent his head to her breasts, until he felt himself grow hard. Then he kissed her on the lips, moving inside her as he moved his tongue in her mouth and soon she came again, with a long sigh of satisfaction, and clung to him, kissing his face all over with tiny, butterfly kisses.

When they saw that the darkness was thinning, too soon, they rose reluctantly from the wooden bench and he dressed, helping her to put on her clothes. They negotiated the stone stairs and he locked the door behind them, but in the gloom of the pathway, between the old building and the manor house, he stopped and pulled her against him, holding her face fiercely between his two hands.

'Marianna – I don't want anything you can't give. I don't want anything but this. I'll be as respectful as you please in public and in private too, if that's what you wish. I'll take care of your estate as if it were my own. And I'll say nothing to anyone else. But please don't pretend that this never happened. Please.'

'I'll not deny you.' Her eyes were wide with desire. 'How could I? Only we must be careful. You have a wife and child. I'm free but you're not.'

It was true. He had almost forgotten about them. She felt him fumble in the dark, taking out the knife he always carried. She saw the flash of the blade and pulled away from him, frightened by his intensity. Quickly, before she had time to comprehend what he was about to do, he turned her hand palm up and, with a quick stroke of the knife, made a small cut there. She gasped and watched the dark blood well up. Still holding her hand, he cut his own and pressed it, palm to palm against hers. There was something so bizarre and savage and yet so sensuous about this gesture that she felt a renewed thrill of desire for him.

'There now,' he said. 'You have the prior claim. Your blood and mine. Together. Always together.'

At the door of the manor, he let her go, wondering what he would say to Halina, how he could explain his prolonged absence. But perhaps she would be asleep. And if not, he would say that he had found one of the horses sick in the stable and had stayed to care for it. She knew how much he loved the horses. She would never doubt him. There was no room in his mind for guilt.

In her bedroom, Marianna examined her body as best she could by candlelight, and was both ashamed and aroused to see the unmistakable signs of passion there: tiny bruises and even the marks of his teeth. She bound her cut hand with a piece of linen, slipped on a nightdress, and slid beneath the sheets, but lay sleepless until the first light of day, her head full of Danilo.

She thought, 'What have I done? What will become of us?'

With the sunrise she slept, only to dream of him. Her first waking thought was of her lover. But she could not find it in herself to regret one second of their lovemaking. While her mind fretted, her body exulted and blossomed. And already she craved more of him.

Chapter Twenty Nine

THROUGHOUT THAT FIRST WINTER, DANILO and Marianna carried on meeting in the Old Steward's House. He had never stopped loving her, and now she was helplessly caught up in her longing for him. They made love whenever and wherever they could. Marianna found it easy to slip out while her small household was asleep. There was no-one to question her, except perhaps Nusia, but Nusia was growing deaf and slept soundly in another part of the house. Essentially, she could do as she pleased.

It was harder for Danilo, but he was determined, lying awake until Halina's soft, even breathing told him that she was asleep, and then creeping out of the cottage as stealthily as a cat. Once, he came back to find her sitting bolt upright by candlelight, watching the door.

'Where have you been?' she asked. 'I was worried about you!'

'Miss Marianna's favourite mare had a touch of colic. Nothing serious, but I thought I'd check up on her.'

'Surely that isn't a job for the steward. Aren't you busy enough without going out in the night to tend to a sick horse, Danilo? That's a stable lad's job!'

He knew that she was angry for him, rather than with him but guilt made him irritable.

'I like to keep them all on their toes. Besides, if I want to go and look at a sick horse, I'll go. Who are you to question me?'

'I don't question you. But I worry about you,' she said. 'You have too much to do. Sometimes I think you'll take a brain fever, you have so much to think about.'

'That's hardly likely, sweetheart.' He had never been able to shift Halina's fixed belief that book work, reading and writing, were somehow dangerous to his health.

'It's not fair that you should take on menial tasks as well.'

'Menial tasks? The nursery maid is getting above herself! I'll do as I please, Halina, and I won't consult you first.'

'I didn't mean that.'

'I don't care what you meant. Go back to sleep. You'll be tired in the morning.'

He blew out the candle and got into bed. She turned over and immediately feigned sleep. After that half-hearted attempt, Halina didn't dare to question her husband further. The idea of his faithlessness didn't cross her mind. He never seemed to notice other women. Sometimes, she thought, he hardly noticed her. The notion of anything other than a strictly formal relationship between her husband and the lady of the house was so unthinkable that it would never have occurred to her.

Many of the Lisko servants were elderly or ageing. The coachman was practically crippled with rheumatism that winter, and instead of employing some young man to help him, Danilo contrived to drive his mistress to and from various social gatherings. This was unorthodox, but Marianna had always been headstrong and it was plain to everyone in her small circle that her steward was a favourite with her. That seemed to be as far as their speculation went. Perhaps they too couldn't conceive of the possibility of any real relationship between servant and mistress. From December onwards, the countryside was snowbound, and Danilo would come to collect her, driving a sleigh, a bed of close packed straw on runners with sheepskins thrown over it. On the way home, they would stop in the shelter of the forest and make love beneath a heap of furs, their breath making faint patterns on the darkness.

Summer made things at once easier and more difficult. Occasionally they would manage to meet out in the more remote fields, among the poppies and cornflowers, or in the warm, sweet-scented hush of the forests that fringed the estate, cushioned by layers of soft leaf mould beneath the trees. She came to rely on him, confiding all her worries to him in the intimacy of what was becoming a marriage in all but name. She could usually lift him out of the black moods that occasionally descended on him.

'I can't go on like this!' he would say. 'It will drive me mad.'

'Then you must just go mad, Danielek. But I shan't mind. I shan't even have you sent away. I shall lock you in my attic and make the best of things!'

She made him laugh, in spite of himself. 'How can you bear it?'

'I bear it because I must. And so must you. What other option do we have? And please don't take it out on Halina. It isn't her fault.'

'No. It's my fault. I should never have married her.'

'Not if you didn't love her. But perhaps you did. Perhaps you do.'

'I didn't love her. I only love you. You know that.'

'Then why, in God's name, did you marry her? I received a dozen offers and never submitted to any.'

'There was a child on the way.'

'And whose fault was that?'

'Don't do this to me. I feel bad enough already without you tormenting me.'

He was angry with himself and with Marianna for the edge of reproach in her voice, angry because he thought that she might be right. And yet what reason had there been for him to have any hopes of seeing her again?

'I'm sorry for Halina,' she said. 'Truly sorry. But I wish you hadn't married her. I know it's unreasonable and unfair of me, but I can't help it.'

'Has she been talking to you?'

'No. But I think you're very short on patience where she's concerned. You must be kinder to her for your son's sake. And if not for his sake, then for mine.'

For the whole month of July, the demands of the estate and a string of visitors from Milatyn and elsewhere made meeting, other than in the most formal sense, impossible. Danilo's time was taken up with haymaking and then planning for the various harvests, as well as autumn sowings and the coming hunting season. He was edgy and preoccupied. Last year, two stacks of damp hay had overheated and ignited, a big loss to the estate for which he blamed himself. The redcurrants and raspberries were, as usual, ripening far too fast and must be sold quickly or not at all. Danilo seemed to be locked in endless haggling with middlemen in the nearby town of Yarychev.

Unlike many stewards, Danilo flatly refused to take advantage of his mistress and make some money on the side. Halina knew it and reproached him for it. She saw no harm in making a bit extra to put aside for winter.

'After all,' she remarked, 'It isn't really dishonesty, Danilo. Everybody does it. You need to make something for yourself. Steward's perks. They all expect it, you know.'

'I don't know what you'd call that if not dishonesty. She's all alone and I won't cheat her.'

'Would she be so loyal to you, I wonder?'

She spoke under her breath, knowing better than to criticise Marianna openly to him. He pretended that he hadn't heard, but it rankled with him. It struck him that Marianna herself probably believed he cheated a little. Halina was right. Maybe she expected it. All the same, he wouldn't do it.

During this time of separation, his resentment against his mistress grew in proportion to his desire to make love to her. It didn't matter that circumstances had hampered them at every turn. He found himself blaming her for the accident of her birth, for allowing him a glimpse of heaven, only to neglect him. One day, when he came to her sitting room for their usual formal discussion, he barred the door with the fragile golden chair, seized her by the arms and smothered her with kisses. Then he forced her down onto the couch, knelt in front of her and buried his face in her lap.

'No, Danilo! No!' She slapped his head, and tried to push him away but he only groaned and held her closer. 'What are you thinking of? Somebody could come in at any moment.'

She continued to fend him off until he retreated. She sat on the couch, glaring at him, fanning herself with her hand. It was very warm in the room. He stood back, glowering, by the door.

'All right, all right. But I'll go mad if I can't love you soon. It's been weeks, Marianna. All I've seen has been the back of your head as you walk off into the distance with a party of ladies and gentlemen.'

'What else could I do? The house has been full of visitors. I didn't dare to slip out at night. Somebody might have heard me. My reputation would be in ruins.'

'Well they've all gone now, haven't they?'

'My brother-in-law is coming here tomorrow.'

He groaned. 'Oh no!'

'I'm very fond of Julian.'

'Then it's a mutual attraction because he surely loves you.'

She stared at him in surprise. He had spoken suddenly, out of a great depths of bitterness and resentment.

'What do you mean by that? Of course he loves me. We've known each other since we were children.'

'I mean he loves you. If he thought you would agree, he would ask you to marry him tomorrow. I see the way he looks at you. Halina used to look at me like that. But he's afraid of being rejected, like all the others, so he keeps his own counsel.'

'Danielek,' she said, in some alarm. 'How would you know all this?'

'I have eyes in my head, haven't I?' he replied, sulkily.

'You mean you've been watching him?'

'Not really. But I watch you. I watch you whenever I can, Marianna. Not to spy on you. I don't mean that.' He sighed. 'It's just that I can't help myself. Sometimes it means I must watch other people too. Julian for one. The way he dances attendance on you whenever he's here.'

'I do believe you're jealous of him,' she said.

He had gone over to stand by the tiled stove and now she came up behind him, her face alight with a kind of perverse pleasure. She tried to slip her arms around him but he turned and seized her wrists.

'Of course I'm jealous! Don't mock me! And don't flirt with me! I won't have it, Marianna. I won't be made a fool of. I can't bear this. If I thought there really was anything between you and Julian I would pack my bags and be gone from here right now. You talk about your reputation but what about mine? What about my wife and child? What would happen to them if we were ever discovered?'

She twisted out of his grasp and watched him warily, massaging her wrists.

'Oh yes,' she said. 'Your wife. While I couldn't get you out of my mind, all that time at Milatyn, there you were courting your Halka. I expect she does exactly as she's told. I suppose she treats you like some sort of God. She's just the type. Well don't expect the same from me.'

'She's a good woman!' he cried, stung into defending Halina.

'A good woman! I hope nobody ever calls me that!'

'You needn't worry. They won't.'

'Well, maybe you've given her a little happiness. Which is more than you've given me,' she said, furiously. 'But don't expect me to arrange my whole life to suit you, Mr Bandura. Don't expect to have your cake and eat it. A wife and a good position and a high-born mistress degrading herself by running after you as well.'

She would have gone on, but he left the room, his face cloudy with rage. She sat down breathlessly, alarmed at herself and yet curiously elated at having been able to provoke such an extreme reaction in him.

As she became calmer, she became anxious about him. She had been unkind and unfair. Might he take her at her word and leave? That afternoon, she walked through the park, taking Zofia with her, but she could find no sign of Danilo. When she arrived at his house, she recognised the heavy scent of raspberry conserve drifting out of doors and windows.

'Hello!' she called out tentatively, and was rewarded a few seconds later by the sight of Halina, rushing onto the veranda, brushing persistent wasps aside and trying to dry her hands on an apron that was sticky with smears of new jam.

'My lady!' cried Halina, curtseying and smiling in a confusion of welcome.

Pavel stood in the doorway and Zofia skipped up to him and planted a kiss on his cheek.

'We're making confiture,' said Pavel, importantly.

'Lovely,' said Zofia. 'Can we have some? mama, can we stay and eat raspberries?'

The two women gazed at each other, the one hesitant and the other painfully shy.

'My lady, would you care to come in? Perhaps you and the little girl would take some cordial.'

'That would be very kind of you, Halina. But I don't want to interrupt your work.'

'No. No. We've almost finished. I expect they'll be busy in the kitchens at the big house too. There are so many raspberries and all ripe together. I've promised to come up and help. That's why I thought I'd get this made today.'

'I'm sure there'll be plenty for you to do. My little girl's very fond of raspberries. I expect Pavel is too.'

Halina poured out fruit cordial and fetched some small sweet yeast cakes and set them out on a cane table on the veranda, begging Marianna to sit down. Zofia and Pavel were already sharing a bowl of fragrant raspberries on the kitchen table, squabbling occasionally over the larger and more luscious fruits. Marianna motioned to the other chair.

'Do sit down, Halina. You look so tired.'

'Well, if the lady permits.'

'I do permit. Sit down and keep me company.'

Until now, her dealings with Halina had been of the most formal kind. She had deliberately kept them that way. She had taken Halina at Nusia's valuation. 'A little mouse'. But this was a pleasant enough mouse, she thought, gazing at her across the table. And a pretty one. The young woman was dainty, with a smear of jam on her cheeks and kindly hazel eyes. She glanced in through the cottage door every now and then, to check that all was well with the two children.

Halina permitted herself the occasional sideways glance at Marianna. She had always been nervous of the tall young woman with the abrupt, almost masculine manner, and had admired her husband's fearlessness when it came to his alarming employer. On the few occasions when she had caught a glimpse of them deep in conversation or even laughing together, it seemed to her that they treated each other very much as equals. But then everyone knew how well Danilo did his job.

As if reading her thoughts, Marianna ventured, 'I wanted to speak to your husband. On estate business. When do you expect him home?'

'I don't know, my lady. I haven't seen him all day. I think he went to discuss something with the miller. He seemed angry about something. They always quarrel, those two.'

'The miller is very independent. Like his father before him, I believe.'

'I believe so.'

'Perhaps you could tell him I want to see him.'

'Is there some problem?' Halina looked worried.

'Not at all. It isn't a matter of any great urgency. Tomorrow will do.'

'I'll tell him.'

The children emerged from the house, mouths stained with raspberry juice, and began to play a complicated game with small stones on the pathway.

Marianna watched the two dark heads so close together for a moment. Young children, she thought, went through a whole series of changes in appearance, so that from time to time you could look at them and see an unmistakeable family resemblance that was not there even a month earlier. Looking at the two of them now, it seemed impossible for anyone not to notice how closely they resembled each other. Pavel might be smaller and stockier than Zofia, but their eyes were the same shade of brown, and there was something about the tilt of each chin, the texture of the hair, the dark brows and the determined expression on each little face that was all Danilo. How could Halina not see it?

'Ah, he is so like his father!' said Halina, complacently. 'And the little girl is so very like you, my lady. Such a pretty child. No wonder our boy is so fond of her. He talks about her so much. Sometimes he tells me that he would like to be Zoshka. Not to be like her, but to *be* her!'

'What strange things they say!' Marianna forced a smile and stood up. 'We must be going. I'll let you get back to your jam making.' She hesitated on the veranda. 'Halina, are you happy here? At Lisko. You don't miss Banunin?'

'No, my lady. How could I? I have my husband and child. I can still go back and see my friends. What more could I want?'

'And is he kind to you, your husband?'

'Why – yes!' Did Marianna hear a slight hesitation or did she only imagine it? 'Our son is the apple of his eye. It's only that – well I sometimes think that I'm a bit dull for Danilo. He's so clever. He's bound to get impatient with me, isn't he?'

'Impatient? Why?'

'I do my best for him. But I can't really talk to him about the estate. Not properly. Whenever I say what I think, it sounds silly. So I shouldn't expect him to confide in me, should I? I keep things nice for him. I make him comfortable. You can see that, can't you, my lady?'

Marianna was taken aback to find her throat constricted as she looked at Halina's eager face. She bit her lip. Marianna's conscience was not easily roused but guilt, an unfamiliar emotion, suddenly nipped at her like a tiresome insect.

She said, 'Halina ...'

'Yes, my lady?'

'He doesn't hurt you, does her? He isn't cruel to you in any way?'

Halina laughed. 'Men are always a little thoughtless, aren't they? They don't know any better. But he doesn't beat me. No. Never. He's not that kind of man. And he's always patient with Pavel. He's a good husband. He takes good care of us. Both of us.'

'I'm very glad to hear it.'

Confused, Marianna called to Zofia and left, thanking Halina again for her hospitality. As they walked across the park, she released Zofia's hand and let her run ahead, fruitlessly chasing butterflies across the grass. The enormity of what she was doing came over her. She thought of the neat interior: the fruit piled high on a platter, the floor clearly scrubbed every day, the intricate cut-out pictures with which Halina had brightened the walls, the flowers, the woven blankets, the painted chest. It was, she thought, as though Halina played at houses every day, keeping things nice for Danilo. With the guilt and the pity came – all unexpectedly – a sharp pang of jealousy.

She thought, I would have liked to do that, to have made a home for him. To have him coming home to me each day. To wake up with him beside me in the night. Something so simple. Why could I not have done that? Oh it isn't fair!

And then, she thought, But it isn't fair to her either. She's a nice woman. I'll have to put a stop to this. I'll have to put an end to this folly.'

At the house, she handed Zofia over to her nursemaid and waited for Danilo, but he didn't come. The sun slipped down the sky. She went to play with the child for an hour, leaving instructions that if her steward came to the house she wanted to see him. She expected every footstep in the corridor to be word of his arrival, but Zofia's bedtime came and still there was no sign of him. Dinner was served, but she was quite unable to eat it. When the dishes were cleared, she slipped on a shawl and walked down to the stables in the cool of the evening, but there she found only two stable lads making the horses comfortable for the night, going about their work with a song that they quickly hushed when they saw her.

She shook her head. 'Don't stop,' she told them, and when they hesitated, 'Please sing. I like to hear your music.'

They took up the song again but they were obviously embarrassed by her presence and she withdrew. There was no sign of Danilo. She walked home by a circuitous route through the parkland, through the orchards and the rose garden, still in heavily perfumed bloom. At last, she sought her own sitting room, called for a lamp and sat down to read, but she couldn't concentrate and presently she extinguished all but one candle and sat by the open window, watching the swift shadows of bats, like night time swallows, chasing insects across the grass.

Time passed.

He'll be in bed by now, she thought. He hasn't come, just to punish me. Oh it's impossible. But perhaps he's gone away! Perhaps he's gone altogether! And what will I do if he has? What will I do without him?

Nusia, who would have lectured her about the dangers of the chill night air, 'pure poison,' she called it, had long since gone to bed. The servants were all asleep and the whole house was quiet. She counted the bustling chimes of the clock up to twelve, sighed, closed the window and decided that she too should go to bed.

She was already in her white nightdress when it dawned on her that she had eaten little at dinner and now, Danilo or no, she was very hungry. She thought about getting into bed, trying to sleep and waiting for breakfast, but sleep seemed a long way off and why should she not raid her own larder if she wanted to? There was no Ma'amselle Jeanne to stop her now. She picked up her candle and went quietly through the house to the kitchens, listening to the familiar sounds as the old building settled itself around her for the night, the cooling timbers groaning quietly.

The fire was raked together, but a comforting red glow came from the stove. One of the house dogs, a shaggy terrier of uncertain parentage that had been taken in one winter by the cook, in much the same way as old Marysia had rescued Danilo, looked up from his bed beside the stove when she came in. He thumped his carrot of a tail once or twice on the floor, in acknowledgement of her presence, then yawned widely, curled up with his nose tucked into his tail and went back to sleep. In the gloom she almost walked into a muslin bag that was suspended from an upside down chair. The cook was straining raspberry juice into a china bowl, to be made into jelly the following day. Like Halina's house, the kitchen was heavily scented with the perfume of the fresh fruit mingling with the faint aroma of yeast cookery. The bread ovens had been in use earlier that day. There would be fresh bread and raspberry preserve for breakfast.

She lit an oil lamp from her candle and then, setting it to one side, foraged in the larder until she found buttermilk and a slice of sweet yeast cake with a crumbly, buttery topping, freshly baked that day. She remembered other, more carefree midnight feasts in this same kitchen. She remembered happy times with her cousin Teresa when they had been scolded by Nusia and the cook for leaving crumbs all over the floor.

'It only encourages the mice!' they had been told but still they had come down in the night in search of cake and confiture.

She was startled by the dog giving a low growl and moving to stand sentinel behind the kitchen door, staring up at it, hackles raised. This door was always locked at night but she saw that the big bolt had not quite been driven home.

Her heart pounding, she leapt to stand beside her fierce little companion, and was just stretching up her hand to push the bolt fully home when she saw the handle being turned. Was it some servant girl, coming home late from the village and hoping that the door had been forgotten? Could it possibly be thieves – or worse? She remembered Podlaski with a tremor of fear. She held her breath while whoever was outside pushed against the door, meeting the resistance of the lock. In the same moment that she lunged to push home the bolt, to make herself doubly secure, she heard a muffled curse from outside and saw the dog beside her let out a welcoming bark and wag his tail in instant recognition of the voice. She slid the bolt back, turned the key and flung the door open to admit Danilo. He almost fell into the kitchen in his surprise at seeing her.

'What on earth are you doing here?' she said.

'I could ask you the same question.'

'It's my own kitchen. I almost died of fright just now.'

'Not you.' He looked at the table with its cake and glass of milk.

'I was hungry and thirsty. I didn't eat any dinner.' She remembered their quarrel. 'And I was worried about you,' she confessed.

'Poor Marianna.' He spoke with heavy irony. She saw that he was not drunk, but that he had been drinking. He sat at the table, seized her glass and took a long draught of buttermilk, then rested his head on his hand as though it ached, which perhaps it did. 'I had this idea the door might be open,' he said, after a pause. Reassured by their presence, the dog turned around three times and lay down to sleep again with a sigh.

'And what if it had been open?'

'I wanted to find you. I would have come looking for you.'

'You forget yourself.'

'I can't forget you, that's for sure.'

'Where have you been anyway? I wanted to speak to you. I couldn't find you anywhere.'

'I had business with the miller. A quarrel if you must know. He's been trying to cheat the estate. He loses grain in the grinding. A sack here, a sack there. Now he knows that I know and it had better stop, because he's well paid. Got a small fortune stashed away there. But it won't stop will it? He'll just lose a bit less, that's all. Would you believe the bugger offered to give me a share if I turned a blind eye?'

'Is he so dishonest?' she asked.

'They all do it. You know they all do it, Marianna. Every single bloody one of them but me.'

There was a rueful note in his voice.

'I know. I do know. And I know you don't cheat me. I'm grateful for it and I trust you. I trust you more than I've ever trusted anyone.'

'That's something, then.'

'Can't we find another miller?'

'Not practical. He's his own man and the only one so close. We can't get rid of him. And besides, he's efficient.'

'Were you with him all day?'

'I didn't know you were looking for me. Do you want me to report to you at set hours? Is that it?'

She sat down opposite him. 'Don't be silly! I was at your house. Your wife was very kind. We talked.'

She caught a glimpse of surprise in his eyes, hostility perhaps. 'You talked to Halina? What about?'

'Nothing much. Just pleasantries. The children. You know the sort of thing.'

'Oh yes. The children.'

'They like each other. Our children.'

'What can we do about that?' He shrugged, miserably.

'You could find work somewhere else. You and Halina and little Pavel. I could find somewhere for you. You're such a good worker that you would have no difficulty in going somewhere else. Perhaps a better position. With more money. A better house for you and Halina. '

All afternoon she had walked around the park, becoming more and more worried that he might have left. Now she was asking him to go. She heard the words coming from her mouth with astonishment. He looked at her as though he could not believe what he was hearing. And yet he himself had ridden around the estate and walked about the village and at last he had sat in the tavern and thought, this can't go on. It's killing me. I must leave. I must leave this place and find work somewhere else.

She was crumbling cake on her plate. She looked young and vulnerable in the long white nightdress, with a shawl thrown around her shoulders.

'Do you mean this? Do you really want me to go away? Can you say that to my face and mean it?'

There was a long pause. The dog snored gently in the heat from the stove. The lamp hissed.

At last, she said slowly, 'Of course I don't want you to go. I just think it would be better for all of us if you did. Better for you. Better for Halina.'

'I'll be the judge of what's best for Halka.'

She shook her head, helplessly. Not knowing what else to do, she got up and moved towards the hall door. There was a crash as his hand and arm moved across the wooden table, sweeping glass, plate and cake crumbs to the floor.

'Marianna, don't make me leave you! For God's sake, don't send me away!'

She was halted by the pain in his voice.

'I'm not sending you away!'

He said, 'I didn't plan it like this. If you tell me to go, I'll go. But what am I to do? If I have to leave you, I'm nothing. What am I to do?'

She came back to him, picking her way carefully among the shards of broken glass. Her feet were bare and she cut herself. He lifted her in his arms, laid her down on the big wooden table and made love to her. As she cried out her pleasure, there was a crash and the bentwood chair with its jelly bag tumbled down, taking the bowl with it, breaking it in two and spilling a great pool of dark red juice on the flagstones beneath.

Miraculously, nobody woke. They cleared up the mess together. The little dog lapped at the sweet juice and the buttermilk, and licked up every last cake crumb, grateful for his unexpected meal; then he went back to sleep with his stomach taut and round. Danilo bathed and bound Marianna's cut foot with great tenderness and took the broken pieces of crockery and glass away with him, meaning to hide the evidence on the rubbish heap as he made his way home.

Chapter Thirty

NEITHER OF THEM SPOKE AGAIN of his leaving. Marianna was afraid of the consequences, for what had happened once could so easily happen again. Sometimes she would lie awake wondering what she would do if she found herself pregnant. She even discussed it with Danilo and for a period of days, weeks and sometimes months, they would make love less frequently. But sooner or later, desire would get the better of them and still nothing happened.

She remembered her illness after Zofia's birth and wondered if this was the cause of her failure to conceive. She had heard of such things. Finally, she accepted her situation with a mixture of relief tinged with just a little disappointment. But when it became clear that the risk of pregnancy was negligible, they began to be more daring. She would even allow him to come to her bedroom, when she was sure that the household slept.

Now, there were some on the estate who muttered that Mr Bandura was very familiar with the lady of the house.

'They're not at all like mistress and servant,' said the miller.

'He's young to be a steward, after all.' The sweep was slaking his sooty throat in the tavern. 'And because she's a woman, he's bound to feel over confident with her. It isn't the same as having to deal with a gentleman, is it?'

'Best not to let Miss Marianna hear you say that. She has a tongue like a knife when she chooses,' said the innkeeper.

'That's true,' admitted the miller. He had felt its sharpness on more than one occasion.

'And he does his honest best for the estate,' went on the innkeeper, who rather admired Danilo. 'No man could do more, even if he were working for himself. Even if the estate was his own.'

During these years, Lisko was thriving, while the country calmed down after the earlier upheavals. Danilo's own people whispered behind his back that he should be lending his energies to their cause rather than the upkeep of a Polish estate, but the two peoples were so intermingled that loyalties were often divided. Ukrainian had married Pole; the son of an old Polish family might now bear the same surname as an Orthodox priest, the one fiercely Polish, the other equally fiercely Ukrainian.

Julian was planning a move to Vienna to learn more about surgery. Floryan was proud of him. His only sadness was that his son had not yet found himself a wife but like Marianna, he sidestepped all serious attachments. One autumn, when he was visiting Lisko, Marianna challenged him with his indifference.

'I've invited a string of pretty girls, Julek. You're very nice to them but then you go home and leave them all pining for you. There must be at least one of them that takes your fancy!'

'I might say the same for you. Why haven't you re-married yet? It can't be because no man has asked you.'

'We weren't talking about me. I've had one marriage already. You haven't even begun yet.'

'And were you so disappointed in the first that you have to refuse all offers now?'

'There have been no offers. And if there were, I should refuse. I like my freedom too much.'

'Then you must surely allow me the same excuse.'

'But men always do have their freedom. They only expect their wives to give up what small independence they may have.'

'You're very bitter,' remarked Julian, rather sadly. They were walking arm in arm. 'Not all men want to impose their will on their wives, you know. Some men ask only for a partnership in marriage.'

'Is that how you feel, Julek?'

'It is. And if I thought that you ...'

She interrupted him. 'Let's talk about something else, my dear.'

He took his cue from her, changed the subject and began to talk about his future plans.

Each Sunday, Halina went to church and prayed that Danilo would love her. She found it hard to put into words what she meant, for he was never violent. There might be the occasional rough word when he had been drinking, but she considered this normal, for it was the way her father had treated her mother. What she found hard to bear was his indifference. Sometimes, he would pat her absentmindedly, as he patted a dog. And although they slept in the same bed, they almost never made love.

She kept their home immaculate, she loved their son, and she helped in the manor house whenever necessary. She was never ill, never complained. She only ever protested on Danilo's behalf, when she thought he had been used unfairly.

What else can I do? she thought, in desperation. What else can I do to make him care for me again?

She was certain that he *had* loved her, for a brief, blissful time. Halina had few women friends in the village and nobody she dared confide in. Nusia was too fond of Danilo to hear a word against him, and told her that she should count her blessings to have such a good man for a husband, but when Halina persisted in asking for advice, she came up with a plan.

'You could brighten yourself up a bit,' said Nusia, 'I've never been married myself, so never had to worry about such things. But you could try to make him notice you again.'

In secret, Halina sewed herself a new outfit, a fine striped skirt, a blouse and a waistcoat with flowers that she embroidered herself when Danilo was out of the house. She had saved a little money and when Danilo went to Yarychev, she contrived to go with him and bought herself a pair of almost new red leather boots, keeping her purchase hidden from him. Easter Sunday was the day she had chosen for the culmination of her plan. She dressed herself in her finery and, as a finishing touch, she wore the amber and silver necklace. Danilo had given it to her to mark their betrothal, when he had told her that she was prettier than any great lady.

As was the custom, she and Pavel took a basket of food to the church: eggs, bread and ham, to be blessed for Easter time. Danilo was sitting on the veranda when she emerged from the low door of the cottage and twirled around in front of him like a young, unmarried woman, so that he could see her petticoats.

He frowned. 'What have you done to yourself?'

'Do you like it? I wanted to look pretty for you.'

'You don't have to go to such lengths, Halka. You've got me. You're holding the proof of that by his grimy little hand there.'

He looked at his son with more affection than he looked at his wife. She had imagined him sweeping her into his arms and calling her *kochana*, darling, the way he used to. Instead she felt foolish and over-dressed. He came to her and lifted the necklace, holding the amber heart between finger and thumb, staring intently at it.

'You never wear this, Halina.'

'Not often, no. But I do treasure it, Danilo.'

'Do you?' He looked momentarily embarrassed. Then he said 'You should treasure it. Not just because I gave it to you. But because its owner was a very great lady.'

'You've never told me where it came from.'

'It's a private matter. It was given to me a long time ago, that's all. And now lent to you.'

'Lent?' She looked at him in dismay.

'By me.' He did a strange thing, then. He bent his head and kissed the heart. She felt his dark hair brushing her face as he did so. She wanted to reach out and touch him but didn't dare. Then he relinquished the necklace and turned away from her.

'Take good care of it. It's very precious to me.'

After Easter, Marianna realised that she had had no show of blood for two months, she was feeling sick in the mornings and her breasts were swelling. It was as though she had been moving through a dream from which she had now woken to find the world a greyer place than she had supposed. She put her hand on the small mound of her stomach and thought, 'Oh God in heaven. What will I do?'

Her mind lurched from one solution to another. Could she select a suitor from those young men who admired her, and achieve a swift marriage? Impossible. Most of her beaux had already found themselves wives and, in any case, she wanted none of them. Besides, the very thought of Danilo's reaction to such a course of action frightened her. What did the village women do, she wondered, if they found themselves with an unwanted pregnancy? And how could she find out without arousing too many suspicions. Was she brave enough to fall down the stairs, accidentally on purpose? And might she not kill herself in the process? Should she tell Danilo? Her mind buzzed around like a fly at a window and at last alighted on the one reliable point in her world. Maybe she could bring herself to tell Julian. Maybe he would help her.

Then she remembered that Julian was in Vienna. He had been at Milatyn for Easter but he would have gone back by now. She wrote to him. He replied promptly but he couldn't come to Lisko. Her letter had been intentionally casual. She couldn't commit such appalling secrets to paper and had meant to explain her predicament in person. He saw no reason to hurry. He was captivated by Vienna. The letter was full of enthusiasm, the words tumbling out onto the page. He had begun to dabble in politics. It was all fascinating. He would come to Lisko as soon as possible, though it might not be for a few months yet. Why didn't she visit him in Vienna instead? She was welcome to bring Zofia with her. Or failing that, he would see her at Milatyn, at Christmas.

Frustrated and angry, she paced up and down until, reverting to the old, wilful Marianna, she flung the letter away, threw herself on the bed, and cried into her pillow. Then she dried her eyes and hoped that her predicament would go away. Miscarriages often happened, didn't they? Perhaps her own body would save her.

For five months, Marianna managed to disguise her swelling waistline with an adroit combination of uncomfortably tight lacing and voluminous dresses. She told Nusia that she believed she was putting on weight and must let out her skirts accordingly. Nusia, who had always fancied her mistress too thin and too tightly laced anyway, thought nothing of it.

Marianna's morning sickness was not severe and she managed to hide that too, even from Nusia. She had put off her customary influx of summer visitors with the lame excuse that she was too busy with plans for new estate cottages to do any entertaining. If the aunts, uncles and cousins were put out, they could hardly descend on her uninvited. 'What does she have a steward for?' they wondered. The weather was unseasonably rainy and she found it easy to shun social contact, easy to linger about the house. Zofia and Nusia, who saw most of her, noticed least. Familiarity and, in Zofia's case, innocence, blinded them to her condition.

It was Danilo who aroused her from this dreamy, disbelieving state. Danilo, of course, who noticed. She had deliberately excluded him from her bed for as long as she could, but eventually, with Nusia away for the day, she didn't see how she could refuse him. As soon as he glimpsed her swollen belly, she saw the shock on his face.

'Oh, Marianna!'

'What's the matter?'

So confused were his emotions that he hardly trusted himself to speak. She stared up at him for a moment, then rolled over on the bed, pulling the covers over herself. He came to sit beside her but when he tried to touch her, she pulled away from him.

'It isn't true,' she said.

'Are you mad?'

'It can't be true. It can't be happening. It mustn't happen!'

'Are you going to deny this one, the way you denied Zoshka?'

'I don't know what you mean.'

'I mean that I know and you know that Zoshka is no more Stanislaw's child than this one will be. Why won't you admit it, Marianna? Even to yourself? Zofia is my daughter. Our daughter. And this ...' He pulled back the covers and laid his warm hand on her belly. 'This is our child too.'

She lay back, too exhausted to argue with him.

'Of course Zoshka's your daughter. She's the image of you and the image of her half brother, though nobody, not even your wife, seems able to see it.'

'I've always seen it. I look into her eyes and see myself mirrored there. Why would you never admit it to me?'

'I didn't dare. She must always believe herself to be a Yelitowska.'

'I agree. I don't want to upset Zoshka any more than you do. But why wouldn't you tell *me*? This has nothing to do with what she does or doesn't believe herself to be.'

'Because if once you were sure ...'

'What then?'

'You would have one more hold over me,' she said, shamefaced.

'Hold?' he repeated the word in amazement.

'Yes, hold. Power. You know all my secrets and I know yours. No – it's more than that. We *are* each other's secrets.'

'All the more reason for us to trust each other.'

'I want to trust you. And I do. I do. But all the same, we've built ourselves a prison made of lies. Sometimes when I'm with you, I think I'll die of loving you. But then another part of me gets frightened and wants to run away. Wherever I turn, there you are.' She closed her eyes. 'Without you, there's chaos. But with you, there's chaos as well. What are we to do?' She turned away from him. 'But that's silly. You're free. You can leave me. I could hardly lay the blame at your door, could I? You could just take Halina and Pavel and go.'

'You're talking nonsense. Where in the world would I go without you? What sort of man do you think I am, for Christ's sake? Do you think I'm a monster?'

He walked away from her to stare out of the window, punching one fist hard into the other palm. She closed her eyes again, locked into some private hell. The baby moved and turned anxiously inside her, as though aware of her distress. At last, Danilo took hold of himself with an effort. There must be some way out.

'Marianna,' he said. 'Can you not go away somewhere? Isn't that what ladies do in this situation? Couldn't you pretend that you're ill and need a change of climate? Go away somewhere where you're not known, have the child and then come back. Pretend that it belongs to some widowed relative. Is that not what sometimes happens?'

She said wearily, 'Oh yes, it happens in books. It happens in fairy tales. But I can't begin to imagine how I would arrange such a thing without the secret getting out. Or where I would go, for that matter!'

He sat down again and took her hand. 'Listen. Perhaps you don't need to go anywhere at all. Perhaps you can just stay here.'

'How can I possibly do that? It'll become so obvious!'

'You've hidden it well for a long time.'

'But now I grow larger every day.'

He couldn't suppress a smile. He would have kissed her hand but she pulled it away. 'This is serious!'

'I know. I know.'

They sat in silence for a while.

'Could it be managed?' she said at last. 'Here? But what about Zofia?'

'Couldn't she go to Milatyn? She loves it there. And they love her.'

'Maybe she could. Let me think about it. It might work. It has to work.'

She made her plans in secret, with only Danilo in her confidence, and then she sent for Nusia.

'Zofia is to go to Milatyn for a while. I'll join her later. We've planned it as a surprise for her.'

It was true enough that Zofia would be enchanted by the visit, though less pleased to find that her mother would be staying behind at Lisko.

'Shall I travel with the little one?' asked Nusia.

'No. It's a long journey for you and besides, I need you here. Grazyna can go in your stead. They'll be company for each other. And I'll send one of the grooms to keep them safe on the road.'

'Are you quite sure, my lamb?'

'Quite sure. Now, would you have Mr Bandura come to me? I have some important business to discuss with him.'

'Marianna, forgive me ...'

'Yes?'

'Are you well? For months now you've seemed ...' The older woman hesitated.

'What?'

'Not yourself, if you'll forgive my saying so. There are many illnesses that begin in this way. I think you should see a doctor.'

'I'll be seeing Julek at Christmas.'

'But could he not come sooner?'

'He's in Vienna. And I don't trust other doctors. Whatever is wrong with me will keep till then. It's nothing serious.'

'Well, if you're sure, I'll send for Mr Bandura. But it's my belief you do too much worrying about the estate. That's what you pay him for. Not that he doesn't make a good job of it. But all the more reason why you don't need to worry.'

She had lied. The problem wouldn't keep. It was growing bigger by the day. Soon it threatened to rend her in two.

When Danilo came in, she told him her plans.

'I've arranged for Zofia and her nursemaid to go to Milatyn. That leaves Nusia, the cook, and a few more.

She counted them off on her fingers. 'Now, Jacek has been very poorly and is confined to his cottage. I had thought of pensioning him off, which I will do immediately, and pay for him and his wife to go to the mountains for a little while, for the good of his health. I was planning to replace him but I won't do that. At least not yet. So that's one problem solved.'

'You'll provide for him after that?'

'Of course. And I need hardly see cook. Nusia can deal with her and the maids. Danilo, I'm going to be ill. Very ill. It will be a peculiarly debilitating illness that means I have to stay in the house, perhaps even in my room.'

He shook his head. 'This is madness. People will call on you.'

'It was your suggestion.'

'I know. But I hadn't thought it through!'

'They may call all they like, but they shan't see me. And after all, it won't be for very long now. I've hidden this well.'

'That's true.'

Well corseted as she was, and wearing carefully chosen gowns, her pregnancy wasn't too obvious.

'There is nowhere else that I can be as secluded as this. This is my own place. I can order everything as I choose.'

'They'll get word at Milatyn. They'll come to see you.'

'No. Zofia will be at Milatyn and my letters to her will be full of good news.'

'You've planned everything.'

'In desperation.'

'Who will you tell? You can't manage alone.'

'Only one other. I shall have to tell Nusia.'

'She must have noticed!'

'She's noticed that I'm not well, but clothes can make a good disguise if you're careful. I have been very careful. And her eyesight isn't what it was.'

'Marianna, the shock will kill her.'

'Nonsense. She won't be shocked. Disappointed, yes. But she's lived too long and seen too much to be really shocked.'

He said slowly, 'I suppose all this might work. There'll be talk of course, but I can quash most of that if I have a mind to. You're suffering from some kind of exhaustion.'

She laughed, though she was close to tears. 'That's true enough, anyway. But I'll be well by Christmas. I'll go to Milatyn for Christmas and then things will be as they were.'

'Not quite. Aren't you forgetting something?'

'I don't think so.'

'For God's sake! What will you do ...?' He hesitated. 'What about ...?'

'No, I haven't forgotten the baby.'

'Then how are you going to explain it?'

'I said I would tell only one other. Nusia. But *you* must also tell somebody else. You must tell your wife. The baby will live with you and Halina.'

He shook his head slowly.

'Are you mad? How can I tell her? *What* can I tell her?'

'Oh not the complete truth. I may be foolish, but I'm not completely mad. Don't worry, Danielek. You needn't come into it at all, or only insofar as I've found it necessary to confide in you. You can tell her what you like about me. Tell her that the child is the product of my illicit liaison with the son of some nobleman. She'll believe you. In fact I think she'll find that far more credible than the truth. And if you tell her to be silent on the subject, she'll obey you without question. She's so loyal, your little Halka.'

'She is,' he murmured. 'She is! Besides, she would love to have another child. She has often said so. Only none came. Not for us.'

'Then you must tell more lies. I'm sorry but it can't be helped. You must explain in the village that the baby is the illegitimate offspring of some distant cousin of your own. They will think Halina a saint for taking in such a child, and some of them may speculate as to the part you might have played, but that will do you no harm at all. Men are allowed such indiscretions. But they will scarcely connect the child with me. Not then. Not if you can spin a good enough tale for them.'

He was astonished by her boldness. Desperation had made her even more daring than usual. He didn't know what to say, knew that he ought to argue but could think of no way of doing so. The plan might work. Besides, there was no alternative.

'I knew you would agree.'

'You take my breath away. Are you so indifferent that you can imagine handing your child over? This isn't some doll, Marianna. This will be a baby. Your son or daughter.'

She had been standing but she sank down suddenly on the couch. When he came to sit beside her, she leant on him with her arms around him and her face against his shoulder.

She said, 'Our baby. Ours. Who else could I leave our child with, but its own father? Anything else would kill me.'

He saw that she was giving him the ultimate gift, that she was making the greatest sacrifice of her life.

'Yes' he agreed. 'Yes, I can see that it's the only way. And who knows? Maybe it'll work.'

Chapter Thirty One

MARIANNA SENT ZOFIA TO MILATYN and then retired from public life. There was no easy way of breaking the news to Nusia, so she simply sat her down and came right out with it.

'I'm going to have a baby.'

Nusia covered her face with her apron and would not be comforted for a long time. 'This would have killed your poor mother.'

'Then perhaps it's just as well that my mother isn't here.'

Nusia stopped crying and lowered the apron from her face, staring at her darling in stunned disbelief.

'All these years, I've loved you and excused you, Marianna. But you seem so callous.'

'I'm desperate. You must keep this a secret. No-one at Milatyn must know. Do you hear me?'

'But surely others will have to know!'

When Marianna told Nusia of her plan to give birth in secret and give the baby into the care of Halina and Danilo, she began to sob all over again.

'Oh Lord! That such a thing should happen to a Diduski. To be raised among peasants. To be given into the care of a Ukrainian peasant. I can't bear it!'

'A Ukrainian and a Pole. Halina is Polish. It's the only way.'

'But what of the father's family? Can they not help? Is there no question of marriage, my darling?'

'No. There is absolutely no question of marriage.'

'Won't you tell me who it is? Who has taken advantage of you like this? Something could be done, surely.'

'Nobody took advantage of me. It was as much my fault as his. And no. I can't tell you, Nusia.'

And I suppose he doesn't know either, whoever he is, the wretch. I suppose he gets off scot free, as men usually do.'

Marianna let Nusia ramble on in this vein for some time, finding it easier to allow her to spend her anger on abusing the unknown father of her child than focussing blame on herself. She felt ragged and strange, as though at any moment her feelings might spill over and engulf her.

'So Mr Bandura knows?'

'He noticed something. I had to tell him.'

'Which is more than I did! How could you keep this from me for so long, Marianna?'

'We don't always look at people properly when we see them every day, do we? But I had to tell him. I need him. And Halina.'

'Dear God. That it should come to this. That you should have to confide in your servants.'

'He and Halina will welcome an addition to their family. He hasn't spoken to her yet, but he will. She'll do as he says. They'll make up a story for the village. And I think she'll love the child.'

'Maybe she will. But I still say it isn't right. They'll have such a hold over you, Marianna. It's so dangerous to give your servants so much power over you.'

'He isn't a servant. And I trust him with my life.'

'He's a Ukrainian servant. It scares me.'

'I know my grandfather sowed a great many wild oats. There are plenty of unknown Diduskis in this neighbourhood. One more won't make any difference.'

Nusia began to cry again. Marianna put her arms around her and kissed her. 'Danilo and Halina will keep the secret. No-one else need know. I made a mistake. I'm sorry. But I'm paying for it now, believe me. I'll go on paying for it all my life.'

Danilo put off raising the matter with his wife until events forced his hand. The cook was away from the house on a family visit and Nusia was in the kitchen when the violent ringing of the bell summoned her to her mistress's room. Marianna was bent double, panting, clutching at the wooden bed-rail, her knuckles white.

'Nunu. It's started. But it's too early.'

'A few weeks too soon,' said Nusia. 'But that may not matter. I have known many an eight month child survive and grow strong. Seven months even, with care!'

The thought entered her head that it might be better if this child did not survive, but she immediately crossed herself to ask pardon for the sin. It was none of the child's fault, after all.

'How long have you had the pains?'

'About two hours. Getting worse.'

'You should have called for me sooner.'

'Why? There's nothing to be done yet. And I thought it might be a false alarm.'

Nusia tried to persuade Marianna to lie down on her bed, but she would have none of it. Instead, she walked about between contractions and then bent over whatever was in her way, her face creased with the pains until they subsided. But there were still long intervals between them. Nusia shooed the two maids who had been helping her in the kitchen out of the house, sending them down to the dairy. Then she brought bread and milk, and encouraged Marianna to eat.

'Those who labour must sustain themselves. Your waters haven't broken yet, have they?'

'No, and with Zoshka that happened first.'

She slumped in a chair. 'I don't feel right. Something's wrong. It doesn't feel like last time at all. It doesn't feel right.'

Nusia felt a cold worm of fear shift inside her own belly. 'All women are afraid.'

'No. Not like this.'

'You've felt the baby move?'

'Yes. Yes, but that's it. That didn't feel right either. Not these last few weeks. Oh I can't explain it properly.'

Nusia made Marianna sit on the bed. Surreptitiously, she took a sip of the French brandy that she had brought, in case it should be needed to revive the mother later. She knew from experience that while such instincts could often be put down to the natural fears of women in labour, sometimes they proved to be all too horribly correct. She had seen a number of women die in childbirth or soon after.

She made Marianna lie on the bed, propping her up with pillows, and then she examined her as she had seen Agnieszka, the village midwife, examine other pregnant women. To be sure, there was something a little odd about the swelling of Marianna's belly. The bump was evidently higher on one side than on the other, and when she felt for the baby's head, she could not distinguish it.

At first, she thought that this was a breech presentation, that the baby was coming feet first, but she herself had delivered one breech baby successfully, and she had watched Agnieszka do the same, by dint of making the mother squat down on the floor and letting, as Agnieszka put it, 'the pull of the good earth do its work and then a little gentle help afterwards.'

This felt different.

'The child is lying across the opening,' she thought, in a panic. 'The shoulder will come first. *And I don't know what to do!*'

Marianna was seized by another contraction. She clutched at Nusia's arm, and bit her lip until it was over.

Once.

Nusia had seen it happen once only with a young girl in the village and Agnieszka in attendance. She felt sick. Turning her back on Marianna, she swallowed another measure of spirits. It had been a young girl, she remembered, delicate as a little bird. In labour with her first baby. Ashka had been her name and her husband had been Jan, who worked for the miller.

The labour had gone on and on, hour after hour, until the girl was shrieking in pain. The men outside could hear her, and her husband had tried to come in, but had been prevented by his fellows. This was women's work. Leave it to the women. She remembered seeing and recognising, not the head, nor the feet, but the tiny shoulder of the infant, knocking against a door that could not grant it admittance, no matter how hard the mother fought. They had bathed the girl's head and given her infusions of strengthening herbs, but it was plain that even the midwife had exhausted her fund of knowledge, and Nusia didn't know what to do either.

She recalled the birth in terrible detail, the picture replaying itself before her eyes: the rupture of the membranes and the water seeping out, the tiny arm that had somehow fought its way through, becoming blue and swollen, the hellish contractions that never seemed to stop until, with a great convulsion, the girl's screams ceased and she fell back on the pillow, unconscious, with the infant dead inside her. Ashka very soon followed her child, never regaining sufficient consciousness to bid her devastated husband goodbye.

Agnieszka had said, 'If the baby is lying across the opening, then say your prayers, Nusia, for there is nothing you can do, and only a miracle will save mother and child.'

Nusia turned to look at Marianna who was pale to the lips, with sweat breaking out on her brow. She smoothed back the tangled hair. Still the waters had not broken. She thought, 'What shall I do? What shall I do?'

'Mr Julek might know what to do, but he's in Vienna and that's no help to us, my darling, is it?'

She thought of sending for Agnieszka anyway, but what good would that do? Agnieszka would only pray and make herbal infusions. Still Marianna laboured. And at last, a despairing cry was forced from her, a long howl like an animal in pain. She roused herself.

'I'm going to die. Help me. Oh for the love of God help me! Do something to help me, Nusia, please!'

She flung herself back on the bed and pulled up her nightdress.

'Nusia, can you see the baby's head? I labour and labour and nothing happens. What can you see?'

Despairingly, Nusia bent down and palpated the swollen belly, aware as she did so of the unusual configuration of the baby beneath. The cervix was dilated and she could see something, but her eyes were so blinded by tears that she could not make it out.

Marianna's contractions were coming more frequently, but still the waters had not burst. 'Open the window, Nusia. Let me breathe!' she cried.

Terrified of the effects of the chilly evening air, but anxious to help, Nusia opened the window. As she did so, another contraction seized Marianna and that dreadful animal howl hung, quivering, in the air.

Chapter Thirty Two

OUTSIDE THE HOUSE, DANILO HAD been hesitating, staring at Marianna's window. He knew that the cook was away and he had seen nothing of Marianna or Nusia. The house looked dead and empty. All day, he had gone about his business with a gnawing worry inside him. As always, when he was angry or distressed, he had gone to his beloved horses. He had begun to groom his favourite mare, one of the trotting horses, and that was when it happened. While he was standing with his head pressed against the warm flank of the beast, trying hard to clear his mind of all other thoughts save the job in hand, he had heard it: a terrible cry, full of fear and torment that invaded his head and his heart, making him flinch and cover his eyes with his hands. The mare shifted uneasily, sensing his alarm.

After a moment, he raised his head and stared at his trembling fingers in the gloom. He thought 'was that real?' He wondered if it was some wild animal, caught in a trap out in the forest perhaps. He collared a passing stable lad. 'Hey you! Did you hear that noise just then?'

'What noise, sir?'

'A cry. Like an animal in pain.'

The young man shook his head. 'No, sir. I heard nothing.'

Danilo let him go and carried on with his grooming for a few moments. But he couldn't settle. Driven by instinct rather than any more rational feeling, he began to make his way up to the house. There he found the doors bolted against him. He walked around the house and stood looking at Marianna's window.

For a while, all was quiet and he was on the point of leaving, for Halina would be expecting him, when the window was opened a little way and he heard it again: that same desolate cry that he had heard in the stables. But he could not have heard it in the stables. They were much too far away from the house. This time it drove him mad. He ran back to the front of the house and began to hammer wildly at the door, crying out, 'Let me in! Let me in!'

The maids had been sent away for the day. There was no-one to answer.

In her room, Marianna heard him. Nusia wrung her hands in desperation. 'Hush! It's Mr Bandura. He has heard you crying out!'

Nusia turned and saw a strange, eager light in Marianna's face. She had raised herself on one elbow.

'Go and speak to him. Let him in.'

'My dear Marianna, my darling, my lamb! How can you think of such a thing? What can he do to help?'

'I don't know. I only know that you must go and speak to him. Now!'

'I can't leave you alone.'

'I'll be all right for a little while. Please. If you never do anything else for me, do this one thing. He has never let me down. He won't let me down now. Go and let him in and tell him ...' She faltered, then cried, 'For God's sake just go and tell him that I shall die!' in such a voice that Nusia fled the room. She rushed along corridors as fast as her legs would carry her and opened the door to admit Danilo.

He pushed her aside and headed towards Marianna's room with Nusia in pursuit, calling out, 'No, no, Mr Bandura. You mustn't go in!'

He hesitated just long enough for Nusia to catch up with him. She collapsed breathlessly into a chair. 'Oh, Mr Bandura!'

He grasped her hands. 'Tell me what's the matter. Quickly!'

'It's the mistress. She's in labour.'

'But it's too soon.'

'A few weeks. Yes. But that's not the problem.'

'Then what is? For Christ's sake, woman, tell me!'

A feeling had captured him that time was vital, that something must be done now. If not, it would be too late.

Nusia stumbled over her words. 'The baby is lying all wrong. Neither head first nor feet first. It's lying across the opening. I don't know what to do, Mr Bandura. She'll die. The child will die inside her and she'll die with it.'

Strangely, all his fear and panic left him. It was as though a cool hand had been laid across his forehead and he thought afterwards of Antonina's hand, soothing the boy he had once been. He released himself from Nusia's grasp.

'Let me go in to her.'

'You?' She was horrified, convention overriding her fear for her mistress. She opened her mouth to protest but he silenced her with a look.

'Do you want her to die?'

'I would give anything for her to live.'

'Then you must let me try.'

'You? What could you do? What do you know?'

'I've delivered a few hundred mares of their foals in my life so far.'

Now she was really shocked. 'Mares?'

'You've always said you trust me. Then trust me now.'

She was too old for this sort of thing. It wasn't fair of Marianna to inflict this on her. Her legs were giving way and now here was this Ukrainian upstart being rude to her, pushing her about. But he seemed so sure of himself.

'What can I do?'

'You can fetch me some oil from the kitchen.'

'Oil?'

'Yes. Clean oil of some sort. I don't care what it is, so long as it's clean. Even soft butter will do. Now, go! Quickly!'

He found Marianna crouching on the bed at the bitter end of a contraction. Her vulnerability and the terror in her eyes made his heart contract too with fear and love, but he had himself well under control now.

'Help me, Danilo!'

'I will, I will. But you must do exactly as I say.'

He looked around, found her jug and bowl and washed his hands as best he could, scrubbing at them with the soap, rinsing them in more cold water. Then he made her lie down with her knees in the air. She tried to object, asking for Nusia, but he said, 'Nusia is fetching something for me.'

'This isn't right.'

'Why not?' he asked gently. 'This is my child, our child. Remember how we made it?'

She fell silent and let him do as he wished. He felt her belly and then slipped his hand between her legs. 'Have your waters gone yet?'

She shook her head.

'That's good. And these contractions? How often do they come?'

'Every few minutes now.'

He frowned. 'Not long. Well, it will have to do.'

Nusia came into the room, carrying a bowl of fresh butter. It had been set before the fire to melt for baking and it was soft and oily.

'Perfect,' he said, glancing at it briefly. 'Now go! You don't need to see this. It's better if you don't.'

Nusia looked at her mistress.

'For the love of God, do as he says!' Marianna whispered.

'I'll be outside the door. Call me if you need anything.'

He waited until Nusia had left the room, then he lay Marianna back on the heaped pillows and felt her abdomen carefully, until he thought he had located the head, back and legs of the child, lying awkwardly across the opening. He waited for the next contraction, letting her hold him as the pain gripped her, soothing her, rubbing her back, mopping her brow. Then he poured a large glass of the brandy that Nusia had left in the room and made her drink.

'All of it. This will hurt.'

'It's already hurting,' she gasped, but he smiled grimly.

'This will hurt much more. So drink. It'll take the edge off the pain. The baby is lying all wrong. It's not even coming feet first. We might manage that. In fact we *will* manage it quite soon. But it's lying across you now, with its shoulder in the opening. That's why Nusia didn't know what to do. That's why she's so scared.'

'Oh dear God!'

'There's only one way and that's to turn it. I'm going to have to put my hand inside you. I've done it before, with a mare and her foal. I have to try to find the foot and bring it out a little way. Then things may go better.'

He made her drink a few more big draughts of brandy. He was afraid of tearing her, inside and out. He was afraid of damaging the child in some terrible way. But he must try. It would help, he knew instinctively, that the waters were still in place, for that would cushion both herself and the child somewhat. Afterwards it wouldn't matter. He made her lie down with her knees well apart.

'Try to calm yourself. I know it's hard, but try to breathe slowly. If a contraction begins I'll have to stop.'

He coated his hand and arm with quantities of soft butter. Then, as carefully as he could, holding his breath, he reached his hand, palm down, into her body, feeling the body of the child beneath it. He had it firmly fixed in his mind that the feet were to the left, the head to the right. Then he felt another contraction beginning and withdrew as smoothly as he could. He waited until it was by, but it was a small one, which was just as well. He was afraid of the waters seeping out before he could do his work.

As soon as the contraction was over, he began again, feeling carefully inside her body, afraid of rupturing the delicate organs there. It was a strange feeling. He had lain within her body so often, but this was different. Intrusive. Invasive.

He closed his eyes and thought, 'She is my sorrel mare. And this is my little foal. I must go carefully and not injure either of them.'

She lay fearfully beneath his hand. She felt blind and mute with pain, but she trusted him.

He had the unmistakeable sensation of a tiny foot in his hand, and he brought this gently through her cervix and down, aware of the intense pain he was causing, aware that she was grunting with deep, dreadful noises, but intent only on what he was touching, seeing nothing. He reached up until his other hand was on top of her abdomen and, feeling for the head beneath the skin, he pushed it gently but firmly upwards.

He felt a rush of warm fluid on his hand. Marianna was aware of the liquid leaving her. The next contraction was much stronger and he had no time to congratulate himself. He saw that the birth would come soon. She was almost unconscious and he dashed water on her face.

She gasped, 'I want to die. Let me die and then the pain will stop.'

'You're not going to die. I won't let you. You're going to live and give birth to this child.' He swung her round, so that she was sitting on the edge of the bed. 'Come on. You can help yourself now. Yourself and the baby.'

She summoned strength from some remote part of herself, from her mind rather than her body, perhaps most of all from him. She grasped his shoulders and pushed. He saw the feet and the buttocks come down and gently pulled on a loop of the cord and waited. Would she be able to do it or must he intervene again? She was very tired. But the weight of the buttocks themselves brought the shoulders down. Her womb contracted again and she pushed. The hips were slippery, and he took one of a pile of linen towels that Nusia had left there and wrapped it around the baby to assist him. One shoulder came out and he raised the child up a little, to allow the other shoulder to be born.

At last, he helped the child to disengage its head from its mother's body. He was aware of the delicacy of the neck. He had come this far and must make no mistakes now.

He said, 'Breathe – breathe the baby into the world, Marianna!' and she breathed deeply and regularly and his child was born.

She heard it crying, saw it in his arms and, exhausted as she was, held out her own.

'It's a girl,' he said. 'Another little girl.'

He was weeping. He put the child into her arms while, half blinded by his own tears, he dealt with the afterbirth.

The baby was small, with a tuft of damp, black hair. She was battered from her unconventional journey into the world but pink and healthy. She seemed to him to be the most beautiful thing he had ever seen or touched.

Nusia, hearing the cry of the infant with astonished disbelief, came hurrying into the room to find the child in its mother's arms and Danilo with his arms around both. She went to the kitchen in search of hot drinks, food, swaddling clothes for the baby. She didn't know what to say. She didn't know what to think. She thought of the tall dark man and the dark girl child, with dawning comprehension. She began to cry with weariness and gratitude.

After a while, she pulled herself together, went back into the room and bustled about, trying to make her mistress more comfortable, bending over the child with exclamations of delight. Then, she turned to look at him.

'Your wife will be wondering what has become of you, sir.'

'Yes, she will.'

'I could manage to walk as far as the stable and send a message with one of the lads to say that you had been detained. The walk might do me good.'

'That would be very kind of you.'

'And then you could stay here with my mistress until she falls asleep. There's no-one else in the house. You needn't fear discovery.'

'Are you sure'

'Mr Bandura, you need have no fears on that account.'

She left them alone together, casting one last glance back at the dark head of the child, tucked up close between its exhausted mother and the man she now knew to be its father.

Chapter Thirty Three

MARIANNA WOKE A LITTLE WHILE later to find Danilo still beside her, the baby curled up close. He had sung to her softly in Polish before she fell asleep:

'Once upon a time there was a princess,
And she lived in a house made of butter,
And the house was full of marvellous things ...'

It wouldn't be possible for her to keep the child a secret in this house for any length of time. She lay back against the pillows, despairing and exhausted.

'Take her. She's your child. Take her to Halina.'

'But Halka knows nothing about her. I thought I had a few more weeks to prepare her. I kept putting it off. What am I to do?'

Marianna turned her face away from him. 'Then tell her whatever you like. Tell her whatever lie you can think of. Tell her that the baby is an aristocrat's daughter, which is true enough. Your wife won't turn this child away. But you'll have to employ a wet nurse from the village. I'll pay.'

Already she felt her own breasts swelling with the milk that her daughter would not drink. Soon they would be painful. Nusia would bind them up for her until the milk dried.

'I can pay for that myself,' said Danilo. 'And I know a suitable girl. She lost her own child a few days ago, poor girl. She'll help Halina about the house and be glad to do it. I've thought about this. In fact I've thought of nothing else. I just couldn't bring myself to tell her. We'll say the baby is my cousin's child. They all know I came from the east, but nobody knows where. And you can come and see her. Oh God, Marianna, you must see her.'

'But not now. It would kill me. As soon as I can walk, as soon as I can move, I'm going to Milatyn.'

'You always fly to Milatyn!'

'Where else can I go? I must have time to get used to this. There's a knife in my heart and you're twisting it!'

He bent his head over the sleeping form of their child. 'Do you think I don't know what you're feeling? I've felt it too. Watching Zoshka grow. Not being able to take her in my arms and kiss her, but always with that distance between us. I know exactly what you must be suffering.'

'And are you glad of it now? Now that you have your revenge?'

'Revenge? I wouldn't wish such misery on anyone, least of all you. But what other solution is there?'

'None.'

'Then will I take her?'

He was still reluctant, holding out the child to her one last time. She seized the bundle and kissed the velvet skin, then surrendered her baby into his arms, lay back and closed her eyes.

Just as he was leaving, she raised her head and said, 'Danilo? Will you call her Antonina? After my mother. Will you do that for me?'

'Of course. It's a good name. She could be Tonia.'

Tonia she was. He was responsible for her life, responsible for her birth, and he loved her.

Within a few weeks, Marianna had recovered enough of her strength to manage the journey to Milatyn. Her confidence in Halina had not been misplaced. She took the child in and was content to spread the word in the village that Tonia was the daughter of a distant relative of her husband. Danilo had told Halina that the baby was Marianna's, but had told her no more than that, and certainly not about the part he had played in the child's birth.

Halina was deeply shocked. 'I can't believe it of her. To find herself in this situation.' The tears sprang to her eyes. She felt more sympathetic than ever before. She couldn't imagine anything worse than having to surrender a baby to another woman's care.

'And the father?' she asked.

'Why would she confide in me? Some young nobleman, probably. A brief liaison at a house party. These things happen all too often, you know.'

'Oh, the poor lady.'

Danilo said, 'I doubt if she would welcome your pity. And as for you, Halka, you were very nearly in the same situation yourself, once. Or would have been, if I hadn't made an honest woman of you.'

'I was always honest!'

For once, he relented. 'I'm sorry. I shouldn't have said that. Of course you were. I'm very tired. It's all been a shock. For me too.'

She clutched the baby against her breast, as though to ward him off with it. 'I know what my situation was then. And I meant no harm to her. It wasn't pity. It was sympathy. She must have been very much in love and very lonely to allow herself ... That was all I meant, Danilo.'

'Take no notice of me. She seemed so helpless and friendless, Halina. And you're right. She's very much alone. She trusts us. To give the child to anyone else might have broken her heart.'

'You must tell her to come and see the child whenever she wants.'

'I already have. But she's going to Milatyn as soon as she's able to travel, and perhaps that's just as well.'

'Perhaps so. Yes, I can understand that she would have to go away. But the poor lady. The poor, poor lady.'

Danilo stared at her for a moment and then he left her with the sleeping baby, and went out into the woods, wandering among the trees until he could regain control of his emotions.

Later, he went to the village to secure the services of a wet nurse and then walked briskly to the tavern, where he took good care to spread the word about his cousin's baby being abandoned to Halina's care.

'The baby was smuggled into the village in a peddler's cart at dead of night. It came as such a shock to us!' He added a few lurid details of the free and easy way of life lead by the fictional cousin, who was supposed to have died giving birth to this same infant.

'But retribution came at last,' said Janusz, the miller, very piously for a man who had fathered one or two infants on the wrong side of the blanket. Danilo would have liked to punch him but he didn't dare to make trouble. For once, he needed the miller on his side. 'And what of the dead girl's mother? Could she not take the child?'

'Dead too,' said Danilo, marvelling at his own invention. Needs must, he thought. 'Weak lungs. Ran in her family. That was how the girl began to go wrong. No mother's influence you see. There was only a drunken old aunt to take care of her. But my Halina will make a fine mother to her.'

'She will. Oh she will. Your Halina is a good lass.'

'We wanted more children, but haven't been blessed so far. This will be a sister for Pavel.'

'And you've a good position on the estate.' The miller nodded into his glass and Danilo bought more vodka. They quarrelled with great frequency, Danilo and the miller, but each time they took good care to make up and drink together to seal the bargain. Janusz had some influence in the village, and Danilo walked a fine line between pandering to the man, and letting him know who was boss. Janusz reminded Danilo of his grandfather. A bully when allowed to get away with things, he collapsed like a house of cards when confronted with evidence of his misdeeds. Now, his support would be useful.

Danilo thought it best to introduce the most dangerous topic himself, without having it dragged out of him. So, after a short pause, and another round of drinks, he said, 'And the mistress has been ill as well. It never rains but it pours.' He shook his head. 'Nusia feared for her life. Some kind of wasting sickness.'

'Ah.' The miller nodded, sagely. 'There has been talk. We daily expected the doctor to be sent for, but none came.'

'She would have none, save her own brother-in-law, Mr Julian. And he's in Vienna. I think he was advising her by letter. And she's a little better now, I fancy. Nusia always panics over nothing.'

The miller pulled on his pipe. 'That's often the way of it. Doctors can do more harm than good.'

'I believe the mistress is going to Milatyn for the Christmas season.'

'So she's well enough for that?'

'Oh, I think so. Zofia has been there since the summer. I think she has just been pining for her daughter. You know what women are like!' He smiled knowingly at the miller. 'And her absence will give me and mine a peaceful Christmas.'

The miller winked at him, grotesquely. 'You mean she keeps you hard at work. Well she always was an imperious little madam, even as a child. But she's fair. You must say that for her.'

'I'll say more. She's a great lady and a good employer. But her absence will give me time to draw breath. With a young baby in the house, that's exactly what I'll need.'

'Indeed. Indeed.'

It was done. The miller went home, replete with vodka and goodwill, nodding sagely. It was done so casually, so carefully, so innocently, that he had believed it all. Danilo had almost believed it himself. If Janusz believed it, he would tell his wife, and then the whole village would know by tomorrow, how the mistress was well enough to spend Christmas at Milatyn and how, much more interestingly, Danilo and Halina had taken in the poor bastard child of Danilo's cousin and were going to rear her as their own.

Many remarked, and carried on believing, that the child might be more closely related to Danilo than that. It was a nine days' wonder. Rumours flew about the village for some time with accompanying speculation about the identity of the child's mother, but there was no real evidence, no certainty. As is the way of these things in villages, some new scandal eventually overrode the gossip about the child. As time passed, they simply accepted her as the foster-daughter of the estate manager and his wife.

A few weeks later, Floryan and Ursula welcomed Marianna back to Milatyn. There were more children in the house, two growing boys and a baby girl. Julian's younger brother, Anton, was still at home, and Julian himself was expected any day, along with Floryan's grown-up children and grand-children. Milatyn would be full for Christmas.

When Zofia first saw her mother, she rushed over to plant a kiss on her cheek and then danced off with a swish of her tartan silk skirts.

'Do you like my new dress, mother? And my hair? Ursula says I'm so pretty that it's a pleasure to look at me!'

'You've always been pretty, Zoshka. But it isn't very nice to flatter yourself. You should leave other people to do that for you.'

'We're going to stay here for a long time, aren't we? Oh I do like it here! There's so much to do!'

'We'll see.'

Marianna watched her dancing daughter wearily. She found it hard to drag her mind from the infant she had left behind. She felt as though a limb had been hacked from her body, leaving a raw wound that ached and festered. When they questioned her haggard appearance, she told them that she had been unwell but had not wanted to worry them. On the day of Julian's arrival at Milatyn, she took to her bed again, mildly feverish and complaining of pains in her stomach. The family's anxious enquiries were almost more than she could bear. Julian finally overcame her protests and insisted on examining her. When the elderly woman servant who had been present for propriety's sake finally left the room, he sat down with his head in his hands.

'Well?' she said at last. 'What's the matter with me, Julek? Can you cure me?'

'You should know. You've had something similar before. You need plenty of rest.'

There was a long pause while Julian searched his mind for appropriate words. At last he said, so quietly that she found it hard to hear him, 'I'm no fool, though you seem to think I am.'

'What do you mean?'

'I know when a woman has just given birth. I believe the evidence of my hands and eyes. I know.'

'I was planning to tell you. I was going to confide in you, Julek. I wrote, asking you to come to me. Don't you remember?'

'If only I had known!'

'I couldn't commit such a thing to paper, could I?'

'Oh God, I should have been with you, Marianna. Who did this to you?'

'Nobody did it to me. It was my own fault. No-one else's. I can't give you a name, Julek. It wouldn't be right to burden you with that knowledge.'

'And there was no question of marriage?'

'None whatsoever.'

'Where is the child now? What has become of it?'

'Halina and Danilo Bandura have taken it in. Nobody knows it's mine. Except those two, of course, and Nusia. A little girl. A beautiful little girl.' She began to cry. 'I asked them to call her Tonia. They'll bring her up as their own, but they've spread the word that she's the orphan child of Danilo's cousin.'

'Bandura and his wife? Nusia is one thing, but you confided in your *steward*?'

'He's always been loyal to me, Julek. I know I can trust him.'

'How can you be sure? With such a secret as this?'

'I just know I can. And Halina is a good woman. I've grown very fond of her.'

'I don't doubt it. But on a matter such as this! My God, it gives the man such power over you. Such a terrible hold over you.' He shook his head. 'I don't like it. I can't approve, Marianna.'

'There was no other way, believe me.'

'If I had known. I could have brought you to Vienna.'

'What good would that have done? There would still have been a child to consider.'

'Teresa and Michael would have taken her.'

'But then they would have known. And if they knew, everyone would know. I love them dearly, but gossip is meat and drink to them and you know it.'

He paced the room, rubbing frantically at his hair until it was standing on end. She lay back on the pillows and watched him until he came to a halt. He put a cool hand on her cheek.

'You know, you probably can't have any more children? After Zofia, there was some damage. Now, I think you might find it very hard to conceive again. Wanda knew but I think she decided not to tell you in case you wanted to marry again. She said nothing was certain.'

'I'll never marry again, Julek. That much is certain. I know I'll never marry again now.'

Marianna was reasonably well in time for Christmas. She joined in with all the family celebrations, sang the old carols, and even ate the traditional *Vigilia* feast of fish dishes and sweetmeats. Julian was very polite and kind, solicitous even, making sure that her chair was comfortable, and that her plate was full, her glass never empty, but he avoided being alone with her.

One night, when they were in company, she sat beside him in a quiet corner and said, 'Well, Julek. Have you found a Viennese wife for yourself yet?'

'A wife? For me? Ah no. No, Marianna.'

'But you must have the ladies flocking round you there, just as you do here. You are so eligible, Julek!'

He pulled a face. 'I'm too busy to think of marriage.'

She looked up at him and sensed a definite withdrawal from her. She said in a low voice, 'I've disappointed you, haven't I? I'm so sorry.'

He seemed embarrassed by her frankness. 'Disappointed? I don't know. I think, after a time, one grows tired of giving where so little is given in return. But I do wish you well, Marianna. I wish you all the happiness in the world.'

As soon as politeness allowed, Julian packed his bags and returned to Vienna, telling her that if the opportunity arose, he would take up a political appointment in the city and make his home there. She saw that she had gone too far. She had wrecked their friendship on the precipitous reef of her clandestine love for Danilo. And it seemed to her that this was one more price she must pay for that love. The debts were mounting. How much higher must they go? Soon after Christmas, she returned to Lisko, taking a protesting Zofia with her.

Chapter Thirty Four

WHILE TONIA WAS STILL TODDLING about Lisko, clinging to Danilo's fingers or riding on his shoulders, the Austrians suffered defeats that marked the beginning of a crisis for them and their empire. The Poles seized the opportunity to carry out their own reforms and begin a process that was to give them some measure of freedom and independence.

'Good for the Poles, but not so good for us,' said Danilo.

Although he might talk big about the plight of his fellow Ukrainians, the villagers muttered that he did little enough to help them. All his early enthusiasm for change seemed to have evaporated. Perhaps the strain of keeping his affair with Marianna a secret had hardened him. It was true that some of the most tumbledown cottages had been renovated and a few new houses built, but not much else had been done to help the poorer workers, although the estate was thriving. He seemed as strong as ever, but his hair was turning grey and there was something of iron in him. Or ice.

'He acts as if he owns the place,' they said, behind his back.

He behaved with an unswerving loyalty to the estate but he never, for one moment, forgot that he was the steward. He might be as familiar as he wished with Marianna when they were alone together. He loved her with a terrible determination, but he always kept up the deferential public front.

For her part, Marianna became ever more eccentric, although her singular beauty seemed undiminished by the years. Her neighbours began to avoid her, finding her unpredictability embarrassing. She was either elated or gloomy. If she drank too much wine, her dinner partner might glance across at her and be alarmed to see tears coursing down her cheeks. It was uncanny, this silent crying.

She had, however, become great friends with Halina, and would spend hours at the steward's house, playing with little Tonia, while Zofia showed off to Danilo's shy son, Pavel. Zofia would rather have been at Milatyn, but she liked Pavel well enough. She could order him about as she pleased, and he always did as he was told.

Dark, thin faced Tonia, loved the lady who came to play with her. One day, when Halina had given her a scolding for some small misdemeanour, she said, 'I want to come and live at your house, Aunt Marianna. You're never cross with me!'

Over the child's head, the women's eyes met and then their gaze shifted. Gently, Marianna disengaged herself from Tonia's too-loving grasp.

'Your mother's right, darling. You mustn't be so bold. Your mother's right to scold you. She only does it because she loves you.'

When she was not spending time with Tonia, Marianna liked to pass her evenings in the kitchen with Nusia, reading by the dim light of a lamp, or simply sitting on the rug by the fire with her head on Nusia's lap, staring into the flames and dreaming. She would have long periods of inactivity followed by great bouts of energy, when she would turn the whole house upside down with her imperious orders.

At such times, she was very hard to please, quick to anger and difficult to placate. There were only two people who could calm her. One was Nusia, who simply ignored her tantrums, and the other was Danilo. When the mistress was in one of her moods, when young serving maids had fled in tears, and when even Nusia couldn't cope, then the steward would come to the house and afterwards the mistress would be subdued but as sweet as honey nevertheless.

Their lovemaking at this time was a dreadful, wordless striving after satisfaction that left them sated but exhausted as they lay in each other's arms. They had taken what they wanted, and now they were paying for it. Her sacrifice of her child to him had changed them irrevocably. Marianna could imagine that if circumstances had allowed, they could have grown old together in contentment. Instead, Danilo took out all his frustrations on Halina.

She continued to keep house, to cook and sew for him, to care for Pavel and Tonia as best she could. Danilo was never unkind to the children, but it hurt Halina that he seemed to adore Tonia with a love that she could not match. If the child so much as fell down and grazed a knee, Danilo would carry her about like a small princess.

Once, Marianna brought some dresses that had belonged to Zofia, the silk and muslin still fresh and faintly scented of rose petals. When he came in that evening, Danilo snatched up the pile of radiant skirts and brandished them at Halina.

'What are these?'

'My lady brought them for Tonia. They were Zoshka's.'

To her astonishment, he flew into a rage, threw the dresses down on the stone floor and began trampling them, muddying the bright silks. When she tried to stop him, horrified at the wanton destruction, he pushed her backwards so that she stumbled and sat down, shocked by his vehemence.

'Who does she think she is, to give the child Zoshka's cast-offs?'

'But they're not cast-offs!' Halina sobbed. 'They're almost new, Danilo. These are not play clothes. Miss Zofia wore them for a while and then grew out of them. Her grandfather bought the silk. It's lovely. It's gentry silk!' Feebly she snatched at the garments. 'Oh don't destroy them, Danilo. Why are you so angry? These belonged to Miss Zofia! I thought you were fond of her.'

Danilo stopped and, catching up the sheaf of dresses, put them to his face and breathed deeply. They smelled of Marianna. They smelled of Zofia. Why shouldn't the clothes be passed between sisters? His breath caught in a sob. He buried his face in the silk, his shoulders heaving. Only a few years ago, Halina would have tried to comfort him, but now she stayed where she was, despising him, puzzled and angry and desolate.

I hate my life with him, she thought.

That night, he went up to the yellow house with the garments in his arms and when he came back, still carrying the dresses, he was much more subdued. A few weeks later, a trunk full of new clothes arrived for Tonia. Halina spread them out, unable to keep the delight from her face.

'They're beautiful. Just beautiful. The others were fine but these are even better. Oh but she will get them dirty, Danilo.'

'Then we can use the other ones for play clothes.'

'How did you do it? What did you say to her?'

'Who?'

'Why, to my lady, to get her to agree to this.'

'It's her daughter after all. Why shouldn't she have the best?'

'Hush!' She looked around as though spies were lurking outside the windows. 'This is better than the best.'

'I persuaded her.'

'How?'

He shrugged. 'I've worked for the bitch for long enough. I have ways.'

She was shocked. 'Don't speak like that about Miss Marianna. It's not right.'

'I speak as I find,' he said, sullenly. 'She always was a spoiled bitch and she's not going to change now.'

Halina was silent again. It would never do to agree with him too vehemently. Once she had done so, and even gone so far as to criticise Marianna within his hearing, but he had turned on her.

'Never say that about my lady. Never let me hear you say such things again!'

'You say them and worse.'

'It's my privilege. I say what I like.

Throughout the winter of 1860, Halina struggled to keep the cottage warm and dry, to amuse the children and to keep Danilo happy. Sometimes, she went out to the privy where she could sit in the earthy, pungent darkness and cry. She was always red eyed but that too infuriated Danilo. She knew that he didn't love her. Perhaps he never had. For the first time it occurred to her that she didn't love him either. Not now. His indifference had all but destroyed her affection.

She thought of taking the children and going home to Banunin, but she was certain he would come and take them back to Lisko. She loved them and couldn't bear to leave them behind. Her parents were dead and she had only an unsympathetic aunt and a clutch of cousins to turn to. They would blame her for having married a Ukrainian in the first place. They had never really approved of Danilo.

She tried to confide in some of the older women of the village, but they seemed to think that these kind of tribulations were to be expected in a marriage. She had always thought so too. but she could not seem to make them understand that, though he never touched her in anger, he was cruel to her in other ways. They would never understand how he froze her out of his life all the time, until she felt as though she were growing physically smaller. She ate little and grew pale and thin.

She began to neglect the house, though never the children. She was unfailingly kind to the children. Sometimes she would wake in the night and listen to his steady breathing beside her, and terrible thoughts would run though her mind. She would imagine herself taking one of the big kitchen knives and plunging it with all her strength into the vulnerable back or breast or neck of the man who lay beside her. Once, when she had been feeling bleaker than usual, she even confided in Marianna, prompted by the other woman's sympathy.

'What on earth is wrong with you, Halina?' she asked. 'You seem terrified all the time.'

'My heart pounds so. I don't know why. It's like a knot of something terrible and terrifying inside me. I can't stop it.'

'But there must be some reason. Does Danilo work you too hard?'

It was a damp March day. The snow was thawing and they were sitting in Danilo's house on either side of the tiled stove. Pavel was out and about around the estate with his father; Marianna had come to watch three year old Tonia, who was absorbed in playing with a doll and a pile of wooden blocks that were by turns a bed, a kitchen, a carriage.

Halina sat with her hands twisting and turning in her lap. Marianna noticed that her apron was grubby, her cheeks thin and so pale that they looked yellow. She reached out and seized Halina by the hand.

'Halina, my dear, you're not well. It's warm in here, but your hands are icy!'

Halina shook her head but said nothing. She found that when she wanted to speak, tears welled up and choked her.

'I feel sad,' she said at last, struggling with her sobs.

'You must tell me what's wrong. I'll help if I can. Is it money? Are the children too much for you? What's the matter?'

Again, Halina shook her head. 'It's Danilo. '

'Danilo!' Marianna spoke sharply, making Halina jump. 'What about him?'

'You asked me once if he treated me well. He used to, but he isn't very kind to me now.'

'Why? What does he do? Does he beat you? Tell me! Maybe I can help.'

'No, no. He hardly lays a finger on me. I try to do the best I can for him, but I never know what will please him and what will make him angry.'

'He shouldn't be angry with you. You of all people. Do you want me to speak to him for you?'

'Oh no, my lady. He would be even more angry. He values your esteem so much, I know.'

'Does he?'

'Of course. And he's a good steward to you, my lady. You must know that. I think he would give his life for the estate.'

'I think he would. But that's no reason for you to sacrifice yours to him.'

'What do you think I should do?'

Marianna sighed. 'Could you bring yourself to leave him?'

'I can't leave. I couldn't take the children away from him.'

'No. No, of course not.'

'I must just bear it. But it helps to speak to somebody.'

'He may grow kinder.'

'I don't think so.'

'Time and circumstance have made monsters of us all, Halina. You must forgive him. I'm sure he doesn't mean to hurt you.'

Halina didn't understand this last observation. It sounded as if Marianna were speaking to herself. Still, she found the woman's sympathy comforting.

In spite of her promise to Halina, Marianna found herself broaching the topic with Danilo. His anger didn't frighten her.

'Has she been squealing about me? Has she been complaining about her treatment at my hands?' he asked.

She turned on him. 'Don't be so ridiculous. I made her tell me what was wrong. She seems so ill. Can't you see what you're doing to her? If you can't love her, then at least have some pity on her. She's the innocent in all this. We aren't.'

'You don't have any pity on me.'

'Why should I? You're strong. And so am I. You *must* be kinder to her. If not for her sake then for mine. I can't bear to see her made so miserable. Knowing that it's my fault.'

'It isn't.'

'Of course it is. I'm as much to blame as you are.'

They were in her sitting room. She had long ago allowed him to do as he liked in this place. No-one ever disturbed them here. He rested his head wearily on her lap. She stroked the dark hair, shot through with a little grey now, and ran her hand over his cheekbones. As he grew older, he seemed to grow stronger: hard and thin and wiry, all muscle and sinew. She felt the weight of him dragging her down.

He sighed. 'I know. I know.'

He pulled her to the floor beside him, pinned her arms and kissed her, lying almost on top of her, beginning to caress her.

'Such a simple thing,' he said. 'Such an easy thing to cause so much trouble for so many people.'

She shifted away from him. 'You needn't be so superior. You can't do without that simple thing yourself! But I wish we could be as we once were. I wish we could love each other as we once did.'

He pulled her into his arms and held her close, rocking her backwards and forwards. 'I do still love you, Marianna. You must know that.'

'And I love you. I'll always love you. So do this one thing for me. Try harder. Be good to her.'

Chapter Thrty Five

FOR A LITTLE WHILE, HE was kinder to Halina. But his store of patience was not very large and she exhausted it.

It was the amber heart that brought matters to a head.

Just before Easter, Danilo visited the town of Kamionka on estate business. He had promised to fetch a wax doll for Tonia and some fishing tackle for ten year old Pavel. Zofia had overheard the transactions and demanded that he fetch her a gift as well. He found the fishing tackle easily enough and bought a silk shawl for Zofia, spending more than he had intended, but he couldn't find a doll. Then, becoming absorbed in his other business, he forgot the time until it was much too late to make any purchase at all. So he arrived home with a gift for his son and one for Zofia, but nothing for his little Tonia.

She was not a particularly acquisitive child, but she had been looking forward to the doll. When she burst into tears of disappointment, Danilo went to Halina's chest and fetched out the amber necklace that Antonina had given him.

'Look, sweetheart!' he said. 'This can be yours. It's better than any old doll!'

As he fastened the butter yellow and silver filigree heart around the child's soft neck, he glanced defiantly at Halina. She was staring at him in dismay.

'She's much too young for such a gift. She'll break it or lose it. Tonia darling, take off the necklace now and let mama put it away for later, when you're more grown up.'

Tonia made a great fuss and Danilo snatched her up into his arms. 'Hush, my darling. You *will* have the necklace in spite of what she says.'

'Be sensible, Danilo. '

'I'll do what I like with what is my own.'

'But it isn't your own.' The words burst out of her. 'You gave that necklace to me. It was mine. A wedding gift from you. I would gladly have given it to Tonia as soon as she was old enough. You've spoiled it now. Why are you so angry with me all the time when I do nothing to deserve it? Why must you spoil everything?'

He had been drinking in the town. The grassy vodka was a haze in his head. He said scornfully, 'Our daughter, our daughter? She's no more *your* daughter than Zoshka. But that necklace is hers by right, and she shall have it. I told you once before, it was only lent to you. Well now its rightful owner has come along, and I'm giving it to her.' He set the child down and she stood, sucking her thumb, looking from one to the other in amazement, the necklace already forgotten. Danilo patted her. 'Go and play. Your brother's outside. Go and play, Tonia.'

Halina was bewildered. 'What do you mean? Its rightful owner? Who did the necklace belong to? What does it have to do with Tonia?'

'It was her grandmother's. What a fool you are, Halina, not to see what is under your nose. Her grandmother, Marianna's mother, Antonina. Antonina Diduska who used to live right here, at Lisko. That's why she's called Tonia. After her grandmother.'

'Yes,' she nodded, feeling very foolish. 'Yes, I know all that. But the necklace. How can it have been Antonina's? How come *you* had it?'

He sighed, hesitated, but he was feeling too angry, too reckless to stop now. The vodka still sang in his head. 'Well, the Diduski family had an estate at Podlaski, and that's where I was born.'

He had never told her about Podlaski. Whenever she had asked him about his background, he been vague. 'To the east,' he had said.

'When I was twelve, the Diduski family spent the summer there. Marianna's mother helped my mother when she was sick with the smallpox. She gave my mother the amber heart. But the smallpox killed my mother and it killed Antonina too. I kept the necklace for myself. My grandfather wanted to sell it, but I kept it in memory of Antonina Diduska. She was very kind to me.'

Halina slumped on the wooden bench by the window. 'I don't understand. I never knew that you had any connection with the family, Danilo. But if you were at Podlaski, all those years ago, that must mean ...' She struggled to absorb these new facts, to make sense of them. 'Wasn't *Miss Marianna* at Podlaski when she was first married? Wasn't that where her husband was killed?'

He nodded.

'And you, Danilo? Were you there back then? Did you know her there?'

'You're a fool, Halka. And I can't pretend any longer. I've known her since we were both children.'

She let out her breath in a long sigh. It was a relief to speak about it at last, to have it all out in the open. But the full implications of what he was saying were only beginning to dawn on her.

'And then at Podlaski,' he continued, 'When they murdered her husband, they would have killed her too. But I saved her. I saved her life and took her back to Milatyn.'

'*You* took her to Milatyn?'

'The house at Podlaski was burnt to the ground. I took her to her father-in-law at Milatyn. But I couldn't stay there.'

He had sat down, his head in his hands, remembering. 'I couldn't stay there,' he repeated. 'I had to leave her there.'

'But you didn't go back to Podlaski?'

'Of course not. Are you stupid? It would have meant a death sentence. I almost died anyway. It was a cold winter. But Yuri's mother took me in at Banunin and I managed to find work there. Learned to read and write. Made something of myself.'

'Married me,' she said forlornly.

'Yes. Married you. But then Marianna decided to come home to Lisko.'

'Where you were waiting for her,' said Halina, slowly. 'What a loyal servant you have been to her all these years.'

It was like some image that, when seen from a distance, is blurred and strange and you can't tell whether it's a tree or a cow or even a human figure. But then you come closer and you say, 'Ah, that's what it was all along.'

She saw it in an instant. It explained everything. Everything.

She said, 'Tonia. She's *your* child, isn't she? Not some young noble-man. She's yours.'

He gazed up at her from where he sat, sober now.

'Yes.'

'And Zofia too? Oh God help me, Danilo, she's the image of you. The living image of you. Why has nobody noticed? Why did I not notice? They are *both* your children. Yours and hers. You and she ... all these years ... oh God help me! God help me!'

She rushed outside and was violently sick into the bushes. When she came in, wiping her mouth, her face had become stony. She wouldn't speak to him or even look at him, no matter what he said or did. He tried to take her hand, already regretting his confession, but it was limp in his own. She would neither move nor look at him. He put the children to bed.

Pavel said, 'What's the matter with mamma?'

Danilo shushed him. 'Go to sleep now. Your mamma's not very well.'

He slept badly that night. Even when he dozed, he was aware that Halina was not beside him. In the morning, he found her in the same place, on the bench beside the window. He tried to go about his work as though nothing had happened. When he came home at breakfast time, she had roused herself and the children; they were washed and dressed and there was food on the table. She was talking to them and looked almost herself again, but she spoke to him as little as possible, and her eyes wouldn't meet his.

It was the end of March, a chilly, early spring day, and the whole village was celebrating *Marzanna,* the death of winter. They had made a figure of straw representing winter, and they planned to carry it in procession round the village. At Podlaski the *Marzanna* was ceremonially burned near the parish boundary post. But in Lisko, as at Banunin, the custom was different. Here, the straw *Marzanna*, with winter's face, was taken to the stream that flowed through the village and drowned. Later, they would make a *Gaik*, a small branch covered with young leaves and decorated with coloured ribbons. This, representing the coming spring, would be carried around the village.

'We have banished *Marzanna*,' they would sing at the tops of their voices. 'And now we are bringing you the lovely young *Gaik*. Rejoice, rejoice!'

Marianna brought Zofia to the village to watch these festivities. She was thirteen now, very smart, in a fashionable gown, white stockings and a warm winter cape, for the weather was still very chilly. Pavel followed her like a dog, thought Danilo scornfully, but if he did, at least she petted him and made much of him.

Danilo had promised to take his little Tonia to see the death of the *Marzanna* and when the time came, he made sure that he was back at the cottage with a broad backed mare to carry them both. She ran out to meet him and he swung her into his arms. Setting her before him, he said, 'Is your mother not coming with us?'

'She said I was to go with you, daddy. Pavel has gone to find Zoshka.'

'But is she not coming?'

Tonia shook her head. 'No. She's not coming.'

Danilo shrugged. He couldn't bear the thought of those reproachful eyes. He didn't go inside the cottage, but raised his hand in a half salute in case she should be watching from the window, and took Tonia on horseback to the village. She loved to ride with him and he with her.

In the village, he found Marianna sitting in a droshky with Zofia and Pavel squeezed in at either side of her, the better to see the procession. When she waved to him, he went over and kissed her hand formally, as he always did in public.

'My lady. So you have come to see the death of winter too?'

'May she rest in peace,' said Marianna, who hated winter. 'And may spring come swiftly on her heels!'

Zofia and Pavel made room for Tonia in the little cart. As Danilo waited with them the memory of Halina, bringing him a thunder candle, came into his mind. She had not made them this year, nor for some years past. He remembered swinging Halina round and round, light as a feather in his arms.

'Winter is dead and spring is coming,' she had told him, joyfully. He could hear her words. 'Oh sir, aren't you glad?'

And he had replied 'Yes, Halka. I'm glad.'

Perhaps just for that short time, he had loved her.

Now the *Marzanna* was coming. Winter was dying. Drowning in the floods of spring. With a lurch of his heart, he thought 'Oh, Halina!' He had a sensation of falling into darkness. He dug his heels into the flanks of his horse and, seeing Marianna's surprised face, called out, 'Take care of Tonia! I must go!'

He galloped back to the cottage, but she was not there. It was emptier than he had ever known it. She had left it very clean and tidy, the fire banked down so that it would be easy to blow into life. She had left a few early catkins in a glass jar on the table. Also on the table he found the amber necklace which, ashamed of his outburst, he had taken from around the neck of his sleeping daughter and put back in its usual place, in Halina's wooden chest. But now the necklace was there for him to see, the amber heart glowing softly in the middle of the table, as though she had just dropped it and left.

The horse was cropping at the short grass by the gate. He leapt astride it and paused for a moment, unsure what to do next, where to go. Then he was off again, riding hard, back to the village, back to the stream. As he approached, he heard the noise of the procession but it was not as he had left it. He heard lamentations rising into the air, and his heart quailed with a dreadful certainty. They should not be lamenting the death of winter, the death of the *Marzanna*, surely? They should be rejoicing at the coming spring.

He heard the wailing women, the shocked murmur of their menfolk. He saw a group of people down by the river where they had gathered to drown the figure of straw. But instead, they were pulling something out: another figure, limp as the *Marzanna*. Only this figure wore a sodden dress, trailing muddy ribbons. As he passed, he saw Marianna sitting bolt upright in the cart with her arms around the children. Tonia was still smiling, a little uncertainly, but Pavel and Zofia were watching, their expressions strained and uncanny.

He dismounted and, as he did so, he felt people catching hold of him, trying to keep him back, but he brushed them aside. Upstream from the village were narrows where the river, the Dumny Potok, ran deep and swift. The spring thaws and rains had made a torrent of the waters. Down here, were rocks and eddies and the water opened out and ran shallower. Branches and dead leaves swirled into the bank, caught in pools. He sniffed at the scent of wet earth and decay and new green: the bitter-sweet scent of spring.

The men down by the river had formed a chain and were bringing the body to the shore. Her face was bruised and muddy but he could see at once that it was Halina. An old man stooped over her for a moment, then shook his head. Danilo heard his own voice, raised above the cries of women behind him, the murmurs of the sad group before him, the noise of running water.

He said '*Marzanna* is dead. Spring is come and *Marzanna* is dead.'

Chapter Thirty Six

HALINA WAS BURIED IN THE graveyard on the estate. It was decided that she had gone down to the river for some reason – although nobody could think why – slipped and fallen into the springtime flood. The Catholic priest agreed with this interpretation readily enough. It would be much too cruel for the children to have their mother labelled a suicide and buried in unhallowed ground. Besides, Danilo wouldn't have stood for that and everyone was wary of him; some, including the priest, were downright afraid of him. But no-one really believed the explanation: not the villagers, not Marianna, certainly not Danilo. Only the two older children, Pavel and Zofia, accepted Halina's death as some dreadful accident. For a long while, Tonia couldn't understand why her mama had departed so abruptly from her life. She became silent and withdrawn and Danilo, try as he might, could not console her. Eventually, he left her to Marianna and threw himself into the work of the estate as a means of drowning his guilt. And if he noticed that the villagers and the workers gossiped behind his back, he maintained a dignified silence. Tonia, seeking the physical comfort that only a soft, female body could bring, turned instead to Marianna. The child was unnaturally quiet at first, sitting for hours in Marianna's pretty room, clutching at one of Zofia's old dolls. From time to time she would say in a small voice, 'Where's mamma? Where's my mamma? I want her.'

At last, driven beyond endurance, Marianna enveloped the child in her arms and whispered, 'I'm here, my darling.' Tonia looked confusedly at her for a moment, sighed and then, all at once, laid her silky head against Marianna's breast and sucked at her thumb.

Marianna had hardly spoken to Danilo since the tragedy, and he had deliberately kept away from the house.

Eventually, she confided in Nusia. 'I don't think I can bear to be here any longer. I must get away for a while. I used to love this place, but it's become a kind of purgatory. I can't stand it.'

'Is your conscience troubling you, my lamb?'

'What can you mean?'

'I think you know well enough!'

'It wasn't *my* fault. I did nothing to Halina.'

'Did you not?'

'Oh let me be, Nusia. You know nothing about Danilo and me!'

'I know enough.'

'No you don't. You think you do, but nobody does. Nobody understands. It's so oppressive here. It isn't good for the children either. I shall go to Vienna for a while. And I think I shall take Zofia and Tonia with me.'

'Tonia? Oh Miss Marianna, do you think he will let her go?'

'I don't see why not. The change will do her good. I'll ask him. I'm sure he'll agree.'

She went to Danilo's house early one morning taking Tonia with her. The sun was already warm enough to dispel the early mists. Marianna's spirits rose a little. It was impossible to be wholly sad on such a day. She caught Danilo before he set out on his day's work. Wordlessly, he held the door open for her. The house smelled stale and there were flies buzzing at the windows. He motioned her to sit down, but she shook her head.

'I've decided that I'm going to Vienna to visit my cousin Teresa and her family, and I wondered if you would allow me to take Tonia with me. I thought it might be good for her. But only if you agree.'

Danilo stared at her for a moment, with a kind of dumb incredulity.

'Well?' she asked. 'What do you think?'

'Vienna?' he repeated, hoarsely. 'You're going away?'

'Just for a little while. But I'd like to take Tonia with me, if you'll allow it. I think a change of scene may be good for her. Will you give me your permission? We won't be gone for too long, I promise you.'

Danilo looked from her to the child. Tonia smiled at him but made no attempt to come to him. Her arms were wrapped tightly around Marianna's neck.

'Do you want to go, Tonia?' he asked. 'Do you want to go with the lady to Vienna?' His eyes were bloodshot. He looked vacant and stunned, as though not quite aware of his surroundings. Behind him, food lay untouched on the table: a stale loaf and a piece of dry cheese. There were patterns in the dust. It seemed that Pavel was making some attempt to keep house, but he wasn't very good at it.

Tonia nodded, but she didn't understand what Danilo was asking. She had never been further than the countryside around Lisko

Pavel came into the room, shrugging off his coat. He looked from one to the other.

'What's happening?' he asked. Since his mother's death, he seemed to have grown older and more serious, watching his father with grave concern.

'I'd like to take your sister away for a little holiday, but only if your father agrees. I'd take you too, Pavel, but I think your father needs you on the estate.'

'I wouldn't leave him anyway. There's too much work to be done. And he needs me. Don't you, father?'

'Of course I need you.'

Unexpectedly, it was Zofia who demurred about the planned trip to Vienna.

'What will happen to Pavel when I'm gone?' she asked anxiously, concerned for her playmate. 'Who will he talk to if he doesn't have me?'

'His father. He'll talk to his father.'

'His father isn't always kind to him. And who will look after them, now that they don't have Halina?'

'They've been managing fine.'

'They haven't. You know they haven't. Mr Bandura does nothing but mope about after his poor Halina, and Pavel can't cook! I'll be worried about him all the time we're away.'

Marianna knew how determined Zofia could be.

'Well, I'll have to find someone from the village to come in and cook and clean for them. But Pavel isn't your concern, Zoshka.'

'He is. He's my friend.'

'Pavel will be busy working on the estate. He's a big strong boy now. And you'll love Vienna, I know you will. But I'll find some help for them, if that will content you. I don't know why I didn't think of it before.'

Marianna looked for a housekeeper for Danilo, but it was difficult to persuade any woman from the village to cook and clean for him and his son. Superstitiously, people shook their heads and crossed themselves.

'For heaven's sake,' she said. 'He isn't a monster. He's just a man like any other. Whoever works for him will be well paid.'

Still they were reluctant to commit themselves, and eventually it was Nusia who persuaded the unmarried sister of a poor farmer to take the job. Yushka had been offered marriage on more than one occasion, but she had refused all her suitors. She had no maternal instinct whatsoever, which meant that far from trying to mother Pavel, she treated him as an adult. Since Pavel would have despised any attempt at mothering, this suited him well enough. When he came in from his early chores, Pavel even began to be glad to find her presiding over a decent breakfast in a warm cottage. Danilo was polite but distant with her, giving her a free hand in everything. Yushka was a good worker and organised things for Danilo in a most satisfactory manner. He hardly saw her, but came home to a good meal and a clean house every evening, and that was enough for him.

Marianna and the girls set off for Vienna without seeing Danilo again, leaving written instructions about various pieces of estate business. Teresa and Michael accepted her explanation for Tonia's presence.

'How sad,' said kindly Teresa. 'How sad for your steward to lose his wife in such a dreadful way. But it's very good of you to take care of the child.'

'It's no hardship, Teresa. She's a darling.'

'She certainly is.'

Teresa and Michael's overcrowded home resembled Milatyn, all those years ago. There were so many young people in this house that two more made no difference. Zofia was soon carried off on city pursuits by her older cousins. Little Tonia was quickly coaxed into conversation again. Soon she was running, jumping, squealing with pleasure as she was chased and tickled and generally fussed over.

In the last fifteen years, Teresa had grown very fat. When she walked beside her husband they looked like a number ten. Michael had moved his family into a small house in Hietzing, near the Vienna Woods. Teresa basked in her husband's continuing success and spent his money on ornate crinoline dresses that looked comical rather than elegant on her rotund figure. Her hair had only a sprinkling of grey, but her eyes seemed as small as currants in her plump face. She bought gorgeous jewellery for herself and expensive toys for the children. Michael was vague, easy-going, charming and – said Teresa privately to Marianna – 'very fond of the ladies.'

'You mean he ...?'

'Oh, he strays occasionally. Like all men. You were wise not to remarry. But I can't complain. He's a good husband and tells me all about his affairs.'

'He *tells* you?'

Teresa laughed at her astonishment. They were drinking coffee and eating a cake so dense and so full of chocolate that it made Marianna feel light-headed. Teresa tucked into her portion greedily.

'Oh, he tells me all about Katarina and Sissy and Adele.'

'But how can you bear it?'

'My dear, don't be so ingenuous. I don't mind in the least. To be sure, I sometimes find it quite exciting and so we make more babies. I don't know how Sissy and Katarina and Adele manage these things but they don't seem to make babies. If there is a secret I wish he would tell me. They say that there is something the man can wear, you know? And perhaps Michael knows about it but he won't wear it for me!' She had put her mouth close to Marianna's ear and for an instant, Marianna was a girl again, in their room at Lisko or at Milatyn, light-heartedly talking of love.

She said impulsively, 'Oh it's so good to be with you again!'

'Why won't Julek come to see you, Marianna?' asked Teresa. 'I always thought you two were very close, so why does he ignore all my hints that you would be glad to see him?'

'I'm longing to see him. But we had a disagreement.'

'Let me guess. He wanted to marry you and you sent him off with a flea in his ear.'

'Something of the sort,' she said, vaguely.

'But of all people, I have to say that he would make a good husband for you.'

'He's too young.'

'Four years? That's nothing. And let me tell you, Marianna, he's as soft-hearted a man as ever walked this earth. You would want for nothing and have your own way in everything. And I suspect that he would be faithful to you. There would be no Katarina or Adele or Sissy in his life. There is none now!'

Marianna squirmed beneath this praise of her cousin. She said, 'There's more to it than that. I think he disapproves of me.'

'Julek? Never! You probably surprise him all the time, that's all. You surprise me. When I told him that you were bringing your steward's child as well as Zofia – but she's not even that is she? – his adopted child then – he was astonished. In fact he couldn't speak for several moments. I think he was moved by your kindness.'

Marianna coloured, not sure how to respond to this. 'I've grown very close to Tonia.'

'And what does Zofia think about that? Isn't she jealous?'

'A little. But Tonia is so much younger.'

'And Zofia is quite the young lady.'

'She is.'

'I must say, you look very worn and tired. Country living is bad for your health. We must get you some new clothes, for yours are fearfully unfashionable, and you have the figure for the new gowns, much more than I do.' She patted her stomach complacently. 'Too many babies for me, and too many good pastry cooks in this city.'

Marianna began to be enchanted by the city. Like a woman in a fairy-tale, she thought that she might go home to Galicia and find that she had been away for hundreds of years and that everyone had grown old and died in her absence. She even forgot for a while that there were other sides to the life of the city, places of extreme poverty where barefoot children picked their way through a foul morass of household slops. When she thought of Vienna afterwards, she always imagined it in terms of touch and taste. She sank into this life of pleasure and over-indulgence as into a sumptuous feather bed and she was able to forget Lisko, to forget the damp huddle of Halina's corpse, even to forget Danilo.

Her body, pampered by scented baths, fine silk underwear, new clothes and heavenly food, almost forgot him and her endless hunger for him. She did not need him here. Only in dreams did she see his face, always the young Danilo, fine featured, swarthy, scowling or smiling at her, multiplied a thousand times like a face in two mirrors, endlessly turning away from her. But that was when sleep took volition from her. Mostly she tried hard not to think of him at all.

She did, however, both think and fret about Julian who had not yet come to see her. When they finally met, it was at a ball, in honour of the younger daughter of a Viennese banker. Teresa was well aware that Julian had been invited too. As the son of a Polish aristocrat, a doctor and a potential politician, besides being heir to a small fortune, unmarried and not yet thirty, ('not even ugly', the mothers said, almost smacking their lips with glee) he was invited to a good many functions, most of which he refused. This invitation, however, was almost a royal command, and he could not decline.

Teresa had gleaned this useful information at one of her tea-parties. Much as the fashionable Viennese ladies might privately despise her foreign looks, she was accepted in society, her connections too important to be ignored. She had managed to secure an invitation to the ball for Marianna, feeling sure that, were Julian and Marianna to meet, the quarrel between them would soon be forgotten.

Marianna found Julian in the supper room. He was deep in conversation with a fellow medical man and Marianna lurked behind him, listening to their discussion. She heard them talk about a certain Ignaz Semmelweis of Vienna who believed that fever was conveyed to pregnant women by the doctors who were treating them.

'The idea is a slur on our whole profession,' said Julian's companion.

'Not at all,' Julian replied, his face alight with passionate interest. 'It's perfectly reasonable. I have seen young doctors go straight from working with cadavers to handling women after childbirth. The disease may be carried in the blood for all we know. We should take proper precautions!'

'So you say!'

'I do say. In Poland, even the horsemen who look after our mares when they are in foal are taught to wash their hands first.'

Marianna had always loved to hear him speak about his work, but the topic embarrassed her for more than one reason. She listened for some time before making herself known. He stood stock still for an instant. Then, remembering his manners, he took her hand and kissed it.

'Marianna! I had no idea you would be here.'

His companion tactfully excused himself and left them standing alone.

It was a fine summer night and Julian suggested that they go out into the garden. They walked arm in arm, until they came to a fountain with a heap of naked stone boys cavorting about its centre.

'Why didn't you come and see me?' she asked him. 'You knew we were in the city.'

'I thought you might still be angry with me.'

'Me, angry with you? I thought you were angry with me.'

'My dear, I didn't know what to say, so I found myself saying nothing.'

'You were very disappointed in me. I know you were.'

'Not exactly disappointed. Surprised. Then sad for you.' He paused for a moment. 'Marianna – this child, this little girl that you have brought with you – she's your daughter, isn't she?'

She said, 'Yes. Tonia's my daughter too. Although she doesn't know it, and Zoshka certainly doesn't know it. I would happily have left her in Halina and Danilo's care if it hadn't been for the accident. Poor Halina died you know. She drowned. And now Danilo is devastated by her death.'

'So I heard.'

'But they were very good to her. And to me. Generous beyond belief.'

'And what do you propose for her now?'

'I don't know. I may decide to keep her with me.'

'Tongues would surely wag. '

'Not necessarily. She has no mother.'

'And no real father too, it seems.'

'I can't speak of her real father, you know that.'

'I know that you *won't* speak of him.' He shook his head, sadly. 'Oh, Marianna.'

'I must seem very shameless to you. But it's a secret that must never be told.'

'What about your steward? Hasn't he grown fond of the child? He's been a kind of father to her, surely.'

'He has. But he has no claim on her.'

'Isn't that a little high-handed?'

'Not really. He's still mourning the loss of his wife. He lives with his son. And the estate keeps both of them very busy. It's not a suitable home for a little girl now. There's nobody to take care of her. She needs a mother. Or a family home of some kind.'

'You could do worse than leave her here for a while, you know. Her and Zofia both. I'm sure Teresa wouldn't mind.'

'I've thought about that already. We've even spoken about it. But I think I would miss them too much.'

'Then why don't you stay here with them?'

'I don't think I could bring myself to forsake Lisko entirely.'

Zofia and Tonia were very happy in Vienna, and Teresa had already made a tentative suggestion about extending their visit. Marianna could not explain about Danilo. Julian would never understand. He who could understand and accept almost everything about her, lovingly and forgivingly, would never understand and accept her feelings for the Ukrainian.

'If you do decide to leave the girls here for a while, I could keep an eye on them, you know,' he ventured.

'Perhaps they could spend some time here and some at Lisko.'

'Yes, perhaps they could. You both could. I'll be coming to and fro anyway, and I could bring them with me. You can make me their guardian if it suits you.'

'How generous you are. And how good to me!'

They sat down beside the fountain and listened to the swish of water upon the stone skin of the little boys. He bent and kissed her cheek. He smelled faintly of soap and wine.

'Oh, Julian, I have missed you. I've missed your letters and I've so missed knowing that you were with me in spirit. Right from that first time at Milatyn, when you showed me the Winged Hussar, I always felt we had a special kind of friendship.'

'Let me show you the city. I always wanted you to come here. There's so much to see. But I know what Teresa is like. She'll show you the interiors of a hundred salons and drawing rooms and nothing else.'

She laughed. 'Well that's true.'

'Then come with me and let me show you another side of this wonderful place.'

Chapter Thirty Seven

FOR THE NEXT FEW WEEKS, they were inseparable, driving here and there about the city. As a respectable widow, escorted by her brother-in-law, Marianna was shielded from the gossip that might otherwise have attended such excursions. Sometimes Tonia and Zofia came with them, but even when she took lunch or tea alone with Julian, the anxious mothers who had set their sights on him as a suitable son-in-law confided hopefully in each other that the pair 'have been like brother and sister since childhood. There's nothing in it but friendship.'

They saw buildings, galleries, gardens. They lost themselves in the music of the city. They drove out into the countryside and drank white wine beneath the vines from which it had come, sweet scented and heady. She saw everything through his eyes, for he had grown to love the city, however fiercely Polish he might remain. He had made good friends among the Viennese. It was impossible not to admire their zest for living. They were perhaps the most civilised of the conquerors of his country, and it looked as though a kind of independence might be gained, not in a glorious revolutionary fashion certainly, but bloodless, which would be better.

'It's always better to talk than to fight,' said Julian. 'I know how difficult broken bodies are to put together again. I've had plenty of experience of that!'

They ate together, and the city's obsession with food began to enchant Marianna too. Often, Zofia and Tonia would accompany them on their cake tasting excursions. Julian told Marianna how a century earlier, Ludwig Dehne, a pastry cook from Württemberg had opened a shop close by the old Burg Theatre. From there, ices and coffee were taken to the box holders to keep up their flagging spirits during performances.

Afterwards, stage door admirers would take their ladies to Dehne's sugar bakery for ice creams and pastries, cakes and biscuits.

'After Dehne's death, his widow became sugar baker to the imperial household,' explained Julian.

Marianna only nodded, with her mouth full of chocolate cream.

'Three years ago, Dehne's grandson decided to exchange pastry cooking for politics.'

'No!'

'Oh, there are great similarities. Both need great quantities of hot air!'

'And what did he do with the business?'

He sold it to his first assistant, Christophe Demel. But the cakes are just as good, if not better.'

'Tonia has chocolate all over her face,' said Zofia, disdainfully.

Marianna leaned over and wiped Tonia's mouth. 'It doesn't matter, Zoshka. You've got a bit round your mouth as well. And look at the colour in the child's cheeks and how she's filling out. We're all the better for sweetmeats. Aren't we, Tonia?'

Tonia grinned happily and licked chocolate from her fingers. Zofia nibbled her pastry daintily and frowned at the younger girl. She took a tiny lace hankie from her pocket and dabbed at her mouth. 'This is what you do, Tonia!'

From then on, Julian wooed Marianna with pastries and puddings of the most delicious kind. He engaged a *Mehlspeiskochin,* an elderly lady who specialised in home-made desserts. He invited Marianna to his apartment and fed her on cream cheese dumplings as light as feathers, sour cream pancakes, little bits of nonsense whipped up with eggs and almonds, or chocolate puddings both light and dense that made the head spin as though drugged for hours afterwards. He gave her *Palinentorte* and *Giselatorte, Linzertorte* and *Nusswaffeltorte,* cakes light and heavy, rich and smooth, plain and crisp. When she protested but half-heartedly because her greed overcame her, he only brought her more: *Apfelstrudel* and *Sachertorte, Josephinentorte* and *Neapolitantorte.* He wooed her with pastries and their unlikely histories. He did not talk to her any longer of politics or medicine or even of love, but of cakes.

When they ate chocolate *Indianers* stuffed with cream, he told her how they were called after a Hindu tightrope walker who had come to Vienna ten years previously, and how that man used to perform on a tightrope, suspended from two towers, balancing his way along them with the aid of a stick. A baker had taken his wife to task for staring at the man, but she had thrown a lump of dough at him, and it had fallen in some hot fat and inadvertently cooked itself, whereupon the *Indianer* was born. When Marianna objected that the *Indianers* were obviously baked, not fried, Julek merely looked blank and shrugged his shoulders.

'Who cares?' he said. 'It's a good story anyhow.'

He even took her with Tonia and Zofia to a pastry cook's shop very early one morning, to watch how the *strudels* were made. They saw two gnarled old men, pulling and stretching the dough slowly and steadily until it became thinner than paper, so thin at last that you could see through it, as it hung down over the edges of the big table.

'Wedding veil thin,' said Julian and it did indeed look like fine cloth.

He brought them gingerbread pictures: Orpheus with his lyre for Marianna, a pair of aristocrats in fine clothes for Zofia, and for Tonia, a splendid Winged Hussar on horseback, pictures which seemed to Marianna's dazed eyes far too beautiful to eat.

At last, after several weeks of this sweet wooing, Marianna protested that all her dresses had had to be let out and she noticed Julian himself becoming fatter. She said, 'You'll send me home looking like Teresa.'

'Must you go home?'

She paused with a forkful of *strudel* on its way to her lips. 'Of course I must. Sooner or later. I've loved my time here. But my darling Nusia is getting old and rather frail. And I worry about my estate.'

'What about your steward? Didn't you leave him in charge?'

'My steward has lost his wife. I haven't heard anything from Lisko for weeks. My estate may be going downhill fast. I have to go home and sort things out.' Marianna resented him at that moment for bringing Danilo into her mind. She wanted to stay here in the sugared cocoon of Julian's admiration and her daughters' love. She didn't want to have to go back to Lisko at all. She had even begun to come round to Julian's suggestion that she might be able to rent an apartment in Vienna, send for Nusia, and have the house at Lisko closed up, leaving Danilo to look after the estate in her absence. It all seemed quite feasible.

'And then,' she thought 'We could all eat cake together.'

'Maybe I could go in your stead. Maybe I could look after the estate for you. Make sure all's well with your steward.'

She sighed. 'No. I don't think so. Not that I don't trust you, because I do. But this is something I have to do myself.'

One night, after she had been to the opera with Julian and her head was full of music, after they had eaten a lavish supper together in his apartment and had drunk a great deal of champagne, he was about to summon a carriage to take her home when she stopped him. Very deliberately, she took hold of one of his hands and laid it on her breast, sliding it beneath the silk of her gown. She bent over and kissed him on the lips. His mouth was cool and dry. There was no explosion of sensation in her, but she thought it was very nice to kiss him, all the same. When she pulled him closer she could feel the satisfactory pounding of his heart against her breast.

Emboldened by champagne and by his wonderful familiarity, she encouraged him to help her undress and then lay on the couch and welcomed him in. He wanted her too much and came very quickly while she was hardly roused.

'Never mind,' she said. 'Never mind, my darling.'

She made him take her to his bedroom where she slipped beneath the sheets and told him to lie beside her, told him to touch her. 'This pleases me. And this. And this.'

He forgot himself in loving her and soon became aroused again. This time it was better. She clung to him, feeling him inside her, moving very gently, murmuring words of love in her ear.

'And I love you too,' she replied sincerely.

'My darling Marianna, you will marry me, won't you?'

She turned into the warmth of his arms. 'Ask me in the morning,' she said.

But in the morning, she rose early and dressed.

He woke and watched her. 'What are you doing?' he asked.

'Julek, my darling, I'm going back to Lisko.'

He stared at her in utter disbelief. 'You told me you loved me.'

'It was the truth. I do love you. Very much indeed. But I can't marry you, Julek. I'm sorry. I only wish I could.'

'Why not?' His hair was tousled with sleep. He looked dismayed, like a little boy, deprived of some long anticipated treat. 'What else can I do, Marianna? What must I do?'

'Find someone else.'

He shook his head, but she persisted. 'Marry someone who loves you and only you. Someone who wants nobody but you. Someone who will give you an heir.'

'How can I possibly do that when I love you?'

'Men marry women they don't love all the time. And for all kinds of reasons.'

'Not me,' he said firmly.

'I can't marry you.'

'Then there must be somebody else.'

She saw that she must be brutal with him. 'There is.'

'But you won't marry him either?'

'No. I shan't marry again, Julek. It was true what I said. Every word of it. I do love you but ... I can't explain this very well, even to myself. It's as though some vital part of me belongs to another person. I could never make you happy. There's an ingredient missing. All the cakes and pastries in the world won't supply it. Only promise me something.'

'Anything.'

'Don't leave me alone again.'

He looked at her in exasperation. 'But you're leaving me alone!'

'I don't mind if you marry somebody else. How could I object? But I can't bear it if you withdraw your friendship. I need it. You're my rock. Say you'll always be my friend.'

'You know I always will be.' He spoke sadly but helplessly. 'And you're definitely going home?'

'Yes. I must. But I'll come back now and then.'

'What of the girls? Have you made any decisions about them? Zofia would be devastated to leave the city, she's so happy here. And Tonia's growing as fat as a puppy on all that *strudel*.'

'They can stay on for a while. I'll miss them, but I don't think Lisko would be good for either of them at the moment. There are things I need to sort out there first and they'll be safe here. I'm torn in two as usual. Perhaps you could bring the girls home at Christmas? It's one way of getting you to come to Lisko.'

'What will your steward say? He did take Tonia in, after all. He must think of her as his daughter.'

'If he objects, he can come and fetch her himself. But he would never dare.'

Julian was surprised by the sudden rancour in her tone. She could be as high handed with Bandura as if he were a serf. Marianna herself sometimes marvelled at his blindness in this respect. But she supposed that for her to be anything more than an exacting employer to her Ukrainian steward was so far beyond belief that it had never even crossed his mind. Honest and upright as he was, Julian was also, in many ways, a deeply conventional man.

She went back to Lisko.

The girls wept to see her go but were comforted by promises that Uncle Julian would bring them home in time for Christmas. Tonia was too young to have any real idea of the time involved, while Zofia was just old enough to be distracted by the promise of a new bonnet and a trip to Rust, to see the storks that nested on the chimneys of that town every year.

Chapter Thirty Eight

THE STAY IN VIENNA HAD done Marianna good. The cakes and puddings had fattened her body while Julian's affection had fed her mind, and she felt able to deal with anything and anybody, even Danilo. This was just as well, because on her return, she found the estate on the brink of chaos, Danilo in a state of habitual drunkenness and gossip rife in the village about the dubious relationship between the steward and his dead wife. People whispered that he had been cruel to Halina, which was more or less true, and that he had beaten her, which was not. Yushka had stayed on with father and son, ignoring every savage outburst, determinedly doing her job. One of Marianna's first actions on her return was to give her a generous sum of money, far beyond her agreed wages, and several gifts, including a big box of Viennese chocolates and a shawl in fine Kashmir wool.

'Oh God love you, you needn't have bothered yourself,' said Yushka. 'Although it's kind of you and I'll not refuse. But my brother is far worse in drink than Mr Bandura.'

'All the same, it must have been difficult for you. It must still be difficult.'

'No, no. I just ignore him and let him get on with it.'

'Well, that does seem to be the safest course of action for you. But it's one that I certainly shan't take.'

Nusia related that one evening, Danilo had marched into the elegant drawing room and erupted into drunken anger there, breaking the golden chair and smashing several pieces of china before he could be stopped.

'I came in to find him with the little God and Goddess in his hands. You know the one your father-in-law gave you? The rude one. He was staring at it and the look on his face terrified me. I thought he was going to smash it to the ground, but he simply went on staring at it.'

'Poor Danielek!'

'I'm glad you say that, for I felt sorry for him too. But I didn't know what to do.'

'So what *did* you do?'

'Nothing. I stood and watched him for a while, and at last he set it down on a table and just sort of shuffled out of the room.'

'Oh, Nusia!'

'I didn't have the heart to scold him. He has been missing you terribly. You must have known that. Why did you go away and leave him?'

'I had to go, for my own sake. And for the girls. But I'm back now.'

'If anyone can bring him round, you can.'

Very early the next morning she sent for Danilo. He didn't come immediately, but eventually he slouched into her sitting room, his face sullen and unshaven, his hair unkempt. He stared dully at her.

'So you've decided to come back at last.'

She ignored his insolence. 'Danilo, what is the meaning of all this?'

'All what?'

'How can you have let yourself and Lisko slide like this? I left it in your care and what do I find when I come back, but this mess? Do you expect me to pay you? Do you expect me to trust you after this?'

He raised his hands slowly from his sides and let them fall again in a gesture of despair.

She looked around the sitting room and he caught her gaze. He had the grace to blush, a faint colour appearing beneath his pallor. 'I'm sorry. I broke some things. I've paid for them, or as much as I can. And it won't happen again.'

'No. It most certainly won't. If it wasn't for Pavel, I would dismiss you right now and find myself a steward who will work for his money.'

'I've always cared for this place as though it were my own.'

'But not for the last few months. Or your ideas of caring have certainly taken a turn for the worse.'

'You've no pity on me, have you?'

'You haven't even asked about Tonia. Or have you forgotten all about her?'

That roused him a little. 'Where is she then?' he asked, but he couldn't care very much. He was quite numb. He thought he would never feel anything again, neither love nor hate. His mind was full of darkness. Sometimes he fought to push it aside, but it enveloped him and he had no strength to fight it.

'I left Tonia in Vienna for a while,' she said. 'With Zofia. They're living with Teresa and Michael. I thought it would be for the best. She's happy and secure there.'

The workers had certainly carried on working, taking good care not to anger him, but often he was too drunk to bother. Goods and gear had gone missing. Wrong decisions had been made or not made at all. In the office, bills, receipts, lists of stores and sales were all jumbled up. Even the horses were looking neglected. She had glanced briefly around the stables last night and pursed her lips at what she saw, really worried. If Danilo didn't care about the horses, things must be desperate. And vital work that ought to be well under way at this time of year had been delayed.

The thought of all this made her flare up again. 'It's obvious to me that you've used your so-called grief as an excuse to neglect my estate!'

'So-called grief?'

'Crocodile tears, Danilo. You mistake guilt for grief. Acknowledge your guilt and have done with it.'

'I made her desperately unhappy. I needn't have done that.'

'You made *me* unhappy too but I've not yet drowned myself.'

'How can you be so cruel?'

'Me cruel? And *you* were never cruel I suppose? To me? To Halina?'

'I never ran away from my problems anyway. And how can you say I've made you unhappy? We've made each other unhappy.'

'Each other then,' she admitted.

'All our lives we've done nothing but cause each other the greatest possible grief. I wish I'd never set eyes on you.'

'We've given each other the greatest possible pleasure as well.'

'That too. I know.'

'And you saved my life.'

'All we've done is strive after something that neither of us could have. It's been a kind of sickness in us. Worse than the sickness that killed your mother and mine.'

'I agree with you. And we're both so scarred by it now that we must just live with it. But it will do neither of us any good to let the estate slide into ruin. I've pulled myself together and you must do the same. If you don't, I'll send you away and find myself a new steward. Do you think I wouldn't do it?' she added, furiously. 'Do you?'

He shook his head. This time he thought she might. She had grown strong again. She would always survive, always get on with life. It was part of what he loved in her. She was vastly relieved to see the backward movement of his shoulders, to see him looking straight into her eyes.

'That's better. That's my Danielek.'

No-one else had ever called him so affectionately, except her mother, all those years ago. The ghost of a smile crossed his lips.

'About the girls. Julian will be their guardian. While they are in the city, at least.'

'So I've lost her. My little Tonia?'

'Not at all. I know the journey is a long one, but he has promised to come for Christmas. You'll see Tonia then. And Zofia.'

'Did you think about me at all in this? Do you think I have no feelings?'

'I know you have feelings. But the girls must come first. And there's something else.'

'What?'

'When Julian comes here, I shall ask you to respect him and his judgement and be prepared to take his advice about the estate. He knows a great deal, and will be a help to both of us. I've been cocooned here for far too long. I'm going to bring Lisko to the world and the world to Lisko. So you may as well accept it, or leave now!'

He had been standing by the window, staring out at the park, deliberately not looking at her face as she lectured him. When she paused for breath, he said, 'Perhaps you're planning to marry again. Perhaps you're planning to bring a new husband to the estate as well?'

'No.' She shook her head. 'I shall never bring a new husband to the estate. You have my word on that. My solemn promise. There will be no husband. None but you.'

He would have come closer, but she moved away from him, shaking her head. 'Not yet. Perhaps not ever.'

'Then what am I to do?'

'I've told you, you must agree to my terms or leave.'

'It seems I must agree. I don't know where else I would go. I have no heart for another place.'

'Then stay. Stay with me.'

'There is so much talk in the village.'

'It'll die down. They'll grow bored and talk of somebody else. The sooner normality is restored here, the better.'

'I'll do whatever you want, Marianna. But don't expect me to be happy about it.'

When Nusia heard that both girls were going to be staying in Vienna, she began to cry. Marianna had told her in the kitchen, where she was helping the cook to make plum preserves. A fine crop had just been brought in from the garden. But if Marianna believed that by telling her in the cook's presence she would forestall any objections, she had underestimated her old nurse.

'Have I nurtured a monster in my poor old bosom all these years? Leaving Tonia and my darling Zoshka with those wretched bohemians. How am I to bear it?'

Marianna put her arms around Nusia and motioned to the cook to bring her a glass of vodka. Nusia pushed it away. The cook, embarrassed but unable to leave the kitchen for fear of spoiling the jam, continued to stir her plums and sugar, swatting the occasional wasp out of the way.

'I went away at the same age and it did me a world of good.'

Nusia wiped her eyes on her apron. 'Yes and I lost you then, as I will lose my darling Zoshka now. When she comes back at Christmas, she'll be a young lady, all elegant clothes and not wanting to kiss me for fear of getting her skirts crushed.'

'When did I ever refuse to kiss you for fear of crushing my skirts?' Marianna asked, indignantly.

'I'll allow that you were different. It would have been better for you if you had been less of a tomboy.'

'You're not making sense. You'll see her again. Often.'

Nusia shook her head and got to her feet with some difficulty.

'Where are you going?'

'I'm going to sort out my belongings.'

'But why?'

'It's as well to be prepared. I don't want to leave any mess behind me when I go to meet my maker. You'll give my christening coral to Zoshka for her firstborn child, won't you? And I'm to be buried in the graveyard on the estate, for I'll not leave Lisko.'

Amused and exasperated, Marianna agreed, and together she and the cook watched Nusia walk out of the kitchen, sniffing with relish at the scent of boiled fruit as she went.

'You'll break my heart,' she stated calmly. 'You've been trying for years, Miss Marianna, and at last you'll succeed. You mark my words, you'll surely break my heart.'

Chapter Thirty Nine

SOME WEEKS AFTER MARIANNA HAD returned from Vienna, she was sitting in her room, waiting for Nusia to come and do her hair. She came each morning as she had once come to Antonina, and if her stiff fingers found it hard to cope with the long tangle of her mistress's hair, Marianna had never been fussy about neatness. This morning, however, Nusia was late. Marianna went to her room, and found her lying cold and still in her bed. Marianna couldn't believe the evidence of her eyes at first, and shook her by the shoulder, but Nusia had died as quietly as she had lived, slipping away peacefully in the night. When it became clear that she would never be roused again, Marianna sank down beside the bed and wept bitterly.

Nusia had been a faithful servant to the family for a very long time, and the funeral was well attended. Danilo helped to carry the coffin. He had not yet offered his condolences to Marianna, nor did he do so at the funeral. All their meetings were very formal now. He seldom came to the house, but he had stopped drinking, smartened up his clothes and himself and begun working in earnest. The estate was running smoothly again.

Without his precious Zofia to confide in, Pavel had become a rather solitary boy. Halina, Zofia, Nusia had all been kind to him but now the three of them were gone: Zofia to Vienna and Nusia to join his mother in heaven, wherever that might be. When he tried to question his father about heaven, Danilo gave a scornful laugh and said, 'Oh, a far better place!' with such heavy sarcasm that Pavel didn't know what to think or believe. Pavel took himself off to the woods and found a starling with a broken wing. He brought it home and tried to fix a rudimentary splint to it. Then he fed his patient on worms and other insects that he found and set about trying to teach the bird to talk, for he had heard that starlings were great imitators.

Danilo, watching him at this task, was poignantly reminded of Ivan, the kitchen boy at Podlaski. He wondered what had become of the lad, and if he had survived into manhood. He wondered what had become of his grandfather. He must be long dead by now. Danilo had scarcely given them a thought for many years, but now the past came rushing into his mind and with it a remembrance of that first passion for Marianna, the intense sensations that had once possessed his body, whenever she was near, the almost painful feeling of attachment, as though a web of fine lines lay between them, spun from one to the other.

A few days after the funeral, Marianna sought out Danilo. He was working among the beehives, wearing a wide brimmed hat and a great curtain of netting, anonymous, mysterious, blowing puffs of smoke into the hive so that he could steal a little of their honey. She waited in admiration as the bees covered him in a sleepy, tumultuous crowd while he removed a comb. Then he replaced the lid of the hive, talking to the bees as he went, and came towards her, flicking bees from himself and carrying the honey carefully.

When he had taken off the netted headdress and brushed the last of the bees from his body, she let him come closer. He showed her his bee stings, of which he had several on hands and arms, pulling the stings out with his teeth and spitting them away, but they didn't seem to hurt him as they hurt other people.

'I used to feel them,' he said, with a grin, 'But not now. They say they are good for rheumatism.'

'I think I'd rather have the aches and pains.'

'Nusia wouldn't have agreed with you.'

'Oh Danielek, I do miss her! I miss her scolding me and lecturing me and telling me what I ought to do. What will I do without her?'

He couldn't resist saying it. 'Do what you told me to do, Marianna. Get on with things.'

She sighed. 'But it's hard.'

'Of course it's hard. I was telling the bees about her death. They like to know of these things: births, marriages, deaths. The great events in life.'

He sat down on the springy turf and she joined him. He took out his knife and cut off a piece of comb, dripping with golden honey, holding it out to her on the point of the knife. When she put out her hand, he gestured it away, holding the wax closer to her face. She opened her mouth and he inserted the knife gently between her teeth, pausing for a moment before withdrawing it, his eyes never leaving her face. He cut off a piece for himself and they chewed the wax together, extracting the honey. She spat the piece of beeswax into the palm of her hand and rolled it in her fingers, making a little candle shape out of it. She had done this often enough as a child. They sat quietly for a while in the sunshine, eating honey, making waxen shapes. She stole the occasional glance at him, glad to see that he was more like the old Danilo, greyer and with more lines around eyes and mouth, but less haggard, more in control.

'I'm very sorry about Nusia,' he said. 'I know you were very fond of her and she was always kind to me, even when others weren't. I'll miss her and I'm sure you will.'

'Are we friends again?' she asked.

'Were we ever enemies?'

'Not really. You know I can't do without you.'

'You don't have to. You'll never have to. I promise you.'

She slipped her warm hand into his. He grasped it tightly and they stayed like that for a long time, leaning together in the slanting, late summer sunlight, with the low hum of the hives and the scent of honey permeating the air all around them.

Chapter Forty

Years passed. Floryan had been dead for some time, killed in a hunting accident. With Julian still in Vienna, his younger brother Anton was in charge at Milatyn. Meanwhile, Lisko seemed caught in a timeless bubble. Danilo, at almost sixty, delegated work to his son wherever he could, but Pavel didn't have his father's flair for management.

'If it was up to you, this estate would go downhill in no time at all. You have to get tough, Pavel. You're too anxious to please people.'

'You hardly ever give me a chance.'

'I give you plenty of chances. Tradesmen do the dirty on you and you don't even spot it. You want to be liked. You've just got to get in there and get on with it. You need to be fair, that's all. No more, no less.'

Danilo was still physically strong, stronger than his son. He looked as though he might survive for ever, untouchable and unapproachable. The young estate workers and servants in the house were frankly wary of him. The older men, some of whom had known him for years, were cautiously friendly, but knew that they must never overstep the mark, never become too familiar. There was one person only who was unafraid of him and that was Marianna. In her mid fifties, her dark hair was belatedly greying. There were laughter lines around her eyes, her waistline was plumper than it had once been and she hardly bothered to lace it in at all.

They still made love, but not very often, and when they did it was with affection rather than passion. Sometimes it seemed to be enough for them to find a quiet place where they could sit close, listening to the whispers of the forest, laughing at this or that piece of local gossip: how young Komorowski kept a pet monkey that had run off with his father's expensive new false teeth and hidden them; how the priest's dog had been caught carrying a boiled chicken but nobody knew where the animal had stolen it from. There was no fire in them these days, but still they clung together, as necessary to each other as the very air they breathed. They were so close that they could read each other's thoughts and finish each other's sentences.

When Pavel was in his thirtieth year, a young Ukrainian girl called Konstanta came to the village. She was very lovely, with black hair and a rich pomegranate bloom to her skin. Her father had lost his job on an estate some miles away, and they had moved to Lisko to live with relatives, but her mother was anxious to marry off this eldest and most beautiful daughter. Konstanta could cook mouth-watering dumplings and make ambrosia of the cheapest cuts of meat. She could kill and salt a pig with no waste at all. She could spin and weave and sew a shirt.

'Can she spin flax into gold as well?' asked the village gossips, bored with the endless catalogue of Konstanta's virtues.

When the steward from the big house came to call, proposing a match with his son, Konstanta's mother couldn't believe her luck, but the girl herself disliked the idea of marriage to a man so many years her senior. All the same, the parents agreed that the match would be a good one, if only the couple could be persuaded.

Konstanta was curious about Pavel, in spite of her misgivings. The thought of being mistress of her own house, of having a little wealth, a position in the community, children – these things were attractive.

'Make him your friend,' said her mother. 'Don't decide anything yet.'

With her mother's blessing, Konstanta went walking about the estate in hopes of meeting Pavel; Danilo sent his son to work where he knew Konstanta would be walking. Gradually Pavel felt himself at ease with her and began to be disappointed when he didn't see her. One day, she came across him in a clearing, felling the remains of a tree that a recent storm had brought down. He paused, glad of the respite from his work, and they sat together on a fallen log. When he pulled her close and kissed her, she didn't object. Then, finding her lips cold, for the day was chilly, he took a bottle of honey liqueur out of his jacket pocket and, drinking a mouthful, put his lips over hers and let a little of the fiery liquid flow onto her tongue. They were married a few weeks later.

The summer of 1881, the year after Pavel's wedding, was a particularly fine one. Marianna gave splendid picnic parties for a procession of visitors. These included Tonia and, less frequently, Zofia, who had remained unmarried. Marianna suspected that there had been a string of more or less unsatisfactory lovers, and a string of extremely satisfactory rewards, which allowed her elder daughter to live in comfort. Zofia had her own apartment in Vienna. She had servants, fine clothes and two small, yapping dogs. She dressed them in jewelled collars, sat them on her lap and fed them from her plate. She seemed content with her lot, but self centred. There would, thought Marianna, be no first-born child to inherit Nusia's christening coral.

Tonia lived in Lemberg with her husband, a Polish musician she had met in Vienna. She had grown as tall as her mother and very slender, with a face that might be called uncommon rather than pretty. It seemed that Zofia had taken all the looks and Tonia all the character. The girls were cordial enough in company, but distant. Zofia seemed reluctant to acknowledge the adopted daughter of an estate manager as her friend, particularly when the girl was such a favourite with her own mother.

Julian also spent time at Lisko that summer, and rode with Marianna or Danilo, noting the smooth efficiency with which everything was run.

'My dear,' he said to Marianna, 'If I decide to retire from politics, might I count upon a room in your house?'

'There are plenty of rooms and you would be welcome to any or all of them. I suppose at our age there would be no scandal in my brother-in-law coming to live with me.'

It was a golden autumn day, with the apple trees heavy with fruit, and they were taking tea off a scrubbed table in the orchard. The samovar had been brought out, as well as gilded bentwood chairs. It all seemed very elegant, luxurious even, although Julian observed that there were flies in the preserves as usual. He heard a little sigh escape from Marianna.

'What's the matter?'

'Nothing. I always get tired at this time of year. Too many visitors. And not all as undemanding as you. But I'm going to have a lovely, quiet autumn and not let anybody else come here to disturb me.'

Julian wandered off to smoke a pipe and finish a watercolour sketch. Encouraged by Tonia, he had taken up this hobby a few years ago. Marianna poured herself a last glass of tea and lingered over it. She thought, as always at this time of year, how sudden silences fell, so that it was possible to hear the approach of winter, stealing quietly over the fields.

'But I wish winter wasn't coming,' she thought. 'I'm happy. I really am very happy now. I wish everything could stay like this for ever.'

She looked up to see Danilo coming across the lawn towards her and, still warmed by the realisation of her own contentment, motioned him to sit down and poured him some tea. He had been in the stables as usual, his refuge. He glanced down at his grubby hands and she remembered across all the years, the gesture that he had once made when she sat, young and pretty, upon a horse from which she could not dismount without help.

She said, 'Never mind your fingers. I love them just the way they are,' and then looked at him to see if he remembered too, and smiled because it was plain that he did. He sat down and took the tea that was offered, as well as a piece of cake.

'Now isn't this nice? I was just thinking how happy I am. Aren't you happy, my love?'

'I never think about it. But perhaps I am, now that you ask. Only I wish sometimes that things had been different. I wish we could have been married. I wish we could have sat here and taken tea together as husband and wife.'

'Isn't that what we're doing now?'

'You know what I mean.'

'You would have grown tired of me long ago,' she said.

He smiled at her. 'Not me. And you're fishing for compliments, my darling. Does one grow tired of the changing seasons?'

She sipped at her tea. 'Do you remember that day in the meadow at Podlaski? I keep thinking about it for some reason. I almost tripped over you and covered you in flowers.'

'I remember. I was only pretending to be asleep, you know.'

'Were you? I never knew that!'

'I didn't know what else to do. Anna in the green meadow. Give me your hand and take my ring. That was what you were singing.'

'So I was. How clever of you to remember.'

'I remember everything. Every single thing. You were so beautiful that day.'

'And you were so handsome that I felt my heart turn over with love for you!'

'I was never handsome.'

'Oh but you were. You were so wonderful. So tall and strong.' She reached out impulsively and touched his cheek. 'I loved everything about you. I wanted you so much. You can't imagine.'

And then she made the remark that was to haunt him. She said, as lightly and breathlessly as a young girl, 'Why did you never ask me to marry you, Danielek? Why did you never give me your ring?'

'Marriage?' he echoed. 'To the estate manager?'

'It's not unknown.'

'It's practically unheard of. Would you have married me?'

'You never asked me. And you know, when it became possible, after all these years, if you had plucked up the courage to ask, I might have dared to consent. Who knows?'

She smiled at him and then rose and, bending over him, kissed him tenderly on the forehead, stroking his hair.

'What an old bear you are,' she remarked. 'They're all a bit afraid of you still, you know. But not me. I never was. Not really. Not even that day when my husband took his whip across your face and I thought you might retaliate.' She stroked his cheek. 'I was always more than a match for you. And besides, I do love you so very much.' She laughed. 'I adore you. I always have. I always will.' She kissed him again, on the lips this time. 'Goodbye, my Daniil, Danilo. My dearest, darling Danielek.'

He watched her moving over the long grass of the orchard in her green dress, and he let her words sink in, finishing his tea, chewing the cake mechanically, hardly tasting it.

After dinner, while she and Julian were reading, she in the big window seat of the drawing room and he in an easy chair near the stove, he heard a gasp, no more than an indrawn breath and turning, saw that she was slumped forward, her face pressed against her hand, against the window, as though she were looking out at somebody.

He rang for help and carried her to bed, where he did all that he could, but he knew that the seizure would be fatal. In spite of all his skills, he thought that she would not even regain consciousness, and his pain was only moderated by his intense efforts to bring her round. When it was all over, he knew that he would hardly be able to bear the sorrow, his heart like a frozen limb that, with returning heat, regains life and instant pain.

Seeing her pale face and hearing her laboured breathing, it occurred to him that he must send for Danilo. He had never quite understood the relationship between these two, but he felt as though someone were standing over his shoulder, urging him on. Danilo must be here.

The man strode in with an expression of agony on his grim features such as Julian had never seen before.

Danilo gazed at Marianna, propped up in the big feather bed. 'When did it happen?'

'After dinner. She was reading. And then suddenly ...'

'Can you make her better?'

The naivety of the question wrung Julian's heart. 'I only wish I could. But I've done all I can.' His voice broke on the words.

Danilo read the tragedy on his face and in his voice. He read it on her face too.

'Then there's no hope. No hope for her and – oh Jesus – no hope for me either.'

To Julian's dismay, Danilo elbowed him aside, snatched Marianna up in his arms and held her close, almost shaking her in an effort to bring her round. She lay limp in his arms, her eyes closed.

'Danilo, please!' Julian moved forward to restrain him, but Danilo only turned away, clutching her closer.

'Open your eyes!' he said. 'Open your eyes, Marianna! For the love of God, open your eyes for me!'

Julian put a hand on his shoulder but Danilo shook him off. 'Leave me alone! Leave us both alone!'

He bent closer to Marianna and whispered in her ear. 'Marianna, don't do this. Oh Christ, please, please don't go. You can't go and leave me. I won't let you. I've saved you before and I'll do it again. I won't let you go, do you hear me?'

Julian was amazed to see Marianna's limp fingers move, and then grasp hold of Danilo's hand. Marvelling, he watched consciousness return to the still-lovely face. The eyes flickered open. Julian stood back, afraid to intervene. Danilo bent over her, straining to hear, and there was such tenderness on his face that Julian felt himself moved to tears. Marianna gazed up at Danilo, smiled, actually smiled at him, then shook her head minutely, closed her eyes, gave a little gasp and lay still against him.

Danilo would not move. He stayed holding Marianna in his arms until, when he laid his head on her cheek, he felt it grow cool beneath his own. Julian had left him alone for a time, but when he came back into the room, he saw that Danilo had laid her down on the bed and was sitting beside her, stroking her forehead.

Julian himself was numb, for he too had loved Marianna, but he saw that here was one who had a greater claim to farewells. His own must wait for later. When he had seen the expression on Danilo's face, had seen her hand reaching up to grasp his, it had been as though a puzzle was suddenly solved in his mind. Many things had fallen into place. And he knew now, with absolute certainty, who Tonia's father was.

Danilo sat drinking brandy in silence, cupping the glass in his rough hands.

'I always thought it would be me to go first. I'm older than she is. I never even imagined – I always thought it would be me.'

'If it's any comfort, I would never have expected it either. I would have said she was as fit as a fiddle.'

'She told me, she said – ' Danilo stopped, unable to get the words out. He looked at Julian and shook his head. 'I never did ask her.'

'We had such a fine afternoon together,' said Julian.

'She said goodbye to me, you know. I thought it was odd. She was just going back to the house, but she said goodbye. Do you suppose she knew?'

Julian shook his head. 'I can't give you any comfort. I have none for myself. Except ...'

'What. Except what?'

'Except that she opened her eyes for you, Danilo. Not for me.'

Danilo got to his feet and shambled out of the house. Julian watched him go. To his amazement he found that his chief emotion was jealousy. He thought, 'I offered her cake when all she ever wanted was good rye bread.'

Chapter Forty One

IN THE ESTATE GRAVEYARD, DANILO stood alone. The weather had turned cold and he was swathed in a long wool coat, unapproachable in his grief. Pavel stood beside his father, but when he reached out to touch him, Danilo shook him off.

'Let me be!' he groaned. 'Just let me be, Pavel.'

'She's gone to a much better place,' said Pavel. 'But you're here and there's work to be done.'

'Then you go and do it. A better place eh? A better place! And I suppose you've been there, so you would know all about it?'

After the funeral, Tonia went wandering through the woods, looking for somewhere to be private with her grief, and came upon the Old Steward's House. Remembering it vaguely from her childhood, she pushed open the door, but she was alarmed to hear a voice calling down from the upper floor, 'Who's there? Who is it?'

'It's only me. Tonia.'

There was a rush of footsteps, and Danilo came into view.

'Who were you expecting?' she asked.

He shook his head and a strange smile crossed his face. 'Oh, no-one. No-one. It was a sort of mad hope.'

'Did Marianna come here?' she asked.

'Sometimes. She liked this place very much. We both did. I believe she spent a lot of time here when she was young. Before I came here.'

'Show me.'

She went upstairs with him, and they sat together on the window seat. Tonia looked around. 'Was I in here when I was a child? It seems very familiar.'

'I used to bring you here when you were living with me and Halina.'

'Did you?'

'Yes. I used to come in here at harvest time. You liked to come with me. I would carry you on my shoulders and you liked to hold onto my hair. It was longer in those days.'

'Long and dark. I remember it. I used to pretend that you were my horse!'

'You did. We would bend down to get through the door and then you would hold onto me very tightly because it was dark in here and you were a bit afraid.'

'Nobody could be afraid if they were with you. You gave me apples to eat.'

'Apples, pears, plums, anything you wanted. You were my little princess for a time.'

'I remember,' she said, sadly. 'I thought you were my father. I wish you had been. But nobody seems to know who my real father is. And they tell me my mother died when I was born.'

'You came to Halina and me when you were just a baby. And I would have carried on being a father to you, if you hadn't gone to Vienna.'

'Why did she do that? Why did Aunt Marianna take me to Vienna with her?'

'She thought it was the best thing for you, after Halina died. Did you not like it there, Tonia?'

'Oh, I loved it. They made a great fuss of me, you know. And yet I was very happy before Vienna as well.'

'What else do you remember?'

'I always thought you and Halina were my real father and mother. Then Zoshka told me that you had only adopted me. She was quite sharp about it. I think she thought it would hurt me. But it didn't. I was too secure at Teresa's house by that time, and I never felt strange coming home to Lisko either. But why did I always stay with Marianna? Why didn't I stay with you?'

'Because Halina was dead. And I suppose Marianna thought it would be better for you at the big house.'

'But didn't you have any say in the matter?'

'Not much, no.'

'Oh, you were my hero. You were, you know.'

She saw his face relax into a genuine smile. 'I loved you very much, Tonia.'

'I remember Halina too but not so well. She used to cuddle me and let me fall asleep on her lap. But Aunty Marianna was always there too, wasn't she? I remember once telling her I wanted a doll, and the very next day, there was this beautiful old doll beside my bed. She has a whole wardrobe of clothes!'

'What became of the doll?' he asked. He was remembering another little girl, all dressed in white, clutching a doll, stamping her foot at him.

'I've got her still. She's very precious to me. I wouldn't lose her for the world!'

'It was your ... it was Marianna's. When she was young.'

Tonia threw him a puzzled frown. 'I suppose it must have been.'

'What else do you remember?' he asked.

'I remember sitting in an open carriage, a droshky. I was all squashed in with Pavel and Zoshka. We were going to see something lovely. And then suddenly everybody was crying. I suppose that must have been the day when poor Halina had her accident.'

'That was the day.'

'I wanted to get away from all the fuss, I remember that. So I went with Marianna, and the house was very calm and quiet. I slept a lot. And then she said we were going to visit some nice people in a big city and off we went. But I didn't want to leave you. We went through the gates and I started to cry and said, 'Where's my daddy? I want my daddy?'

'Do you really remember that?'

'Oh I do. She put her arms around me and comforted me and Zoshka told me not to be silly. But it was you I wanted. It was a long time before I saw you again, and then everything was different and even I was different.'

'You were the apple of my eye,' he told her, oddly comforted.

'Then why did you let her take me away from you?'

'She did as she pleased. She always got her own way, with me at any rate.'

'Like Zoshka?'

'Marianna wasn't quite like that. Just very strong-willed. And she was right. I was in no condition to look after you properly, Tonia. I doubt if you would have been as happy here with me and Pavel as you were in Vienna.'

'Perhaps not.'

'And I did see you from time to time.'

'But never so close again.'

'No. Never so close.'

She got up. 'They'll be looking for me. I must go. Are you coming?'

'No. I'll sit here for a while yet.'

'May I write to you?'

'If you like.'

'And will you answer? There's no point in my writing if you don't answer.'

'I'll try. But I'm no great correspondent.'

'A line or two would be enough.'

'You look like her you know.'

'Who? Halina?'

'No. Marianna.'

'But she wasn't really my aunt.' She stared at him. 'Was she?'

He shook his head. 'No. No Tonia, she wasn't your aunt. But perhaps we grow to look like those we love.'

'You cared for her very much, didn't you?'

He said nothing. She came up to him and planted a soft kiss on both cheeks, and when he raised his head, she had gone.

Marianna had left a decent sum of money, some jewellery and other items to Zofia. More surprisingly, she had left the same bequest to Tonia. Zofia was not happy about it but hid the fact of her displeasure beneath the black Chantilly lace of her veil. The rest of the estate, the house and most of the land, was left entirely to Julian, with the proviso that he should either retain Danilo Bandura as steward, or provide him with a house and enough land to maintain himself for the rest of his life. At the end of the will, there was a curious and intriguing sentence.

'To my dear steward and best of friends, Danilo Bandura, loyal for so long and so very far beyond the call of duty, I leave the green and gold Italian box of which he knows, that lies in my little drawing room.'

'It's worth a fortune!' whispered Zofia. 'Floryan gave it to her. It's a great treasure. It shouldn't leave the house.'

If this was a surprise, the very last line of the will caused a mild sensation among the listeners, conscious that they were, after all, in mourning.

'All else that I could possibly give him is already in his keeping.'

Hearing the terms of the will, Danilo fought with his disappointment. He had begun to think of the estate as his own. Instead Marianna had done the expected thing and left it to Julian. He had been deluding himself.

A Pole to the last, he thought. Well, Polish lady, you had to see the land in Polish hands, didn't you?

For a time, he was very angry, but it was a strange, desolate kind of anger. He wanted to summon her back, to argue with her, to cross verbal swords with her once more, and then to make up the dispute with kisses and caresses. His anger dissolved in bitter grief. What was the point? He had always known it would be like this. He had seen the pathway, even as he set foot on it, had followed it with clear eyes all the way to the far horizon.

Then he remembered what she had said to him on that last day: 'Why, Danielek , you never asked me,' and the thought occurred to him that perhaps it was all his fault. Why had he not asked her to marry him? Perhaps, after a suitable time had elapsed following Halina's death, a marriage between them would have been possible, and then he would gradually have been accepted as the admittedly unorthodox master of Lisko and they could have lived together. The girls would have made the yellow house their home, he would now be the owner of the whole estate, and Pavel might be quite the gentleman. He went on like this for a time, building fantasies of what might have been, but they were wormwood to him.

He thought, what does any of this matter if I can never see her again, never touch her again, never hold her in my arms or sit with her by my side? He was cast into another black depression and went about his work with a heavy heart.

Chapter Forty Two

Not long after Marianna's death, Julian moved to Lisko, leaving his brother, Anton, in possession of Milatyn. He brought with him the collection of antiques and militaria that he had inherited from Floryan: embroidered sashes and swords, coins and saddles, and the Winged Hussar that he displayed in his drawing room for all his visitors to see.

When Danilo came in to discuss estate business, Julian found him viewing the eagle armour with a compound of awe and dislike.

'Beautiful but terrifying, isn't it?'

'It's very Polish,' said Danilo.

'The wind whistling through those eagle feathers must have made a dreadful sound. Like avenging angels.'

'Impressive,' said Danilo, shortly. But it seemed to stand for something he had lost, or for something he could never have. He felt like pulling it down, stamping it into the floor. Its presence here was like a conquest of all that he had once held dear.

'I hope we can work together,' said Julian. 'You won't find it the same as working with Marianna. I think she gave you a very free hand.'

'She did, sir.'

'And I shall too. But perhaps not quite so free. I intend to invest time and money in this place, and I shall want things done my way and not yours. Nor perhaps hers.'

'I understand, sir.'

'I know you understand, but can you accept it?'

'I have no choice in the matter.'

Julian had resolved to be diplomatic. He could not dismiss the man out of hand, but he knew that Danilo was too used to going his own way. There was bound to be a confrontation. When it came, it was an argument over some small matter of estate business: the purchase of new machinery from the city. Danilo didn't think it was necessary. They bandied words until Danilo said wearily, 'You must do as you please, sir.'

'Yes, I think I must.' Julian spoke very gently.

Danilo sighed. The fight had gone out of him. 'I'm getting too old for all this. I'm not up to it any more.'

'It's simply that you're not used to being overseen in this way. But I must run the place as I think fit. The Ukrainians have a bad time of it, but the poor Polish farmers are only a little better off. And you know as well as I do that badly managed estates grab the lion's share of what little spare money there is.'

He saw Danilo bridle and quickly corrected himself. 'Oh, I'm not saying that Lisko is badly managed. Far from it. You've worked miracles here. It's just that for years, our gentry have been keeping the wolf from the door at the expense of your people, and many of our own too.'

'Well, there's some truth in that.'

'I have money to invest in this place. More ready money than Marianna had, anyway. I want to make the whole estate more efficient. But I want to make it more profitable as well. It pains me to see people resentful and miserable, but it pains me even more to see them hungry and sick. I'm going to do the best I can to remedy that.'

'Then, good luck to you. I know you're right. And it isn't that I disagree. It's that I'm no longer my own master. It was different with Marianna.'

'Yes, it was different. But I'm in charge now.'

'I don't know what the answer is, sir.'

'You still miss her very much, don't you?'

'All the time.'

There was a moment's silence between them. Then Julian said tentatively, 'There was very much more to the relationship, wasn't there? More than steward and mistress, I mean.'

'I thought you must know.'

'For years?'

'For many years. Ever since that night at Podlaski when your brother was killed. And even before that, I think.'

'Good God!' Julian was genuinely shocked.

'Oh, for a long time it was unspoken. There was nothing improper back then. She was very unhappily married, but she was a lady. I was a servant. A stable boy.'

'So what happened?'

'I helped her to escape that night. I had no hand in the killing, no hand in any of it. I swear to you. But I helped her to get away.'

'You were the one. You saved her life!'

'I did.'

'But she said ...' Julian hesitated, trying to remember her exact words.

'What did she say?'

'Nothing. Just that somebody had helped her. And then? What happened next?'

'Briefly, we became lovers. It seemed inevitable. Not just to me, but to her, too. I didn't force her. You have to believe me. We loved each other. And then we parted. What else could we do?'

'She spoke of somebody helping her. But she told me the man had been executed, when my father took reprisals.'

'I think she said that to protect me. And herself. I never went back to Podlaski. I found my way to Banunin. And then on to Lisko.'

'So Zofia is your child. Zofia is yours!'

'She told you?'

'Only half the story. '

'Sir, you mustn't ever let her know. Poor Zoshka would be devastated.'

Julian allowed himself a wry smile. 'It would make or break her, true.'

So many secrets, he thought. How had Danilo borne it for so long? His sympathy for the man increased by the minute.

'And Tonia?' he asked, though he already knew. 'She's Zofia's sister?'

'She is.'

'And she knows nothing either?'

'No. I saved the child's life. It was an impossible delivery. Nusia was there and could do nothing. Marianna would have died, and the child with her.'

'So what did you do? What could you do?'

'I'm a horseman, sir. Always have been. Horseman first, steward second. I did what I would have done for a mare, and saved the baby's life, and the mother's life too.'

'You take my breath away. And it worked, this procedure?' he added, his curiosity as a doctor for a moment over-riding everything else.

'I turned the baby inside her. It wasn't easy but there was nothing else to be done. She'd have died otherwise. We were all desperate.'

'So you were twice responsible for saving Marianna's life?'

'I wish there could have been a third time.'

'What a tissue of falsehoods you have had to spin over the years, my friend,' said Julian.

'I know. You tell one lie and before you know it you're enmeshed in dozens of them.'

'I think, if you'll take my advice, that Tonia at least should know.'

'Do you think so?'

'She should know of the relationship. She's quite different from her sister.'

'Perhaps you could tell her?'

'No. That must fall to you.'

'Then maybe I will tell her. The problem is that I want nothing now. I think you should find yourself a new steward, for I can't do the job any more.'

'Are you sure?'

'I'm sure, sir. I want no quarrel between us, but I've no heart for the work.'

'Well, if your mind is made up, I won't replace you yet. I'll do the work myself.'

'Will you?'

'And I can consult with you, whenever I need advice?'

'Gladly, sir.'

'Do you think your son will continue to work for me?'

'Of course. Where else would he go?'

'Then you must carry on living in the cottage. Unless you want a house of your own? I can arrange that for you, if you prefer.'

'No. No, I'm fine as I am.'

'I'll give you some land, so that you won't be relying on Pavel and Konstanta's good will.'

'That's kind of you.'

'No. It's the very least I can do. It's what Marianna wanted. You know I loved her too.'

'And she loved you. After all, she gave you her most prized possession, didn't she?'

Julian gazed through the window, across the lawns. 'You mean Lisko? No. Not quite. There are not many things more precious than land. At least, not to a Pole. But some things are beyond price. It seems to me that in saving her life you took it into your own keeping.'

'I knew her before. When she was a child,' said Danilo, impulsively. Suddenly he needed to tell someone. Julian ought to know the whole of it. There would never be a better time.

'When she was a child? How could that be?'

'They came to Podlaski when she was a little girl. I was just a boy myself. Antonina – her mother – came to visit my mother when she had the smallpox. And afterwards they both died.'

'Good God, Danilo. I didn't know any of this. Well, I knew poor Antonina had contracted smallpox there, but nothing else.'

'No. It was our secret. Another secret. But you see it was as though we were always linked in some strange way. It was as though we were meant to be together. We couldn't get on without each other. We were constantly being drawn together. But we were a Ukrainian and a Pole, and that pushed us apart. It was cruel.' Danilo tried to smile, but only grimaced, painfully. 'She loved you as well.'

'But she loved you more, Danilo.'

'Maybe. All I know is she couldn't rid herself of me. I think she tried when she went to Vienna. But I was like some terrible obsession with her.'

'She told me she couldn't marry me. She said there was somebody else. But she wouldn't tell me who.'

'We couldn't help ourselves. Later on we became more comfortable with each other. It was better in a way. But we lost something as well. We lost our – '

'Passion?' asked Julian gently.

'Yes. We lost our passion for each other and somehow we lost our passion for life as well.'

Julian patted him on the shoulder. 'I understand. I do understand, you know.' But he wondered if he really did.

Chapter Forty Three

IN LATE SUMMER, TONIA CAME back to Lisko, bringing her daughter Ludmilla with her. The child was a roly-poly toddler with chubby limbs and silky brown hair. Tonia needed no persuasion to go and see Danilo, but Julian warned her, 'He is neither well nor happy, Tonia. Be careful how you speak to him.'

'Do you think I should take Ludka?'

'I think maybe you should. I'm sure he would like to see your daughter.'

She walked the short distance to the cottage with Ludmilla, but it was slow progress. The toddler was distracted by flowers, worms, fallen leaves and shiny black beetles. Tonia wore a striped taffeta dress that she had had during her pregnancy, though it was now much too big for her. Her hair was tied up behind with a bootlace. Zofia always remarked scathingly that Tonia looked as though she had flung on the contents of her rag bag each morning, but her husband, who loved her dearly, didn't seem to notice or mind.

Pavel was not at home, but Konstanta asked her to sit on the veranda and produced a glass of cherry vodka. She admired Ludmilla and Tonia admired Konstanta's beauty.

'Do you have any children yet?'

The young woman shook her head sadly. 'Not yet. But if the good Lord wishes it, we will have a large family. Pavel is very fond of children.' She lowered her voice and looked over her shoulder 'We feel it would help my father-in-law too.'

'Is he at home?'

'He's indoors. He sits by the fire a lot and dreams like a very old man, though he isn't so old.'

'Will you ask him if he'll speak to me?'

Tonia saw Konstanta's lip tremble and thought, 'Why, she's afraid of him!'

'Don't worry,' she said. 'I'll speak to him myself.'

She got up and strode inside, carrying Ludka with her.

'You never wrote to me, Mr Bandura! You promised you would.'

'I'm sorry.' He roused himself to smile at Ludmilla. 'What have you brought to show me? Who's this?'

'I thought you might like to see little Ludka.'

He held out his arms wordlessly, and the child trotted into them. He bent down and kissed the starfish fingers.

'Dada!' she said.

'She calls all men that. It's a bit embarrassing.'

'She's very like your mother.'

'Is she? But you would never tell me anything at all about my real mother. Nobody would. They said she was some relative of yours or Halina's who got into trouble and died when I was born.'

Konstanta, who had been hovering by the door, called Ludmilla to her, enticing her with sweetmeats.

'Konstanta,' said Danilo. 'Do me the favour of taking the child for a walk. I would like a few moments alone with Tonia.'

Konstanta did as she was told. She loved children and was eager to please her father-in-law. When Ludmilla had toddled off, Danilo rose and went to a chest that stood in one corner of the room, opened it and began to rummage inside. Presently, he turned towards her, holding the amber heart.

'Once upon a time there was a princess,' he said. 'She lived in a house of butter.'

'And the house was full of marvellous things. Yes. I know that lullaby. Aunty Marianna sang it to me. And I sing it to Ludka sometimes.'

He put the warm resin into Tonia's hand, closing her fingers over it. 'There. That's for Ludka. When she's old enough.' He paused. 'The amber belonged to her great grandmother.'

'My grandmother? But this is such a beautiful necklace. A valuable necklace.'

'Yes. And it belonged to a very great lady.'

She sat down suddenly, her legs shaking.

'Tell me. What lady?' But she knew. She had known it in her blood and in her bones.

'Your grandmother was Antonina Diduska. You were named for her.'

'Antonina. Tonia. So you're saying Marianna was my mother?'

'Yes. You really are a Diduska, you see. Whatever Zoshka may think of you.'

She put a hand over her eyes.

'Are you all right, Tonia?'

'I feel a bit dizzy. Just give me a moment.'

He watched her in silence, half reaching out a hand to touch her, but then withdrawing it.

'So, how do *you* come to have the necklace?' she asked at last.

'Antonina gave it to my mother, many years ago. As a gift. Now I'm only giving it back where it belongs.'

She drew a deep breath. It was now or never. 'And you can do that because *you* are my father, aren't you?'

He nodded.

She screwed up her face into a frown. 'I always thought there was something. But I pushed it to the back of my mind. I never allowed myself to make the connection. Until now. Who else knows?'

'Only Julian.'

'Uncle Julek?'

'He was a good friend to your mother.'

'So he knew and he never told me!'

'He didn't know the whole of it until very recently. And then he thought it was up to me to tell you.'

'Why didn't you tell me sooner?'

'All my life, Tonia, I've had to tell so many lies. I promised your mother I would say nothing. But you were mine. You are mine. In fact, I brought you into the world. I helped your mother give birth to you in secret. You would have died if I hadn't been there to help. You and she both would have died.'

'Is that true?'

'It's the truth. I swear it.'

She gazed at him in silence.

'I'd better not tell Zoshka,' she said at last. 'If Marianna is my mother that makes Zoshka my half sister and she wouldn't like *that* at all.'

He looked at her gravely for a moment. 'Oh, sweetheart. You're even closer than that.'

There was another pause while she absorbed this astounding information.

'Zoshka too? Oh Lord.' She began to laugh but he saw that the tears were streaming down her face. She wiped her eyes on her sleeve. 'I can hardly believe it. Oh don't worry. I'll keep the secret. Though it seems a shame that I should lose a sister for the sake of propriety. But I won't be without a father any more.'

'For what that's worth. For what I'm worth.'

'You're worth a very great deal to me!'

'Halina always knew that you were Marianna's daughter, but for most of our marriage, she didn't know who your father was. She thought you were the daughter of some young aristocrat that your mother had had an affair with.'

'And then she guessed?'

He hesitated. 'Yes. Sadly she did. So you see I'm not much of a discovery as a father, am I? A liar and a cheat. Although I did love your mother. I loved her very much indeed.'

'But I've always loved and admired you!' She looked at him through her tears, suddenly anxious. 'And I want to keep you. You must look after yourself in future. Do you hear me?'

'I don't want anything. I just want people to leave me alone.'

'But there's so much to live for.'

'You have to go home, Tonia. Your husband needs you. And little Ludka.'

'Then why don't you come to Lemberg with me?'

'No.' He shook his head. 'I'll not leave Lisko now.'

'Are you sure?'

'I can't leave here.'

'Then I'll come back as soon as I can.'

'Don't worry about me. It's enough that you're not ashamed of me.'

'Ashamed of you? Never!'

They heard Konstanta coming back with Ludmilla, talking to her in loud, cheerful tones.

Tonia said quickly, 'Does Pavel know all this?'

'No. No, and he mustn't. It's better that he doesn't.'

She sighed. 'So many secrets.'

She fetched the child from the veranda and held her up to him. He kissed her soft forehead and then planted the same kiss on Tonia's cheek. She looked at him, a tall, powerful man still, though his face was lined with suffering. She had a sudden inkling of the sheer magnetism of him, and what her mother must have felt for him.

A few days later, just before she and Ludmilla set off for Lemberg, she leaned down from the Lisko carriage and took Julian's hands in her own.

'Keep an eye on my father for me, Uncle Julek.'

'Of course I will.'

'I have this terrible fear that I won't see him again. Oh, it's bitter. Bitter to find him and lose him again so soon.'

Surprised, he said, 'What can you mean? He's strong and fit and he'll live for years yet. And he won't leave the estate. I won't send him away and why else would he go?'

'God forgive me, but I see only death in his face.'

Chapter Forty Four

SUMMER GAVE WAY TO AUTUMN and with it came the anniversary of Marianna's death. Nobody had seen Danilo for days, and when Pavel went hunting for him, he found his father upstairs in the Old Steward's House, lying on the bench by the window, his face livid, the skin stretched over the bones beneath. Pavel had brought vodka. At first his father refused to drink, but eventually his son's alarm seemed to penetrate Danilo's consciousness and he did as he was told.

'I thought she might come here. I waited and waited for her, but she never came.' He caught pathetically at Pavel's arm.

'If you mean Miss Marianna, she's dead.' Pavel was exasperated. And angry on his mother's behalf. 'She won't come back. I know you miss her, but she won't come back. You have to accept that and get on with life.'

'But you know there are demons that haunt the night-time fields. And noon ghosts too that come in the daytime. You believe in them, don't you?'

'Maybe.'

'I've seen them. We saw, oh, we saw something. Marianna and I. That night on the road from Banunin. And then up here afterwards.' He looked around, recalled bitterly to the present and Pavel's puzzled gaze. 'So why will she not come? I call to her and call to her but I feel nothing, not even a whisper to comfort me.'

On All Soul's Eve, Danilo went to the graveyard and left an offering of bread and cheese in the barrel provided for the use of the priest and the holy men who travelled about, seeking alms. It was the custom at this time of year to put candles or lamps on the graves of the dear departed. Danilo had never attended church much, neither his own Orthodox church nor the small Roman Catholic church that sat just beside the estate. Now he found some comfort in the murmur of prayers, the calling of the names of the dead, and the chanting of admonitions to God, to the saints, to Jesus Christ to grant them eternal rest. Here was a mother, sobbing over the grave of a child, and there was a husband, broken heartedly mourning his young wife.

Danilo was comforted by this communal misery and yet he couldn't truly join in, for how could he pray for eternal rest for her, when he was not resting with her? But he had always heard it whispered that on this one night, the souls of the departed might be allowed back to visit those still on earth, and although in the years of his youth and strength he would have scorned such notions, now he was clutching at straws.

Presently, he left the main burial ground and made his way through the chilly, misty night, heavy with the scent of decayed undergrowth, towards the old graveyard where Marianna was buried. They had wanted to take her back to Milatyn, but Julian had not allowed it, insisting that she remain at her beloved Lisko. Marianna was, after all, a Diduska and might lie in peace beside her mother and father, close to her nurse and her own Diduski forebears.

It had once been the custom to leave food on the graves so that the hungry ghosts might eat. Now, most of these provisions were donated to the priest instead. Danilo carried his own lantern that gave off only a glow-worm flicker in the absolute dark. Around him were memorial stones, protruding from the undergrowth like decayed teeth, some so old that they had tumbled over to one side, leaning like drunken men, some with the names almost erased by time and lichen. The name Diduski predominated, but there were older names too. He wondered if one of them was the grave of Stanislaw the Devil. Perhaps there were the graves of his many victims. He shivered in spite of his woollen coat. But the importance of his mission came back to him, and he found Marianna's stone cross, close by the gate.

Danilo drew out of his leather bag a honey cake that Konstanta had baked the day before, a piece of salami, a flask of mead and a wedge of cheese. These, he placed on the grave and then knelt down. Again he looked about him. No other person had come to this place. All were forgotten. If Julian was mourning Marianna on this night, he had not come to her grave to do so. Danilo felt inside his coat and took from his bosom a red rosebud. It was one of the last in the garden, surviving there in spite of frosts. He had gone up to the house and cut it when no-one was looking. And this, too, he placed with the provisions on the stone, and then sat back, saying brokenly, 'Come to me, Marianna. Come! Eat and drink with me, my darling.' He felt foolish and clumsy, saying the words aloud, but they seemed to him like a magic spell, an incantation.

He sat on until his lamp burned low and went out, leaving him in darkness. He sat until his limbs almost froze to the ground, for a heavy frost had come, but there was no sound, no vision to excite him. At last, he staggered to his feet with rime on his coat and on his hair, and went home to lie fully clothed on his bed, his teeth chattering with the cold.

The next morning, he had a fever. He rambled incoherently and sometimes he seemed to think that he was at Banunin, sometimes elsewhere.

'He talks so strangely!' said Konstanta.

'It's the fever. Ignore it,' said her husband.

He recovered his health somewhat and passed Christmas indoors with Pavel and Konstanta, who was overjoyed to discover that she was pregnant.

Julian came to check on her health, and to visit Danilo at the same time.

'There's life in you yet, and you could enjoy it if you had half a mind.'

'You give me no good news. Tell me I have a weak heart. Tell me my blood is poisoned. Tell me anything but how strong I am.'

'But you aren't going to die all in a minute like Marianna. You'd better accept that. You're on the mend. And now there's a grandchild on the way. You could live to be eighty, see it grow up.'

'That's my misfortune,' said Danilo and lay back on the pillows. Julian felt an immense sympathy for him. He thought of Marianna every day. Lisko was full of her.

'You strive too hard. She's here you know. Under your very nose. You try so hard to see her that you're blinded by your own misery.'

'What must I do?' asked Danilo.

'Let her go and she'll come to you. I don't know how else to put it.'

Danilo shook his head. 'How can I? I'm afraid of losing her completely.'

'Not you.'

'I can't do it.'

'Then I can't help you.'

'No. I must help myself. Leave me alone and let me think.'

After Christmas, a *kulig* came to Lisko, one of the great travelling parties that went about by sleigh from estate to estate, gathering young participants like a snowball, eating and drinking people out of house and home along the way. Lisko was their last port of call. Julian welcomed them all and they shortened the long nights with good food and wine, pleasant conversation, music and merriment.

In their cottage, Pavel and Konstanta kept themselves to themselves, snug and warm and well fed, watching Konstanta's belly grow bigger, but Danilo roamed about in the frosty night and coughed when he went to bed, waking them up.

'He'll kill himself, you know,' said Pavel. He was rolled up close against his wife, chest to back, and belly to buttocks. His arms were around her, his hands on her stomach and he felt the sudden, miraculous movement of the child inside her.

On a bitterly cold February night, Danilo went down to the stables, saddled up one of Marianna's old horses, another gentle sorrel mare, and rode off through the estate. He took the road to Banunin, and found himself in the big field where he and Marianna had seen the strange creature that had leapt into the air, bending backwards and forwards as it went. The night came back to him with great clarity. He thought about all that had happened afterwards, and yearned for one more glimpse of his darling.

There was a full moon. The night was cold and still, and the sky was eerily clear, the frosted snow shimmering on branches and fences. Distantly, as on that other night, he saw lights in cottages. He felt warm in spite of the cold and dimly discerned that his fever must have returned. His body felt very light. It seemed to have no weight at all. He slid down from the horse, but he was unable to stand upright for very long, so he sat down in the snow for a while, listening to the animal's warm breathing and snuffling, close beside him. Worriedly, she butted him with her soft nose, but he pushed her away and she wandered off, looking back at him occasionally. She was cold and wanted her warm stable.

'Go home,' he said, though his voice was a whisper. 'Go home. I don't need you now.'

As though assenting in this, the animal set off at a careful canter, picking her way down the long lane to Lisko.

Danilo lay down in the snow and looked up at the moon. He thought how beautiful it was.

'Why, it's almost as clear as day,' he said aloud. 'And warm too.'

He closed his eyes for a moment, just to rest them, and then, seeing light behind the closed lids, opened them again. The sun blazed down above him, where only moments before the moon had been. He was lying in a meadow on a hot summer's day. He looked down at his hands and saw, quite without surprise, that they were young and strong again, and that the brown marks of age had faded.

He raised himself so that he could peer between the growing stalks and saw Marianna coming towards him, all dressed in white. She raised her hand and freed her hair from its constraint, and it tumbled down her back in a mass of brown curls. Her arms were full of meadow flowers: cornflowers, poppies and yellow cockle. She was coming closer, so close that she almost tripped over him. But this time she didn't start at his presence. Instead she bent down as though she had expected him to be there and, still holding a few flowers in one hand, reached down with the other and pulled him to his feet.

He was as light as a snowflake.

He looked into her eyes. 'I thought I'd lost you.'

She was smiling at him. 'You've been looking for me in all the wrong places, my love. But here I am. I've come to the meadow to find you. Steward of my heart.' Then she put her face up to his and kissed him gently on the lips. 'My darling Danielek,' she said. 'Oh my darling, I'm here. I'll never leave you again.'

The sorrel mare returned, alone and riderless to her stable. The groom, who had just discovered her absence, raised the household. Julian, already suspecting the worst, went to Pavel's cottage and roused him and Konstanta. Danilo was not in his bed. His clothes were gone but not his outdoor coat.

They rode in search of him and, instinctively, Julian lead the little party along the road to Banunin. Just before they reached the gates of that estate, they saw a dark figure lying huddled in a field, the lines of it made sharp and distinct by the moonlight, which was, as Julian said, 'as clear as day'.

Julian dismounted first and, grasping Danilo's muscular wrist in his fingers, felt for a pulse. But the hand and arm were cold, and no heart was beating within his body.

THE END

Author's Note

ALTHOUGH *THE AMBER HEART* IS fiction, some of the events described in these pages really happened to my family, and some of the characters, for example Marianna's brother-in-law Julian and Floryan of the many wives, are very loosely based on real people. Even Danilo himself was inspired by extraordinary facts that came to light while I was researching my family history. My family came from those same eastern borderlands where Marianna Diduska spent her life, and Lisko is based on the estate where my father, Julian Czerkawski, was born and spent his early childhood. He too remembered 'parking' his horse in a ditch so that he could climb on, when he was too small to mount in the normal way. The strange, demonic creature in the field is also based on a true – and truly terrifying – encounter.

Many thanks are due to my much loved Polish relatives and friends, but especially my late father, Julian Czerkawski and my dear late great uncle and aunt, Karol and Wanda Kossak, their daughter Teresa and her partner Andrzej, whose stories of the old days proved so interesting and inspirational when I was a young woman, visiting Poland for the first time.

Since I wrote the very first draft of this novel, many years ago now, I have done considerably more research about this time and place. This is a novel, a love story written from the heart, but The Last Lancer, coming soon, will be a factual history of my Polish family, my grandfather in particular.

– *Catherine Czerkawska*

About The Author

CATHERINE CZERKAWSKA IS AN EXTENSIVELY published writer of fiction (novels and short stories) non fiction and award winning plays for theatre, BBC radio and television. Born in Yorkshire, of Polish and Irish parentage, she has spent most of her life in Scotland, with time also spent working in Finland, Poland and the Canaries.

Her novels include *The Physic Garden*, set in early nineteenth-century Glasgow, *The Jewel*, about the life and times of Robert Burns's wife, Jean Armour, both published by Saraband, and *Bird of Passage*, a powerful tale of cruelty, loss and enduring love. In 2019 Contraband published *A Proper Person to be Detained*, a personal family story that takes us from Ireland to the industrial heartlands of England and Scotland, giving voice to people often maligned by society and silenced by history – immigrants, women, the working classes.

Her stage plays include two full length plays commissioned by Edinburgh's Traverse Theatre: *Wormwood*, a play about the Chernobyl disaster staged in 1997 and *Quartz*. She has written plays for Glasgow's Oran Mor, as well as various community theatre projects, television drama and more than 100 hours of drama for BBC R4.

Her other interests include antique textiles, local and social history. She has served on the committee of the Society of Authors in Scotland and spent four years as Royal Literary Fund Writing Fellow at the University of the West of Scotland.

https://www.catherineczerkawska.co.uk/
Facebook: https://www.facebook.com/writerczerkawska/